I0678705

CLANDESTINE

HOUSE OF OAK BOOK THREE

NICHOLE VAN

Fiorenza Publishing

Clandestine © 2015 by Nichole Van Valkenburgh
Cover design © Nichole Van Valkenburgh
Interior design © Nichole Van Valkenburgh

Published by Fiorenza Publishing
Print Edition v1.0

ISBN: 978-0-9916391-5-1

Clandestine is a work of fiction. Names, characters, places and incidents are the products of the author's imagination or are used fictitiously. Any resemblance to actual events, locales or persons, living or dead, is entirely coincidental.

All rights reserved. No part of this publication may be reproduced, stored or transmitted in any form or by any means without the prior written permission of the author.

To Andrew,
For seeing me through so many firsts:
Photography, writing . . . motherhood.
Don't forget to be awesome.

To Dave
For giving me Andrew.
And for the record—you never forget to be awesome.

Prologue

EXCERPT FROM THE JOURNAL OF GARVIS SAMUELSON

LONDON
APRIL 14, 1828

This was the one—I was sure of it. The wound that would finally kill him. I watched the knife sink deep into my employer's shoulder. I fired at the assailants, but they melted into the London mist. My master collapsed in the dark alleyway, blood rapidly darkening his greatcoat.

I was part of his crew, as he sometimes called us—the group of men who protected and served him. For our part, we simply called him W.

W had survived so much, but as I turned him over, I feared the nasty wound would turn inevitably gangrenous. All the money in England would not be enough to save a man from such an injury. Not even the infamous W, who owned a good percentage of that money.

"Garvis," W said to me between clenched teeth, "in my coat pocket . . . there is the information Wellington seeks. Ensure he receives it."

I nodded my agreement. More men than just W had bled for the information those documents contained. The fate of the British Empire hung in the balance.

How I got W back to his townhouse, I cannot remember. Once there, I handed off the blood-stained letter with strict instructions to place it directly into the Duke of Wellington's hands.

Two footmen carefully lifted W into a clean bed. Lean and tall, W still had the vigor of a man ten years younger, despite the gray creeping in at the edges of his dark hair.

"You know the drill." W fixed me with his pale eyes as a valet cut away his gory clothing. "That special poultice I discovered while in Brazil. Flush the wound with my best brandy before stitching it closed, and do not let anyone— on pain of death—come near me with a leech or bloodletting lancet."

These instructions were not new. W had this same odd ritual around all his wounds. The valet and I flushed and stitched the wound, applying the poultice of herbs and honey. All the while, W mumbling strange sentences, like 'Hope tetanus vaccine is solid' and 'What I wouldn't give for an antibiotic.'

But this, also, was nothing particularly unusual. W occasionally said inexplicable things like 'whatever, man,' and he had a strong affinity for the word awesome. By this point, I had given up making sense of it.

As we were wrapping the wound in clean muslin, W grabbed my hand tightly. "If I end up delirious, do not believe a word I say."

W did well that first night, sleeping fitfully. But despite all our precautions, a fever set in the next morning. W descended into delusional ramblings.

Naturally, I had been through this before with my employer, but usually W's mutterings were quiet and indistinct. This time started like all the others with W murmuring phrases like 'mustn't go back' and 'she's well.'

However after a day, W became more agitated. I woke from dozing in a chair to find him thrashing about. Jumping to my feet, I instantly tried to still him before he reopened his wound. W continued to toss his head back and forth.

"Please, sir, you must calm yourself," I pleaded.

W hissed and opened his eyes, scanned the room and then focused on me. His eyes narrowed in confusion.

"Who are you? Where am I?" he whispered.

"You are in your townhouse, sir. In London. I am Garvis—"

"This isn't my house." W opened his eyes wider, darting a glance around the room again. Staring at the bed hangings, the candles burning, the fire flickering in the hearth.

"No!" W heaved his body, nearly breaking my hold. His eyes rolled back into his head. "No, this isn't right. It can't be."

I needed to calm him. "Everything will be all right, sir. You just need to compose your—"

But W continued to thrash his head back and forth, muttering.

"No! No, I was there. In the cellar of the house . . . falling . . . so long ago . . . cottage . . . Duir Cottage."

"Sir, calm down."

W fixed me with a terrified look. "What is the year?" he asked, licking his lips.

I paused. How gone was he into his delirium? "1828, sir—"

"No! Oh heavens, no!" W groaned. "No, that's not right. It makes no sense." He grabbed my arm with his good hand, holding fast. "Tell me you lie. Tell me the year is 2014—"

Horror flashed through my soul at those words.

"Sir, you are fevered—" But my words fell on deaf ears. W had closed his eyes, murmuring again.

"It was there—there in the cellar. The portal." He started thrashing about again. "My name. What is my name?"

"Please, sir, calm down. You mustn't be so wild—"

"Wild!" W suddenly laughed—a crazed, maniacal sound. "It's all wild, wild, wild! Marcus Wilde!"

Chapter 1

Marc Wilde *should* have been having a good day.
A *fantastic* day, even.

But, of course, something *would* have to come along and mess it up. Whatever. Just his luck.

On the surface, his day seemed so perfect. A flat out ten out of ten in nearly every category.

Location = 10/10.

He was on a photoshoot for *Vogue Thailand* with Australia's Next Top Model, who posed nearby in a gossamer gold silk gown. The ocean lapped soothingly against the rusted hull of a nearly century-old shipwreck nestled romantically in the sugar-white sand.

What wasn't there to love about the whole scene? Standing on a shipwreck in the midst of exotic scenery? A beautiful woman at his side? It was every man's fantasy.

Career = 10/10.

His latest film, *Croc-nami*, was a huge commercial success (well, at least in Southeast Asia), and Marc—martial artist turned stuntman turned leading man—could practically taste his growing fame.

Out of the corner of his eye, he could see a promotional poster for *Croc-nami* taped to an awning behind the art director's head. The image depicted Marc—his face grimy with blood, dirt and scruff—holding aloft a chainsaw with an enormous tsunami rearing behind him, gigantic crocodiles lunging out of the frothing water.

Words blazoned across the bottom:

The crocs are coming and they are hungry for YOU!

It was the moment in the film where Marc turned to the camera and uttered that infamous catch phrase. Deadpan and threatening:

"Later, alligator."

Granted, *Croc-nami* wouldn't be winning an Academy Award, but he viewed the movie as a stepping stone. The film would give him visibility, opening up other roles and cross-promotions. Case in point—this uh-mazing photoshoot.

Weather = 10/10.

The sun beat down with the bone-melting warmth of summer in Australia, a welcome change from February in New York or London. Marc kept tilting his face toward it, soaking in the vitamin D.

So yeah. Everything picture perfect. Literally.

Basically a ten out of ten day all around.

Except for the teeny, tiny matter of the note he had received earlier that morning.

It had landed on his perfect day like a six-foot-eight guy in front of Marc's fifty-yard-line Bronco's football seat.

Ruining the entire experience.

The letter was terse and anonymous.

I know what is hidden in the cellar of Duir Cottage in Herefordshire.
A time portal would be of extreme interest to the rest of the world.
I have definitive proof of its existence.

My silence comes with a price.

Place thirteen yellow roses in the front window of Duir Cottage
to acknowledge you have received this missive.
Instructions will follow.

The chilly words had chased his spine.

It just figured. Awesome day fumbled away by an old-school black-mail threat.

Classic.

Lack of Lame Extortion Notes = 0/10

The worst part? This was no idle threat.

Duir Cottage did indeed have a time portal in the cellar—a simple slab of stone which stood guard over a wormhole of sorts to the same date and location two hundred years in the past, linking 2014 and 1814 tightly together.

How had someone found out about the portal?

Marc's younger sister, Emme, had been the first to stumble upon the portal nearly two years ago. This had resulted in a trip to 1812 where she had met her husband, James Knight, a nineteenth century aristocrat raised at Haldon Manor, the nearby estate which owned Duir Cottage in the past.

But before the spring of 2012, the portal hadn't been traversable. And since that time, the portal had been a carefully guarded secret known to fewer than ten people, all of them family and friends. So none of them would have ever breathed a word about it.

The list of those who knew about the portal was short:

Marc, obviously.

Emme and her husband, James, the present-day owners of Duir Cottage.

Emme's best friend and self-proclaimed mystic, Jasmine.

James' sister, Georgiana, and her husband, Sebastian, currently living in 1814.

Arthur Knight, James' younger brother and the owner of Duir Cottage and nearby Haldon Manor in 1814.

That was it.

No one else knew.

Except *someone* apparently did.

But how? And who? How much money would 'silence' cost?

And why link the portal with him, Marc Wilde?

He wasn't the current owner of Duir Cottage and had no known obvious connection with the building beyond staying there occasionally.

He doubted Emme or James had received a similar note, as the note had been forwarded *from* Duir Cottage. The letter had been placed in the postbox, not mailed, and the elderly handyman who periodically checked in on the cottage had sent the letter along via Marc's publicist.

If anyone else had received a note as well, Marc would have heard about it long before now.

Why *him*?

It made no sense. None.

But as he was in Australia and too far away to do anything about it at the moment, Marc tried to mentally set the letter aside. He had this ten-out-of-ten, perfectly amazing day to focus on first.

It wasn't like the letter was earth-shattering or even life-threatening. It could wait a few hours before being dealt with.

But the knowledge of it buzzed in the back of his head. An annoying insect he kept batting away.

Focus. He could focus.

Just enjoy the weather, the scenery . . . complete the photoshoot.

Then, he would call Emme and James and talk about what to do.

But the blackmail bad luck spread like contagion through his should-have-been-totally-awesome day.

The sun, though brilliant, had turned the humid air thick. Walking began to feel like swimming, plastering his clothes to his body. Worse, blond dread-locked wig insulated his head, sending the heat into suffocating territory. Marc wanted nothing more than to dive into the ocean.

But *that* lovely relief was definitely out of the question. Glancing down at the clear blue water, Marc searched for evidence of the box jellyfish infestation swarming the shore. Tiny, transparent and therefore nearly invisible, the jellies turned swimming into a lethal game of maritime Russian roulette. It didn't help that the Australian photography crew had spent half the morning loudly swapping box jelly horror stories. The waves lapped a taunting litany.

To make matters worse, someone had read the tide table wrong and the tide was coming in, swirling around the rusted hull of the ship. If Marc had been allowed to keep his *boots* on, the water with its nearly invisible menace would not have concerned him.

However, after a heated discussion with the photographer, the stylist had forced his boots off, leaving Marc barefoot in cuffed, torn jeans and a military-style vest. The stylist had seemed callously ambivalent about his overall health and the death threat lurking in the water.

With the water lapping in, Marc had to continually climb higher up the rusted shipwreck, praying he didn't cut his bare feet on the metal hull. If a box jelly didn't kill him first, tetanus would probably finish the job.

The icing on the cake, as it were, came again from the photography crew. Every time Marc almost teetered into the water, they would all shout a teasing, "Later, alligator," in their broad Australian accents.

Where had it all gone so wrong?

Blackmail. Ah, yes. That was it.

Marc glanced over at the AusNTM model. Primped, painted and artlessly vapid in her clinging gold dress. She epitomized the kind of rail thin, stylized version of womanhood that Hollywood preferred. A pretty girl who hid insecurity behind a too brittle laugh, barbed comments and thick layer of make-up.

Marc had spent most of his adulthood surrounded by women like her.

They really weren't his type.

But . . . here Marc heaved an enormous sigh . . . *Sara* was here too.

Sara—vivacious with dancing blue eyes and a quick smile.

Sara—the stylist who had offed his boots and was definitely pulling for a box jelly to do him in.

Sara—Marc's ex-girlfriend.

He had been palpably shocked to see her when he arrived that morning, nearly fidgeting as she jammed the dreadlock wig on his head. None too gently.

Love Life = 2/10. If he were going to keep track of that today too. Which it appeared he was.

Sara *was* more-or-less his type. Intelligent, loyal, witty. Tall and pretty without a trace of vanity, despite working as a stylist.

Their break up the year before in Bali was still a vivid memory.

"So this is it," Sara had said, tapping a high-heeled foot. "Just like that—we're done." She adjusted her large sunglasses and swallowed. That hard swallow which fought to keep tears at bay.

Marc shifted uncomfortably. He hated scenes, hated strong emotions and, even worse, talking about them. Why did things always end this way? Ugly, messy. Hurt.

"Sara, look, I'm so sorry. Really, I am." He truly was. "I never intended to lead you on. You want more. I get it. But I just . . . can't . . . be more for you right now."

"Can't or won't, Marc?"

Ugh. He also hated that question.

More foot tapping.

"Both, I suppose," he said, knowing it was the wrong answer. "I'm just not a touchy-feely kinda guy."

A long pause. More tight swallowing.

"Well, I hope she destroys you."

"What? What are you talking about? Sara, there isn't anyone else and—"

"Oh, I know there's no one else. Not yet. But, someday . . . someday there will be. Someone who makes you want to open up to her." She paused, glanced to the side and then brought her gaze back to him. "And I hope she bloody destroys you."

So . . . yeah. That was Sara.

Marc considered all of this as he scrambled up the shipwreck, balancing above the model on the jagged edge of the hull, hefting a massive chainsaw above his head. Wig plastered to his sweat-covered face and shoulders, a heavy ammo belt slung over the vest.

The problem was this: Marc had liked Sara. He truly had.

But he just didn't do intense, consuming emotions. It wasn't his thing.

He wasn't a let's-hang-out-and-talk-about-our-*feelings* kinda guy.

More of a when-is-kickoff and pass-me-the-bacon kinda guy.

Not that he was a jerk. He loved his mother. He loved his sister. He took care of them both, respected them, laughed with them, enjoyed spending time with them. He had always felt close to Emme and his mom, particularly as his British father had up and left when Marc was only eight. They were his life and he would gladly die for them.

But when it came to women he wasn't genetically related to, Marc struggled. It wasn't the women he dated, really. He recognized that. The problem, it seemed, was within himself.

Though he had, at least, been smart enough to avoid saying the dreaded *It's-not-you-it's-me* line to former girlfriends.

Even though the phrase sorta hit the proverbial nail on the head.

He often wondered if maybe the crushing pain of his father's abandonment had broken something inside him. Something that couldn't be fixed. Dooming Marc to live with a heart incapable of 'til-death-do-us-part love.

Sara and the string of girlfriends before her had all been perfectly lovely people. Women for whom he felt affection and camaraderie and attraction.

But capital-L Love? The kind of love that poets sobbed over and singers crooned about and men fought wars for . . .

Nah. Nope. Never.

Not even a glimpse.

And after thirty-two years of life, if he hadn't felt anything like romantic love by now, he probably never would.

Marc just figured he didn't do big emotions. Some people didn't. That was fine. Just part of who he was, like his green eyes and love of martial arts.

He should probably settle down with someone like Sara and figure that was that.

But there was this nagging sense of . . . unease. That affection and similar goals weren't enough to last through a lifetime of challenges. That he would end up like his father, walking out the door without looking back.

And given what a mess *that* decision had made of his own childhood, he couldn't risk doing something similar to anyone else.

So yeah. His love life wasn't in the best of places.

"Higher if you can, Marc," the photographer called. "I need the chainsaw to clear your head. Oh, and keep that right shoulder down. I don't want the ammo belt drifting over your face."

Marc made the adjustments, ignoring the burn in his biceps. He had given up trying to understand what the ammo belt had to do with a chainsaw. He secretly thought it was Sara's passive-aggressive way of sabotaging him. Making him look ridiculous while simultaneously sending him into heatstroke with all the extra weight.

The whole day had turned into just a little bit of Hell wrapped up in taunting tropical splendor and topped with a generous dollop of blackmail.

But Marc, being Marc, did what he always did in such situations.

He smiled. He was easy-going, game for anything. The man that could brush anything off. It was the reputation that gave him his living.

"How hot does it have to get before I *want* to be jellyfish bait?" he called to the lighting crew, grinning at them.

"Sara, it's really nice to see you. How's your mom doing?" Fine. Her mother was just fine.

And didn't blink when every five minutes he heard, "Layteh, allagay-teh," followed by raucous laughter.

Humor and deflection. It was like breathing.

Did anyone notice that his smile was somewhat strained? That his nonchalance wasn't exactly non-chalanty?

Someday he would laugh at the absurdity of this day.

Someday. But not yet.

Finally, the art director called a break, and Marc, gratefully, jumped his way to shore.

Marc sank into a beach chair under one of the awnings, gulping down an absurd amount of water, wishing desperately for a cool breeze to relieve the heat.

His mind circling back to that note.

Blackmail was an ugly business. The monies paid would never stop. And what evidence did this unknown person have? Who were they?

And with all his contacts, did Marc know a guy who knew another guy who could effectively ferret out the answers for him?

Swallowing more water, he pondered his options, staring sightlessly. People were still standing around in small groups, discussing (more like arguing) model posing and running mascara.

Marc's phone chirped. A text from Emme.

DO NOT read FauxPause today. Just don't.

He sent her back a smiley emoji because Emme hated emoji and would be less likely to ask probing, *concerned* questions if she were annoyed at him.

Standard emotional deflection.

Of course, that didn't mean Marc actually *trusted* Emme's advice.

Sara and the photographer were now arguing with the art director. It sounded like Sara wanted to add ninja knives and a quiver of arrows to the ammo belt (definitely passive-aggressive sabotage). Fortunately, she was getting some pushback.

In other words, nothing was happening any time soon.

So Marc instantly went to the bookmarked website on his phone: www.FauxPause.com. (Tagline: *Grab a coffee and sit for a Pause.*)

The loading icon spun and spun. Cellar wi-fi was slooooooow on Fraser Island. Text messages, however, were not.

Marc, I know you're not listening to me. I am serious. DO NOT GO THERE. For once, trust me.

He texted back a kissy-lips emoji.

Marc loved FauxPause. Granted, pretty much anyone with an internet connection loved FauxPause. It was *the* website right now. Hip. Current. Everyone who was anyone found their way into its commentary.

I mean it, Marc. Don't ignore me.

Marc ignored her.

He was having a bad day and if anything could cheer him up, it would be FauxPause.

With sections entitled *Faux Sure* (modern culture in the *now*) and *Fashion Faux-ward* (fashion trends, bad and good), FauxPause curated all the ephemera that made modern civilization, well, modern.

Slick and ironic with often biting humor, all reflected in the website's design: black and white Parisian-inspired minimalism with punches of mustard and teal. Marc had this secret fantasy that someday he would be featured on the website. A glowing review under *Faux Sure*.

The managing editor, La Pochette, wrote a section dedicated to cultural missteps: *Oh the Urbanity!* Her charcoal image in a retro teal dress peeked cheekily at the viewer, hand reaching into a mustard purse slung on her shoulder, ready to pull out another biting piece of hilarious media satire.

Her last post had been classic: an anti-Valentine's Day rant entitled *The Boy-cott* which advocated taking back the upcoming Valentine's Day and focusing on inner, not outer, validation.

Cupid's stupid. Last thing I need is a naked man-baby packing antiquated weaponry manipulating my love-life, she wrote.

La Pochette didn't pull any punches.

Which was why, when the website finally loaded, Marc realized he probably should have listened to his sister.

There it was under *Review of the Preview*—a scathing dialogue between La Pochette's id, ego and superego critiquing theatrical trailers.

Comedic gold.

Except when the movie in question was his own.

Review of the Preview:
Because all the good parts are in the trailer anyway . . .

Today's Preview: Croc-nami

Ego: *Let's start with the name. Croc-nami? Really?*

Id: *It's like a flashback to 2005 to when I opened my niece's closet to an avalanche of smelly plastic shoes. The 240 seconds I spent watching this preview were 230 seconds too long.*

Superego: *Be nice, you guys. Good people worked hard to bring this movie to life, and we should respect—*

Id: *Respect?! Whatever. Don't even start that Pollyanna routine of yours.*

Ego: *Patience, children. I want to know more about this lead actor, Marc Wilde? A.k.a, the Crocinator?*

Id: *Some D-list wannabe.*

Superego: *I am sure he is a very lovely person with a winning personality.*

Id: *[sarcastic eyeroll]*

Ego: *I looked him up on IMBD.*

Id: *Liar. You did not.*

Ego: *Okay, you're right. He's not on IMBD.*

Id: *D-list wannabe, I'm telling you.*

Ego: *But I did find a couple of his earlier films. Most notably, a little pearl entitled, Ninja Pirate 3: The Last Arrrrghonaut.*

Id: *Shut up! No! Take it back!*

Superego: *Ah, a cinematic gem, you say?*

Id: *You're making my eyes bleed just reading this.*

Ego: *Which, of course, begs the question. Ninja Pirate 1 and Ninja Pirate 2?!*

Id: *Again . . . I just . . . I can't . . .*

Superego: *Marc Wilde is a martial artist—*

Id: *Artist? Did you really just go there?*

Superego: *Point taken. But he is sorta hot in a karate kid meets surf bum kinda way. And he is supposed to be Australian in the movie, so the surfer thing works on many levels.*

Id: *I cannot believe those words actually came out of your mouth. There is NO level at which this movie works . . .*

Ego: *I'll grant you the hot surfer look.*

Id: *Fine. Hot, maybe. But NOT Mr. Wilde's epic fail at an Australian accent. It's called a dialect coach, people. Look it up.*

Marc grimaced. He had *told* the writers over and over that he couldn't do a convincing Australian accent. Just because Marc had a perfect English accent (courtesy of his British grandmother) along with his American one, it didn't mean he could do other accents flawlessly. Another fact the Australian photography crew had rubbed in over and over today.

Ego: *And those blond dreadlocks?*

Id: *Ick. They're like a mangy sheepdog hugging his head.*

Superego: *Yeah, I'm with Id on this one.*

The dialogue went on, slamming the movie's plotline (Ego: *So a tsunami somehow snags saltwater crocs off the coast of Africa and pushes them over five thousand miles to New York City?*) and even worse CGI (Id: *Photographing a toy crocodile in front of a green screen does not a convincing terror make.*). Superego, at least, seemed to like him.

Superego: *Okay, granted, the plotline and special effects are terrible. But Marc Wilde is at least a little bit of eye candy, right? All those muscles and impressive fight moves and gratuitously ripped shirts?*

Ego: *Maybe, but I did mention the dreadlocks earlier . . .*

Id: *And though I do appreciate a nice set of pectorals, I discovered you actually can have too much of a good thing. I counted over eleven close-ups of Mr. Wilde's abs in the theatrical trailer alone. Is that the best thing the movie has to offer?*

Superego: *Yes.*

Ego: *Hell, yes.*

Superego: *I understand the movie is a runaway hit in Singapore and Thailand. They love* Croc-nami. *You can buy t-shirts in Malaysia with anime-esque crocodiles, pleading with their cute huge eyes,* Beware the Croc-nami!

Id: *I think that pretty much sums it up, doesn't it?*

Ego: *It does indeed.*

Marc shook his head and stared at lapping waves.

Emme's text popped onto his screen. *You didn't listen to me, did you?*

No, he did not.

Social Media Exposure for the Day = -11/10

The problem, of course, was that everything La Pochette said was sort of true: *Croc-nami* was not a phenomenal film. It was a low-budget B-movie.

But it wasn't as awful as she painted it either. The special effects weren't that bad and the martial arts in the film were top notch—Marc's expertise ensured that much. It was a campy, action romp with a broad international audience.

The problem, of course, was easy to spot: La Pochette's scathing review had just sealed his tomb.

Curse her.

He was going to be pigeon-holed as that-actor-from-*Croc-nami* for the rest of his life. No respected director would touch him now with a ten-foot alligator-repelling pole.

Blackmail, box jellies, scorching heat, Sara and now a scathing, highly-visible movie review?

He was sure today was karmic retribution for something. His break-up with Sara hadn't been *that* callous, had it?

With a sigh, Marc dialed Emme's number. It was time to chat about that blackmail note.

Because if the universe insisted on him having a bad day, he was taking his sister down with him.

Chapter 2

Kit Ashton was having a horrid day.

Oh, who was she fooling.

She was having a horrid *month*. Perhaps even a horrid year. And her situation did not promise to turn a corner any time soon.

Well, it *could* improve rather rapidly. If she managed to find Daniel.

But in typical Daniel-like fashion, her younger brother had run to ground.

Again.

And, as usual, she was not sure where to find him. Assuming he even *wanted* to be found.

Daniel could be a serious trial.

Kit carefully surveyed the items on the desktop. A fire burned low in the grate doing little to warm the winter-cold air. The candle in her hand flickered, casting ghoulish shadows on the dark paneled wood lining the walls, illuminating the eyes of a painted lynx staring at her above the stone mantle. As if the large cat could divine her purpose here, would hunt out her secrets.

She shivered. That would be bad.

Voices echoed quietly down the hallway, soft murmurs of discussion and the clink of teacups from the drawing room. She had so little time. Cautiously, she sifted through each item on the desk, meticulously placing it back exactly as before—an inkwell and heavy emblazoned family seal, a well-used blotter and neatly trimmed quills, estate correspondence stacked according to the sender's perceived importance.

Mr. Arthur Knight's desk captured the man himself: tidy, organized, somewhat pretentious around the edges.

She surveyed the desktop one last time.

Nothing.

Or rather, nothing more than she had expected.

But there *had* to be something somewhere.

Daniel had left her very few clues before disappearing. Just that vague note which led her to the town of Marfield and then on to nearby Haldon Manor, where she was now living.

Nothing more.

Did Daniel realize how desperately alone and penniless she found herself? How difficult he had made it for her to return home?

She thought not.

Being her brother's keeper had never been easy. Keeping him out of trouble, out of debt, out of prison even.

For his part, Daniel was adept at keeping her *out* of his life.

What, precisely, was her brother up to this time? The few ideas she did have were terrifying in their scope. None of them ended well. He appeared to have landed himself in a mess of epic proportions.

The only solution was for Daniel to return home as soon as possible, firmly sweeping this episode under a very heavy rug, maybe placing some hefty furniture on top of it for good measure. Ensuring that no whiff of this ever escaped to the world at large.

Granted, she had to actually *find* Daniel before she could do any of that.

Dismissing the desktop, Kit moved to the drawers, quietly opening one and then another, carefully lifting ledgers and sifting through papers. Documents she had no business looking at.

You really should not *be doing this. It's not worth the risk*, her Virtuous Angel whispered.

Don't listen to her. That was her Wicked Angel. *We need to find Daniel. Any means justify the end.*

Daniel had always mocked her for turning internal moral dilemmas into silly dialogue between Virtuous Angel and Wicked Angel. Kit preferred to think of it as carefully assessing her options from all points of view.

One of them had to.

But then Daniel didn't seem possessed of a Virtuous Angel, so the whole concept of 'moral dilemma' was a bit of an oxymoron for him.

Kit, on the other hand . . .

I do understand what is at stake here! Virtuous Angel was indignant. *Trust me, I want to return home too. But this is the wrong way to go about finding him. Who says there will be any information in here?*

Wrong shmong. Wicked Angel shrugged. *This is our only option. Just keep looking.*

Kit shivered and tugged her red shawl tighter around her shoulders. The intelligence she needed *had* to be in here somewhere, didn't it? Had Daniel had any correspondence with Arthur Knight?

Someone *had* to know something. She just needed to find the right information, which would (hopefully) lead her to Daniel, which would allow them to (finally) return home.

Just sneak back into their former lives. No one the wiser.

That was the most important part, really. No one could ever know about this little . . . episode. Because if someone, *anyone*, found out . . . about Daniel's suspected behavior . . . about her time here at Haldon Manor . . .

Kit swallowed. Hard. Her heart suddenly racing. Panic tasted metallic and cold in the back of her throat.

Shaking her head, she tightened her jaw. Swallowed. Angled her candle and dug more thoroughly through the desk drawer.

Arthur Knight, her employer, seemed an upstanding sort of person, unlikely to be wrapped up in the nastiness of Daniel's life.

But Kit had learned from hard experience that *everyone* had secrets. No matter how honest and upright they appeared, every person had something they didn't wish others to know. Some hidden pain which kept them up at night, mentally picking, trying to close the nagging worry but instead only deepening the wound.

Kit was so eternally weary of secrets. Lies and half truths and clandestine things one couldn't fathom.

Things Kit *would* never fathom, because there was one truth—and one truth only—she had learned:

Secrets abandoned you . . . left you.

They left you standing in the entryway of your house, the slam of the front door still echoing. They left you holding your crying little brother, unable to understand or explain *why*. They left your father half a man, disappearing bit-by-bit into his research until he faded all together. They left you wondering if your mother would ever return.

Secrets left you with only one thing—more secrets.

And once secrets took someone, that person never returned. She understood *that* bitter lesson early on.

Secrets were thieves, stealing joy.

Kit Ashton *hated* secrets.

Hypocrite, Virtuous Angel murmured.

Kit bit her lip. Despising herself a little.

She had deserved that bit of recrimination.

For someone who abhorred deception, she did have rather more than her share of secrets currently. Fairly riddled with them.

She *was* the worst sort of hypocrite.

Though if her mother's secret had been something of *this* magnitude, Kit might have felt more pity for the woman.

She finished rifling through the drawer, resisting the urge to slam it shut. Nothing. She swallowed tightly and pulled out the next one.

Gah. She never thought about her mother. With both her father and mother now dead, it was pointless to dwell on the past.

It was probably just this room with its dark paneling and large, stone fireplace. Her father's study was like this. She could practically smell his musky cologne lingering in the air.

Both rooms even sported a similar painting of a lynx over the mantle.

It sees hidden truths, the lynx does. All ancient cultures believed so, the Greeks, the Norse . . . She could almost hear her father's voice—calm, quiet, withdrawn. Reciting historical facts. Asking questions about his research had been her only way of connecting with him.

She felt the cat's eyes on her now. Accusing.

Kit shook her head, banishing the maudlin thoughts. They wouldn't help her achieve her current goals.

Determined to drag her brother out of his current mess and back to home, she had followed Daniel's cryptic note to Marfield, arriving a little over a week ago. But she hadn't planned ahead—long story there—and had found herself penniless and wardrobe-less in an unfamiliar village. Bless the kind-hearted vicar and his wife for taking her in and, even more, arranging an interview for a post.

All of which had resulted in Kit being hired earlier in the week as a companion to Lady Ruby Knight—Arthur Knight's aunt visiting from Shropshire—when the woman's previous companion had unexpectedly resigned her post. The daughter of an earl, Lady Ruby had married decidedly down in life when she eloped with the younger son of an untitled gentleman, Arthur's now-deceased uncle.

If Lady Ruby found her reduced circumstances a trial, it was hard to say. The lady had a mercurial temperament. No situation was so grand that Lady Ruby couldn't find fault with it.

Quite frankly, Kit didn't care. The employment was a godsend, giving her a much-needed roof over her head, food in her belly and a chance to live in Haldon Manor, the place her brother had indicated he was heading. The place she hoped to find him. Before Daniel did something incredibly stupid and ruined the future for both of them. But discreet inquiries had yielded nothing, forcing her to adopt more direct measures.

Kit needed answers *now*. She could only hide her true identity for so long.

Something or someone would betray her eventually. Nothing in her upbringing had prepared her for this situation.

Well, to be a lady, yes.

A paid companion, however? Not so much.

It was only a matter of time before Arthur and Lady Ruby realized it, before she exposed herself for the fraud she was.

She didn't do well being ordered about by others. Nor could she keep opinions to herself.

Every morning, she ruthlessly pinned her mass of unruly hair to her head, buttoned herself into a second-hand serviceable frock and swallowed every last dry, dry, dry remark down her throat.

But like too many goose feathers stuffed into a pillow, eventually someone would hit her on a weak seam, causing a virtual explosion of *Kit* to burst out of her mouth.

Take this evening, for example. Everyone had stared when Kit disagreed with Lady Ruby, insisting that buttercup yellow was a horrid color for just about any complexion and no woman with taste would ever wear it.

Ruby had *not* been amused.

You really need to hold your tongue. The risk is too great, Virtuous Angel chided.

But only for now. Once we find Daniel, you can march right up to Ruby and tell her that no amount of rouge will make her look thirty again, Wicked Angel snickered.

Kit studied the drawer currently opened. Again, expense ledgers and filed correspondence. She tilted the candle to better examine the papers. Nothing.

She drew in a deep, stuttering breath.

She had maybe five more minutes before her absence from the drawing room was considered overlong and someone came looking for her. Though hopefully that someone would *not* be Mr. Jedediah Knight, Arthur Knight's cousin and Lady Ruby's son.

She now knew *why* Lady Ruby's previous companion had quit so abruptly. A week of fetching shawls and dodging Jedediah Knight's wandering hands had shown her, more than anything, how protected, pampered and *sheltered* her life had been up to this point.

Ironic that. Particularly given how *un*-protected and *un*-sheltered she had always assumed herself to be.

She had just opened the last drawer in the desk when footsteps sounded in the hallway. Kit slid the drawer shut and froze, listening intently. The rumble of Arthur's voice reached her, talking with another low male voice. They wouldn't come into the study, would they?

The door handle moved.

Why, *yes*, indeed, they would.

Instantly, Kit snuffed her candle and dove under the desk, grateful for its paneled front hiding her from view. It was a tight squeeze as she had never been accused of being a smallish sort of woman.

Tall and overbearing? Yes.

Statuesque and shapely? Certainly.

Petite and demur? Uh . . . no.

She had spent years coming to terms with the fact that men would always be intimidated by her size. Probably because most had to look *up* into her eyes.

Well, who was she fooling? It was still a struggle. Did any woman truly love everything about herself?

Men either treated her as uninteresting wallpaper or viewed her as some freak-show trophy to be shown off.

Though, being about five inches shorter would be helpful in a situation like this. Kit winced as she wedged her knees tightly against her chest, ensuring all of her dress made it underneath with her. Her head twisted awkwardly against the under side of the desktop.

It was a literal reminder of her current situation. Stuffing herself into a too-small container.

The door creaked and two sets of footsteps sounded through the room. She rested her head on her knees and took several slow breaths, trying to quiet her thumping heart.

"I tell you, Linwood, I have no information about Miss Emry's brother." That was Arthur. Kit knew his voice by now.

Which meant the person with him was that haughty viscount she had met earlier at dinner: Lord Linwood.

"Come now, Arthur. I cannot believe that to be the case." Linwood's voice dripped sarcasm.

Kit could see Linwood as he had looked all evening. Dark haired with nearly colorless pale gray eyes. Meticulously—she would say even fastidiously—groomed in a glove-tight blue coat and tan trousers. And tall. He topped her five-foot-ten-inches by half a head.

The chilly February weather had swept inside with him, literally and figuratively. He had responded icily to all inquiries during dinner.

Even Marianne, Arthur's wife and Linwood's younger sister, could not thaw him. Not even when she encouraged him to hold her tiny two-month baby, Isabel—Linwood's only niece. The baby had cooed at him, adorable and trusting. Though as a glowing new mother, Marianne had been too caught up in her baby's charms to notice her brother's uncomfortable stiffness.

"Miss Emry died with James in that carriage accident. You yourself went to identify the bodies," Linwood said.

Kit's interest peaked. She had heard about James Knight, Arthur's older brother who had died just eighteen months before.

"After such a tragedy, you did not attempt to contact her brother—Marcus, was it?—to inform him of her demise?" Linwood continued.

A clink of metal sounded, followed by rustling and popping. Someone was stirring the fire to life. Arthur, perhaps?

"Things were not that simple after James' . . . death." Was there a pause in Arthur's voice as he said that? Odd. "Tracking down Miss Emry's brother was not an immediate concern at the time. I honestly cannot remember if Marcus was contacted or not. I most certainly have no knowledge of his whereabouts. To be frank, I do not understand why he is of concern to you."

Someone shifted, pacing the floor, boot heels clicking.

"There have been several attempted thefts at Kinningsley over the last two weeks," Linwood said. "Twice someone has entered the house. Just yesterday, I awoke to find my guard dog dead and my office ransacked."

Kit stopped herself from sucking in an audible gasp. *Oh dear.*

Was Daniel involved with these break-ins? And if so, why? What exact mischief did he have planned?

Kit chewed on her cheek, mind churning through the possibilities. None of them pleasant.

"I had heard," Arthur replied, his voice placating. "Robberies are not uncommon, as you well know. Why someone poached three hens from our coops Thursday last, and Sir Henry's butler caught a maid red-handed with a cravat pin."

The footsteps came closer to the desk. When Linwood next spoke, the sound came from directly over Kit's head. She held her breath, praying he didn't walk *around* the desk.

"No. The attempts at Kinningsley are more serious than hen-rustling or a servant's petty theft. I have several footmen keeping round-the-clock watch, but to truly stop these would-be-thieves, I must find the mastermind behind the scheme."

Did Linwood seem agitated? Was that even possible? The viscount seemed incapable of agitation. Obdurate even.

"And you think Miss Emry's brother is this mastermind?" Arthur sounded skeptical.

Linwood shifted something on the desk above Kit's head. She silently ordered her hammering heart to stay in her chest.

"I am not sure," Linwood said after a moment. "But as you well know, Napoleon is on the run, pulling back farther and farther into France. Victory is close. However, the French have spies among us who are determined to thwart this war at any cost, particularly with Napoleon in retreat. Miss Emry admitted to working within the greater spy network of Europe. We both know the future of Europe hangs on a knife's edge right now. One tiny push one way or another, the slightest advantage, could make all the difference."

Kit tensed, teeth grinding. That same panic welled again. *This* was what she most feared. Daniel was so impulsive. Hasty. Impetuous. *Please let him have nothing to do with this.*

But Linwood's words buzzed angrily in her head. *The French have spies among us . . .*

"Miss Emry and James were killed in that carriage accident nearly eighteen months ago," Arthur said. "Why haven't you pursued Miss Emry's brother before now?"

Linwood drummed his fingers on the desktop.

Is that actual emotion I am sensing from him? He seems too antisocial for that. Wicked Angel murmured snidely. But then, Wicked Angel was almost always snide.

"I am sure I do not need to impress upon you the confidential nature of this conversation." Linwood's fingers continued beating a steady rhythm: *ta-ta-tum, ta-ta-tum, ta-ta-tum.* Arthur must have nodded his consent because Linwood continued, "I have recently been given reason to believe that James and Miss Emry's death was no accident."

Silence for a moment. And then Arthur laughed, stiltedly.

"Truly, Linwood, I would not have thought you capable of a flight of fancy. James' death was tragic but most decidedly an accident—"

"I must beg to disagree, Arthur. My sources would hint otherwise. James' death was decidedly suspicious."

"Linwood, you cannot believe—"

"Arthur, you are being obtuse. We know there were spies in this neighborhood just last year. Your trusting nature blinds you to the realities of life—"

"That is hardly the case." Arthur let out a bark of laughter.

"I fear I shall have to be more specific." More finger tapping on the desktop. "As you know, the Home Office has operatives from all walks of life who provide the British government with information. Several weeks ago, the Home Office lost contact with one of their most-trusted clandestine agents. A member of the aristocracy. But before disappearing, this agent informed the government there was an individual here in Marfield with connections to French intelligence gathering."

"Heavens!"

"Indeed. Aside from trying to locate this agent, the Home Office is desperate to understand the nature of the threat in this area. Marcus is known to be a man of some fighting skill who has been intimately involved with international spy activities. Due to his sister, we know those covert operations encompassed Marfield at one point. Therefore, it stands to reason Marcus has, at minimum, valuable information. At worst, he might be an informant himself."

"I am still not quite sure I understand your reasoning, Linwood. We are in Herefordshire. *Rural* Herefordshire. Why would the French have any interest in this part of the country? It makes no sense."

Linwood shifted, his trousers brushing against the desk. "There are reasons."

A pause.

"Something perhaps related to the attempted break-ins at Kinningsley?" Arthur asked, pointedly. "Seeing as you are sharing confidences, what are these would-be thieves looking for?"

Again, a pause. A shifting of feet. And then:

"I am not at liberty to say."

"I see." Though Arthur's tone indicated he clearly did *not*. "Well, if I hear from this Marcus, I will inform you immediately." He sounded . . . amused, was it? As if he were humoring Linwood.

"I appreciate your cooperation in this matter. I have also been making inquiries into all newcomers. This new paid companion of your aunt's, Miss Ashton, is it? From whence does she hail?"

Kit held her breath. *Oh no.*

"Yorkshire, I am told. She had been staying with the vicar but had glowing references from Lord Curtis."

Kit grimaced. False references she wrote with her own hand.

See, this is why you should never, ever tell a falsehood, Virtuous Angel whispered.

The answer seemed to mollify Linwood, however, as the drumming fingers stopped.

A knock sounded at the door.

"Come," Arthur called. The door swung open.

"I say, most sorry to interrupt." Jedediah Knight's nasal words skittered down Kit's spine. Like squeaky chalk on slate, that voice. "My mother sent Miss Ashton to fetch her embroidery, but Miss Ashton has not yet returned. Have you seen the chit?"

Kit could almost see Jedediah's long nose twitching as he spoke, flushed and clashing with the striped orange and pink waistcoat he wore.

Both Linwood and Arthur disavowed knowing her whereabouts.

Jedediah grunted. "Hopefully she has not taken to sneaking whiskey in her chambers. Mother's last companion spent every day half-sprung."

The *nerve* of the man! Kit clenched her teeth. Though if anyone could drive someone to the bottle, it would be Jedediah Knight. Kit could hardly blame the woman.

Truth be told, if her situation became any more intolerable, whiskey could start to look like a viable solution.

Which merely underscored the point more fully. The sooner she found her brother, the better.

Daniel could try to shut her out of his life, but Kit was made of stronger stuff. She just needed to find him before he did something colossally stupid.

And even if he did, she would not abandon him. Ever.

Chapter 3

Thirteen yellow roses sat gracefully in the windowsill as Marc pulled up to Duir Cottage—their cheerful blooms mocking the seriousness of his current situation.

Granted, the roses looked right at home with the honey-colored stone and thatched roof of the cottage. Ivy covered the fence surrounding the house, and an enormous old oak tree arched protectively over the entire building. The sunny yellow roses were just golden gilding on all the oozing English charm.

Marc had arrived at Duir Cottage six days ago. Both Emme and James were currently in Seattle and had reacted to the blackmail threat much as Marc expected.

James, laughing: "What a devilish mess. Adds a dash of excitement to everything, doesn't it?"

Emme, puzzled: "Are you sure this isn't one of your friends' ideas of a practical joke? Like they just made a super lucky guess?"

Marc had no real answer for either of them.

Unfortunately, Emme and James had an off-the-grid trek through Mongolia planned, starting the next week. And in Emme's own words, "No blackmail traveling disaster is going to derail this trip. Period."

So . . . yeah. Emme and James would come straight back to Duir Cottage in March. In the meantime, Marc intended to uncover information about the blackmail and stall for time to sort out a solution.

His efforts, so far, had been disappointing. The blackmail letter had been slipped into the post box and that was it. No more letters had arrived. No one suspicious had been seen lurking around the property. Google found no digital chatter anywhere about the portal.

Just nothing. Not a single lead. All Marc could do was hope the blackmailer contacted them again.

He *hated* waiting. Simply sitting around, everything on hold.

Not cool.

So after a couple restless days, he took the bait and purchased thirteen (obnoxiously chipper) yellow roses and placed them in the mullioned front window, just as the letter had directed. His attempt to flush out the blackmailer. The flowers waved an affectionate 'hello' every time he pulled up to the cottage, looking absurdly pleased with themselves.

Why would a blackmailer choose *yellow* roses? It seemed so . . . friendly. Neighborly, even.

He had pointed this out to Emme's best friend, Jasmine, when she called to check up on things.

"They're worse than a puppy. So sunshiny. It's like they want me to pet them or something," he had said.

Jasmine chuckled. "I would pay good money to see you pet roses—"

"Jas . . ." Marc warned.

"—but I hate to be the bearer of bad news. Yellow roses don't always represent friendship. In many societies, they mean the exact opposite:

treachery and death." Trust Jasmine to set him straight. "Besides, there are thirteen of them. That's never a good number of anything."

"Nice. So you're telling me that my cheery roses secretly want to stab me in the back with their thorny claws?"

"You have to admit, it would make for a great movie. You could call it *Thorns of Menace.*"

Silence.

"You think you're hilarious, don't you?" Marc made his voice suitably grumpy.

"Absolutely." Her laugh sounded tinny through the international phone connection. "Just imagine. You could dress up yellow roses in little dread-locked wigs and make them tiny chainsaws out of grass—"

Marc had practically hung up on her.

Stupid, stupid flowers.

But even with the roses displayed as directed, there had been no more notes from the would-be blackmailer. Just complete radio silence.

One more thing for his overflowing Inbox of Frustration.

La Pochette's scathing review of *Croc-nami* had gone viral. Insanely viral. Marc had begun avoiding the internet altogether, as the memes, parodies and links were non-stop. Some enterprising person had even created an animated gif that moved between Marc saying, "Later, alligator," hefting that chainsaw above his head, and the big-eyed anime crocodiles pleading, *Beware the Croc-nami.*

Emme found it hilarious. Apparently, anyone with an internet connection found it hilarious.

It wasn't as if Marc couldn't laugh at himself. Really, he could. And often.

The problem was his future as an actor in the industry.

Would he ever be able to live it down? Or was he now doomed to forever be the *Croc-nami* guy?

Though *if* knowledge of the time portal were leaked to the press, Marc could claim that it was a promotional stunt for a new movie. A time travel romp with Marc portraying a Navy SEAL turned swashbuckling pirate. It would be more believable than actually *having* a time portal in one's cellar.

Ninja Pirate 4, anyone?

He could only imagine the heyday that FauxPause would have with *that* juicy bit of news.

Driving past the front of Duir Cottage with its jaunty flowers, Marc parked the car in the old stables and collected his groceries from the backseat, pondering the blackmail problem.

Even if the world found out about the portal, it wasn't as if the portal were a revolving door, allowing any passerby to stroll through. It wouldn't work for just anyone.

No. The portal had a mind of its own. An agenda.

Jasmine, resident mystic and knower-of-all-things-weird-and-arcane, explained it best.

Past and future formed an eternal *now*. So to the portal, time was not a river, but a vast ocean where the lives of every person who had ever lived existed simultaneously as concentric rings rippling on its surface. As if each life were a stone dropped into the water by some unseen hand. And where the expanding ring of one person became tangled with that of another, the portal provided a link, a pathway that could be traversed.

But only those who had a connection with someone in the past could travel the portal. Therefore, as a method of transportation, the portal was decidedly unreliable. It usually just sat in the cellar, a slab of carved rock pulsing with unseen power. Marc had spent the last two years jokingly touching it, rubbing it like a lamp, tempting fate to release a genie.

Nothing ever happened.

Not that he expected anything would. How could he—a football-loving, martial-arts-doing, twenty-first century actor—have anything in common with a nineteenth century person? The very idea was laughable.

Shrugging, Marc walked through the overgrown back garden to the kitchen door, balancing his groceries while he dug a key from his jacket pocket. He had the key in the lock and the door open before he noticed that the room was not as he left it.

Nothing had been disturbed per se. The modern kitchen with its marble countertops and stainless steel appliances sat gleaming to his left. The huge, rough-hewn dining table still rested directly in front of him.

And the enormous fireplace with its wingback chairs and overstuffed sofa beckoned cozily to his right. Everything in its place.

However, the unexpected addition of a beaver top hat and old-fashioned greatcoat draped over one of the dining table chairs caught his attention. Stark and ridiculously anachronistic.

Beyond the table, he had a clear view of the central hallway. The door down to the cellar—and the time portal—stood open. A large antique-looking wooden trunk sat in front of it.

Every one of Marc's senses instantly ratcheted to high alert.

Silently, he set his keys, phone and bag of groceries on the wooden kitchen floor. Stepping fully inside, he quietly closed the door. He scanned the room, noticing no one, hearing nothing.

Had he interrupted someone just arriving in 2014?

The entire set-up smacked of planning. One didn't accidentally *fall* through the portal with a trunk that size. No, someone had prepared to do this. And was that someone still in the cellar, bringing up more items?

Most importantly, was *this* the person behind the blackmail attempt? It was too much of a coincidence to not be related. If so, what was this person's link to him and the twenty-first century?

Stealthily, Marc edged around the table, cursing his squeaky leather shoes, praying he was being quiet enough. He touched the greatcoat as he crept by—both it and the top hat identical to those James would wear.

He paused at the edge of the hallway, listening again. Nothing. No one.

Should he say something? Try to lure the person out?

As usual, he felt no fear, just the heart-pounding rush of adrenaline. He had spent over twenty-five of his thirty-two years studying martial arts and street-fighting. His bare hands had always been protection enough.

Cautiously, Marc peered around the door frame, through the trapdoor in the floor and down into the cellar. The wooden stairs descended steeply to packed earth, empty. But he couldn't see into the back of the dark cellar where the portal hummed. Was someone down there?

Cloth suddenly clamped around his mouth, a strong hand pressing into his face. Hard.

Marc breathed in a sickly sweet smell, making him instantly woozy. But years of martial arts training sprang into action, despite his suddenly spinning head. He shot back an elbow, delivering a sharp blow to his attacker's ribs, getting a low grunt as a response.

Male, his mind absently noted. His attacker was definitely a man.

Marc hooked the unknown man's leg with his own, while simultaneously grabbing the arm which held the cloth over his mouth and twisting it outward painfully, breaking the man's hold. Allowing Marc to snatch a breath of much-needed fresh air. Even so, the room spun crazily.

Marc sensed blackness creeping in at the edges, enhancing his light-headedness, making his movements less precise than usual. Relying on muscle memory, Marc used the twisting momentum of his body to throw his attacker to the ground.

But the man was not entirely unfamiliar with street fighting, and Marc was sluggish. So instead of tumbling down the stairs alone, the attacker had time to grab Marc, sending them both spinning toward the ground. Marc found himself face-to-face with a brass button embossed with a vine-covered crest. And then they were both rolling, rolling down the wooden stairs.

Marc instinctively braced for impact, but it never came.

Instead, he just continued on . . . falling, falling, falling . . . the button flashing before his gaze, searing into memory.

Until blackness took him.

THE OLD BOAR INN
MARFIELD, HEREFORDSHIRE
FEBRUARY 19, 1814

Lady Ruby's instructions had been extremely clear:

Take this letter straight to Mr. Millet at the Old Boar Inn to be posted. My nephew's butler has shifty eyes and is not to be trusted with my correspondence.

Kit had stared at the letter as she drove the Knight's gig into the nearby town of Marfield.

Firstly, the Knight's butler, Finley, seemed a perfectly fine fellow with nary a hint of shiftiness about his person.

Secondly, Kit could not imagine—even if the butler *were* shifty—why he would be interested in letters to a Mrs. Boring of Quiet Street, Bath.

Yes. That *really* was the address, neat and plain. Mrs. Boring. Quiet Street. Bath.

It was fairly ridiculous.

But nearly every day, Lady Ruby sent Kit into Marfield on some errand or another.

"Poor Jedediah is in need of more blacking for his boots. Off with you."

"See that Mr. Millet posts this letter to Plymouth. And be sure to ask if any correspondence has arrived for me."

"The feathers in my purple velvet turban have quite drooped. I believe the haberdasher has some lovely peacock ones you can fetch."

Kit had become quite adept at navigating the few miles between Haldon Manor and Marfield in the gig. Fortunately, the roads were well-maintained, allowing for easy travel despite the gloomy February weather.

Today, the sun broke through the ever-present clouds.

Away, away, away, Wicked Angel whispered. *Let's fly away. Just take a ring or two from Lady Ruby, hitch up the gig and we'll be in the next county before anyone realizes you're not coming back.*

Do not *listen to her.* That was Virtuous Angel. *First of all, you are not going to add theft to your growing list of crimes. Second, they would catch you. Third, where would you go? You can't go home without Daniel, and home is the only place you want to go. You have to find your brother, which means remaining at Haldon Manor. He has to be around here somewhere.*

But despite her constant searching, Kit still hadn't found him.

Was Daniel here? And if so, what were his exact plans? The snippet of discussion she had overheard between Arthur and Linwood had only fanned the flame of her worry. It was *exactly* the thing she feared.

Secrets. Always secrets. She was so eternally weary of them.

Kit just wanted her brother. She had practically raised him after their mother left and their father buried himself in grief and his books. Six years her junior, Daniel hadn't understood or even seemed to care that he had no mother. And just like their mother, wanderlust gripped him. Daniel could never stay in the same place for more than a month or two.

With their father's death the previous year, Daniel was all the family she had left. Without Daniel, she would have no one. *He* would have no one. Who would bail him out of his scrapes, if not her?

And if he continued down this path, she wouldn't have a roof over her head to return to.

They *needed* each other. Didn't Daniel see that?

Kit stepped out of the Old Boar Inn—the letter having been safely delivered into the hands of Mr. Millet—and tilted her head back, attempting to dispel her anxiety by basking in the warm sun.

Well, warmish-for-February sun. It still felt lovely and helped banish some of the chill which seeped through her winter pelisse and wool cloak.

With a sigh, she walked over to the gig. How long could she stall before returning to Haldon Manor? Lady Ruby would expect her back promptly. And then there was the matter of Jedediah Knight, who had become more aggressive, always appearing where least expected.

"Miss Ashton, how surprising to find you here," he'd said, cornering her in the still room off the scullery, blocking the door. "And all alone. If I didn't know better, I would say you have been waiting for me."

She hadn't. And she had seen how both scullery maids and the cook had ducked out of sight as soon as they heard his voice.

"Mr. Knight," she replied with a bobbed curtsy. "I was just fetching some dried lavender for your mother. If you will excuse me, I am sure she is waiting for it."

He crowded her into the small workspace, forcing her to shoulder her way past him to escape. He took full advantage of the proximity to press against her. Kit jabbed a seemingly accidental elbow sharply into his ribs, causing him to fall back with a grunt.

"Have a care, Miss Ashton," he had hissed. "You will not always be able to escape."

A shy, smaller, more retiring woman would have caved to his pressure by now or run off in fear.

Fortunately, *shy* and *retiring* had never been words in her vocabulary. And at her age—thirty, last November, firmly *on the shelf* as Daniel kept reminding her—she had no patience with such men. Bullies always raised her hackles.

So far, her sharp tongue and even sharper elbows and knees had kept him at bay. Men the likes of Jedediah Knight would never cow her. But without her place in society to protect her, she had few other resources beyond quick wits and even quicker reflexes. And, really, it was only a matter of time before she offended him enough to put her position in jeopardy.

Lady Ruby would hardly side with Kit over her wayward son. And Kit could ill afford being tossed into the street.

So she just bottled it all up. Swallowed the scathing retorts. The hissing comebacks. Crammed, stuffed and squeezed it back inside her until she threatened to burst.

A couple rings and the gig. I'm telling you—it's a good plan. Wicked Angel wouldn't stop tempting her.

She was not naive. She knew that the game—the thrill of the chase—was a large part of the fun for men like Jedediah. Her life before Haldon Manor had been filled with parties and dinners and never ending socializing. She was no stranger to aristocratic men and their machinations.

Fortunately, standing in the middle of Marfield with her gig, she remembered she had no worries about running into Jedediah today. Arthur and his cousin had strode off that morning in the woods, rifles slung over their shoulders—gamekeeper, servants and a pack of hounds in tow.

She tugged her plain bonnet loose, allowing it to hang on its ribbons. Again, tilting her head back and feeling the sunshine on her face. She righted her head and made a studious show of petting the horse hitched to the gig, putting off returning to Haldon Manor for at least a few more minutes.

A group of day laborers strode up the high street, jackets dusty, sledgehammers over their shoulders. Two servant girls passed them, giggling and whispering.

And then a figure down the street just past the apothecary caught her eye. A taller man, lean with close-cropped hair in a dark blue coat and gleaming boots, turning to walk down the alleyway between two buildings. He came into profile as he turned, nodding a greeting to the laborers.

And in that second, Kit's heart stopped.

She would know that profile anywhere.

Daniel.

Hallelujah. At last!

He watched the laborers, never fully turning his head toward her. Too far away for her to yell and capture his attention.

Drat.

He hadn't seen her. And even if he had, how likely was he to recognize her? Heaven knew Daniel had never seen her dressed in a gown like this.

Suddenly, he pivoted entirely and disappeared down the alley. Frantic to reach him, Kit darted across the street, lifting up her long skirts as she picked her way toward the alley.

So her brother really *was* here. That note she found had been right. But *why* was he here? What was his connection with Haldon Manor? And please, oh please, let it have nothing to do with French spies and the current war with Napoleon.

Jumping over a pile of manure as she passed the apothecary shop, she realized it didn't matter anymore. She didn't care why he was here, what had driven him. He just needed to come home.

If he came home without doing damage, everything would be all right. Their lives would go on just as they had before.

She was almost to the alleyway when a now-familiar voice accosted her.

"Miss Ashton, how delightful to see you."

Kit turned to the gloved hand touching her arm and the round, smiling face of the vicar's wife, Mrs. Smith.

Drat, drat and triple *drat*!

Kit owed the miniature Mrs. Smith a tremendous debt of gratitude. She and her husband had welcomed Kit into their home when she had nothing more than the clothing on her back. In fact, Kit's current serviceable brown dress, pelisse and cloak had belonged to the vicar's late sister—fortunately a taller woman for Kit's sake. The second-hand skirts were only a little short on her.

Even with Daniel perhaps lurking around the corner, every ounce of gratitude and politeness and good breeding in her soul knew that she could not snub Mrs. Smith.

Argh!

More's the pity.

With one longing look to the corner where Daniel had just disappeared, Kit bobbed a polite curtsy in greeting.

"And you too, Mrs. Smith."

Mrs. Smith was one of those tiny humans, the kind who made Kit feel just that much larger. As if nature had laughed when it made two women so impossibly different.

And so Kit found herself looking down, down, down into Mrs. Smith's kind brown eyes. The vicar and his wife made an odd pair—him tall and gangly, his wife tiny and round. The top of Mrs. Smith's head barely reached her husband's ribcage.

"You look well, Miss Ashton." Mrs. Smith appraised Kit's clothing. "I take it Lady Ruby and Haldon Manor agree with you."

Mrs. Smith, it seemed, took great pride in having helped Kit become placed as Lady Ruby's companion. As though Kit and Lady Ruby had been courting, and Mrs. Smith had facilitated a match.

It was oddly disconcerting.

Biting back her impatience, Kit responded to Mrs. Smith's inquiries.

Kit was well. Lady Ruby was well. Baby Isabel was a dear little thing. Haldon Manor was a lovely home. Yes, the Knights did employ an excellent cook.

And then, she moved on to give polite replies to Mrs. Smith's worries. How terrible that Mrs. Croft had still not forgiven Mr. Smith for that incident involving his heifer and her vegetable garden. Yes, Kit would try to attend the next meeting of the Marfield Temperance Society. Indeed, liquor was the Devil's own brew.

Wicked Angel snickered at that.

All the while, Kit prayed that Daniel was still down that alleyway, that she would be able to find him.

Her foot wanted to *tap-tap-tap* with impatience.

Though I deeply appreciate her and all that she has done, Mrs. Smith needs to move along. Virtuous Angel murmured.

Indeed. Doesn't she have some do-gooder stuff to attend to? Wicked Angel asked.

It was a sign of her impatience and desperation when both angels concurred on anything.

Finally after Kit agreed to give a speech on the deleterious dangers of whiskey (causing more snickering from Wicked Angel), Mrs. Smith hurried off to chat with Mrs. Millet at the Old Boar Inn about the evils of ale.

Kit wished her luck and ducked down the alleyway.

But she had taken too long; the alley was decidedly empty. Just a pile of refuse and an old barrel. Nothing more. She walked through the narrow corridor, which opened up to another small street leading to the village green.

No Daniel in sight.

Kit sighed and leaned against the alleyway wall, resisting the urge to slowly pound her head into the brick.

It figured. The man *had* been Daniel. She would know her brother anywhere. Even here.

Frustrated, Kit spent the next thirty minutes walking the length of town, finally looping back to the gig and her patiently waiting horse.

Still no Daniel.

Had she truly seen him? Or was she just so desperate to find him that she was now imagining things?

And she had to get back to Haldon Manor before she lost her post. Chewing her cheek in frustration, Kit patted the horse again, forcing agitated tears back. She *never* cried. Crying solved nothing and would only give her a headache. She took in several lungfuls of air, trying to center her breathing.

In, out . . . in, out.

Giving the horse one more affectionate pat, she climbed into the gig.

Daniel was here. He was. She *had* seen him. She refused to doubt it.

She would find him, remove him from whatever nonsense he had gotten himself into and return home. End of story.

Chapter 4

The pounding in Marc's head pulsed viciously. Like someone playing whack-a-mole with his eyeballs. Groggily, he opened his eyes to a spinning world.

And then promptly shut them again as bile rose in his throat.

He lay on ground that was far too hard and cold. The musty air chilly. But mostly, it was the startling lack of sound. His ears hummed noisy, empty static.

He felt like he was coming out of anesthesia, where every sense was hyper-aware but still shockingly befuddled.

Taking in a couple of deep breaths, he forced his mind more awake, centered his focus.

Tried to remember what had happened.

The greatcoat. The beaver top hat. The trunk.

Blackmail. There had been an intruder. A man. And a fight. A sweet-smelling cloth over his mouth. That button with a shield surrounded by twining leaves.

And then . . . falling.

Gingerly, he opened his eyes again. The headache receded somewhat but the room still spun around, though a little less than before. He was lying on his back in the cellar, the portal humming against the top of his head, the stairs rising up at his feet. Dim light filtered down from the trapdoor.

Cautiously, Marc flexed his hands and then his feet. Aside from all his senses being acutely heightened, he seemed to be all right. There must have been some drug on that cloth. Like a handkerchief full of chloroform or something equally Sherlock Holmes-esque.

Each deep breath cleared more of his fuzziness. The nausea retreated. Listening intently, he still heard nothing. No sound of movement from above.

Feeling more alert, he carefully sat up and then paused, allowing his head to stop spinning.

So far, so good.

Pulling to his feet, he took in a few more slow breaths. Better. He was improving, the mental fog retreating.

He needed to call the police about the break-in. And then James and Emme. This whole situation was getting more serious. The man who attacked him had to be involved somehow with the blackmail attempt. The events were too coincidental not to be related.

Marc climbed up the steep wooden stairs and stopped in the doorway to the hall, clutching the jamb, closing his eyes against the spinning world.

Okay, so maybe he wasn't quite a hundred percent. More like seventy-five percent. A couple more deep breaths and a cool hand against his forehead helped.

He would grab his phone from the kitchen and then lie down before attempting to make any calls. He could deal with all of this a lot better once he was lying on his back.

He opened his eyes again and stared down at the wood floor. The trunk was gone. Whoever had broken in was obviously no longer here. What a mess. Was some nineteenth century nut-case now loose in modern Herefordshire?

Sighing, he turned to walk into the kitchen and then froze. His heart rate kicked into high gear.

The kitchen wasn't there. Well, *something* was there, but it was most definitely *not* the 2014 kitchen he knew.

Breathing shallowly, Marc scanned the hallway. It was eerily the same with its dark oak paneling. But no light fixtures hung from the ceiling, no switches poked out from the wall.

Adrenaline pumping, he walked fully into the back of the house, where the modern kitchen/great room should have been. The enormous fireplace still dominated the left side of the room, but it now hung with work pots and baskets of dried herbs.

All signs of modernity gone.

"No!" Marc gasped. "Nonononononono!"

Clutching his aching head, he stumbled back down the wooden stairs and collapsed against the stone at the far end of the cellar. The portal thrummed under his hands, potent and alive. But nothing happened. Not the swooping, falling sensation that Emme and James described.

Wait.

Falling. He *had* fallen.

No!

This couldn't be happening. Was he in 1814? He was definitely going to be sick.

Darting back up the stairs, Marc barely made it to a bucket in the primitive kitchen before losing the contents of his stomach. Shaking, he collapsed on the cold wood floor, one arm still looped around the bucket.

This couldn't be happening. He didn't have *time* to be trapped in 1814.

He needed to be home, meeting with his agent and coming up with a strategy to combat the whole FauxPause mess.

He needed modern medicine and wi-fi and ESPN and . . . and . . . deodorant.

And what of his attacker?

They had fallen down the stairs together. Had the blackmailer returned to 1814 with him? Or was the man now, indeed, traipsing around 2014 causing trouble?

And how could Marc possibly discover the answer to those questions?

Damn! What an ghastly mess!

He hung his head over the bucket and threaded his fingers into his hair, trying in vain to massage the tension from his skull.

How would Emme and James ever figure it out?

And why had the portal let him through? He had jokingly tried for nearly *two* years to take a trip back in time. Granted, he had never been serious about it.

But the portal only allowed you through for a reason. Your life had to be entangled with that of someone else—at least, according to Jasmine. The path of your life had to *require* a trip through time.

Who could he be connected to in the past? This attacker/possible blackmailer who was now (maybe) creating havoc in 2014 Marfield? That made no sense.

And what was he, Marc Wilde, to do here? What did 1814 have to offer him? And vice versa?

He was a British/American martial arts actor, raised in Denver, living wherever his acting took him. The only constants in his life were his mother, his sister and Broncos football. Precisely in that order.

Of all his dreams and ambitions—of which he had many—living in the early nineteenth century was decidedly *not* one of them.

How soon could he return to his own century? And even worse, *would* he be allowed to return?

His stomach heaved again, requiring him to clutch the bucket tightly. After completely emptying his gut, the nausea receded. A few minutes later, Marc struggled to his feet. He emptied the bucket into what looked like an outhouse of sorts behind the house and took a drink from a well in the yard. Then, he trudged back down to the cellar.

The portal still pulsed mockingly. But again, no amount of thinking positive twenty-first century thoughts and hugging the stone—and then kicking, swearing, pounding it—returned him home.

Sighing, he sank back down to the dirt floor, holding his head in his hands.

Trying to gather his fuzzy thoughts together.

Okay, assuming he might actually be stuck in 1814, now what?

He was lost in another century, far from friends and home and everything that was familiar.

Well . . . that wasn't entirely true. He actually *did* know people in 1814.

One person, at least—Georgiana.

Georgiana, James' younger sister, was here with her husband, Sebastian. Marc knew Georgiana well, as she had spent over a year in the twenty-first century. She was like another sister to him. But Georgiana and Sebastian weren't anywhere near Duir Cottage, of that he was quite sure. Sebastian was the Earl of Stratton, so he and Georgiana were probably in London or living wherever nineteenth century earls lived.

So they probably weren't an immediate help.

However, Arthur Knight should be nearby. James' younger brother who had inherited Haldon Manor when James and Emme were supposedly 'killed' in a carriage accident.

Marc had never met Arthur, obviously, but he *was* family of a sort—being Marc's sister's husband's brother and all.

That should count for something. Arthur would help him, right?

Well . . . maybe . . .

Hadn't James and Georgiana reminisced more than once about Arthur's stodginess?

Not that it mattered at this point. Stodgy or no, Marc needed help. Needed to pick himself up off the floor and head up the road to Haldon Manor. Fate would take things from there.

Breathing deeply for another fifteen minutes helped immensely. Most of the nausea passed, and Marc's head felt nearly better.

As he sat there, Marc took stock of the situation. He couldn't just walk up to the doors of Haldon Manor in the jeans, t-shirt and leather jacket he was currently wearing. He needed to look the part of an arriving gentleman who might be friends with Arthur Knight.

Right. How to do that?

Fortunately, Emme had made Marc go to the Jane Austen Festival in Bath more than once. Not to mention the Bosom Companion of the English Regency meetings he had attended a couple times with Georgiana. The kind ladies there had drilled him over and over on how to speak. Marc had finally figured out that he just needed to use the fanciest, biggest words he knew. That usually did the trick.

So he had a general understanding of how a nineteenth century gentleman should dress and act.

And *Ninja Pirate 1* had been a historical film (loosely interpreted, but he had worn pantaloons, a cutlass and had learned how to bow like a gentleman). So really, he wasn't entirely clueless. Thank goodness.

But it did mean finding more period-appropriate clothing.

Pushing to his feet, Marc climbed out of the cellar (again) and explored the cottage. It was eerie to be in a building he knew so well—that looked so much the same—and yet was not. All the floors smooth and level, the wood brighter and un-aged. Walls didn't bulge and lean. Everything crisp and new.

It was like seeing a younger, less drunk version of the house.

In a wardrobe upstairs, he found some men's clothing, finely woven and tailored. Judging by their size, they must belong to someone taller than his own six feet. Sebastian, perhaps? Hadn't James said he was tall?

It didn't matter. The clothes would work.

A few minutes later, Marc stowed his modern clothing in the bottom of the wardrobe and assessed himself in the wavy mirror in the corner of the room.

He didn't look too bad. The fawn colored trousers bunched a bit at his ankles and the blue wool coat was a little long in the sleeves, but his broad shoulders filled out the rest nicely. He wasn't drowning in it. The silver-striped waistcoat fit well. Granted, a gentleman usually wore boots, but his dark leather shoes weren't entirely anachronistic. Some things just never went out of style.

Best of all, he had managed to tie the cravat in what James called a mail coach knot. It was the only knot Marc knew.

But, seriously, how many twenty-first century men could confidently dress themselves to look like a gentleman from 1814?

He felt absurdly proud of himself.

Though, running a hand over his scruffy chin, he would probably need a shave. The scruff Marc religiously maintained, his I-haven't-shaved-in-a-week-stubble would have to go. He was quite sure a permanent five o'clock shadow wouldn't become vogue until Don Johnson and *Miami Vice* circa 1984. Unfortunately, the cottage didn't have a straight razor, so shaving would have to wait. He probably needed a hat and gloves too, but those items were not to be found.

Though after a little more digging, Marc did uncover a caped greatcoat in another closet (again, probably Sebastian's judging by the size) and shrugged into it, glad to finally feel warm under so many layers of clothing. The February chill had definitely permeated the house.

So that was that. He was as ready as he would ever be.

Squaring his shoulders, Marc marched down the stairs, intent on the front door and Haldon Manor. But as he turned to walk outside, he saw that the door down to the cellar still stood open. No sense in advertising to the world there was something of interest down there.

He took two steps down the hallway and shut the closet door. But as he turned back toward the front door, he caught a flash of white out of the corner of his eye.

There, on the floor, lay a folded square of cloth. Hidden behind the open closet door. Bending down, he gingerly picked it up. Noting the yellow liquid which stained its center. A careful sniff revealed the same sickly, sweet smell. Chloroform or whatever had been used to help subdue him.

This *had* to be the same cloth his attacker used. But how had it ended up here, just outside the closet door in the hallway?

There was really only one answer. In order for it to be here, the man had to have fallen through the portal with Marc. And then, he had accidentally dropped the cloth while leaving the cottage. Marc felt a sense of relief that the man wasn't running rampant through 2014.

But it was all too fleeting.

Why was someone trying to use the portal? Why the blackmail? Why would the portal allow this attacker to travel back and forth? Had Fate linked him to this man for some reason?

And how was he to apprehend a man he hadn't seen? His memory of that button was all he had to go on.

So many unanswered questions. And no Google or modern police forensics to help him.

Marc pocketed the square cloth and surveyed the hallway one more time, looking for any additional clues. But there was nothing more.

He just needed to find Arthur and formulate a plan. An unknown man with proven nefarious intent and knowledge of the portal was on the loose in Marfield. Who knew what might happen. The man couldn't be stopped soon enough.

With a deep breath, Marc stepped out of the front door of Duir Cottage. And swallowed.

He hadn't really thought through how much things had changed in the past two hundred years.

The house was completely different. There were no sunny yellow roses in the window, obviously. But also gone were the graveled drive and lush front garden. The stone fence was starkly new, bare of any covering ivy. The enormous oak tree to the right of the house was a tiny sapling, recently planted and spindly. Forest surrounded the house.

The silence was even more unnerving. No hum of the nearby motor-way. No rumble of a tractor or burst of a car alarm. Just the chirp of birds and rustle of leaves.

It all underscored the reality of his situation.

A lane still wandered off to the left, disappearing into the trees, hopefully leading up to the front door of Haldon Manor.

Straightening his shoulders, Marc stepped through the garden and onto the lane. After a few minutes of walking, he saw the lane intersected with a wider road in front of him. Haldon Manor should be down that road to the left.

Suddenly, gunfire cracked sharply through the woods, followed by the frightened whinny of a horse and the loud jangle of a harness.

But it was the sound of a woman screaming in terror which sent Marc sprinting up the lane.

Chapter 5

The echoing gunshot shattered the peaceful calm, startling Kit. The bullet ricocheted right over the top of the gig, causing her to jump and lose her grip on the reins.

But even more critically, the flying bullet spooked her horse. The poor gelding flinched in his harness and then took off at a run. The sudden movement, combined with Kit's own slack hold, tore the reins entirely from her hands.

With a terrified scream, Kit clung to the frame of the gig as it hurtled down the lane, watching the driving leathers bounce uselessly on the ground behind the galloping horse. No way to retrieve them.

The lane extended straight ahead for the moment, crossing over a small bridge. But beyond that, the road curved sharply to the right, and the horse showed no signs of slowing down. At her current pace, there was no way the gig would make the turn without toppling.

Holding on desperately to the bone-jarring carriage, her options quickly dwindled to just two less-than-ideal choices. She could jump from the runaway gig and hope she wasn't too injured. Or she could stay in the carriage and pray the horse calmed before the curve. Which, given the poor thing's frantic pace, seemed unlikely.

The gig clattered over the bridge, the fateful bend in the road looming closer and closer. Jumping looked more and more like the better idea. At least that way she could *choose* where she fell.

It just figured she would (finally!) see Daniel only to be crushed to death under a runaway carriage. Given everything she had been through in the last month, she refused to have it all end like this.

Kit tried to assess how fast she was truly going. Could she release the gig long enough to gather her dress in one hand before leaping out? She didn't want her skirts to snag, dragging her underneath the carriage instead of away from it.

Staring along the left side of the road, she was debating whether grass or mud would make for a better landing, when a man burst from the bare trees next to her horse, running full tilt.

She caught the general impression of a billowing caped greatcoat and dark, curly hair as the man came alongside the horse. Effortlessly, he grasped the harness and launched himself onto the animal's back in one smooth motion, wrapping his arms around the beast's neck and grabbing the reins. Leaning backward, the man pulled on the reins, gradually calming the terrified horse. Stopping its frantic gallop.

Kit gasped. Astonished. It had all been so fluid, done with such seeming ease.

The entire scene was surreal, like some trick from a traveling gypsy circus. Maybe the man was a gypsy himself, come to think of it.

Kit could only stare as the gig slowed and then came to a stop right before the dangerous turn in the road.

All in all, the entire incident had lasted less than a minute.

Breathing heavily and shaking from delayed shock, Kit watched as her rescuer patted the horse's neck, making soothing noises and calming the frightened animal. With the same easy grace, the man dismounted, holding the lathered horse still and keeping a reassuring hand on the animal's neck.

And then he lifted his head and turned his attention to her.

Oh my, whispered Virtuous Angel.

Oh my, indeed.

Dark, wind-blown hair curled over his ears and coat collar. A day or two of beard growth stubbled his cheeks. His tanned skin hinted at a life spent outdoors. A caped greatcoat clung to his shoulders and then dropped straight to practically brush the ground, a blue jacket peeking out underneath. The wild chase had rumpled him, leaving his coat askew, chest heaving for air.

But it was his eyes—vividly green against his tanned cheeks and dark hair—that held her attention. They thrummed with life, promising a rogue's tongue and unruly past.

A far cry from the pampered, fussy, *civilized* men who inhabited her life.

Uhmmm . . . suggestion, murmured Wicked Angel. *When we abscond with a couple rings and the gig, I nominate we take* him *too.*

Kit sighed in agreement.

Not helping, Virtuous Angel muttered. *The last thing we need is a pretty-faced distraction right now.*

But, oh, what a delicious distraction . . .

Who was he? And how had he happened to be along the private lane to Haldon Manor?

Though bedraggled, the fine-cut and fabric of his clothing spoke of refinement and money. Her mystery man cocked his head at her, continuing to pat the horse comfortingly, catching his breath.

"Good heavens," Kit murmured. Though the word came out as more of a breathy sigh than an exclamation.

Not *exactly* the best beginning. She tried again.

"Thank you, sir." She nodded at him, unable to tear her eyes free. His striking gaze pinned her to her seat.

"Are you . . . unharmed?" His low, cultured voice was still somewhat winded but confirmed him a gentleman.

"I am well. You have my deepest thanks." Kit blinked. Surely her eyes were too wide, wide, wide.

She smoothed her hands against her skirts and used the excuse to cast a quick glance down at her clothing.

Drat.

Her cloak had swung around to her front and her bonnet was gone, torn from her head by the terrifying ride, no doubt. In her peripheral vision, she could see locks of hair dangling free from their pins. She actively resisted the urge to pat them back into place. Not that it would help, really.

She didn't need a mirror to know she looked a fright.

And even with everything set to rights, she would still be wearing a second-hand brown wool dress—a lady of genteel birth fallen on hard times.

Which, currently, described her situation quite accurately.

How would this man react if he could see her as she looked at home in her own clothing, coolly confident? Well . . . at least as confident as she could be. And how *pathetic* she even thought such a thing.

He could never see her like that. It would risk too much. A man like him would never be welcome in her world.

He said nothing, but merely scrubbed an ungloved hand through his mussed hair, somehow rendering it just that much more tempting.

How could a man sprint onto the back of a runaway horse and come out looking even better than before? Not that she had seen him before, but still.

It wasn't fair.

Kit generally considered herself immune to attractive men. Inoculated against them.

She had been raised with her handsome brother after all, and the men she associated with before landing at Haldon Manor were an urbane lot. Clever, sophisticated, moneyed.

In short, Kit Ashton was *not* the sort of woman to become infatuated with a handsome face.

So it came as no surprise that the gentlemen she had met so far at Haldon Manor scarcely turned her head. Jedediah Knight . . . uh, obviously no. Lord Linwood was not un-handsome, but his starched demeanor and cool reserve easily counteracted his good looks.

But *this* man . . .

He seemed elemental. Untamed. Dangerous.

The kind of man who would entice a woman to make poor life choices.

The kind of man her mother would have warned her to stay far, far away from.

What a *pity* she had never had a mother's influence.

Wicked Angel snickered at the sarcasm.

Really, he needs to come along with us, Wicked Angel urged. *He could be the scenery.*

You are such a trial. We are not running away, remember? No matter how lovely the scenery, Virtuous Angel chided.

Kit batted both thoughts away, but she did give in and straightened the cloak around her shoulders.

"I cannot imagine my fate had you not happened along." She pasted on a bright smile.

Mmmm, perhaps a little too bright. Star-struck. She dimmed it a bit. Tried again.

"How does one ever learn such a remarkable trick?" She gestured toward the horse.

He stared for a moment, giving her a chance to study the carved planes of his face.

Yes. Still handsome.

Drat him for making her *want* to flirt.

A lady's companion did not flirt. Of *that* she was quite certain.

But he was just so irresistibly . . . male. So self-assured and capable in that romantic greatcoat which made his shoulders seem enormous.

And, heaven knew, she had *such* weakness for broad shoulders. They made her want to place things on them . . . like her hands or head or . . . her problems.

How wonderful would it be to have such strong shoulders as a sanctuary? A place to rest from her troubles.

But she had promised herself she would be good.

That thought settled it. No flirting then.

He shrugged and said, "Happy to be of service," while continuing to pat the horse's neck.

Completely ignoring her question.

Hmmm. Why avoid the question? Apparently, she wasn't the only one with secrets.

A soft breeze tugged at Kit's hair, implying that more of it was down than she had initially thought.

Blast.

Pausing, as if unsure, the man gave her a brief bow.

Kit blinked and felt her smile falter.

So was he dashing, handsome, secretive and . . . rude?

He had turned back to the horse, continuing to soothe the lathered beast. She studied the man's dark curls for a moment and then her eyes met his as he raised his head again.

He didn't look particularly haughty. More like harried.

Odd.

So perhaps not . . . rude? Dashing and handsome went without saying.

But still definitely secretive.

Her eyes narrowed. How to prod him?

"Miss Katherine Ashton, pleased to make your acquaintance." She nodded politely. And then waited for him to do the same.

He said nothing. Did nothing. Just continued to stare at her with those rather unnerving green eyes.

He was clearly going to need more prodding.

She leaned forward, as if imparting a confidence. "In a polite conversation between a lady and a gentleman, this is the point where you, sir, introduce yourself." She paused. Waiting.

Again, he said nothing and instead widened his eyes, as if her suggestion had startled him. As if the entire scene with her were overwhelming in some way.

The silence lingered a little too long.

"Let's just say that I am a . . . friend," he finally responded with a wary tip of his head.

"A friend?"

He shrugged.

"That is all the answer you will deign to give me?"

He raised an amused eyebrow, his face showing a sudden hint of mischievousness.

"I did just save your life. I should be allowed an eccentricity or two."

Unbidden, Kit found herself matching his tone. "I believe *incivility* was the word you wanted there."

"Excuse me?"

"An orange cravat or flower in your hat would be an eccentricity. A refusal to introduce oneself is something else entirely."

"Ah." His head reared back. "And you feel *incivility* fits the bill?"

It was Kit's turn to shrug. Saucily mimicking his nonchalance.

He gave a wry grin. Though . . . it was so much more than just a grin, really.

He had one of those slow-burn smiles. The kind that started small and then grew wider and wider until *pow!* You forgot how to breathe.

Stupid, handsome man.

"After such a scolding, I can hardly introduce myself now, can I?" He added a cocky smirk to his ridiculously charming smile.

Both her eyebrows went up and she folded her hands in her lap. Mostly because they itched to swat that grin off his face. "You must forgive me, sir. I am not adept at following astonishing jumps in logic."

Impossibly, his smile broadened, crinkling his eyes. "That was nicely done."

"Excuse me?" It was Kit's turn to look confused.

"All of it. The cutting remark, the self-righteous folding of your hands—"

"Self-righteous?! Gracious! And you call yourself a gentleman—"

He laughed good and loud at that. His head went back and his eyes disappeared.

And at that precise moment, Kit realized she was in serious, deep-water trouble.

Handsome, dashing, *charming* man.

With obvious secrets to hide.

Curse him.

Still chuckling, he gestured toward her. "Well, if I introduce myself now, it would smack of surrender. And I assure you, I never raise a white flag."

He did not, however, refute her accusation of his un-gentleman-ness. Interesting.

They stared at each other for a moment.

"Well, I thank you for rescuing me," she said at last, not wanting to seem churlish. "'Twas most fortunate."

He patted the horse's neck again. Shrugged. "I am glad that today has been fortunate for one of us, at least."

Marc swallowed and let out a slow breath, continuing to rub the horse. Mostly to give the illusion of being busy.

Wow. He was *so* utterly out of his depth.

Ninja Pirate 1 had most definitely *not* prepared him for situations like this.

Though who knew all the horse jumping training he had undergone for that western cattle-heist flick (*The Quick and the Spurious*—it was huge in India) would prove so useful.

He had stopped the horse based entirely on muscle-memory and then turned . . .

. . . to find *this* woman staring at him.

He didn't know what he had expected a nineteenth century woman to look like . . . but she was most certainly not it.

She sat on the carriage bench swaddled in a cloak and seemingly twenty layers of clothing. Composed and steady, despite the undoubtedly frightening ordeal with her horse. She didn't seem like a woman who could be easily rattled. More like a fierce huntress with her hair torn loose and fluttering wildly around her face, spilling onto her shoulders.

Brown-ish hair . . . though it wasn't exactly brown. It glinted with reds and golds too and curled everywhere.

Definitely not simple brown, now that he considered it. He was sure Emme would have an exact word for the color. Auburn, maybe?

And huge, wide-set brown eyes that somehow matched the color of her hair, golden and warm.

So again, not quite brown really.

They looked out inquisitively, framed between dark arching eyebrows and high cheekbones. He could tell she was tall, even seated.

And then there was her feisty, quick wit.

All in all, she reminded him vaguely of Katherine Hepburn in her prime. An *Adam's Rib* Katharine Hepburn.

Bottom line . . . she was stunning.

Which was entirely unexpected. Why had he always assumed that women in the past would be more quiet and submissive? Somehow . . . less than women in the modern age.

This woman was clearly none of those things.

What had she said her name was? Miss Ashton?

She *clearly* hadn't appreciated his teasing refusal to introduce himself, but Marc was hesitant to tell anyone his name until he had chatted with Arthur.

Though, would it hurt to tell her his first name? He hadn't considered that. Was he being rude? He didn't want to be rude. Particularly not to her.

Just so . . . out of his depth. The sooner he found Arthur and had a crash course in nineteenth century etiquette, the better.

She shifted on the carriage seat. "Well, as you are a *friend* . . ." She lingered on the word, rendering it so very, very dry.

"Marc," he said without thinking.

"I beg your pardon?"

"If we *are* to be friends, call me Marc. All my friends do."

Miss Ashton stilled, giving him a puzzled look. So maybe that hadn't been the best idea after all. Women probably didn't call unknown men by their first names. Ouch. What a terrible faux pas—

"I am so sorry. I did not mean to . . . give offense—"

"No, no need to apologize." Miss Ashton waved her hand in a dismissive gesture. "I am not so missish as to stand by ceremony. I was just . . . surprised, is all. I do believe I heard a certain gentleman declare just moments ago that he never raises a white flag." She raised both eyebrows. Challenging.

"Perhaps this certain . . . gentleman is willing to make an exception for a *friend*." Marc matched her challenging look.

"Perhaps." The lovely Miss Ashton tapped a gloved finger against her lips. "Though such turnabout smacks of a fickle nature. Not something I should wish in a friend."

Ah. Clever. She *would* be clever.

"Not even two minutes into our friendship, and you are already taking me in hand, trying to reform me. Change my very nature—"

"Precisely. How fortunate for you to recognize early on the value of our friendship." Miss Ashton smiled, her expression a heady mixture of charm and wicked delight. "But if you are to be Marc to me, then I must be Kit to you."

"Kit." Marc tried out her name, liking how it captured her. Bold and strong.

"Marc," she responded, tipping her head at him as if in greeting. Which he supposed they were finally doing.

She paused and then continued. "Is that short for Marcus, perhaps?"

She asked the question innocently enough, but there was a hesitancy in it. How could his given name mean anything to her?

"Why, yes, in fact it is."

She nodded. "May I ask how you happened to be along the lane to Haldon Manor? I thought I had been introduced to all the gentlemen in Marfield."

Right. How to explain his presence here?

Wait. How nineteenth century-ish did his language need to be in order for him to blend in? Damn . . . or, er, drat. He needed to pay more attention to the words leaving his mouth.

He had been thinking about it as adopting a character, like he was doing research for an upcoming film project. Something suitably Jane Austen-ish, using his most posh British accent.

So far she hadn't seemed too surprised by his language.

He could do this. He had read *Pride and Prejudice and Zombies* after all. He just needed to keep using fancy words. Lots of them.

"I do not hail from Marfield, so it would be unlikely for us to have formed a prior acquaintance."

What a mouthful. Though he was quite proud of himself for it. Did it sound stuffy enough?

He assessed her. She sat coolly composed in the carriage, pulling her cloak more tightly around herself.

No reaction. That was good, right?

"Naturally, I had surmised as much," she said. "Yet how does a gentleman find himself upon a private lane without carriage or horse?"

Yeah. That was an excellent question. How *does* a gentleman end up on a private lane without a carriage or horse? What logical explanation could he possibly give?

Trust Miss Katharine Ashton—Kit, he mentally corrected—to be stunning, feisty *and* intelligent.

Things he generally loved in a woman . . . under different circumstances. But for the moment . . .

She stared at him intently, as if seeing right through his bumbling facade. Politely waiting for his reply.

And then Marc hit upon the perfect explanation.

"I fear I was robbed."

Kit looked gratifyingly shocked.

"Robbed? Heavens! How terrifying!"

"Yes, indeed it was." Marc adopted his movie-mournful face—the one he perfected when playing a doctor dealing with terminal patients in *The Docs of Hazard*. "Highwaymen. Four of them. They came upon me as I traveled this morning, forced me off my horse at gunpoint and galloped off with all my possessions. At least they left me my clothing." He gestured down at the greatcoat.

Kit seemed concerned. Perhaps *too* concerned.

"How horrid. What did the men look like?" She leaned forward, eager for his answer.

"Uh . . . it is hard to say. They had kerchiefs tied around their faces and hats pulled down low," Marc said and then instantly rethought his words.

Is that how highwaymen dressed in 1814? Or was he just thinking of John Wayne westerns?

Kit didn't seem to find his description odd. She pursed her lips.

"So would you say the men were fair or dark? Tall or short?"

Why the follow-up questions?

"I . . . hardly remember. A little of both I suppose."

She gave an exasperated huff. "How can the criminals be apprehended if you cannot provide an accurate description of them?"

Damn.

That was the last thing he needed. Innocent men being arrested because he fingered them in his fictional robbery.

"Well, I shall think upon it carefully and see what I can remember. I would hate to provide a false description . . ." That, at least, was the truth.

Again, the silence stretched a little too long.

Her gaze narrowed. "I had thought you were perhaps an escapee from the circus."

"Circus?" That startled a laugh from him.

"The jumping onto the horse and all . . ." She trailed off helpfully, giving a flick of her wrist.

Marc finally caught the teasing glint in her eyes.

"Or perhaps you are more clown than acrobat?" Her eyebrows raised a sardonic inch.

Ah. Stunning, intelligent *and* snarky.

A lethal combination.

Unbidden, he smiled. Snark was a language he spoke fluently. Was nineteenth century snark any different? He sincerely hoped not.

"Indeed. How did you know?"

She grinned. "Consider it a fortunate guess."

"'Tis such a pity. My parents had such hopes of a fine career as a lion tamer, but alas, I am always bound to disappoint. I was more suited for clown-ery in the end."

Wait. Was he *flirting* with her?

"Clown-ery? Really?"

"Clownishness?" he offered.

"How about we settle on buffoonery?"

Slowly, they both smiled at each other. She had a lovely smile, wide and full of mischief.

He reflected it right back at her.

A shared sense of . . . awareness passed between them. One creature recognizing another of its same species.

Yes, there was definitely some flirting going on.

Heaven help him.

Chapter 6

I say, Miss Ashton, was that you?" A voice suddenly called from the opposite side of the road.

Marc whipped his head around and looked over the top of the horse to see two gentlemen nearly running out of the trees, hunting dogs yapping around them. Dressed like himself in long overcoats that fell to their heels, rifles tucked against shoulders, though both men sported beaver hats and leather gloves. Right behind them came what must be three servants in rougher clothing.

The taller of the gentlemen gestured with a concerned look. "Jedediah's shot went wide, and we heard a woman scream."

Kit gave a forced laugh. "Mr. Knight, I am quite well, as you can see. Though the shot did startle my poor horse."

"Dash it, Arthur. I told you it was nothing." The shorter of the gentlemen—Jedediah, Marc presumed—grimaced in annoyance as they came near. "'Tis only Mother's companion and everything is obviously set to rights." He pulled off his hat and wiped his brow.

Kit stiffened in her seat.

Had the man been offensive? Marc wasn't sure.

But wait—hadn't he just referred to the taller man as Arthur?

Marc nearly sagged with relief. Hallelujah! And not a moment too soon. Arthur would know how to smooth all this over.

The men stopped alongside the gig, the hunting dogs continuing to run round and round. One of the servants called the dogs to heel, and then everyone finally spotted Marc standing by the horse's withers on the opposite side.

Noticing their stares, Kit gestured toward Marc.

"This kind gentleman appeared at just the right moment to stop the horse. I am quite sure he saved my poor neck." Her laugh seemed a little forced.

"Well, a proper thank you is in order then." Arthur nodded his head in Marc's direction.

"It was remarkable. He leapt onto the back of the galloping horse." Kit gestured. "And right after being accosted by highwaymen too."

Arthur's head jerked to attention.

"Highwaymen?"

"Yes, this gentleman had his horse and possessions stolen out from underneath him at gunpoint."

The servants let out gasps of alarm while the dogs, sensing the instant tension, started running in circles again. Arthur called them to heel.

"Gracious!" Jedediah exclaimed. "I say, Arthur, what kind of place is Herefordshire turning into? First all those robberies and now this?"

Arthur shook his head. "'Tis most disconcerting, to be sure." He gave Marc a shrewd, assessing look.

For all his stuffiness, Arthur Knight was not a fool.

"You have brought quite a bit of excitement to our corner of the world, sir."

Arthur gave Marc a polite bow and then waited expectantly.

Marc gathered this was the point at which he was supposed to introduce himself. But given what a mess he had made of introductions so far, he would be better off holding his tongue.

With a tight smile, Marc walked around the horse and gave both men a polite bow. At least, he hoped it was polite.

"Mr. Arthur Knight, I presume."

"Indeed, I am he. It seems we are in your debt, Mr. . . . ." Arthur let his voice drift off, obviously expecting Marc to finish the introduction.

Unsure, Marc shot a glance at the crowd of people and dogs, all watching with interest.

"Might I have a word with you in private, Arth—uh, Mr. Knight?" Marc gestured for them to walk up the road a ways.

Arthur dragged his eyes up and down Marc's clothing. No doubt noting his odd footwear and lacking hat and gloves.

"If you wish." Arthur nodded after a moment. "I would appreciate a recounting of the robbery which landed you here."

"Naturally, of course. There is much to discuss."

Arthur raised his eyebrows at this, but said nothing more. Instead, he handed his rifle to one of the servants and instructed them to see Miss Ashton back to Haldon Manor. He then gestured for Marc to walk beside him up the lane toward the house.

Out of the corner of his eye, Marc studied his brother-in-law—for lack of a better way to describe the brother of his sister's husband.

Though Arthur's hair was more sandy than Georgiana's blond and his eyes more gray than James' blue, Marc could easily see the family resemblance between the three siblings. The same shape of the eyes, the same long nose. Arthur was somewhat taller and leaner than James and, as expected, his eyes lacked the mischievous sparkle of his brother and sister.

But, all in all, he seemed a good enough sort. Stiff and serious but also conscientious and kind.

Arthur said nothing and Marc waited for the gig to pass them with Jedediah now driving. Once everyone was safely out of earshot, Marc stopped.

"Marc Wilde." He offered his hand with a smile.

Arthur's eyes widened considerably under the brim of his hat. "Well, well, this is unexpected," he said, giving Marc's hand a firm shake. "Very unexpected."

Marc's laugh came out strained. "That makes two of us."

They assessed one another for a moment.

"Well, well, well," Arthur repeated, as if the reality of Marc's presence was settling in. "I take it you are Emme's brother from the twenty-first century? The one who fights in that Oriental style?"

Marc nodded, resisting a smile. He was quite sure every martial artist on the planet collectively shuddered at their sport being referred to as 'that Oriental style.'

"I can see the family resemblance. But your clothing . . ." He gestured toward Marc's long greatcoat.

"Ah, yes, well—I didn't want to make a scene, so I helped myself to some things left in Duir Cottage. I hope that was all right. The fit isn't too off—"

Arthur nodded. "You did quite right."

Marc breathed easier. It was nice to be with someone who knew his true past. He didn't have to stress over every word out of his mouth.

"And the highwaymen?" Arthur asked.

"Man, I *am* sorry about that." Marc gave a rueful laugh. "I totally made it all up. Miss Ashton was asking me all these questions about who I was and where I came from and the whole robbery thing just popped out. "

Arthur blinked at him. "I take it you mean to say the robbery is fictitious?"

"Exactly." So yeah. Maybe he needed to watch his speech after all. Nothing was going to be easy, was it?

Arthur nodded. "You did right. It is as good an explanation as any for your appearance, I suppose." Arthur gestured for them to walk up the lane.

"I *am* terribly sorry to trouble you." Marc nodded at the road ahead.

"No, no, 'tis no trouble." Arthur waived his hand. "James and your sister . . ."

" . . . are doing great," Marc finished for him. "Happy and ridiculously in love. I wish I had my phone, so I could show you a photo or two—"

"No, no, that would not be necessary." Arthur's expression instantly became strained.

Ah, right. Arthur disliked references to twenty-first century technology too. Marc wasn't going to be able to relax his guard at all.

"How about yourself? You and the family doing well? I am sure James would love to know."

Arthur's entire expression changed at the mention of family. His face softened and got a sort of wondrous look.

"We are well," he said. "We welcomed a tiny addition to our family just before the new year. Isabel Augusta Knight. She is small but fierce." Arthur laughed at the oblique Shakespearean reference.

Ah, so that was the source of Arthur's change in manner. A daughter.

"Mother and baby are well?"

Arthur nodded, a deeply satisfied look on his face.

"I take it your trip through the portal was, uh, unintentional then?" Arthur changed the subject.

Marc gave a small burst of laughter. "Putting it mildly."

"Did you try to return?"

"Several times. It seems the portal wants to keep me here for the moment. A man attacked me in Duir Cottage—in 2014—half-drugged me and then tumbled us both through the portal. I'm still trying to figure out how it all happened."

Arthur's eyes widened with alarm.

"So someone else came through with you?"

"Yes. I'm afraid so. But if it's any comfort, he seems to be from the nineteenth century too."

Walking along the lane, Marc told Arthur about the blackmail attempt, arriving to find the nineteenth century trunk and clothing in Duir Cottage and then the attack from behind by an unknown man. That distinctive brass button with the vine-covered shield crest. The drug-soaked cloth which indicated the man had come through the portal too. How were they to track down Marc's attacker with so little to go on?

"Blast! What a mess." Arthur let out a long breath of air.

"I really don't know what to make of it, Arthur," Marc continued.

"James and I couldn't find anything anywhere that hinted at someone else knowing about the portal in 2014. But obviously someone does. Is it possible that someone here found out about it?"

Arthur gave a bewildered shrug. "I have told no one about the portal, though obviously Sebastian and Georgiana know. Possibly . . ." Here Arthur paused, looking into the trees, thinking. "The superstitions about the old oak tree which once guarded the portal still abound in the area. Perhaps someone took them to heart and experimented. I shall have to ask my gamekeeper if he has seen anything unusual on the grounds as of late."

"Have you thought about having a guard of some sort for Duir Cottage? I'm not sure how you could phrase it, but with more people knowing about the portal, it really should be watched more carefully."

"Agreed." Arthur nodded. "Perhaps your story of robbery and highwaymen can be put to good use. It will allow me to set a guard to the cottage without arousing suspicion. It is not quite planting season yet, so there are several tenants and their sons who would be happy to have the extra work."

They walked in silence for a moment longer, Arthur shaking his head. Troubled.

"Deuce take it, things are unsettled at present," Arthur said. "I must thank you for not introducing yourself to others. I would have had a devil of a time explaining your presence here."

Marc cocked his head, questioning.

"Your sister caused a bit of . . . trouble before she left, particularly with Lord Linwood—"

"That's Emme!" Marc laughed. He had heard all about Linwood from Emme and James. Neither had a particularly favorable opinion of his high-and-mighty lordship.

"Yes, well, she more-or-less told Linwood you were a spy—"

"What?! Emme never mentioned she turned me into a spy."

Arthur gave a humorless chuckle. "Well, she did. And Linwood latched onto that small piece of information and is utterly convinced you are somehow involved with a spy ring. He is just trying to determine which side you spy for."

"Which side?" Marc scrambled, trying to remember his British history.

"Exactly. Are you spying for the British, the French or the Americans?"

Marc blinked. Well, *that* decision was simple enough. "The Americans, of course. My father may be British, but my mom isn't, and I was raised in the U.S. Not that I'm *actually* a spy, but if I had to choose—"

"You do realize we are currently at war with the United States, do you not? That just being known as an American citizen puts you at risk of arrest?"

Ah. He had *not*, in fact, known that. How very educational.

Of course! Americans referred to the Napoleonic wars as the War of 1812. Duh.

Crazy what a difference a hundred years would make in British/American relationships. But for the time being—

Marc swallowed.

"Even worse, if you are a British citizen and guilty of spying on your countrymen, betraying us to the enemy . . . Well, there really isn't anything worse you could do. Such traitors are hung, drawn and quartered. Even more, the family of a convicted turncoat is also ostracized. All their lands, titles, monies . . . everything seized by the crown."

Marc paused. He was missing something here, he was sure.

"But why would Linwood care about me?"

Arthur gave a fairly hefty sigh, tapping a gloved hand against his thigh.

"The story is somewhat involved, so I'll be brief. A spy within the British aristocracy has gone missing and left information that French agents were active in this area. Linwood is convinced some of the attacks have been targeted at his estate, Kinningsley. I would wager Linwood has something to hide. He sits in the House of Lords and is privy, I am sure, to affairs in the Home Office."

Arthur shook his head and then continued. "The problem is this. In an attempt to explain her sudden appearance, your sister stated that you and she were spies intent on destroying Napoleon. She claimed you were employed by Princess Pepsi of Toyota Camry and Calvin Klein, the

Duke of Kleenex. Emme asserted she had been attacked by a French agent who had left her for dead here in Marfield. This explained her sudden presence, but unfortunately, left Linwood with many unanswered questions, particularly about you and your role as a covert agent."

A groan escaped Marc's lips. Princess Pepsi of Toyota Camry? The Duke of Kleenex?

Emme was a *riot*. He was going to kill his sister.

Arthur continued on. "Even worse, Linwood is now convinced that French agents caused the carriage accident that, uh . . . killed James and Emme and that you, as Emme's brother, must have knowledge of this—"

"Damn! What a mess!" A mirthless laugh escaped Marc. He ran both his hands through his hair, tempted to pull it out by the roots.

Granted, Emme had a way of making him feel like that.

"Precisely," Arthur agreed with a weary smile. "And I have been unable to distract Linwood from the trail. He is convinced of your involvement. And now you arrive with this true tale of blackmail and threats to the portal . . ." Arthur's voice trailed off.

"Is it possible they are related? The blackmailer, local burglaries and the possible French agents in the area?"

Arthur shrugged. "I was just asking myself that very question. It raises the possibility something more sinister is afoot, particularly if a British agent has gone missing. Linwood's concerns must have some merit after all."

They walked in silence for a moment.

"I know that James would want me to make you feel at home, so you are obviously welcome to stay for as long as you wish," Arthur said.

"Thanks. I really appreciate it. To be honest, I'm feeling way out of my depth. I would love some help on the finer points of . . . etiquette. Ya know, bowing and the whole lot."

Arthur turned to him, eyes wide with surprise. "Etiquette cannot have changed that much. Gentlemen do not bow in 2014?"

"Not particularly," Marc chuckled, "and definitely not Americans."

Arthur looked suitably scandalized. "Well, I shall have my valet assist you, both with matters of etiquette, as well as your speech."

Of course. Marc definitely needed help with that too.

Arthur continued. "Michelle is well-versed in all things that pertain to being a gentleman."

Another pause.

Wait—Arthur had a valet named Michelle? A female valet?

That didn't really make much sense—

It all seemed a little progressive for early nineteenth century Britain. But before Marc could ask a follow-up question about *Michelle*, Arthur had moved on.

"We will need to provide you with a history." Arthur tapped his fingers against his thigh. "We will say that you are an old school friend of James' just returned from the East Indies. That will explain your sudden arrival, your tanned complexion and the general . . . uh, shall we say, *rustiness* . . . of your speech and manners. The robbery will be an excellent cover for your lack of possessions. You were accosted by highwaymen outside of Leominster—which also safely removes the robbery from my jurisdiction as magistrate—and then made your way here on foot, arriving just now. You have been devastated to learn of James' demise and, considering your grief and loss of possessions, I have graciously invited you to stay as long as you would like." Arthur gave a decidedly smug smile.

Marc could practically see James rolling his eyes and making some comment about Arthur always wanting to be the hero.

But, as far as plans went, it was actually an excellent one.

"Now, I just need to create a plan to track down your blackmailer," Arthur said. "The man sounds too dangerous to be roaming about the countryside—"

"You?" Marc asked. Talk about wanting to be a hero. "No offense, but why should you be the one to track him down? The man has been specifically threatening me and I'll need something to do anyway—"

"Are you mad?!" Arthur whipped his head around, staring like Marc had just sprouted fairy wings. "Did you not clearly understand everything I just said about Linwood and the danger around those suspected of spying activities? If Linwood gets wind of this, you could find yourself incarcerated, particularly if you are found doing anything suspicious. You need to lay low here. Do nothing to attract attention to yourself.

Bumbling around and asking questions about shady characters would be the *worst* thing you could do. Besides, I will not risk the reputation of my family if anything were to happen. As my guest, your behavior reflects upon me too."

Marc wanted to pull his hair out. *Here* was the Arthur he had heard about. More concerned about appearances than reality.

"But there is no truth to any of this—"

"Yes, but Linwood does not believe that fact. You are just going to have to trust me," Arthur said. "Someone in the village may have seen something. I know the right people to ask discreet questions and will be able to send out tentative feelers without raising any eyebrows. Your job" —here Arthur fixed Marc with a stern look— "will be to stay put at Haldon Manor and work on polishing your manners."

Marc chewed on his cheek for a couple seconds. The idea chafed. He *hated* sitting and not doing.

That said, given his ignorance of this time period, he could easily find himself on the wrong side of the law. Besides, he had no clue how to conduct a criminal investigation in 1814. And, really, given his situation, Arthur did call the shots.

"Fine." Marc nodded in capitulation. "I'll lay low."

"Good. Now, we just need to give you an alias."

Ah. An alias . . . that could be fun.

"Do you have any thoughts as to a name?" Marc asked.

Arthur shrugged. "Something innocuous would be best."

"Say like Albert Einstein?" Marc laughed, expecting Arthur to join him.

Arthur didn't. He just looked confused.

"If you are to be an old school friend of James', you probably would not be German," was all he said.

Marc blinked. He really *was* in 1814, wasn't he?

"So would Gregory Peck or Cary Grant be better?"

Arthur nodded. "Solid British names those. Either would work well."

"Clark Kent?"

"That does have a nice ring to it. It really does not matter which name you choose. It should just have a generally British sound."

Marc thought for a few moments, the grin on his face becoming more and more maniacal. The options were endless . . . if he could choose any name, who would he want to be?

"Uhmm . . . I'm thinking maybe something a little more formal. Darth Vader perhaps?

"Darth?" Arthur considered for a moment. "That is an odd first name—"

"Garth then?" Marc groaned and then slapped his leg in irritation. "No, it won't work. I'm an idiot. I already slipped up and told Miss Ashton that my first name is Marc—"

"Dash it!"

"I know. So I think we have to leave my first name as Marc. Which is *such* a pity, as being Garth Vader would have about made my year."

Arthur grimaced. "Well, we will leave your first name as Marc. There's no helping it. But to prevent mentioning your first name too much, we should make you a lord."

Marc pinched his lips together, holding in a decidedly un-manly giggle.

"So . . . you're saying . . . you want me to go by Lord Vader?" he managed to gasp out.

"Does that work?" Arthur asked, his eyes completely innocent.

Marc could only nod.

"If you are a lord, then no one really ever needs to use your first name to introduce you. You can just be Lord Vader to one and all and—I say, are you quite all right?" Arthur paused, looking at Marc with concern.

Marc's lips were twisted into a tight grimace, trying valiantly to hold back explosive laughter.

Get it together, man!

But . . . Lord Vader! It was just the funniest—

Why, oh why, wasn't there someone here who could laugh with him over this?

Life was so unfair sometimes.

Marc let out a long, slow breath of air, forcing his giggles back.

"That is settled then." Arthur gestured up the road. "Lord Vader, allow me to welcome you to Haldon Manor."

A peaked roof came into view, punctuated with gables and mul-lioned windows. Winter-bare wisteria vines climbed over red brick and a multitude of chimneys rose to the sky.

Marc frowned for a moment. He had been expecting to see Haldon Manor, but this house wasn't it.

Oh, wait. Now he remembered.

The Haldon Manor of 2014 was a somewhat newer building—a Vic-torian Gothic mansion turned into a hotel and day spa in the 1950s. But this building was much older, from the time of King Henry VIII if he remembered right. Which explained the sprawling structure and crenel-ated gables.

A touch of fear crept in. So far, Marc had been calm . . . just doing what needed to be done. But now . . . what if he were stuck here? What if the portal never let him return?

His breathing sped up. Panic stuck in the back of his throat.

Staying in 1814 was just not an option.

Not. Going. To. Happen.

Even people bowing and calling him Lord Vader didn't compensate for losing his twenty-first century identity.

Though . . . almost. Really, it *almost* did . . . but not quite.

He just needed to figure out what the portal expected of him, sort out . . . whatever needed to be sorted . . . and then he would be on his way.

It was that simple.

Chapter 7

The cut of zees coat suits you well, my lord."

Arthur's valet brushed Marc's shoulders free of invisible lint.

Michel—not Michelle—it turned out, was definitely male and decidedly French ("You call me *Mee-shell*, my lord, like your Engleesh Michael.").

Marc had also mentally dubbed him 'Most Likely to Win a Nicolas Cage Look Alike Contest.' Really, the resemblance was uncanny. His bright blue eyes were wide below his expansive forehead, his lean frame constantly in motion.

Upon arriving the previous evening, Marc had been introduced to Arthur's petite wife, Marianne, as well as two house guests: Lady Ruby

Knight and her son, Jedediah. They all had questions about his sudden appearance—awkward questions that Marc struggled to answer.

Arthur had come to his rescue almost immediately, saying Marc needed time to deal with the news that his friend, James, was in fact deceased. Everyone had backed off, saving Marc from saying something incriminating and allowing him to retreat to his room.

The rose bedroom, Marianne called it. Named not for the color of its draperies (which were an uninspired gray), but rather the extensive profusion of rose-themed objects decorating the room: rose vases on the fireplace mantle, an enormous rose painting over the bed, roses twining through the floor rug.

Not the most masculine of rooms, but . . . whatever.

Sometime in the middle of the night, as Marc lay staring at the shadowy rose-embroidered pillows on the window seat wondering what time it was—the room sadly lacked a rose-painted clock—it hit him again (and again and again) that he really *was* in the past. Unmoored from everything he had ever known.

Cast out to sea, to use a nineteenth century metaphor.

He was going to need to get used to speaking like that anyway.

He was in 1814. What was he supposed to do now?

Lord Linwood suspected him of being a spy for Princess Pepsi of Toyota Camry (!) with possible knowledge of local French espionage (!!), forcing Marc to adopt the pseudonym of Lord Vader (!!!).

What was it they said? You can't make this up, people?

Stranger than fiction?

Yeah, definitely.

Though Emme *had* made it all up, curse her.

But that didn't answer his question. What was he supposed to do? Who was his life linked to?

In short: what did he need to do in order to return home? Preferably as soon as possible.

He could practically hear Jasmine's voice in his mind, chiding him.

Relax, Marc, she would assert. *Just enjoy the process. The universe has your best interests at heart.*

Easy for Imaginary Jasmine to say. *She* wasn't the one trapped in 1814 with no Sports Center. Or refrigeration. Or even indoor plumbing.

Or, quite frankly, a clock.

After mulling over the problem of how to return to his own time, he had landed on an answer.

Namely, the blackmailer was probably his link. But knowing that didn't help much.

Arthur had made it clear Marc was not to interfere. Arthur had plans to track down the man, and Marc needed to lay low. Avoid hitting Linwood's radar. Marc would just be a blundering idiot crashing his way through rules and laws he didn't fully understand.

That didn't make it any easier to sit still, doing nothing.

Arthur had pathetically little to go on. Just a description of that distinctive brass button with the vine-covered shield crest.

How did one conduct a search of coat buttons in 1814? For all he knew, that particular button was extremely common in nineteenth century Britain.

Finding it could be like a proverbial needle in a haystack.

Again with the nineteenth century metaphors.

Maybe he *could* do this.

After all, he had held his own in that brief conversation with Miss Kit Ashton of the snarky wit and tumbling hair.

Not that Marc had seen her again. Yet.

Kit who he had discovered worked as a paid companion to Arthur's aunt, Lady Ruby. He remembered Emme and Georgiana talking about it once. An unmarried woman of genteel birth with no money or relatives to support her had few respectable avenues of employment. Working as a governess or paid companion were nearly the only options.

Marc's mind boggled at such a life. So that was it for Kit, was it? She would spend her days doing . . . whatever it was a paid companion did? All that vitality eventually snuffed out of her through the sheer drudgery of life.

Something within him rebelled at that thought. It seemed so terribly unfair. Kit should be free to be anything she wanted to be: the head of a company or a lawyer arguing cases in court or . . . or a lion tamer in a circus. Something more than a paid-companion-nobody to a snooty aristocrat in the rural backwaters of nineteenth century England.

No wonder women had fought so hard for change over the last two hundred years.

Marc twisted to lay on his back, pushing thoughts of Kit aside.

She wasn't his problem. Though part of him wanted to *make* her his problem. Interesting idea that. What had prompted it?

Which was his last thought before drifting off to sleep, only to wake hours later with the sun high in the sky and a maid placing a breakfast tray on the table next to his bed. She bobbed him a curtsy and then exited the room.

Breakfast in bed. *That* he could get used to.

Michel arrived just as Marc finished the last of his bacon. Thank goodness there were still smoked breakfast meats!

Servants trailed behind the valet, carrying coats and pants. Not pants . . . breeches, Marc mentally corrected himself . . . or were they pantaloons?

In any case, Michel had instantly begun the process of transforming Marc into a Gentleman of Quality, as he put it.

Michel was a master of the craft. His own words.

This started with a bath, for which Marc was grateful. Though bath was perhaps too generous a term for a large bucket filled with water. Michel called it a hip bath, which seemed appropriate, as only Marc's hips got wet.

And then there was that incredibly awkward moment when Marc realized Michel and a footman were going to *watch* him bathe.

Talk about Not. Going. To. Happen.

After a not-so-subtle cough and jerk of his chin, they exited the room.

After the bath, Michel had proceeded to ruthlessly scrape every whisker from Marc's face with a straight razor and then styled his curly dark hair into a wild, tousled look Michel called *a la Brutus*.

All the while, Michel spouted a non-stop stream of instructions and advice.

"When zee lady enters a room or stands, you must stand as well. When you bow, you may hold a lady's hand and lean over it, but you do not kiss it." Michel made a *tsking* sound. "Zat is not the done thing in England nowadays."

The list went on and on. Marc felt like he was preparing for a new film role. Which, in a sense, he supposed he was.

It would be like playing Mr. Darcy . . . though really that sounded quite stuffy and not fun at all. Who was the scoundrel in *Pride and Prejudice*? Whitman? No. Witless? Wickham! That was it.

Marc would just pretend to be more like Wickham. Only without the seducing of innocent girls (obviously). Just someone with a little more dash than Darcy. He could do that.

As Michel continued his monologuing, servants presented a selection of coats, shirts, pantaloons and other clothing—all borrowed from Arthur's closet—for Michel's inspection. Michel had an opinion about everything. *None* of which he kept to himself.

"Lord Vader you are most fortunate in your physique. Zee ladies, they like the broad shoulders, *n'est-ce pas?*"

And then a moment later, after assisting Marc into a pair of skintight buckskin breeches—

"Your fit into the pantaloons is adequate, my lord. Though you should consider exercises to increase the size of your thighs. They are well-muscled but could perhaps have more girth."

Marc just really . . . he had no words in response to *that* observation.

At one point, Marc made the (apparently) cardinal sin of touching his styled hair.

Michel let out an exasperated sigh. "No, no, my lord. That will not do. You must not touch zee hair once I have done with it. You will appear a very ninnyhammer."

Michel also used words like *ninnyhammer*.

Was Marc supposed to adopt words like that too? Because he didn't think he had it in him. At least, not without busting out laughing.

All in all, it was a decidedly illustrative couple of hours. At the end, Michel meticulously brushed the dark green coat free of tiny specks of lint. As he did, Marc glanced at the coat buttons. Plain silver.

"Do buttons ever have a design on them?" Marc asked. "Like something in brass with a crest and vines?"

Asking a simple question about buttons couldn't hurt, right? He wasn't doing any investigating. Nope. He was just trying to understand the culture better. That was all.

Michel paused in his brushing. "Silver buttons are the mark of a truly wealthy gentleman, my lord. Why should you wish for brass buttons? Though if you desire, we could have a family crest worked into your buttons—"

"So a crest on a button would perhaps belong to a family?"

Michel shrugged. "Not always, but it eez a possibility. *Voilá*. You look *magnifique*."

Marc studied himself in a mirror, turned sideways, studying the effect of the coat over a cream waistcoat shot with subtle gold stripes, tan buckskins disappearing into the top of polished Hessian boots. Marc and James shared the same shoe size, which was fortunate, as it allowed Marc to appropriate all of his brother-in-law's footwear.

Though James would certainly snicker at the sight of Marc in full Regency regalia, knowing him for the impostor he was.

Marc nodded at his reflection. "I look good."

"Of course you do, my lord. I would expect nothing less from myself."

Humility was also not Michel's forte.

And with one last swipe of his brush, Michel proclaimed himself done. Releasing Marc to do . . . whatever it was that nineteenth century gentlemen did . . .

Which was *what* . . . exactly?

How *did* one pass the time in 1814?

"So, now I . . . " Marc trailed off as Michel turned to exit the room.

The valet blinked. "I shall return at six to dress you for dinner. Until then, you may do what you will, Lord Vader. Perhaps you wish to take a walk in zee garden? Or visit zee library for something to read? I am sure that Mr. Knight has a copy of *Debrett's Peerage* you may study to remind yourself of the order of precedence."

Debrett's Peerage? Right . . . Marc had a vague memory of his English grandmother talking about *Debrett's*. It was a catalog of every living (and many dead) members of the British aristocracy. Anyone with a title would be listed in its pages. His grandmother had been obsessed with it.

Marc and Emme had spent summers in Britain with their father's mother who had drummed into her American grandchildren all the important parts of British life. Like having clear upper-crust elocution, a confident seat on a horse and knowing how to dine within the peerage. He could still hear his grandmother in her crisp, polished tones, *You must never forget that we are third cousins to the Dukes of Devonshire on my grandfather's side of the family.*

Perhaps a refresher on the British peerage wasn't such a terrible idea. He needed more ammunition to help him stay in 'character.' And seeing how all in-depth sleuthing was denied him . . .

Marc paused. "Right. Well then, show me the way to the library."

THE LIBRARY
HALDON MANOR
A FEW MINUTES LATER ON FEBRUARY 20, 1814

Kit turned the page of the book. Again. Still not reading a single word. Concentration escaped her.

Nestled sideways into cushions on a window seat with her back against the deep window embrasure, she sighed and stared sightlessly into the library. Or, at least, the sliver of the library she could see through the edge of the drawn window curtains.

The library was one of her favorite rooms in the house, with floor-to-ceiling bookcases and dark wood lining nearly every surface. An immense fireplace dominated the left end of the room opposite the doorway. So large Kit and several of her friends could practically stand up in it. The fireplace recalled Haldon Manor's beginnings as a Tudor estate when life was more communal. A cheery fire roared in it, sending seeping warmth through the room.

Two overstuffed chairs crowded close to the fire, separated by a long sofa. A large console backed the sofa, sporting wide drawers along its length which were said to house the late Mr. James Knight's impressive collection of maps.

Quite frankly, it all reminded her of home. Her father loved rooms like this. He would have spent days closeted with the maps, dragging old tomes off the bookshelves and perusing them lingeringly.

Kit's throat tightened. She blinked fiercely several times.

Now was *not* the time to think about her father. Even though it had been nearly a year, his death was still raw. He may not have been the most attentive of fathers, but he had loved her in his way and she still missed him.

She pulled her feet under her, tucking them firmly out of sight with the rest of her. She liked this little corner of the library, sandwiched between the window hangings and the tall, paned window. It was always full of light, despite the dreary overcast skies outside. Best of all, it hid her from the rest of the room, particularly the doorway.

That was crucial.

Lady Ruby was taking one of her 'restoratives'—which was what Ruby called a glass of brandy and a lengthy nap. Despite it not even being noon yet.

The problem, of course, was Jedediah. Ruby considered it a 'restorative,' but Jedediah thought of it more as 'open hunting season.'

Fortunately, Jedediah Knight had a strong aversion to libraries—Kit supposed it was the possibility of accidentally learning—and so had yet to find her here.

Granted, hiding in the library also meant no one *else* would find her.

Particularly not the dashing man who had stopped her runaway horse.

More's the pity.

Marc. She whispered his name. And then paused. Marc felt a little too familiar for a lady's companion to call a visiting lord.

Marcus, then. The same name that Linwood had mentioned to Arthur. Miss Emry's brother. Who may or may not be a spy.

Coincidence? Or subterfuge?

And if *subterfuge*, it explained his reluctance to properly introduce himself.

But he had retired early, and she had been unable to get another word from him on the matter. Or even a passing look.

That said, Kit had found out from Fanny, the upstairs maid, who had it firsthand from the second footman, Gilbert, who had overheard the cook talking with the housekeeper about how the stranger had been accosted and had probably killed one of the robbers with his bare hands before being grievously wounded himself, left to stagger his way to Haldon Manor half dead (None of which made any sense with what the man, himself, had told Kit, but who cared? It was an entertaining story . . .), when the butler, Finley, interrupted and called a meeting in the staff dining hall to set them all straight.

Though the facts themselves were not uninteresting, despite Finley's dry, monotone recitation.

The stranger was actually Lord Vader, a longtime school friend of Mr. James Knight, who had recently returned from a lengthy stay in India.

Marcus, Lord Vader . . . which was just an unexpected surname, really.

Was it a British name? It sounded more German, truth be told. She had even asked Gilbert and Fanny about it. Gilbert had simply shrugged, but Fanny insisted her father's cousin knew a family of Vaders who lived near Hereford. So perhaps it wasn't as odd as it seemed.

In any case, Marcus, Lord Vader, had been robbed while en route to Haldon Manor to visit his former friend and had been left to find his way on foot. Lord Vader had been devastated to learn that his friend, James, was now deceased. But Mr. Arthur Knight had seen fit, in his goodness, to provide Lord Vader with clothing and allow him to stay as long as he wished.

Furthermore, Finley did not want to hear any more speculation about Lord Vader killing anyone or being wounded.

Additionally, in response to Fanny's question, Finley did not wish to speculate on Lord Vader's marital status, or as Gilbert put it, his 'history with the ladies.'

And, no, Lord Vader had not provided a description of the robbers, and Finley hardly felt it relevant to his position to ask. Miss Ashton would be wise to remember that and keep her curiosity to herself.

Which effectively shut off the string of follow-up questions Kit had poised on her tongue.

Everyone was summarily dismissed.

Kit really needed more details about the robbery.

Had Daniel been involved with it? It seemed unlikely . . .

Well, actually, it didn't seem unlikely at all. That was the problem. Daniel was probably desperate for cash, and highway robbery would be just the romantic thing to appeal to him.

She hoped Lady Ruby would send her back into Marfield once she woke up. Kit was desperate to find and, this time, actually *talk* with her brother . . .

The door to the library creaked open, followed by muffled footsteps on the wood floor. Kit instantly stilled, practically holding her breath.

Drat. Had Jedediah found her at last? The curtain was excellent at hiding her, but it also had the disadvantage of hiding the room from *her* view.

The footsteps drifted toward the bookshelves away from the window. A cabinet opened and Kit heard the *shush* of books being pulled from the shelves and then *snicked* back into place.

Was it Jedediah?

The steps started again, this time drawing closer and closer. A hand appeared on the edge of the curtain and began to pull it back.

Lord Vader—*Marcus*, Kit reminded herself— poked his dark head around the edge of the fabric, eyebrows hiking up at finding the window seat occupied. Kit locked eyes with him just as a voice sounded from the doorway.

"I say, there you are, Lord Vader." Jedediah's nasal wheeze unmistakable.

Marcus turned back toward the room, leaving Kit with a view of his tailored broad shoulders and tight buckskins. His body and the window curtain hiding her from the rest of the room.

"Uh, yes. Here I am." Marcus clasped his hands behind his back but did not move away from the window, protecting her from Jedediah's view.

Jedediah grunted.

"May I help you?" Marcus gave a polite nod.

"Don't suppose you have seen Miss Ashton skulking about, have you?" Jedediah gave one of his signature sniveling sniffs.

Oh dear . . . would Marcus betray her?

"Skulking?" Was that humor in Marcus' voice? "I can't say that I have seen Miss Ashton display any tendency toward skulkery."

Marcus crossed his fingers behind his back, causing Kit to smile and relax slightly.

Jedediah humphed. "Dashed hard to keep track of that chit. Always snooping about where she shouldn't and not respecting her betters. Not quite sure why Mother hasn't sacked her yet."

Kit sucked in an outraged gasp.

Ugh! He was *such* a creepy cad.

Though you have been snooping about, Virtuous Angel pointed out.

But not skulking, Wicked Angel countered. *And you definitely respect those who have admirable qualities. Jedediah is just not one of them.*

Marcus canted his head toward her and then stilled. "Well, if I see any unauthorized . . . skulking . . . from Miss Ashton, I will be sure to inform you."

Ah, bless Marcus for defending her.

A pause.

"I thought I saw Miss Ashton headed down to the lake just a moment ago." Marcus bounced on his toes, still keeping his fingers crossed behind his back.

"The . . . lake?"

"Yes . . . or at least I supposed that was a lake I saw out beyond the walled garden. It looked largish and full of something liquidy and wet, so naturally I assumed—"

"Thank you, my lord." Jedediah sounded even more stiff than usual.

Marcus waved a hand. "Think nothing of it, old chap. I would be more than happy to help you identify other physical landmarks, as well. I do believe I also saw a thing called a 'hill' in the distance. It is quite large and rises from the ground as a high protuberance complete with these white fluffy dots I have on good authority are referred to as 'sheep'—"

Kit clamped a hand over her mouth, stifling her laughter. The man was truly incorrigible.

Jedediah made a choking sound. "I am well aware of what a hill looks like, Lord Vader."

"Ah, well, that is a relief. But if you need any pointers about trees, just let me know. They are those tall, spindly things you see jutting up everywhere. Quite bare this time of year, but if you are patient, come April—"

"I said thank you, Lord Vader. I shall leave you to your perusal of my cousin's library." Jedediah practically snarled the last sentence and stomped out.

Jedediah's angry footsteps fading, Marcus turned around to Kit on the window seat, hand still over her mouth, eyes dancing with laughter.

He pushed the curtains back to reveal more of the room and folded his arms across his chest, leaning a shoulder into the window jam, a roguish gleam in his green eyes.

Taking up more than his fair share of air in the room.

"That," he said, nodding toward the doorway Jedediah had just vacated, "is one remarkably repulsive human being."

Kit dropped her hand, freeing her laughter. It felt *so* good to laugh. Particularly with Marcus smiling at her.

He had changed and was now shaved, styled and immaculately turned out in a tight coat and those thigh-hugging breeches, looking every bit a gentleman of station and breeding. Altogether striking.

But his eyes betrayed him. He could be buttoned up into civilized clothing and starched within an inch of his life . . . but the rumpled gypsy sparkled underneath.

She sensed he wore being a gentleman like a cloak. Something to be easily tossed on or off.

She found the thought entirely too compelling for her peace of mind.

How did the East Indies shape a man? What experiences readied one to effortlessly leap onto the back of a galloping horse? How wild and untamed was he underneath that veneer of urbanity?

And did she really want to know?

Nothing can come of it, Virtuous and Wicked Angel sing-songed together.

How unkind of Fate to toss such an attractive man into her path when she was absolutely *not* in a place to do anything about it.

In contrast to him, she wore a twice-turned muslin gown with faded gray stripes and a fraying hem, her hair pinned to her head as best she could manage by herself, stuffing her curls into a large knot. Kit didn't know the first thing about creating the intricate hairstyles she saw ladies like Mrs. Marianne Knight wear. In the past, someone else had always done such things for her. Granted, she had tried to enliven her current outfit by wrapping a ribbon around her head and draping a red paisley shawl over her shoulders, both gifts from the kind Mrs. Knight.

Though she still looked poor and frumpy. *Sigh.*

"Thank you for not giving me away, my lord." Kit's hands twitched, reaching to smooth her skirts and fluff her hair. To preen under his gaze.

Gah. Marcus, Lord Vader made her feel so self-aware. She *never* felt awkward around men. What was it about him?

"Think nothing of it," he returned, eyes flicking to her hands with the smallest grin. Probably sensing the effect he had on her.

Drat him.

Why did she *care* what he thought of her?

"Though you will have to avoid any and all skulking activities you had planned this afternoon, as I would hate for you to make a liar of me," he continued. Still with that knowing grin hovering around the edges of his mouth.

He really was a marvelous specimen of manhood. Leaning against the window jamb, arms crossed, making his shoulders seem enormous.

Again with the broad shoulders. They almost taunted her.

Shoulders which could hold things . . . like her sorrows and troubles, her endless responsibilities and secrets . . .

Or you, Wicked Angel said. *They could also just hold you.*

Yes. There was that too.

Kit squelched her wistful thoughts.

Not helping.

A beat of silence.

"I thought we agreed to be Marc and Kit to each other? None of this 'my lord' nonsense." He gave one of his slow burn smiles. Mischief-lit. The kind that said *I'm a rascal, but you will love me anyway.*

Both her shoulder angels exhaled in delight despite themselves.

Stupid, charming man.

No flirting, remember? You promised to be good. Virtuous Angel chided.

Don't listen to her, Wicked Angel chimed in. *You deserve some fun.*

True that. And how could a little flirting hurt? She wasn't actually going to confide in him or cry on those (large, inviting, attractive) shoulders . . .

Every facet proclaimed him a man who joked his way through life without ever engaging his emotions. Infinitely attractive and lively to be around. But she knew from her long experience in society to never take such men seriously. Woe to the woman who ever gave her heart to one. Once a rogue, always a rogue . . .

Exactly! And spending time with him isn't helping you find Daniel. Virtuous Angel could be such a kill-joy sometimes.

Not true. Remember he was robbed. He might know something about Daniel. You definitely need to flirt the information out of him. Wicked Angel said, smugly.

That was too true.

She *did* need to know more about that robbery and Daniel's possible involvement.

So, really, she was merely engaging in a little bit of investigative inquiry. That was all. She would *not* lose her head over Marcus, Lord Vader.

The flirting was just a means to an end, right?

And to that end . . .

"No skulking for the rest of the afternoon?" Kit made a small moue of distaste, drawing her shawl around her. "That does put such a damper on all the activities I had planned."

Marc gave a small laugh, tilting his head toward the window. The overcast light raked his face, painting it half in light, half in shadow.

"Ah. I *had* nurtured a private hope that the erstwhile Kit Ashton had a dark secret or two." He winked.

Kit managed a nervous chuckle.

He had no idea.

"Well, skulking without a secret is quite pathetic. And I generally try to avoid being pathetic." She leaned toward him as she spoke, as if imparting a confidence.

That statement won her another crinkle-eyed grin.

"You seem like a man with secrets of your own," she continued.

No sense beating around the bush, as it were. Get straight to the heart of the matter.

"Don't we all?" He shrugged, his grin un-faltering, his face giving away nothing.

Kit matched his grin. His smile was like a contagion. She dared anyone who saw it not to automatically reflect it back.

Charming, stupid, *secretive* man.

"I wager you have delicious secrets." She lent a husky edge to her voice, angling her head in such a way as to invite him to share his.

He chuckled. A deep, rumbly sound that she felt to her toes.

"Naturally. Is there any other kind?" He waved his hand dismissively. "Though, I like the thought of you having a secretive history. It makes your life seem more interesting than simply reading or . . ." He trailed off, gesturing vaguely with his hand.

"Embroidery?" Kit supplied.

"Yes . . . embroidery." Marc looked perplexed. "Is that all you do? Read and embroider?"

"Oh no, not at all." Kit went wide-eyed, pasting on her most innocent expression. "I also *fetch* reading and embroidery for Lady Ruby. Or, best of all, read to her *while* she embroiders. It's a complex system."

"Really?"

"No, not really."

"It sounds heinously boring."

"It is, I assure you. Just a step above watching paint dry." Kit cracked a mischievous smile of her own.

Marc nodded thoughtfully, that grin tugging at his lips, and then gestured toward the book she held in her hands.

"So . . . are those truly your only two options of things to do? Reading or embroidery?"

"No, a selection of handy crafts is open to the modern lady who is adept with a needle. We also while away our time at knitting, darning, tatting and even quilling."

Marc gave her a confused look and sat down on the window seat, angling against the opposite side of the window embrasure. He leaned against the cushions, stretching his legs out along the floor next to her. Kit couldn't help but notice how the window light caught the sheen of his dark hair curling around his ears.

The entire scene conspired to make his shoulders as broad and problem-supporting as possible. Drat him.

"That sounds . . . monumentally boring." He looked speculative. "And you spend your entire day doing this?"

"Why yes. Of course, ladies also engage in such *thrilling* pastimes as strolling in the garden, changing our attire for dinner and, if we are most fortunate, practicing a musical instrument—"

"Please tell me you are joking?" Marc's look turned strained.

Kit gave a wry smile. "No, I'm afraid I am not. Which explains why everyone drinks and gambles. It's the only way to make all the rest of it palatable. I should think even quilling would seem exciting if one were drunk enough."

"Truly?"

"No, I am completely lying. I don't think *any* amount of alcohol could make quilling interesting, but it *might* be worth a try." Kit gave a rueful shake of her head. "You know, as a way to break up the monotony of everything else. Perhaps we could even bet on the outcome."

Marc laughed. Head back, eyes scrunched nearly shut, flashing surprisingly white, straight teeth. He had an exceptionally nice laugh, deep and robust.

"No wonder you harbor secrets then." His laughter faded into a broad smile.

He quite scattered her thoughts.

She would not fidget with her skirts. Or check her hair in the window's reflection.

No, she would not.

When was the last time a man had made her *this* self-conscious? She tried to remember.

There *had* been that dinner party at Lady Spencer's where Kit met a dreamy French painter with long tawny hair and passionate blue eyes. Nearly a caricature of the sweeping romantic *artiste*. He had whispered to her at length about the transitory nature of perception. She remembered fidgeting as he spoke, angling to catch her reflection in a silver candelabra to make sure her earrings were hanging straight. But in the process, she accidentally bumped her wine glass, spilling red Bordeaux down the front of her white evening gown . . .

So mortifying. She had never seen the French painter again.

Why, oh why, did she *now* meet a charming man with a clever sense of humor?

It was all just so . . . unexpected.

Some hint of her wonder of him must have shown on her face, as their eyes met. And then held. And held.

And held.

Until the silence stretched and Kit could feel the awareness growing between them.

His grin faded slowly by degrees, until it was only the suggestion of a smile. His eyes turned intense, gleaming bits of bright jade nestled into his tanned face. As if he, too, were not unaffected.

And in that moment, she had a flash of . . . something.

Something beyond herself.

A sense of familiarity, of recognition.

That perhaps in some former life, in some way, she had known him. That this meeting of minds was not entirely serendipitous.

But possibly more directed. A boon granted by Fate.

A rightness. That he was *meant* for her.

Her breath caught at that.

How impossible!

Given her life—past, present and future . . . for more reasons than she cared to list. Nothing could ever come of attraction between them. He would unravel all her secrets.

Unravel *her*.

There could *never* be a permanent place in her life for a man like Marcus, Lord Vader. For any man she met here in Marfield, for that matter.

She just needed to find Daniel, go home and move on.

And forget all about a certain wind-swept, horseback-leaping gypsy.

No matter how charming his smile.

Chapter 8

Silence hung in the library.

Marc stared helplessly into Kit's eyes. Luminous and velvety . . . not a deep chocolate but a lighter brown . . . more the color of draft beer with reds and golds mixed in.

Not that she would appreciate the comparison, he was sure.

It really did match the color of her auburn hair which she had attempted to ruthlessly pin to her head, but curls still escaped to frame her face and dance along her neck. Emblems of the woman herself, trying to stuff herself into a life which clearly didn't fit.

She seemed so fearless. Impervious to what the world thought of her . . . what *he* thought of her.

Unapologetically herself. Take it or leave it.

Heaven help him, he *adored* women like that.

Confidence like hers was never bestowed. It had to be worked at and fought for and *won*.

What fiery crucible had given Miss Katherine Ashton such unshakable composure? And why did he want to know the answer to that question so badly?

Now he would meet someone like her. Stripped of his life as he knew it and in no position to pursue anything with her.

It just figured.

"How did you come to be at Haldon Manor?" he asked, unable to resist.

"Me?" she squeaked, looking somewhat startled. "I am sure you cannot be interested in the sad vagaries of my history—"

"Is this part of your secret life then?"

He loved the idea she might have a secret past. That, somehow, the entirety of her existence was more than the small sphere she currently occupied. That perhaps a more adventurous future awaited her. Or that her life had not always been so bleak and solitary.

She laughed weakly. "Nothing about working as a lady's companion is secretive—"

"Perhaps not. But I know very little about lady's companions. So it makes you a lady, obviously." And then Marc remembered something Michel had said earlier. "Wait. If you are a lady, I probably should not be alone with you like this, right? Isn't it a risk to our reputations?" He gestured between them.

His mind still boggled a little over that idea. That just being alone with a woman was a problem.

Kit's eyes widened. "That . . . is true. Though" —she glanced toward the library door Jedediah had left ajar— "with the door open, all propriety should be met. Besides, as lady's companion, I am not held to the same strict standards as, say, a young debutante."

"That makes sense. So you . . . work for? . . . serve? . . . Lady Ruby?"

Again, how did such a striking woman end up in her situation? Or rather, how did a woman retain such a strong sense of self, given her circumstances? Confidence emanated from her. Such self-possession was certainly purchased at a price. What had been the cost for her?

"Yes, I serve Lady Ruby. I mostly assist her and ensure that her days aren't too boring."

"Back to that are we? Does Lady Ruby like to—"

"Embroider?"

"I was going to say drink and gamble . . ."

Kit laughed. "She does indeed."

Marc nodded. "And before finding a position with Lady Ruby, where were you?"

Now there was definitely panic on Kit's face. Skittering and then gone. How . . . interesting.

She really did have a juicy secret or two. One could always hope.

"Providing for myself, as I am sure you know." She continued to laugh, though it acquired a brittle edge.

"No, I don't know. As I just said, I know little about what it means to be a lady's companion, having never been one myself."

That got a more genuine laugh from her. Marc was starting to thoroughly adore her laugh, throaty and low.

She didn't elaborate however.

"So that's all you're going to say then?"

She slowly nodded. "Yes, I believe so."

"Just shut me out—"

"It's not like that. My life before here was . . . complicated."

"Ah. And you assume I can't understand complicated things?"

"Don't be difficult." She shot him a withering look. "I simply can't talk about it."

"You *do* have secrets." A small thrill chased his spine.

Kit shrugged. She turned to look into the library, the books ranged on the shelves. Filtered daylight caught the highlights in her hair, turning it to gilded bronze. He studied her profile, strong and elegant, just like the rest of her.

She turned back to him. "How about you? I understand you recently returned from the East Indies?"

Clever girl to turn the tables like that. Now it was his turn to scramble a little.

"Yes."

She cocked him a questioning eyebrow. And then rolled her hand. *Go on.*

Now it was his turn to shrug. "I don't know that I can talk about it." He leaned toward her and whispered from behind his hand. "It's a secret."

Her eyes narrowed. "Going to play like that, are you?"

"If I must."

He fixed her with a frank look, bouncing his eyebrows conspiratorially. Challenging her to tell all. Not that he had a clue what he would say in return if she did.

She broke the gaze first. Pursing her lips, she stood and walked over to run a hand along the table situated behind the sofa, her red shawl slipping to her elbows.

Remembering what Michel had counseled, Marc instantly stood himself.

She adjusted a book on the top of the table and then turned to him, allowing the light of the window to fully hit her.

Yes, he hadn't been amiss about her height or her figure. Heavens but she was tall, merely an inch or two shorter than his own six feet. And her figure could only be described as statuesque. Magnificently so. Curved in all the right places.

Marc was a ratios man. He liked a woman to look like, well, a woman. Hourglass shape with a waist he could wrap his arms around.

Kit did not disappoint. No emaciated, primped, calculated allure for Miss Ashton. No, she was just refreshingly real and solid.

She faced him calmly, drawing her shawl back up her arms.

"Your secret past. It must be good." Marc had to say it.

"Perhaps." She adjusted her shawl and then leaned back against the table. "What about yours? Is your secret good?"

"Amazing," Marc deadpanned.

"I doubt it's as good as mine," she countered.

"Not a chance."

They stared at each other for a moment, at an impasse. She tucked her hands behind her, trapping them between her back and the table's edge.

Finally, Marc grinned. "So let's say we place your secret on a scale that ranges from the number one, which would be hardly any secret at all, to the number ten, being the biggest secret ever, where are you?"

She paused for a moment and then answered. "A ten. Definitely a ten."

"Really? That *is* quite the secret." He smiled, slow and dangerous. "Well, I'm quite sure my secret goes to ten point five."

She laughed at that. "Is that all? Only ten point five? Why not take it all the way to eleven?"

And now he liked her all the more for the unwitting *Spinal Tap* reference.

Marc matched her smile and felt something hard burning in his chest.

How could some nineteenth century woman captivate him like this?

Kit shifted and crossed her ankles, making her legs look just that much longer.

"And you won't tell me this level ten secret?" Marc asked.

Kit shook her head. "Will you tell me yours?"

It was Marc's turn to shake his head.

Silence.

"So . . . we both have terrible secrets that we refuse to discuss. I can respect that. Now what shall we do?" he asked.

"You could tell me about your harrowing robbery—"

Marc tsked. "Perhaps. Or maybe the robbery figures into my ten point *five* secret?"

Kit huffed. "Come now. Admit that you are simply being obstinate because I declined to tell you *my* secret—"

"I will do nothing of the sort."

She shifted and pulled her arms back to cross them, regarding him with pursed lips. Considered a different tactic.

"So you were accosted by several armed men on horseback? What did these men look like?"

"As I said, I am not going to discuss it."

Her eyes narrowed. "So you *are* being obstinate—"

"Not in the slightest. Let's make a pact. You tell me a secret, and I will share a secret with you—"

"Did one of the robbers happen to be about your height and build? Darker hair?"

"My, my, my. What a remarkably *specific* question." Marc raised his eyebrows. "Does this tallish, dark haired man have anything to do with *your* secret?"

She shrugged noncommittally. "Maybe. Again, if I admit to something will you?"

Marc paused, regarding her for a moment, rapidly making deductions based on what Arthur had told him. "You know something about the robberies that have been going on?"

"I didn't say that."

"No . . . but you suspect you know the robbers?"

A hint of panic flickered across Kit's face. "It's possible that I know many things."

"I don't doubt that."

Yes, that was definitely panic he was seeing.

"Well, I think I know at least one of your secrets." She lifted her chin.

That surprised a laugh out of Marc.

"Nice attempt. You can't deflect me that easily. I doubt you know any of my secrets, so I call your bluff."

He gave her his just-try-me face.

Kit narrowed her eyes.

"Very well then. I believe you have a sister named Emry who was here at Haldon Manor and formed an attachment with your old school friend, Mr. James Knight."

Marc couldn't stop a gasp from escaping.

How the——?! How had she possibly connected him with Emme?

She arched an expressive eyebrow. "So as I know one of your secrets—"

"I have admitted nothing."

Kit gave him a scornful look.

"Please! If you had seen your face when I mentioned Emry's name—"

"Miss Ashton!!" A voice interrupted from the doorway. Marc and Kit instantly stood at attention turning their heads toward a small maid who bobbed a curtsy at Marc.

"Beggin' your pardon, my lord, but Lady Ruby has need of Miss Ashton." The girl stood uncertainly for a moment, wringing her hands in her apron.

Kit paused and then pasted a strained smile on her face. "Of course. Thank you, Fanny, for informing me."

Fanny bobbed another curtsy, sneaking a peek at Marc from underneath her lashes before scurrying out the door.

For her part, Kit also dipped him a small curtsy and turned to leave the room. Marc couldn't help but follow her.

"This isn't over, Miss Ashton," he murmured as she crossed through the doorway and into the great hall. She didn't respond, but the sudden stiffening of her spine informed him she had heard.

And if it hadn't, the turn of her head and cocky, challenging lift of her eyebrow as she strode away would have.

Ah, yes. Matching wits with the lovely Kit Ashton was going to prove all sorts of entertaining.

Marc watched her stroll across the great hall and up the staircase which lead to the family apartments, her head held high.

Elegant. Regal. Utterly and absolutely alluring.

The kind of woman who walked at a man's side and even tugged him along from time to time. The kind of woman a man could build a life with.

Whoa. He blinked. Where had *that* come from?

Marc rolled his shoulders, sloughing the thought away.

It was ridiculous. So she was fun to flirt with? So he felt a sense of inexplicable connection with her? So what?

How could Fate think to bring them together? Sure Emme had drug James back to the twenty-first century with her, but their love had obviously been in the cards from the beginning. And James was mentally in a place to deal with moving centuries.

But for him and Kit . . . their lives—past, present and future—were just too different. Despite his attraction, he couldn't imagine her in his world. And he most certainly wasn't going to stay permanently in hers.

So yeah. That was that.

Though *how* had she known about Emme? Perhaps Linwood was

spreading the word about him farther than Arthur knew? It was a puzzle.

He leaned against the library door, staring into the great hall. Its large vaulted expanse sported an enormous bank of floor to ceiling windows on one side and an imposing fireplace on the other. Doors punctuated the walls leading off into the drawing room, dining room and library. At the far end, the stairs to the family wing climbed through a final doorway, flanked by two full suits of armor standing at attention, each holding an enormous broadsword.

At that precise moment, Marc realized Jedediah Knight stood in the doorway of the drawing room, staring at him with narrowed eyes. Watching him.

How long had he been there? Long enough to see Kit leaving the library? Probably.

The points of Jedediah's shirt collar nearly reached his eyes and his absurdly elaborate neckcloth sat atop a bright, mustard yellow waistcoat. His wool coat of turquoise blue had mother-of-pearl buttons. No brass buttons for Jedediah.

Marc realized he would be cataloging buttons with interest for some time. It was about the only way he could help Arthur's search.

Though Jedediah's jacket sported unnaturally large padded shoulders and was cinched more tightly at the waist than any man could manage without the aid of . . . well . . . what? A corset?

Basically, Jedediah Knight was ridiculous.

"Do you risk your eyes with those?" Marc asked without preamble, gesturing toward his own more modest collar.

"I beg your pardon?"

"The points of your collar. They seem dangerously high. Why if you were suddenly startled and turned your head too quickly, I fear one of them should poke out an eye."

Jedediah instantly stiffened. "I would not expect a man of your . . . experience to understand the intricacies of a well-featured gentleman."

And then Jedediah grasped what appeared to be a magnifying glass dangling on the end of a chain, raised it to his eye and ruthlessly surveyed Marc from head to foot.

Marc was quite sure the entire scene was intended as a set down.

But as the quizzing glass—yes, that was it—made Jedediah's blood-shot eye appear huge, it was all Marc could do not to laugh. A smile tugged at his lips.

A fact not lost on Jedediah, who somehow managed to look even more stiff.

And then a thought popped into Marc's head—a thought so utterly magnificent he couldn't just bat it away.

"You wouldn't happen to have a middle name that begins with the letter *I*, would you?"

A question for the ages, that one.

Jedediah froze and then frowned. "It is Ignatius, as a matter of fact. How did you ever know?" He shot Marc a suspicious look.

"Hopeful guess, I suppose." Marc bit his cheek, ruthlessly forcing himself not to smile. "I have always wanted to address a Jed I. Knight."

How Marc managed to say that sentence with a straight face, he would *never* know.

The quizzing glass made another lengthy appearance. Jedediah sensed there was a joke in the conversation somewhere, but he was helpless to locate it.

Instead, he glowered at Marc and walked slowly toward him. Minced, actually, as there seemed to be some sort of padding in the thighs of his coral-colored breeches.

Was *that* what Michel thought Marc should wear too? There was not a snowball's chance in Hell he would ever don anything so ridiculous.

"Do not think I am ignorant as to your game," Jedediah practically hissed.

Marc jerked his head up, realizing he had been actually staring at the man's thighs, which brought the monstrosity that was Jedediah's hair into focus. Wild and uncombed, it looked like it hadn't seen a good sham-pooing in *far* too long. How did one create such a look without getting dreadlocks? Was it really the rat's nest it resembled—

—aaaaaand now he was staring at Jedediah's hair.

Wow. He needed to get a grip.

Jed I. Knight, indeed.

Marc lowered his eyes to encounter Jedediah's baleful blue eyes.

"I know your game," Jedediah repeated, emphatically poking his finger at Marc.

Marc pasted on his cockiest face.

"I highly doubt you know my game," he drawled. "I can't imagine five-card stud poker is popular in this area—"

"Miss Ashton is under my cousin's care, and she does not need some rapscallion sniffing around her skirts." Jedediah gave a supercilious snort.

Marc laughed at that. Honestly, the man was such a . . .

Douche? Cad?

Twit?

"And by rapscallion, you mean yourself, right?" Marc couldn't help it. Jedediah-baiting was his new favorite sport.

Jedediah gasped. "How dare you, sirrah! I have called out men for less offense but, as you are my cousin's guest and newly arrived in England, I shall merely warn you to improve your manners—"

"Call me out? As in . . . fight me?" Disbelief shot through Marc's tone. The thought of seriously fighting this idiot—

Actually . . . the more he considered it, the idea had some attractive merit.

"Precisely! I will have you know, I am a crack shot."

"So pistols are the weapon used?"

"How can you possibly be so unversed in the protocol of a duel of honor?" Jedediah shot him a withering look. "And you have the gall to call yourself a gentleman."

Marc shrugged. "I just wondered if the rules were different here in good old England. Where I come from, my body is the only weapon I need." He cracked his knuckles to emphasize the point.

Jedediah's eyes widened slightly, but he braved onward. "I have done a round or two in Gentleman Jackson's Boxing Salon, I will have you know—"

"Gentleman Jackson's Boxing *Salon*?" Marc instantly had an image of men prancing around an overstuffed room taking wimpy swipes at each other.

Oh, please.

"Mr. Jackson is a champion pugilist and furthermore—"

Marc raised a skeptical eyebrow and drew up to his full height, allowing himself to look down on Jedediah, despite his bouffant hair. Silencing him.

And then Marc smiled. A nasty grin. The kind of smile that was anything but welcoming.

"A fight would be just the thing. Beating you into a bloody pulp would do wonders for my temper." Marc cracked his knuckles again for emphasis, edging his smile into murderous territory.

Jedediah swallowed. And then lifted his chin in a bit of bravado. Marc could practically see his peacock feathers bristling.

"Have a care," Jedediah hissed. "I am a force to be reckoned with, Lord Vader."

"Don't worry, Mr. Jed I. Knight." Marc leaned forward, crowding the smaller man. "I never underestimate the power of the Force."

And with that, Marc turned and strode off past the suits of armor, rapping their hollow metal shells to emphasize his point.

Chapter 9

Marc Marc Marc.

The name tripped through Kit's head in an almost constant thrum. She had practically skipped into the breakfast room behind Lady Ruby. Settling the elderly woman at the table, she was now trying to focus on dishing up Ruby's plate.

Without much success.

Gah! It was like she was thirteen again and dealing with her first infatuation.

How embarrassing.

And, heaven knew, she was *not* one to indulge in puppy love.

No matter how tempting.

Exactly. You need to find Daniel, extricate him from whatever he is involved in and return home. Can you even imagine if you brought someone like Marcus, Lord Vader back with you? Virtuous Angel shuddered.

That is true, Wicked Angel sighed. It was *not* a good sign when Wicked Angel and Virtuous Angel agreed on something. *So . . . nothing will ever happen? We've established that. Move on. What can a little flirting hurt?*

Yes, what could it hurt? Just a light flirtation. Stay in practice, as it were. It was becoming her mantra.

It would at least provide a welcome break from the incessant monotony . . .

There was just *something* about Marc—here she mentally sighed over his name again—that drew her. That sense of similarity.

She could still see him casually stretched out in the window seat, teasingly trying to coax her secret out of her. Clever and handsome with that deep, rumbling laugh. A laugh that shook those broad, broad shoulders . . .

Were they as powerful as they looked? Would his arms wrap around her like twin bands of supporting steel?

Perhaps she should consider confiding in him. Not about *everything*, obviously, but she could at least mention she was looking for her brother. Merely a tiny piece of her secret.

Though she was quite sure she had found Marc's. He was Miss Emry's brother, the one that Lord Linwood had seemed interested in tracking down. His face when she had mentioned Emry's name . . . well, it left her no doubt.

Miss Emry who was said to have died in the same carriage accident as James, Marc's old school chum. The accident that Linwood felt had not been an accident at all but caused by some French spy. Who was now trying to steal something from Linwood and so kept attempting to break into Kinningsley.

Wasn't that what he had said?

And Linwood was trying to find Marc, because Marc was an intelligence agent himself and might have information about the French spies in the area.

It really was quite the convoluted mess, when she thought about it.

Marc seemed capable of being a spy. Quick and intelligent, probing with his questions. And he had just returned from a long stay overseas. Not to mention that fancy maneuver with her runaway horse. Definitely all spy-ish.

Though, he didn't seem as upset over James' death as he should be. *If* he had just found out about the death. But if he knew about his sister's demise already, then he would likely have known about James' too. So then it all made more sense.

Most of all, she *really* hoped Daniel had nothing to do with the entire affair. But knowing her brother—

"Miss Ashton, please pay attention. The bacon must not touch the kippers." Lady Ruby's aristocratic hauteur skittered down Kit's spine.

Right. Kippers. Focus.

"Of course, my lady," Kit murmured in reply, glancing down at the plate she was currently dishing from the sideboard for Lady Ruby.

Back ramrod straight in her chair, Lady Ruby had strong opinions about the world and her place in it. All of which was captured in her love of the color purple. The ancient color of kings, as she was fond of reminding Kit. Every day she wore the same color; only her choice of fabric changed.

Today, Lady Ruby had chosen a velvet theme—a gown of deep purple velvet caught tight around her ribcage, trimmed with silver cording and topped with a tasseled turban. Of velvet, of course.

Lady Ruby's organization of any given day began with her breakfast plate. Ruby insisted it be divided into four parts, each carefully delineated: two rashers of bacon, six kippers of uniform size fanned with tails angling out, a coddled egg and three stacked toast triangles—all in that order running clockwise around the plate with no one item touching another.

"Careful, Miss Ashton. We do not want to have a repeat of last Thursday's debacle." Lady Ruby sniffed.

Ah yes. The Porcine Rebellion, as Kit wryly dubbed the incident. That disastrous moment when a bacon rasher had slid across the plate causing a chain reaction, which ended with the coddled egg trapped between two kippers and speared by a toast triangle. Traitorous bit of bacon.

Ruby had been seriously displeased. As a compartmentalized eater, she found such gastronomic disorder distressing. But, then, most things in her life were compartmentalized.

Case in point. The part of her brain that housed *People Who Are Cads* should have definitely included her own son, Jedediah. But, no, he was firmly ensconced in the section labeled *People Who Can Do No Wrong.*

"Good morning, Mother."

Speak of the devil. Or was it the devil speaking?

Kit swallowed a sigh as Jedediah crossed the room and gave his mother a dutiful peck on the cheek.

Jedediah looked ridiculous, as usual. He had thrown off his knee breeches and tasseled boots in favor of low slung shoes and a pair of skin-tight gold satin pantaloons.

Kit had to repeat it to herself: Gold. Satin. Pantaloons.

Even better, he sported a bright-green velvet coat caught in tight at the waist. A blood red waistcoat peeked out, while the folds of a snowy cravat billowed under his chin.

The entire effect called to mind a rather demented Christmas tree.

Kit knew that Jedediah fancied himself something of a leader of men's fashion. But *should* there be a place in a man's wardrobe for a tasteful pair of *tight* gold satin pantaloons?

And wasn't that an oxymoron? Could gold satin pantaloons *ever* be tasteful?

Arthur and Marianne entered the room on Jedediah's heels, greeting them all—Arthur nearly tripping over his jaw when he spotted Jedediah's trousers. His eyes tripled in size. Marianne nudged her husband before he could say anything, silencing him with a quick shake of her dark head.

Kit thoroughly liked Arthur's quiet, petite wife with her kind eyes and gentle smile. Kit couldn't fathom how the same set of parents had produced both Linwood and Marianne, as the two siblings were nothing alike. Well, they looked alike with their dark hair and gray eyes, but Marianne was as soft and warm as her brother was icy and arrogant.

Pulling her head back to the task at hand, Kit carefully adjusted the last of Lady Ruby's kippers and then strolled to place the plate in front of Ruby, all components at precise right angles to each other.

Lady Ruby inspected her work for a moment and then nodded. A quick up and down jerk. It passed muster.

Thank goodness. Now Kit was free to dish her own plate.

She was contemplating the bacon rashers and wondering how many would be embarrassingly *too* many to take when Marc walked into the room. Tastefully dressed in tan buckskin breeches, polished boots and a tailored dark blue coat.

Not a scrap of gold satin in sight.

More's the pity, Wicked Angel muttered. *I bet he would look fabulous in gold satin.*

Hush you, Virtuous Angel chided. *Not helping.*

He politely greeted everyone and then joined Kit at the sideboard, lifting covers off to inspect his options.

"The bacon is excellent," Kit murmured, careful to keep her voice low as she piled several slices on to her plate. Lady Ruby would *not* approve of any unauthorized flirtations.

In fact, it would be best if Kit mentally staked a sign in front of Marc as if he were part of an animal menagerie: *Do Not Flirt with the Charming Gentleman.*

Well, at least not when Ruby and Jedediah were around.

Though given the warm chuckle he proffered her, that was going to be difficult. He began to stack bacon onto his plate. Slice after slice.

Kit raised an eyebrow. "You are . . . fond . . . of bacon, I take it?"

He shrugged, adding one last rasher to his pile. "It's more a lifestyle than a food, I think. The world really cannot have too much of it. You don't seem so adverse yourself." He nodded toward her plate.

Kit mimicked his shrug. "Far be it from me to not be supportive of your lifestyle choices."

Marc managed to turn his abrupt bark of laughter into a loud cough.

"So is this how we are going to entertain ourselves today?" he asked, recovering. "Bacon analysis?"

Kit scooped a coddled egg onto her plate, deliberately cozying it up to her bacon. Just to be obstinate. "Perhaps. If we are extremely fortunate, maybe Cook will encase something truly repulsive in jelly for luncheon, like eel or whole partridges. Just to break up the monotony."

He shuddered and poked at the kippers. "No, that will not do. I will not lay about waiting for Cook to liven up my day."

"I appreciate a man with ambition." Kit placed four toast triangles on her plate, making sure they looked a haphazard jumble.

Marc moved past the kippers and began inspecting the selection of breads.

"I have an idea." He pursed his lips, thinking. "We are at breakfast. There will, logically, be some conversation. What if we mentally added the words . . . let's say . . . 'with a chamberpot' to the end of each person's sentence?"

Kit blinked and then turned slowly to regard him.

"With a chamberpot?"

"It could prove amusing." His face gave away nothing, though his green eyes let off mischievous sparks.

"Are all men perpetually twelve-year-old boys?"

"Most assuredly." He laid a mockingly-sincere hand over his heart. "Why I am scarcely a day over thirteen myself."

Kit narrowed her eyes at him, a traitorous grin tugging at her lips.

"I say, Lord Vader, finding the kippers fascinating this morning?" Jedediah's high-pitched drawl cut through the room.

Kit noticed Marc's barely suppressed eye roll. "Of course. Do you not? I find they are particularly delicious when encased in jelly." He cocked a challenging eyebrow in Jedediah's direction.

Somehow Kit managed to swallow her mirth, though that stubborn grin still tugged at her lips.

Jedediah scowled, sensing a joke, but helpless to recognize it. "I find jelly quite tedious to eat."

"Due to my festering rash," Kit murmured to Marc as he turned toward the table.

Marc swung his head back to her, looking puzzled for just a fraction of a second. Then comprehension dawned, causing his eyes to spark again. Fire and devilry.

She raised a challenging eyebrow and moved past him.

"Done. The first one who laughs owes the other a secret," he whispered to her back.

Kit stiffened. Drat him! She hadn't intended for the game to have a forfeit.

Marc sat down between Marianne and Jedediah, allowing Kit to sit opposite him, between Arthur and Lady Ruby. Kit eyed Marc for a second.

She *couldn't* spill her secrets.

Though she wouldn't mind knowing more of his.

So . . . she would just have to ensure she won.

Marc raised an eyebrow which asked all too clearly: *Are you going to back down from the challenge?*

She gave a studied toss of her head. *Not a chance. Play on.*

That signature slow-burn smile gradually expanded over his face. All rogue. Marc gave the faintest nod.

Lady Ruby leaned forward, her purple velvet turban nodding haughtily, drawing Marc's attention. "I am delighted by your arrival, Lord Vader. It has been quite some time since I have enjoyed the company of an adventurer."

Due to my festering rash.

The words hung in Kit's head. She shot Marc a quick look. He responded with a slow wink.

Donotlaughdonotlaugh . . .

She forcibly pinched her lips together.

And just like that, breakfast was the most entertaining thing to happen in weeks.

Marc watched Kit bite her lips, a grin slipping through but not a laugh.

She was going to be a tough competitor.

Of course, that's what made the whole game fun.

He studied Kit as she sliced her bacon into neat pieces. She had taken four slices, an amount Marc could respect. She wasn't one of those bird eaters.

He had once briefly dated a French model who never actually ate food, at least not that he had seen. She just considered it something to poke and prod during mealtimes; she had not been particularly curvy.

But Kit dug in to her meal like she had never heard of calories or fat or carbs.

Which, now that he considered it, she probably never had.

She was wearing a simple gray muslin gown with the same red shawl pulled around her shoulders. Her *only* shawl, he was starting to realize.

He could tell Kit was poor. Or, at least, not as well off as Marianne and Lady Ruby, who vaguely shined in their expensive, tailored dresses and perfectly curled hair.

By comparison, Kit's clothing appeared worn and didn't quite fit right. Her dresses were generally too tight through the bodice, too loose in the hips and several inches shorter than he assumed was strictly proper.

Not that he minded. Seeing Kit's trim ankles when he entered the breakfast room had instantly brightened his day.

But in all, her dresses seemed like they had been meant for a different woman. Someone a little shorter and stouter than Kit.

And yet somehow, despite her poorly fit dresses and haphazard hair, Kit shone as the most vibrant part of the room.

She just had a . . . presence about her. As if *she* knew she had intrinsic worth and forget anyone who thought differently.

When would women realize that confidence was the sexiest attribute of all?

Arthur cleared his throat and gestured toward Jedediah and his skin-tight gold satin pants. "Cousin, I thought you intended to accompany me shooting again this morning—"

"Ah yes . . . that." Jedediah cut him off with a careless wave of his hand. "As you can see, I am hardly dressed for hunting today. I am afraid I will have to cry off."

Due to my festering rash.

Marc's lips twitched. Kit lifted her head, meeting his gaze. Amusement tugged the corners of her mouth, but otherwise she held firm. Every line of her body clearly stating, *Bring it.*

"Any particular reason?" Arthur managed to look concerned.

Jedediah shook his head, a little too vigorously. "No, no, none at all. Just not feeling the thing today." He turned to Lady Ruby. "In fact, I was hoping you might help me with a small matter, Mother. You know, that issue we have been having . . ."

Due to my festering rash.

Caught off guard, Marc managed to turn his bark of laughter into a cough at the last second.

That had been close.

Kit maintained her serene expression and took a piously unconcerned sip of tea.

The wretch.

Jedediah looked pleadingly at Ruby, who instantly smiled a little too brightly and reached over to pat his hand.

"Of course, my dear. I had nearly forgotten about that . . . issue. It has definitely been a concern for both of us."

Now it was Kit's turn, choking a little on her tea as she set her cup down.

Man, he loved to watch the play of emotions across her face. The way her beer-colored eyes lit when she was teasing him.

No, not beer-colored. Describing a woman's eyes like that would likely get him slapped.

He thought for a moment. *Honey-colored.* Much better.

Marc dug into his pile-o'-bacon. Mmmmm . . . bacon. He felt magnanimous enough to tolerate the lack of plumbing and Jedediah Knight's idiocy as long as he had bacon as a consolation.

It really made up for so many of life's deficiencies.

Suddenly, the door opened and a footman entered with a bow.

"Lord Linwood," he said in suitably reverent tones.

Right behind, a tall, lean dark-haired man strode in, scrupulously—Marc would actually say *fastidiously*—groomed.

Linwood was dressed and pressed in a perfectly tailored greatcoat which hung in sculpted lines to his mirror-shined boots, a darker coat and ivory waistcoat underneath. Not a hair out of place on his head nor speck of dust on his clothing, despite the fact he must have ridden over.

Everyone at the table instantly stood. It took Marc a second to catch on, and then he scrambled to his feet as well.

Really, he had to *stand up* for this?

Linwood handed a beaver top hat to the footman and removed leather gloves from his hands with precise movements, folding them and placing them neatly inside his hat. All done with military precision.

Marianne instantly went to him, rising on tiptoe to place a kiss on his cheek.

"Welcome, brother. How lovely to see you. Will you not join us for breakfast?" She smiled warmly and gestured toward the table.

Everyone sat down as she said this. Again, Marc was a little late and fumbled back into his chair.

So *this* was the infamous Timothy, Viscount Linwood. The man radiated cool reserve and haughty superiority. Emme had nothing kind to say about him, as there had been a bit of an *incident* which Marc had heard all about. Something about Linwood making improper advances which Emme had to ward off.

Remembering at the last moment that Linwood wasn't to know that he was Emme's brother, Marc fought to school his features into some semblance of blandness.

Or at least not blatant hostility.

He pasted on his movie-pleasant face. The one he used when meeting someone for the first time. Linwood would never suspect a thing. Marc wasn't an actor for nothing. Despite what the occasional scathing online reviewer may say.

Fortunately, Linwood was still focused on his sister.

"No, thank you, sister. I breakfasted before riding over." He gave her a small bow as she returned to her seat. "Besides, I have little desire to sit."

Due to my festering rash.

Unbidden the words bolted through Marc's mind.

Kit choked across from him but bit back her laughter in time.

Ah, so they were still playing despite the interruption, were they? Great.

It would definitely add a whole new level to what was sure to be a dicey conversation.

Linwood entered farther into the room and clasped his hands behind his back, coming to a stop behind Kit's chair. Fixing Marc with his icy gray gaze.

Absently, Marc noted that the viscount sported silver embossed buttons on his coat. Not brass with a crest. So far, Marc hadn't met a gentleman with brass buttons on his coat. Granted, he had only been in 1814 for two days, but that attacker was Marc's ticket home.

"I take this to be your new visitor, Knight." Linwood kept his eyes on Marc, even while addressing Arthur.

"Why, yes, indeed," Arthur said with a strained, forced laugh.

Damn. Now was *not* the time to realize that Arthur Knight was a terrible liar. Arthur cleared his throat. The noise self-consciously loud in the small room.

And Arthur was worried about *Marc* giving something away—

"Lord Linwood, may I present Lord Vader, an old school friend of James' who has just returned from the East Indies."

Marc and Linwood cautiously nodded to each other. Two bulls, carefully assessing strengths. Looking for weakness.

"A pleasure, Lord Linwood." Marc managed to trim *most* of the irony out of his words.

"Indeed," was Linwood's cool response. "I was unaware James had a friend named Lord Vader. Did you meet James during his time at Eton?"

Clever man. Linwood had been with James at Eton, so he clearly already knew Marc had not. Fortunately, Marc knew James like a brother.

"Cambridge," he said, unable to keep the hint of challenge out of his voice. "We studied together there."

"Ah." Linwood flicked his gaze up and down Marc's figure, obviously looking for some sign all was not as it seemed. "I understand James enjoyed his time at Cambridge."

"Naturally. He had me to ensure things stayed lively." Marc allowed himself a leisurely smile. Linwood was welcome to probe his understanding of James' life.

Another quick glance from Linwood. "Were you aware of James' death before arriving here?"

Marc swallowed at the unexpectedly direct question. Weren't people supposed to be all circumspect and closed off during this time period?

"I had heard rumors of James' demise, which given the depth of our friendship, I had to ascertain for myself. I have been profoundly saddened to learn the rumors are indeed truth. James was the best of friends."

Giving a small catch of his breath, as if he were fighting off strong emotions, Marc looked to the side, schooling his face into movie-devastated mode. Marianne reached out and gave his hand a comforting pat.

Really, this was *such* a masterful performance. Too bad a certain snarky online reviewer wasn't here to witness it.

For his part, Linwood merely narrowed his eyes, his body language remaining skeptical.

"I was alarmed to hear you were robbed en route to Haldon Manor," Linwood said. "How unsettling for you."

Linwood regarded Marc with those icy eyes of his. Nearly unnervingly pale and colorless. As if even his eyes would never do anything so messy as have color to them.

Man, he was such a . . . a . . . stuffed shirt.

Marc smiled tightly. "I haven't survived so many years in the East Indies for nothing. I can take care of myself."

Linwood didn't smile. Did the man *ever* smile?

"Of course. Which is why men robbed you and left you with only the clothing on your back. *That* kind of taking care of yourself?"

Marc blinked. Go figure. Linwood was turning all smart ass.

Though wouldn't *arse* be the more appropriate nineteenth century term?

Pity 'smart arse' didn't have the same ring.

Marc allowed himself another grim smile. The kind that didn't reach his eyes.

"I was taken by surprise and decided a horse and pair of saddlebags were hardly worth my life. Given that the thieves only wanted my possessions, I didn't want to do anything . . . *rash*."

Marc lingered on the last word. Knowing Kit, at least, would get the joke.

Out of the corner of his eye, she pinched her lips together.

Linwood stood still, almost unnaturally so. As if relaxing and slouching and the things other humans did were beneath his dignity. He seemed always primed for a fight.

The childish part of Marc wanted to shake a red cape under the nose of Linwood's bull. Just to see if he would charge.

"I am, naturally, relieved you escaped unharmed." Linwood's tone, however, indicated his complete indifference to Marc's health. "As you most likely know, I am one of the magistrates of this area. I would like to ask you some questions regarding this incident—"

"Actually, Linwood—" Arthur cleared his throat. "—the robberies took place near Leominster, so the entire affair is not within our jurisdiction. I do not see the point in questioning Lord Vader."

Linwood turned his stony gaze to his brother-in-law. Only the haughty raising of an eyebrow indicated his annoyance at Arthur's interference.

"Be that as it may, Knight, I am sure Vader would not mind answering a few questions. Given that you and I are responsible for the welfare of those living in this area, it behooves us to investigate any disturbance which might threaten—"

"If you must know," Marc interrupted, "I did not get a close look at my attackers. They had kerchiefs around their faces . . . though I do believe one of the men had blue eyes. Or were they gray? In any case, they were upon me and taking everything, giving me little opportunity to do anything else other than cooperate."

Linwood swiveled his head back to Marc. "And you hesitated to do anything . . . rash?"

Yep. Definitely a smart arse.

"Precisely. I dislike anything to do with . . . rashness."

Kit choked again across from Marc, looking primly down at her hands with her lips pressed firmly together.

Linwood blinked, sensing he was missing something in the conversation, but unable to put his finger on what that would be precisely. Only his fingers tapping against his thigh betrayed his agitation.

"So you can give me no information that would be helpful in tracking down these miscreants?" he asked.

Marc heaved his shoulders in a baffled sort of shrug. The kind that said he wished to be helpful but didn't know how to proceed. He most certainly didn't want some innocent man to be fingered for this fictional robbery.

Though, perhaps, there was *one* piece of information that would be helpful. Would Arthur mind?

"Nothing really." He tapped his chin, as if in thought. "Though I do distinctly remember the buttons on the coat of one man—brass with a raised crest embossed in the center, vines chasing through it. That is all, unfortunately."

Arthur's head instantly snapped up, shooting Marc a quelling look.

Marc shrugged faintly as if to say, *It's no big deal.*

The more people who were on the lookout for that button, the better. Why not link it to his fictional robbery? The man in Duir Cottage certainly hadn't been on the right side of the law. Arthur grimaced subtly, obviously not liking Marc's interference.

Linwood regarded Marc for a moment, face impassive. Did the man even blink? He seemed almost more robot than human.

"A button. That is something . . . I suppose. If you remember anything else, I request you inform me immediately. I feel those involved with this robbery might strike again, and I wish to ensure safety for the good of all."

Kit twisted slightly in her seat, catching Linwood's eye. "Would you say the feeling is like an . . . an itch . . . that you wish to scratch?"

Marc nearly snorted, desperately trying to hold back a sudden laugh. Heaven help him!

She was utterly shameless.

Linwood raised another cool eyebrow, studying Kit. Obviously trying to understand why she would insert herself into the conversation.

"Indeed, Miss Ashton." His voice all icy hauteur. "You might call it an itch that I feel must be indulged."

Kit turned back to Marc as Linwood said this, her honey eyes dancing. The words hanging unsaid between them.

Due to my festering rash.

Marc managed to control his laugh just in time, while Kit forcefully bit her lip.

Oh yes. Miss Kit Ashton was an absolute delight.

Chapter 10

Kit pulled her heavy wool cloak tighter around her shoulders. Though sunny, a bitter winter wind stealthily crept around the Herefordshire hills, jumping out when she least expected it, snatching at her cloak and tugging her bonnet. Leaving her toes hopelessly chilled in her walking boots.

She shuddered but kept her chin up, restlessly searching. Darting glances up and down Marfield's high street, thoroughly examining each and every man.

Five days. It had been five days since she had caught that glimpse of Daniel here in Marfield. But despite canvassing the village each time

Lady Ruby sent her to fetch some bauble or collect the post, there was no sign of her brother.

Drat him.

She had dropped off another letter to be sent from the Old Boar Inn (again addressed to the impossibly dull-sounding Mrs. Boring of Quiet Street, Bath) and was now making the same tour of Marfield she had been doing all week. But with the colder weather, few people were out and about.

Biting back a hefty sigh, Kit found herself in front of the parish church, its gray stone half covered in moss. Only the flag-shaped weather vane atop the steeple tower glinted coppery and new.

Pushing open the gate, she wandered inside, welcoming the calm hush of the graveyard surrounding the church. Trees lined the perimeter of the fence, providing a sheltered respite from the wind.

She ambled through the gravestones, stopping in front of a more recent addition.

In loving memory of
James Richard Knight
Born May 23, 1781
Died Oct 15, 1812
Age 31 years
Beloved son and brother

Ah. Arthur's older brother, James.

The one who died with (perhaps) Marc's sister in that (perhaps) carriage accident. The reason (again, perhaps) behind Marc's visit.

Life at Haldon Manor had certainly become more lively with Marc's arrival.

Despite playing several more rounds of their word game, neither of them had laughed in company yet—the wagered secret still hanging in the balance. Though it had been a very near thing when the phrase was *after licking a toad* and Lady Ruby had said: *I had the most fanciful conversation with the vicar yesterday.*

Despite spending time together laughing and teasing, Kit felt she was no closer to understanding who Marc really was.

The man definitely had his secrets. Where had he been before arriving at Haldon Manor? Was he truly a spy with his sister, like Linwood suspected? What was his purpose here?

He had skillfully dodged every question Kit had thrown his way, taunting her, telling her over and over that she had to win their silly word game before he would give up anything.

All the while, reducing her to weak-kneed laughter with his relentless flirting.

Marc, Kit realized, was a Meringue Man.

And she had *such* a love/hate relationship with Meringue Men.

She knew from experience that some men put up walls of steel and ice, like Lord Linwood. Cold, hard fortresses around their hearts that kept everyone shut out. Ice Men, she called them.

With Ice Men, you knew when you broke through. All their cold reserve would shatter spectacularly in an eruption of emotion. Their coldness could be off-putting, but at least you knew where you stood.

But other men put up walls of soft, sticky meringue. These men were sweet. Delicious to be around, eating up the delight of their company. And at first, Kit found the clever repartee of their company heady and intoxicating. It was flirting at its best. Like World Championship flirting.

However, after a while, all that sweet meringue became a little cloying. It was a sticky defense that bounced back at you. No matter how far you sunk into it, you were never sure when you were through to the heart of the matter. Meringue Men usually didn't explode. They just kept hiding emotions and feelings in increasingly complex layers of jokes, leaving you wondering which was truth and which was deflection.

Why, oh why, did she have to have such a *thing* for Meringue Men? Why did she have to love the language of flirt so well?

It all doomed her to one shallow relationship after another. Meringue Men were the best secret-hiders. They buried everything important so deep inside no one would ever reach the center. Even if you found out one secret, you were still left wondering what other secrets they were keeping from you . . .

Granted, it wasn't as if she had been all that forthcoming with her own secrets. But *her* secrets were truly monumental.

Marc's just involved a deceased sister who might have been a spy with him. Obviously, she could see how being a spy would make you extra secretive, but still . . .

She needed to find Daniel. She wondered for the twentieth time if she shouldn't tell Marc about her brother. With his probable experience as a covert agent, Marc would be just the person to help her.

But . . . it was all the follow-up questions about Daniel she dreaded. Those she wouldn't answer. Though maybe, if she stated the matter obliquely enough, Marc could help her.

Kit was on her third circuit of the graveyard, when a hand suddenly closed over her mouth from behind.

Hard and swift. Kit instantly stiffened.

"Don't scream."

She sagged with relief at the all too familiar voice in her ear. Every last thought of Marc instantly evaporated.

Daniel. Hallelujah!

Jerking her head free, she rounded on her younger brother, throwing her hands around his neck, giving him a fierce hug. His arms wrapped around her, squeezing her in return.

She held him for a moment, relief washing over and through her, wave after wave.

At last! He was here. Together, they could sort this out, stop whatever horrid plan he might have set in motion, find a solution. Go home with no one the wiser. Everything would be okay.

With one last embrace, she released him and stepped back.

He looked . . . well . . . like Daniel. A bit taller than herself, hair two shades darker but glinting with red undertones. Dressed in a long, worn greatcoat over the same blue coat she had seen him in before, a little rumpled and worse for wear. A far cry from his preferred attire but still the same old Daniel. It figured this extreme change in their normal life-style wouldn't affect him as much as her.

Stupid man.

They regarded each other for a few moments, Daniel taking in her brown cloak and the drab gray of her gown underneath. Hair peeking out from under her shapeless bonnet.

"Well . . . Kit . . ." He stared. "You, erm, look . . . great."

She did not.

"I barely recognized you in that dress." Daniel, being his typical self, didn't know when to stop. "I thought I saw you come out of the Old Boar Inn, but I just couldn't believe my eyes. I've been following you for the last little while just to be sure. You're here! I have no idea how or why . . . but . . . but here you are! You just look so different . . ."

Suddenly, all of Kit's relief morphed into rage. After everything that had happened, the impossibly stupid things Daniel had done—this latest scrape being the last in an incredibly long line of frustration-inducing behavior—

And all he could focus on was her attire?

She swatted his shoulder, only barely controlling an urge to full-on punch him. "You idiot!" she hissed.

Daniel wrinkled his brow. "Happy to see you too, sister dearest."

Gah! He had to be about the most clueless, daft, imbecilic—

Kit growled, attempting to control her swelling anger.

She stabbed a furious finger into his chest. "How could you?! How *could* you get us into this mess?"

Gaze instantly shuttered, Daniel batted her finger away.

"Us?" He pointed a similar accusing finger at her. "*You* aren't supposed to be here. *You* were supposed to stay at home."

"Right. Stay home. And what? Deal with the horrid aftermath of your disappearance? Sit around wondering what you planned to do and how much it would affect . . . *everything*? Somehow just give up caring about what happened to you?"

"Kit, I left you that long letter *specifically* to explain everything—"

"What letter? I didn't get a silly letter. All I found were those papers you left in the study in Whitmoor which lead me here. I know you, and I am sure you have something planned—"

"Of course I have a plan. Something I have been working on for nearly a year now. Things just got a little . . . sidetracked . . . shall we say? But I am back on course."

Kit stared at him for a moment. Would there ever be a time when she wouldn't worry about Daniel? Concern for her younger brother was one of the constants of her life.

Like English rain and mud on new shoes, she could always count on Daniel to need rescuing.

"It's not your job to rescue me." Daniel's gaze pinned her down.

Ah, so *that's* how he was going to play.

"No. It's just my job to mop up the messes you make. And this mess"—she spread her arms expansively—"is truly spectacular. I know you think it a fun lark, but this particular adventure of yours could have ghastly repercussions."

They regarded each other. Daniel crossed his arms over his chest and bounced a leg. Restless and bounding with energy. That had always been Daniel's problem. Constant motion—an almost pathological inability to sit still. He needed to be doing, moving from place to place, scrape to scrape.

He swallowed. "Well, I have never asked you to clean up after me—"

"When a disaster of this proportion looms, someone has to—"

"Why don't you let me live my life? Why do you always interfere?"

Kit clenched her jaw. "Daniel, this isn't just about *you*. Why can you not *think* beyond yourself?"

"Don't you *dare* throw this back at me." Anger flared in his eyes. "Just because you don't like my decisions, doesn't mean they're not right. I'm not accountable for your happiness."

So typical, Wicked Angel muttered. *He* never *takes responsibility for anything. Remember the time he got ridiculously sloshed, drove himself home and careened into that ditch—*

He did *apologize to the farmer for the broken fence,* Virtuous Angel countered.

Gah! You're such a Goody Two-Shoes. Don't you remember there was a horse involved with the whole thing? Wicked Angel said. *The poor animal was never the same—*

"Don't tell me you *still* do the shoulder angel thing?" Daniel said, noticing her distraction. He stared at her with a cocked eyebrow, his face a textbook of little brother mockery.

Kit just pressed her lips together. Comments like *that* would get him nowhere.

But it does underscore why *you are here,* Virtuous Angel murmured. *No one else knows you even have shoulder angels.*

No one but her crazy, frustrating, beloved little brother.

Kit swallowed past a sudden burning lump in her throat.

"Daniel, you are the *only* family I have. I cannot and will not lose you."

"I am not your only family." Daniel turned on that annoying-brother smile. "I mean, you *do* have your shoulder angels . . ."

The lump in her throat instantly evaporated. Kit fixed him with her glacial big-sister stare. Teasing was *not* going to get him anywhere.

He squirmed a tad. "Right. Well."

"Daniel, you must come home. If you don't . . . it just doesn't bear thinking upon. I could . . . *we* could lose it all. The house, the title, everything will revert to the Crown. Everything our family has ever been will just . . . *poof*. Evaporate."

Daniel held his arms tighter across his chest. The bouncing of his leg turning to pacing. Back and forth, back and forth.

"Kit, I am truly sorry." Daniel gestured futilely. "But we don't live in the Dark Ages, for heaven's sake. You are a modern woman! You don't need me and my title to provide a roof over your head. You have money of your own—"

Kit fought back the stab of pain which flickered through her chest. Somehow she hoped Daniel had planned on coming home all along. That he truly hadn't simply neglected to think through how his actions would affect her.

Wrong. She had been *so* wrong.

"Money I cannot currently access, thanks to your little shenanigans here. And who knows how things will change if you don't return with me."

"I am hardly your savior, Kit."

Anger nearly blinded her for a moment. How could he *be* so callous?

"Do you think I enjoy working as a paid companion? That I relish hearing Lady Ruby's arrogant voice—"

"Paid companion?"

"Yes, Daniel. I am employed at Haldon Manor as a companion to Lady Ruby."

Daniel stopped his pacing and stared at her like she had sprouted horns.

"But . . . but . . . why?"

"You know, so I can have a roof over my head, food to eat . . . that sort of thing."

Daniel's eyes widened in confusion.

"How—" He shook his head. "Kit, how long have you been uhm . . . working for Lady Ruby?"

It was Kit's turn to tap her foot. "Five weeks, Daniel."

His head reared back as he hissed in a breath.

"Five weeks?!" he gasped. "You have been here for five weeks? Kit are you mad?"

"Daniel, you had disappeared! What did you expect me to do?"

"But . . . but I came back. I just had to go take care of some things, but I returned home—"

"You did? I didn't know that. You just left without a word!"

Ugh! That was *always* his line—'things' that needed to be dealt with. Daniel, at least, had the decency to look slightly chagrined.

"And when you came home, you didn't think to wonder where *I* had gone?" Kit asked.

"Well, I most certainly didn't think for one moment you would be *here*. Kit, how could you?"

How dare he throw this back on her! Kit silently counted to ten.

Daniel continued on, oblivious to her seething. Or, rather, long immune to it.

"This is bad, Kit. People everywhere will be looking for you. I mean, I can disappear and no one will think anything of it, but you . . ."

His voice trailed off. They both knew what her absence meant.

"*Exactly*, Daniel. That is *exactly* the problem—"

"Look, Kit, I am truly sorry. But . . . things are complicated. Give me a couple days. I can probably at least get us some money so you don't have to keep working for your keep. I have found a way to earn some cash already. At least enough money until—"

"Daniel, money isn't the answer here. I need *you*. You need to come home with me—"

Kit stopped abruptly, staring at Daniel's blue coat. Or rather more precisely, the *buttons* on his coat.

Daniel took advantage of her pause to grasp her shoulders.

"Please, I need you to trust me."

But those buttons held Kit's attention. Brass buttons with a raised shield covered in vines . . .

Coincidence? What were the chances?

All the air rushed from her lungs.

"Daniel," she whispered, "how do you intend to get money—"

"Miss Ashton?" A voice called from the other side of the church. An all too familiar voice.

Drat! Any other time, Marc would be a most welcome sight. But right now . . .

Daniel instantly stiffened.

"I'll be in contact with you," he whispered, turning to dart into the bushes.

"Daniel, no! Wait—" Kit grabbed his arm, stopping him.

"Trust me, Kit. Just this once. I *do* know what I'm doing."

Daniel wrapped her in a quick hug and planted a firm kiss on her cheek next to her mouth.

And then he was gone.

Kit stared sightlessly at where he had just been, eyes wide. A sinking sensation rapidly growing in her stomach.

Sometimes she hated that she knew her brother so well.

"Am I . . . interrupting something?" Marc's voice came from right behind her. Far too close *not* to have seen Daniel's exit.

Was Daniel part of the group who had robbed Marc? What would Daniel do next? And would his actions destroy both their futures?

And even worse, how was she going to explain Daniel to Marc?

Chapter 11

Marc had plainly seen the hug and kiss which preceded the disappearance of a man into the shrubbery.

A *tallish, dark-haired* man, to be exact. Precisely as she asked him in the library.

The shock of it hit hard. Like a swift round kick to the head, leaving him reeling and wanting to hurt something. Or, rather, a tallish, dark-haired *someone*.

Was she flirting outrageously with Marc while carrying on a love affair with this other man?

And why had she asked if this man—clearly the one he had just seen—had been involved in Marc's fictional robbery?

Secrets, indeed.

Kit whirled around to face him, a too bright smile pasted on her face.

"Marc! What an unexpected delight to see you—"

"Unexpected *would* seem to be the right word." The drawl just escaped him.

Wind tugged at his hat, swirling his caped coat around his legs. Man, it was bitterly cold today. But the frigid wind hadn't stopped Kit from venturing out to meet this man. She was clearly up to something.

Marc knew he was supposed to be laying low, not wandering out and about. But hanging around Haldon Manor doing nothing to track down the blackmailer . . . he just couldn't sit still a second longer. He had to be *doing*. And so he had asked Arthur to let him ride into Marfield. Begged, actually. Swearing and promising to do nothing suspicious.

But then, at a distance, he had seen Kit darting through Marfield, obviously looking for something, and had to follow her. Maybe hoping to find out more of her secrets.

He had not been disappointed.

The strength of his reaction surprised him. Why should he care who she was hugging and kissing? Sure he and she flirted with each other, but what did that signify?

He flirted with nearly every woman who crossed his path. It was like breathing and eating.

So why was Kit any different?

Though he tried to shrug it away, she *was* different from other women he had known.

The charisma she effortlessly wove? The sense of strength and depth behind her charm? Again, what fire had forged her?

And why, why, *why* did he care?

Nothing could ever come of a relationship with her. So why bother feeling anything other than gentlemanly friendship?

And how to make his wayward heart see sense over this issue?

He studied her for a moment. She *should* look terrible, but instead the wind had burnished her cheeks a rosy pink, turning her eyes more chocolate than honey, accenting the slash of her red mouth. Her cloak pulled tight around her body for warmth.

How he loved her height, the tall lushness of her. He couldn't blame Tall Dark-haired Man for wanting to hug and kiss her. Marc wouldn't mind it himself—

Stop, stop, stop!

Not. Going. To. Happen.

Marc sucked in a deep breath and mentally shrugged off any awareness of her.

He was a twenty-first century man. He could be understanding about the whole scenario. It was not as if he cared.

Liar.

"I don't suppose you would be willing to pretend you didn't just see that?" She regarded him hopefully. And then batted her eyelashes, giving her shoulders a winsome lift.

"Does that actually work? The innocent-girl eyelash flutter?"

Kit batted her eyes one more time and then sighed, dropping the act.

"Sometimes." She shrugged, glancing back to where her gentleman caller had just been.

"Does Mr. Tallish-and-Dark-Haired fall for it?"

She turned back to Marc, eyes calculating. "Would it help if I said yes?"

"Probably not."

"Worth a try," Kit muttered with a grimace.

"I must say, you do seem to get around more than I would anticipate."

Okay, he mentally admitted, so maybe he did care that she was randomly embracing other men. What *were* her secrets?

Her eyes widened. "What is *that* supposed to mean?"

"Nothing really. All the women I outrageously flirt with do this. It's a fairly standard practice—"

"Are you finished?"

"No, no actually, I'm not." And maybe, he suddenly realized, he wasn't interested in being all twenty-first century *understanding* either. "So explain it to me. You play lady's companion by day, while at night—"

"Pardon me, Lord Vader. What exactly are you insinuating?"

Ah, so *now* he was Lord Vader?

"Insinuation? Hardly. The scene seemed fairly self-explanatory to me."

"How dare you!" Kit crossed her arms and glared.

"Who me?" He pointed to his chest in mock disbelief. "I am not the one lurking around shrubbery kissing random men. Which, if I may point out, is really an ineffective way to ensnare a man. The tavern in the Old Boar Inn would be a more fertile hunting ground. Warmer, for one. Not to mention drunks probably litter the floor, ripe for picking—"

"*Now* are you finished?"

"Not a chance. I mean, you could at least share the wealth—"

Kit threw her hands up in disgust. "Now, you are just being ugly—"

"Hardly!"

She was right. He totally was.

But whatever. He pressed on with a bark of laughter. "I think you lost any shred of holier-than-thou high ground as soon as you decided to lock lips with—"

"Lock lips? Either you didn't see what happened clearly, or we need to update your understanding of exactly how kissing works—"

"Hey, I am not judging. What you see here" —he waved a hand in front of his face— "is devoid of judginess."

It was a lie. He was totally judging her. But again . . . whatever.

"You are finished." She silenced him with a slice of her hand. "You clearly have misinterpreted what you *think* you saw—"

"Right. And I am supposed to believe you . . . why?" He cocked his head to the side, voice dripping with sarcasm.

"Marc . . ." said warningly.

At least he was back to being Marc.

"Oh, that's right." He snapped his fingers. "Because I know you are keeping *big* secrets from me, and this isn't part of your big secret because . . ."

Marc rolled his hand encouragingly. *Please explain.*

Her shoulders sagged. "Marc, I want to tell you. Truly, I do but—"

He held up a staying hand and arched an amused eyebrow. Ensuring every part of him communicated his disbelief.

She stuttered to a stop. And then heaved a great sigh.

He just raised his eyebrow higher and crossed his arms, shaking his head back and forth slowly.

"Nice try, but I'm not letting you off that easily. Come on. Talk." He beckoned with his fingers.

Kit fidgeted for a moment, pulling her cloak tighter around her shoulders. A vagrant gust of winter wind darted between them, tugging at Marc's greatcoat and further chilling his toes in his boots. Kit shivered.

Seeing her cold and miserable faded his anger.

She had secrets. So what? So did he. They just needed to trust each other.

Well . . . she needed to trust him, at least.

Glancing back at the church behind them, Marc offered her his arm.

"Here. It's freezing. Let's duck inside the church out of this wind, and you can tell me all your darkest secrets. Also, I do believe there was some mention about broadening my understanding of kissing." He pasted on a cheery grin.

Kit just glared at him, chewing the inside of her cheek. And then with a disgusted shake of her head, hooked her hand into his elbow, allowing him to lead her into the church.

Though no warmer on the inside, the church did provide shelter from the biting wind. Marc's boots echoed on the worn flagstone as he directed Kit to a bench at the back of the short nave. Light filtered dimly through the arched stained-glass windows, dancing in colored beams on the pews as they sat down side-by-side, shoulders nearly touching.

"So, Miss Ashton. I am honored you could join me here today. I believe you had something you wished to share." He mimicked her look from earlier, batting his eyelashes and lifting his shoulders winsomely.

With a resigned shake of her head, Kit laughed.

"Does that innocent-girl eyelash flutter actually work?" she taunted.

Marc grinned and leaned even closer, whispering conspiratorially. "Every. Single. Time."

She pursed her lips together, turning her head to stare into the empty church. And then reached up a hand and untied her serviceable bonnet, pulling it off her head, tossing it onto the bench next to her. Marc followed her lead, placing his beaver hat next to him. Though most of her hair was neatly tucked into a bun, a few curls sprang free to hang along her neck.

Distracting little curls.

"So . . . Mr. Tallish and Dark-haired?" Marc studied her profile.

She was in great poker form, giving away nothing.

"One of your secrets for one of mine?" She raised an eyebrow at him. Questioning.

"Do you really think you are in a position to be making demands?" he countered.

After a moment, she heaved a hefty sigh.

"Fine. I will tell you, Marc," she said. "But you have to promise me you will keep the secret."

He blinked. "Of course, I will. That goes without saying—"

"No. I fear the secret involves you in a way and—"

"Me?" The thrill of surprise chased his spine. "That seems . . . unlikely. But, regardless, you have my word. I will keep your secret, I promise."

Kit nodded. And then took a deep breath.

"Mr. Tallish and Dark-haired—as you call him—is Daniel Ashton . . . my younger brother."

"Your brother?" Marc's head reared back in surprise. "Not a male admirer?"

A wry grin touched her lips. "No. I leave that honor solely to you."

He matched her grin with one of his own. Relief washed through him, ridiculous as it was welcome.

"So . . . your *brother*. I did not expect that."

"Yes. I cannot go into the details of why he is here or even why I am here—"

"Ah, still keeping secrets."

"—but I noticed the buttons on my brother's coat resemble the ones you described to Lord Linwood."

"What?!" Marc said too loudly. "Are you sure?"

"Well, as sure as I could be. They were brass with a raised crest covered in vines."

Whoa!

Marc drew in a long, hissing breath and sank a hand into his hair.

Maybe . . . maybe it was just a huge coincidence. How common were such buttons anyway?

Or maybe it was his key to solving this mystery and returning home.

Rubbing his temples, Marc processed the implications.

First, Kit had a brother named Daniel who lurked about in shrubbery.

Who had buttons that sounded similar to the one he remembered from his scuffle with the intruder in Duir Cottage.

In the twenty-first century.

Was Daniel his man, then? The blackmailer?

A man from the nineteenth century, traveling between time periods, causing who-knew-what kind of havoc?

Or was he part of a larger plot?

For the hundredth time, Marc cursed that he hadn't caught a clear glimpse of the intruder who attacked him. The man who disappeared into the shrubbery could have been his attacker. He looked to be about the correct size. But Marc would have to question Daniel to know for sure.

Despite Arthur's misgivings, Marc had been smart in coming into town to look around.

His lengthy silence distressed Kit.

"Marc, please," —she grabbed his gloved hands in hers— "I realize Daniel most likely was one of the highwaymen who robbed you, but I promise I will find a way to repay what you lost. Just pleasepleaseplease don't turn him over to the magistrate."

Oh right. There was also that . . .

How to respond?

"Kit, this is serious."

"You promised to keep the secret." Her dark eyes looked beseechingly. Her hands tense around his. "I need Daniel. He's all I have left, and I love him more than life. If he continues down this path . . . at best, it will leave me cast out of my family's house. And at worst . . ."

"What do you mean, Kit?"

She heaved an exasperated sigh and pulled her hands back into her own lap. "I came to Marfield to find Daniel, as he had run off. Since my father died last year, Daniel is the only family left to me. Literally, the only family. I fear he is involved in deep things which could keep him from ever returning home, back to our estate, to his place in society. If Daniel doesn't return . . . things would be bad. Despite appearances, I promise he is a good person."

"All right." Marc blinked. "But why are you Lady Ruby's companion if your brother is a man of some property?"

"Well, I left too . . . hastily. I knew Daniel was involved with something in a town called Marfield in Herefordshire, and so I simply left. But I found myself here without any money and no Daniel in sight. The vicar was kind enough to arrange for the position with Ruby to give me a roof over my head. I am only here until I convince Daniel to return home with me. Having lost my father this past year, I can't bear to lose Daniel too. Please don't betray us."

Wow. That was a lot to absorb. Assuming Daniel was the man in Duir Cottage, how was Marc to deal with Daniel without betraying Kit too?

"I have no intention of turning Daniel over to the local magistrates, Kit. But I would like to chat with him about his activities in and around Marfield. I believe he has information that might prove useful—"

"Because of your spying activities with your sister, Emry?"

Man, she was so smart. Quick with a probing question.

"How do you know about Emme?"

"Hah! So you admit she was your sister?"

Marc gave a cheerless chuckle. "Yes, my younger sister. Now you know one of my secrets, so we are even. Again, tell me how you know about Emme."

"I may have overheard Linwood and Arthur talking about trying to find you. They were concerned about the rise in local thefts and thought they might be tied to a French spy ring." She looked at Marc's impassive face. "That information does not appear to have surprised you."

He shrugged. "Arthur told me all about it."

"Ah." She fidgeted, her mouth opening and then closing just as quickly. As if wanting to ask a question, but almost afraid to know the answer. Finally, she raised her chin and dove in. "So . . . are there French spies in the area? And, if so, do you think they have something to do with Daniel?"

Excellent questions. Were there French spies in the area? Did they have something to do with Daniel?

That was a chilling thought.

He could hardly tell her the truth.

Well, you see, I am actually from the twenty-first century, and I think your brother has been traveling back and forth between time periods with potentially disastrous consequences . . .

Man, he really needed to run Daniel to ground.

"I'm not sure, Kit. We need to talk with him to know. Given the nature of the robbery and my, uh . . . past activities, shall we say, I wonder if your brother knows something which may prove helpful."

Kit wrinkled her brow.

"I assure you, Kit, I mean him no harm. I simply wish to ascertain what he knows. That is all. Could you arrange a meeting between us?"

A beat of silence.

"I . . . I don't know." She shook her head. "Daniel said he had some plan to get us money. I don't understand completely what is going on. I didn't see the buttons in time to ask him about his role in your robbery. What is he involved in, Marc? Do you think it truly dreadful?"

Again . . . wow. How to answer that?

"Uhm . . . I can't honestly say, Kit. I suggest we both hold off making any judgments until we talk to Daniel."

She nodded. "Finding him might be difficult. But with your help, I have faith we can track him down. I have a lot more I want to say to him anyway."

Kit nibbled on her bottom lip. They sat in silence for a moment, studying the old church.

Well, Kit studied the church. Marc watched Kit from the corner of his eye, his mind galloping from the revelation.

Kit's brother might be the man who attacked him in Duir Cottage. The blackmailer. Or Daniel, at a minimum, might know who *was* blackmailing him.

And even more importantly, this all brought Marc one giant step closer to finding his ticket home. Arthur could now focus on tracking down Daniel. And perhaps once they put a stop to whatever scheme

Daniel planned, the portal would allow Marc to return.

Hallelujah!

Kit shifted next to him.

Of course, returning home also meant leaving Kit. The thought made his heart give an odd little lurch.

Though, how could Kit ever fit into his modern, twenty-first century life? She would be so lost and alone, even with Marc at her side.

Case in point, Georgiana had spent over a year in the twenty-first century and never felt like she fit in. And Georgiana had James at her side the entire time. Her brother had come *with* her.

But Kit would have to *leave* her brother behind. Something he doubted she would do.

And Marc absolutely refused to give up his career, family and entire life in 2014. Just thinking about it caused a wave of panic.

Yeah.

There was no hope of a future together. Ever. Period.

Though, he was comforted to realize Kit's life had probably not always been the drudgery it was now. That she had a future where she would be free to choose her own destiny. Or, at least, as free as any nineteenth century woman could be.

Kit would flirt, find a nice man, settle down, have a quaint cottage full of babies—

But why did that image make him want to punch something . . . hard?

Okay, so maybe he *knew* the answer to that question. He just needed to be honest with himself.

He *liked* Kit. The way she matched his wit, dished out as much as she took without any apology. The flirty lift of her mouth as she teased him, how she refused to take any of his bull.

It all boiled down to that irresistible confidence. So secure within herself.

Making him *want* to know her better.

How could he possibly feel so drawn to the one person who could never become a permanent part of his life?

Though actually the question provided the answer.

This was just a case of wanting that which he could never have. Kit was unattainable and, knowing that, he longed to keep her in his life.

Like a child who wanted an off-limits toy, making the forbidden item seem impossibly desirable.

Classic reverse psychology.

Yes! That was all it was. Nothing more.

He was fine. Just fine. He wasn't falling for this woman.

Marc relaxed next to Kit on the bench, content his emotions were securely locked away.

For her part, Kit shivered, drawing her cloak around her more firmly, rubbing her arms.

"You know, if you want a hug, you only have to ask," Marc said. "No need to be so awkwardly unsubtle about it."

He turned more toward her, stretching an arm along the back of the bench. Behind her but not touching.

He was emotionally safe, right? So no harm in continuing his shameless flirting.

Kit stopped rubbing her arms and fixed him with a hard stare. And then glanced pointedly at his arm behind her.

"You pull a move like that" —she gestured toward his arm with her chin— "and you call *me* awkwardly unsubtle?"

He winked at her.

"I can't even think of a way to politely respond." She shook her head.

"Here, allow me to help." He cleared his throat loudly and then launched into a credible falsetto. "'Pon rep, Marcus, I daresay you are the most dashing thing to ever inhabit buckskin breeches."

"'Pon rep? Do you enjoy London cant?"

"Who me? I don't. I assure you. It is my valet, actually. He also uses phrases like 'fustian nonsense' and 'all the crack.' Quite educational."

With a helpless smile, Kit stopped rubbing her arms and instead tugged off her worn gloves, blowing warm air on her cold, red fingers.

"Here, permit me." Marc pulled his arm from behind her and stripped off his own gloves.

Without thinking, he took her frigid fingers in his. They were practically ice cubes. *That* was why he felt a zing as he touched her.

Focused on his task, Marc rubbed her fingers and blew on them, gradually warming them up.

After a moment of chafing some warmth into her hands, he looked up. To see Kit staring at him with huge, wide eyes.

Ah . . . right.

He was holding her hands. And, by doing so, had probably broken a book-full of nineteenth century etiquette rules.

He should care. He really should.

But he didn't. And she didn't pull her hands away.

He glanced down at their fingers, intertwined.

Kit had beautiful hands. Soft and cared for—the hands of a lady. Strong with neatly trimmed nails. Long, elegant fingers. Not dainty, but then nothing about her was dainty, thank goodness. She was solid and real and here.

For now.

He rubbed his thumbs along her palms, appreciating the slide of her smooth skin against his.

Some distant part of his brain screamed at him. Insisting that the heart-racing heat he felt in simply *touching* her hands was more than mere polite friendship.

Lifting his eyes back to hers, Marc deliberately engulfed her hands, holding her gaze as he continued to rub warmth into her fingers.

He raised her hands and blew on the backs of them. And then quite deliberately, turned over her right hand and planted a kiss into her palm.

A very *good* kiss, he might add. The kind that sent an electrical sizzle up a woman's arm.

Kit gasped and instantly curled her hand around the kiss, sealing it in. She pulled her hands out of his grasp and back into her lap, clasping them together. Hard. As if she wanted to protect the kiss emblazoned on her palm.

Or possibly prevent him from duplicating the gesture.

It could go either way.

"I like your hands." The words popped out.

"Thank you." She swallowed and turned said hands over in her lap. "They are a little large. To match the rest of me."

She said it matter-of-factly. But he had to wonder if this wasn't a chink in Kit's confidence armor. Was anyone really as confident as they seemed on the outside?

He couldn't stop his curiosity. Had all that confidence been forged as a defense? Was confidence her version of deflection? Forcing hurts and pains to seemingly bounce off of her?

Part of Marc (the part he currently refused to listen to) howled at the thought that this amazing woman would ever, for even a moment, doubt her amazing-ness.

Something panged in his chest, kicking powerfully against the blocks he had built around his feelings for her. He shook his head and reached for her hands again.

"No. They are perfect." He massaged her knuckles, breathing on them anew. "All of you is perfect."

She raised an eyebrow. "Ah. So your lordship likes a proper armful? Not the petite, slender misses one sees in London?"

He grinned. "I like a *woman*, Miss Ashton. And when I embrace a woman, I like to feel I am holding something soft and curved and decidedly female. Otherwise, what is the point?"

Kit gave him a skeptical, I-suppose-I-can-humor-you look. "I think a good many men would disagree. I have listened to their talk enough to know. I am far too tall and—"

"No, there you are wrong. A man wants a woman to be distinctly unlike himself. Women obsess over the smallest things. Are my hips too big? Are my eyes too small? They don't realize it is the *entirety* of a woman which draws a man in. That every little quirk simply becomes part of what makes a woman uniquely special."

Kit stared at him with her enormous honey eyes. Faintly amused but clearly unbelieving.

He *hated* seeing doubt in her eyes. Particularly when it was directed at herself.

That something underneath his sternum thumped again, spreading a painful ache across his chest, tightening his breathing.

He could not stand another moment of her self-doubt. Someday he would ferret out its source, but for now, he merely wanted to combat it. Like a vicious weed that needed to be stamped out.

Without thinking, he stood and locked eyes with her, drowning in their chocolate depths. With a gentle squeeze of her hand, he oh-so-slowly pulled Kit to her feet.

And then, again . . . slow, slow, slowly tugged her toward him. Until her skirts swished around his boots and he could feel the warm puff of her breath against his chin. Her height allowing him to look her straight in the eye.

Carefully, respectfully, he wrapped his hands under her cloak and around her waist, drawing her into his arms. Gently, as if she were a treasure. Something precious to be cherished.

He felt the initial surprise in her body, and then she melted into him, her ice cold hands pressed against his chest between them.

She *was* a delightful armful. Lush and curved, her waist narrower than he had supposed. She smelled faintly of lavender and clean soap.

Why hadn't he thought to hold her before now?

"See," he murmured into her hair, "I was right. Look how perfectly you fit."

The truth of his own words hit hard. She *did* fit perfectly against him.

She gave a muffled laugh that sounded as rattled as he felt.

"You only say that because we're both so cold," she sighed, pressing her frozen nose into the crook of his neck. And then snuggled in even closer, burrowing her ice-cube fingers under his coat and wrapping them around his back. They burned through his waistcoat.

His arms tightened around her. How had he ended up in the deep end so fast?

Why, why, why was he doing this to himself?

Kit was a nineteenth century woman . . . no, lady. A nineteenth century *lady*. And as such, she was used to a life and set of rules he would never understand. Surely, he had broken at least a couple dozen of those rules in the last fifteen minutes alone.

Not that he claimed to be a gentleman, despite all of Michel's coaching.

But, man, it felt good and just plain *right* to have her in his arms. Like every other woman had been the wrong fit. Like he had been born to hold her and only her.

It was a terrifyingly disturbing thought. Because it made him want to hold her more. To keep her permanently, which was an impossibility.

Fate had sent him into the past. There was a blackmailer on the loose who needed to be stopped. He had assumed *that* was his mission. But Kit was now wrapped up in the mess too.

Were they fated for each other like James and Emme or Georgiana and Sebastian? He had rejected the idea just a few minutes ago . . . but now.

The thought thrilled and terrified.

Marc gathered Kit even closer to him, burying his nose in her hair. Inhaling deeply.

Kit's hands moved across his back, pressing through his waistcoat. And then she pulled away just enough to move her hands around to his chest, still pressing. She had a faint frown on her face. Marc forced himself not to study the slight pout of her lips.

That path led to danger and deep waters.

Instead, he lifted a questioning eyebrow.

"Are you muscled everywhere?" she finally asked, feeling the ripples of his stomach. "It's like you're one solid muscle."

He shrugged. It was a by-product of all his muay thai training.

She squeezed one of his biceps. He flexed for her.

Her eyes widened.

"I take it you approve, Miss Ashton?" he asked.

She nodded carefully and then took a cautious step back from him. Swallowed.

"I promise my muscles don't bite."

That got a quiet laugh from her.

"I am not entirely sure of that."

A small pause.

"Thank you," she said softly, eyes calm and sincere.

Marc instantly understood what she meant.

Thank you for making me feel beautiful. For shoring up my wavering confidence.

"You are welcome," he replied just as gravely.

She studied his face, eyes unreadable. "Nothing can ever come of this . . . of us. You know that, right?"

He nodded. "I know."

"It's not that I don't like you."

"I know. I don't . . . not like you . . . too."

They gazed at each other in silence.

She smiled—a weak, weary thing. "Friends, then?" She extended her hand to him.

He wrapped her cold hand in his. "Friends."

And then he tugged on her hand, pulling her back into him, murmuring into her hair, "And as your friend, I can't let you return back to Haldon Manor until you have warmed up a bit."

Her body vibrated with laughter, and she melted against him.

Nothing could come of it—her words echoing through the aching pang in his chest.

Nothing.

Chapter 12

L ord Linwood, thank you again for arranging this delightful party. Your estate is enchanting," Lady Ruby said as she entered the drawing room, the purple satin of her evening gown rustling.

Following right behind, Kit watched Linwood bow politely over Ruby's knuckles. As usual, the viscount was immaculately turned out, this time in a black coat and subtly striped scarlet-red waistcoat. Both fitted to his frame as only the most exclusive London tailor could manage. Weston, perhaps?

Kit looked past Linwood, scanning the room for Marc, noting he wasn't there.

Not yet, at least.

Her talk with Marc in the church earlier in the week had shifted their relationship—solidifying their friendship but adding a robust layer of angst.

She could still vividly recall the feel of his arms around her, the potent breadth of his body. She had wanted to sink into his strength, to rely on someone as she hadn't in a *very* long while. Cry out a lifetime of trouble and sorrow on his solid chest.

He was just so very . . . male. That sense of something wild and elemental within him. Untamed. The opposite of everything she had ever thought she would want in a man.

But she knew why.

He accepted himself the way he was. And, as a consequence, made *her* feel accepted just as she was. No need to change a thing.

It was odd, actually. All her life she had been feted and sought out because of *who* she was. Most people never bothered to see past her social station, family connections and clever wit to appreciate her for herself.

But here, stripped of everything she had ever been, she had only herself to recommend her. And how thrilling to realize she was enough. That someone *could* accept her.

Her throat tightened painfully when she thought about it too much. They had no promise of a future together. No matter what her treacherous heart (and shoulder angels) wanted.

For just a moment, Kit imagined dragging Marc home with her. How all her friends would squeal over an adventurer-turned-spy in tight breeches. A man who spent his time sailing the world on a clipper ship, sails snapping—sword in one hand, pistol in the other. Not that she had seen Marc brandish either weapon, but she was quite sure he would be proficient with both.

A romantic untamed rogue straight from the pages of some sappy novel.

Yes, her friends would all collectively swoon and then read her the Riot Act, listing the many, many ways in which being emotionally involved with Marc was a very, very bad idea.

And they would be right. At least on paper. Curse them.

"Miss Ashton, my shawl, if you please." Lady Ruby walked slowly toward the roaring fire and the settee in front of it, gesturing toward the purple shawl which Kit held over one arm. Startled out of her reverie, Kit instantly crossed the opulent drawing room to her employer.

Linwood had invited everyone from Haldon Manor to Kinningsley for a brief country party. A much newer building than Haldon Manor, Kinningsley had been completed just thirty years prior by the current Lord Linwood's grandfather. With its profusion of marble, fluted columns and soaring ceilings painted with cherubs and country scenes, the entire house was an homage to classical Greek and Roman aesthetics.

Rumors among the servants had it that Marianne had pleaded with her brother to give her some respite from the constant drain of entertaining Lady Ruby and Jedediah. Though no one doubted Marianne found Lady Ruby and Jedediah tedious company, it was hard to believe Lord Linwood would arrange a party strictly for his sister's comfort.

But arrange the party Linwood had, inviting everyone to quit Haldon Manor and join him for several days at his estate. As Lady Ruby's companion, Kit had been allowed to come.

Kit had driven herself and Fanny the few miles to Linwood's estate in Arthur's gig. There was no room for them in the family coach, particularly as Marianne insisted tiny Isabel accompany them, stating over and over how besotted her brother was with his baby niece. Kit kept her opinions about *that* to herself.

Despite everything, the invitation had cheered Kit immensely. Which was truly pathetic, when she thought about it too much. It was more than just a change of scenery (though that too was decidedly welcome). Kinningsley afforded her a different landscape to look for Daniel.

The past few days of searching had proved futile. Marc kept a low profile but frequently rode into Marfield to snoop about. He updated her each day about what steps had been taken and what their next step would be.

Daniel had disappeared, as usual.

Though lovely to have help, she was still nervous about Daniel and Marc meeting. Who knew what Daniel would say?

Certain undisclosed aspects of her family needed to stay just that—undisclosed. Would he understand the danger in telling Marc too much?

Kit settled Lady Ruby onto the settee in front of the fireplace near the vicar and his wife, arranging Ruby's purple cashmere shawl precisely as she liked it (two pleated folds, draped on the shoulders so the shawl hung at precisely the same length on each side).

Jedediah joined them, taking a seat next to his mother, tugging on his pink velvet tailcoat, raking Kit with his gaze. Ruby inspected her shawl, satisfied with Kit's efforts, waving her away with an impatient flap of her hand.

Set free, Kit wandered over to one of the floor-to-ceiling windows which had a clear view of the drawing room door. It also gave her a chance to study the room's ceiling. Gilded moldings held panels depicting pastoral scenes of the various stages of courtship with mischievous cupids wreaking havoc amongst it all.

Kit couldn't help darting a surreptitious glance at Linwood, wondering why the stuffy viscount tolerated naughty cupids frolicking in his drawing room. Maybe he secretly enjoyed them.

The thought put a smile on her face.

Kit ran her hands down the front of her gown. Marianne, bless her good heart, had found several evening gowns which had belonged to the former Georgiana Knight. It was not atypical for members of the aristocracy to pass along unwanted clothing to genteelly-born servants. A few items to help Kit feel less out-of-place while hovering around Lady Ruby and the other house guests. It was yet another example of Marianne's thoughtful goodness.

Kit was taller and decidedly more curved than Georgiana, but Fanny had helped Kit refashion one of the dresses in time for this evening. A simple red silk gown with tiny puffed sleeves and low neckline. The color had never really flattered Georgiana's fair complexion, which is why it had been left at Haldon Manor. But wine-red suited Kit to perfection, giving her skin and eyes a bright gleam. Kit had forgotten how much she loved the feel of silk against her skin.

It was amazing what an elegant dress did for self-confidence. That extra bounce in one's step when wearing something stunning, making it just that much easier to feel poised and collected. Kit had even managed to waylay Fanny for a few minutes to help with her hair, which was now more artfully arranged on top of her head with loops and curls.

All in all, she felt a bit more like Katherine Ashton tonight. A little more like her full self.

She was so absorbed in her cupid watching and dress-musings, she nearly missed Marc's entrance.

He walked through the door with that confident swagger of his, assured his dark green evening coat and understated green-and-gold-shot waistcoat fit him to perfection. A scoundrel dressed up in gentleman's clothing.

Which accurately described him, she supposed.

Marc scanned the room, his eyes drifting right past her. Seeming to look for Kit, but not seeing her. With a faint frown, he strode into the room.

And then his eyes swung back her way; he instantly froze. Recognition flaring, his head rearing back in surprise.

And then that languid smile of his made an appearance, moving straight through a grin into a full-blown laugh. Head back, eyes crinkling.

Kit found it particularly gratifying.

You have absolutely no hope of a future together, Virtuous Angel unhelpfully reminded her.

Exactly. Which is why you need to soak up every second of being in his delicious presence, Wicked Angel said. *Maybe he will even let you touch his muscles again.*

She and her shoulder angels shared a joint collective sigh at the thought.

That would be *so* lovely.

Marc stopped in front of her, surveying her clothing from head to toe. And then bowed.

"Miss Ashton, shame on you. Placing all other ladies in the shade with your radiance."

And just like that, her knees turned to jelly.

He winked and gave her a naughty grin. He knew *exactly* what such comments did to her.

Kit returned his saucy look and willed her traitorous knees steady.

He moved to her side and pretended to study the room. Kit peeked at him out of the corner of her eye.

"You have about thirty seconds before Lady Ruby notices us talking and calls me away," she murmured. Even now, Jedediah shot a backwards glance at them, leaning in to his mother's ear, causing Ruby's shawl to slip. Thirty seconds might actually be somewhat optimistic.

Marc nodded and looked upward, examining the ceiling, all nonchalance.

"So what is our boredom-busting theme going to be tonight?" he asked under his breath.

"I am not telling any more of my secrets."

He shrugged. "Neither am I. But that doesn't mean we can't play."

"But if a secret isn't the penalty, what will the forfeit be?"

He was silent for a moment, still studying the ceiling. "A boon. If one of us laughs, we owe the other a favor of their choice."

A favor? Wicked Angel nearly giggled with glee. *I know exactly what we're asking for.*

Virtuous Angel rolled her eyes. *I don't know how I put up with you sometimes.*

Ruby had leaned forward, engrossed in a conversation with the vicar, causing her shawl to sink another six inches. Kit had maybe fifteen seconds more.

"Done," Kit whispered, barely moving her lips. "What should our game be?"

"Are those naked babies with arrows?" Marc shifted, craning his head sideways.

"Cupids. They're cupids."

"And naughty ones too, it seems. Please tell me Linwood specifically requested cupids—"

"Focus, Marcus."

"Right. Perhaps we could read each discussion as a coded conversation for something else?"

"Mmmm, like incontinence?"

He turned from the ceiling with a raised eyebrow. "My, my, Miss Ashton. Are all ladies perpetually twelve-years-old?"

Teasing, awful man.

She chose to ignore his comment.

"Theater aliases," he continued.

"I beg your pardon?"

"Miss Ashton." Lady Ruby's voice carried across the room. "My shawl has slipped."

Kit shot Marc a wry look.

Turning her head toward her employer, she said, "Coming, my lady."

And then turned back to Marc, giving him a polite, extremely slow curtsy. Marc responded with an equally lingering bow.

"During dinner, combine a color from the clothing of whoever is speaking with the food they are eating," he murmured. "It will become that person's theater name."

Kit nodded and then turned to leave.

"I dearly hope my alias will be Emerald Bacon," he said to her retreating back.

Kit bit off her laugh just in time. Wicked wretch. He nearly won the first round without trying.

Marc tried to focus on dinner. Honestly he did.

But his brain was mush.

That *dress* . . .

Blood red silk that clung to Kit's frame, accentuating rather than hiding.

He had grown used to her shapeless clothing. It was part of her whole shtick. Clever, witty, no-nonsense . . . all hidden behind mousy clothing.

And then she had to go and sucker-punch him with that dress. It had taken two sweeps of the room to recognize her. And when he had . . .

How was he supposed to maintain emotional distance when she looked like *that*? Even worse, he wasn't the only man to notice her charms judging by the admiring looks sent her way.

The woman didn't fight fair.

Though speaking of games . . .

So far, Lady Ruby had been renamed Violet Wine and Jedediah had become Pink Oyster, on account of his glaringly bright tailcoat.

But the *coup de grace* had come from Linwood in his red waistcoat, who took a bite of fowl while discussing the possibility of rain with Arthur, officially naming himself Scarlet Partridge.

Kit had choked on her wine.

Now they were all gathered back together in the drawing room, listening to Jedediah ramble on about his exploits at Gentleman Jackson's Boxing Salon. Though tedious in the extreme for Marc, at least Linwood seemed to be suffering too, judging by how the man drummed his fingers against his thigh.

Marc deemed it a win.

"I managed to land a cross-punch to my opponent when he failed to duck—"

"Enough, dear boy." Ruby cut off Jedediah, thankfully taking pity on them all. "I believe I have had enough excitement for one night. Miss Ashton, if you will, I should like to retire." Ruby rose to her feet, prompting everyone to rise. A chorus of bows and curtsies ensued.

Kit shot Marc a resigned look as she followed Lady Ruby from the room, taking all of Marc's fun with her.

Arthur and Marianne agreed to play whist with the vicar and his wife, leaving Jedediah, Linwood and Marc to gaze tensely at each other.

Yeah. He was *not* going to spend what remained of his evening with those two.

Marc bowed and excused himself, saying he wished to consult the library for a book to read. Anything to escape the drawing room.

Situated across the large domed entry hall, the library wasn't difficult to find. A soaring space of white-washed bookshelves, dotted with tables and a large desk. Someone obviously took their learning seriously. A fire crackled in the fireplace.

Marc had only gone a few steps into the room when a voice accosted him.

"Vader, may I have a word?" Linwood's ultra-cultured accent grated. Or should Marc call him Scarlet Partridge?

Marc turned with a raised eyebrow. The viscount stood inside the library door, his face as inscrutable as ever.

"If you wish, Linwood."

Marc strolled over to the fireplace and leaned a shoulder into the opulent marble mantel. Arms folded across his chest. Waiting.

He was quite sure Linwood viewed their relationship like some giant game of chess, where each conversation was a strategic ploy. To what end, Marc was unable to say. He just found perverse pleasure in watching Linwood try to make heads or tails of Marc's presence in Marfield.

The viscount could make the first move.

Linwood studied him for a moment and then walked over and lifted a thick book from one of the tables and returned to Marc, handing him the book.

Marc reluctantly took the proffered volume. Never breaking eye contact with Linwood.

"A reading suggestion?"

"Something of the like." Linwood shrugged. Even in the dim fire-light, the viscount's eyes were unnervingly pale.

Marc raised his eyebrows, questioning.

Linwood gestured toward the book. "I was hoping you would be able to explain to me where the Barons Vader are to be found."

Marc tilted the book into the light and read the title: *Debrett's Peerage of England, Scotland and Ireland.*

Ah. So *that* was how Linwood intended to play.

"I have searched the book thoroughly and have yet to find any reference to a Lord Vader."

Linwood studied Marc with haughty contempt, his face giving away nothing. Though there was a glint in his eye. Linwood looked positively gleeful. Well, for Linwood anyway.

Adrenaline surged through Marc. He needed to bluff and think fast. He hadn't come this far to reveal himself to Linwood now.

Marc smiled, tight and mocking.

"Vader is a . . . Prussian title. Consequently, you won't find me listed with British peers." He handed the book back to Linwood, who took it grudgingly, setting it down on an end table.

Linwood regarded him again, eyes narrowed now.

"Why do I doubt the veracity of your answer?"

Marc shrugged. Several replies popping into his head at once.

Why are you such a stuffy cad?

Have you considered a theater career as Scarlet Partridge?

Marc settled for saying, "You are entitled to your opinion."

The viscount *was* currently feeding him and providing a roof over his head. No need to be a total jerk.

Go figure. Maybe Marc actually cared about manners after all.

Linwood merely brushed a speck of lint from his coat sleeve. "As I am the one currently housing and feeding you, I feel I deserve to know exactly who you are."

Ah, unless Linwood beat him to being a jerk. *Then* Marc supposed it was okay.

"I believe we already covered the social niceties several days ago, Linwood, but if you would like another introduction." Marc gave a precise bow and a mocking grin. "Lord Vader, at your service."

Linwood's eyes narrowed. Obviously not appreciative of Marc's wit.

"I have been anxious to arrange a meeting with her most royal highness, Princess Pepsi of Toyota Camry," Linwood said. "Are you acquainted with her highness?" He assessed Marc through hooded eyes, obviously searching for a reaction to his words.

Marc instantly swallowed a laugh, though Linwood surely saw the smile which threatened.

Despite being colossally inconvenient, this entire debacle Emme had set in motion was *almost* worth it, just to hear Linwood say the words *Princess Pepsi of Toyota Camry* in his snooty, aristocratic drawl.

"I have never had the privilege of visiting the esteemed country of Toyota Camry. I hear it is quite lovely, being a safe and economical place for families but a little sedate for my tastes." Marc considered himself more of a motorcycle kinda guy. "Though I understand Princess Pepsi has a bit of a temper. If you disturb her over much, she is liable to erupt. Like a shaken bottle of champagne." Marc managed to keep his face straight.

Linwood paused, obviously sensing that he was missing something. A beat of silence.

"You bear a strong resemblance to a woman I once met. A Miss Emry Wilde. Perhaps a relation of yours?" Linwood clasped his hands behind his back.

Damn. Marc reminded himself not to underestimate Linwood's intelligence. Arthur was going to have a conniption over this conversation. He needed to get Linwood off the scent.

"Miss Emry Wilde? That doesn't strike me as familiar. Though perhaps she might be an acquaintance of my sister." Marc pretended to ponder for a moment, tapping his lips. And then snapped his fingers, as if just remembering something. "I do seem to remember my sister mentioning a friend who was once accosted by a dishonorable man. But I can't for the life of me remember her friend's name."

Okay, so maybe baiting Linwood wasn't the best way to dissuade him from this line of questioning . . . but Marc seemed unable to stop himself when around the viscount.

Linwood shifted his weight. Almost as if he were uncomfortable with something.

Marc liked to think it was perhaps some vestige of a guilty conscience.

Though more likely it was just gas.

"Indeed. Well. I shall leave you to your reading, Lord *Vader.*" Linwood lingered ironically upon the name.

And then bowed, stiff and formal, exiting the room.

Chapter 13

That will be all, Miss Ashton." Lady Ruby waved her hand, pulling a lavender shawl tighter around her shoulders. Kit plumped a final bed pillow. "You are free to retire or continue mingling with the other guests. Please see that I am not disturbed."

"As you wish, my lady. Good night." Kit curtsied.

Lady Ruby nodded and reached for a book on her nightstand as Kit carefully closed the bedroom door, balancing a candle in her hand.

Kit tripped down the grand staircase, slippers *tap-tap-tapping* on the marble, eager to return to the drawing room and the company there.

Well, really only one person—Marc.

Scarlet Partridge, indeed.

She left the stairwell with a bounce in her step and started across the soaring entry hall.

"There you are," a deliciously low baritone voice murmured from behind her.

Marc.

Before Kit could answer, a strong hand snagged her elbow and pulled her into the library. Without a word, Marc lifted the candle from her hand and carefully used it to light a standing candelabra next to a table.

He stood back, arms crossed, staring at her. "Really, Miss Ashton, we must stop meeting like this."

"Indeed, my lord. What will people say?"

He grinned.

Kit grinned back.

And then his smile turned quite predatory. A thrill sizzled down her spine.

He took a step toward her. And then another.

She raised an eyebrow at him. Questioning. But she didn't take a step back.

His grin turned decidedly roguish, green eyes glinting catlike in the dim light.

Kit caught her breath. What was it about this man? An adventurer wrapped up in a gentleman's clothing. That combination of tailored elegance and wild unpredictability.

You are in soooo deep, Virtuous Angel whispered.

Mmmmm, can you blame her? I mean, look *at him,* Wicked Angel sighed.

Kit *did* look at him. She wanted to rumple his clothing, to take him back to the man who had jumped onto her runaway horse. Elemental.

Marc took another step toward her, stopping so close Kit could see the faint reflection of the room in his eyes. Could feel the heat of his body.

Her heart sped up.

And then, with that same lazy grin, he reached out and grasped her elbow, tugging her to him.

Kit didn't resist.

He engulfed her in his arms. His incredibly strong, muscled, *male* arms.

The sudden touch shocked her. But right behind the shock came relief.

At last.

As if she hadn't been complete before this. As if every moment spent outside his embrace was only half-lived.

For her part, Kit wrapped her arms around those broad shoulders, leaning on them. Threading a hand into his thick, curly hair.

"Is this your boon?" she asked. "Because though it was a near thing, I never laughed. I admit Scarlet Partridge was a near miss—"

Marc laughed and gathered her closer. "I have been wanting to do this all evening," he muttered into her ear. "All week, really."

Kit resisted a sigh as he tightened his arms around her waist, his thumbs making lazy circles against the small of her back.

He was just so warm, so solid. Heavens but she loved the strength of him. The feeling that he could move mountains for her.

She tried and failed to imagine the path of his life. But she wanted to know all of it. Every last detail that had brought him to this point.

He sighed and somehow clutched her closer.

"When I walked into the drawing room and saw you in this dress . . ." He growled in her ear.

Actually *growled*. Low and rumbly.

"Did you just growl?" Kit laughed quietly.

He growled again. Making her laugh harder.

"If you could see yourself in this dress the way *I* do, you would growl too. If I had my way, I would burn every single one of those shapeless things you usually wear and dress you only in red silk."

Kit stilled. Did he mean that?

He could actually make good on that threat, she realized. He was an unattached gentleman of some means. A baron. Was he contemplating offering for her? Did a man like Marc . . . marry?

Panic edged in. It was just entirely impossible. Her life was just too . . . she mentally flinched away from the thoughts crowding in.

Marc sensed her sudden tension.

"Relax." He breathed in her hair. "Let me have the delight of simply holding a beautiful woman in a breathtaking red dress. Nothing more. Just let me have another growl or two."

Which lead to another deep grumble in her ear.

Kit melted against him, surprised to find her eyes stinging.

Why was Fate being so cruel? Why thrust her into this impossible situation with Daniel and then toss the most remarkable man in her path?

In another time—at another point in her life—Marc would be a godsend. Someone she would dream into her future.

Ruthlessly, she pushed any thoughts of the future far away.

The moment needed to just . . . be. In this beautiful place, with her lovely dress, heady with after-dinner wine . . . and him so gentle and strong and free. It had to be enough.

She sighed and nuzzled her nose into his neck, breathing in the scent of wool and something faintly woodsy. If she pulled back her head, he would kiss her. She knew it.

Mmmmm, yes! What are you waiting for? Wicked Angel urged.

An enormous part of her wanted that. Wanted his kiss.

But . . .

Kissing him would admit, even if only to herself, that she was in too deep. That for all her caution—which, quite frankly, hadn't been particularly cautious at all—she was falling hard for him. And that things were about to get very, very messy.

Exactly! Kissing him will not help you find Daniel. It will not help you solve this mess and return home. It will only make everything so much worse. Dumb Virtuous Angel and her prudent, moment-killing logic.

Kissing *would* just make the inevitable parting that much more painful.

She let out a small growl of frustration of her own.

She felt more than heard Marc's laugh.

"That's my girl." His breath tickled her ear. "Now you're getting into the spirit of the thing."

"I didn't want to leave you hanging like a fool," she murmured back, letting her lips graze his ear in the process.

So much for holding back.

Marc growled again. Her unsolicited touch obviously being all the encouragement he needed.

He responded in kind, nibbling a kiss along the edge of her ear. The touch of his lips like hot satin. Kit tightened her grip on his hair, barely suppressing a full-on gasp.

Way too deep.

Help, she mentally cried.

She was sinking fast.

His lips had found the edge of her jaw and were drifting slowly, slowly, slowly toward her mouth . . .

. . . when chaos erupted outside the library door.

They jumped apart as footsteps pounded across the entry hall.

Through the hubbub, Kit clearly heard Linwood's angry voice.

"There will be hell to pay for this."

Marc glanced at her and then grasped her hand.

"Stay here. I will see what is going on. We can't be seen leaving this room together."

Too true. She did have a reputation to think about, she supposed. Not that she had been thinking much about it over the last few minutes.

Kit nodded, eyes wide. Unsure if the interruption was a welcome reprieve or an unwanted intrusion.

Marc lifted her hand to his lips and pressed a lingering kiss into her palm.

And then he was gone.

The entire house was in uproar.

Linwood stood in the high, domed entryway, calling out orders. Like a general marshaling his troops.

Marc paused for a second, trying to pull his head back to the matter at hand.

Instead of swimming in the memory of Kit in his arms. The heat of her breath swirling around his ear.

That dress, her teasing smile, the lushness of her—both physical and emotional. The sense of connection he felt. He was only a man. How could he resist such a perfect combination?

He felt a lingering sense of unease for kissing her jaw like that. She wasn't some flirty woman he had just met at a bar. She was a nineteenth century lady, completely unused to playing by his twenty-first century rules.

He would do well to remember that.

Man, his mother and Emme would give him *such* a talking to over this. A well-deserved lecture.

Linwood noted him standing off to the side and pointed.

"You!" he intoned, walking toward Marc. "I would speak with *you* immediately."

He snapped his fingers and strode past Marc right back into the library, confident Marc would trail behind him.

The library where Kit most assuredly still was.

Damn.

Which meant Marc *had* to follow him. If only to be sure that Kit's person and reputation were preserved.

Suppressing an urge to hurt something—or even better, a tall, arrogant *someone*—Marc followed Linwood into the library. Feeling like a school boy about to be taken to the whipping shed.

Marc entered expecting to find the viscount confronting Kit. But the library appeared blessedly empty. Only the flickering candles and fireplace winked a polite welcome.

Where had Kit hid herself? The room was half shadows, but Marc caught a glimpse of red disappearing under the desk.

Plucky, adorable woman!

Linwood whirled on him with barely suppressed rage. It was oddly heartening to see him so angry. The man actually did feel some emotion underneath that fastidious veneer. Fire and ice.

"Does this look familiar?" Linwood said, shoving his hand toward Marc.

Hesitantly, Marc looked down. And then scowled himself.

With a sharp intake of breath, he snatched a button from Linwood's grasp and tilted it into the candle light.

A brass button with a raised crest covered in vines.

The button already seared into his memory. It had to belong to the man who had attacked him in Duir Cottage.

Daniel.

But what——?!

"I see you recognize this button, Lord Vader."

Marc nodded. "It is definitely the same as the one sported by the . . . highwayman who accosted me."

He heard a faint hiss that could only come from Kit. Marc instantly coughed to cover her noise.

"Where did the button come from?" Marc asked.

Linwood clenched his jaw. Marc could practically hear his teeth grinding. "It was found lying on the floor of my private study. Which, at some point this evening, was ransacked. With everyone's attention on our guests, it was the perfect opportunity."

Marc's head reared back. Daniel was definitely up to something.

"Was anything stolen?"

"Yes." Linwood nodded once. Curt and precise.

The viscount's demeanor did not invite follow-up questions.

Marc couldn't care less.

"What was stolen?"

Linwood narrowed his eyes. "Don't you wish you knew, Vader?" A healthy dose of sarcasm there. "Or are you in league with these highway-men yourself? In which case, why not tell *me* what was stolen?"

Ah. The man could be *such* a smart arse.

Marc handed the button back. "Please, Linwood. Were I to steal something from you, I would not be so gauche as to leave a button call-ing card and a ransacked room. Give me some credit."

Why, oh why, could he not stop baiting this man?

For his part, Linwood regarded him with jaw clenched, eyes intense and accusing.

"This robbery is a capital offense, Vader. A matter of national secu-rity. Even aiding the robbers would be considered an act of high treason. I would moderate your tone, were I you."

"Well, thank goodness I am not you."

Linwood hissed. Yes, Marc needed to reign in his junior high taunting tendencies.

"Again, what was stolen, Linwood? You are talking in riddles and making threats, but I assure you, I am utterly innocent. I haven't a clue what was stolen or who, precisely, would have stolen it."

That wasn't entirely true, but close enough.

"The French will pay a high price for what was taken. Something I am willing to bet you already knew." A muscle twitched in Linwood's cheek as he spoke.

Marc had not, in fact, known that. Surprise surely showed on his face.

No sense hiding this fact from Linwood.

Did that make Daniel an agent for the French then?

If so, it explained why Kit was so desperate to find her brother.

High treason was an ugly crime, as Arthur had mentioned. It thoroughly tainted every family member it touched. No wonder Kit wanted her brother found and returned home before he was captured.

But what about Marc's interaction with Daniel in Duir Cottage? Was Daniel somehow planning on using information from the future to alter the course of the Napoleonic wars?

Just the thought sent a chill of foreboding down Marc's spine.

"What is your game, Vader?"

Marc blinked. Drat. No matter how careful, Linwood was determined to expose Marc. "I have no *game*, as you put it, Linwood. The button belongs to someone who robbed me. That is all."

A pause.

"And your sister, Miss Emry?"

Back to *that*, were they? Arthur was not going to be happy about this.

"As I have said, Linwood, you have the wrong man."

Linwood drummed his fingers against his thigh, obviously not buying Marc's story. Whatever. It was just nice to see that the viscount had a nervous tick. He wasn't quite as impervious as it would seem.

"Ah. But I believe that I do have the right man," Linwood said after a moment. "My sources point quite squarely to a missing British agent being involved in this. Did I mention that the missing agent is in fact a woman?"

Marc stilled. *That* piece of information was impossibly interesting. And yet . . . explained so very, very much.

Visions of Kit danced through his head. Insisting her brother *had* to come home or all would be lost.

He suddenly had a *lot* more questions he wanted to ask her.

Marc forced his face into a calm mask. Movie-serene.

"And you think Miss Emry is your missing agent?"

Linwood tugged on the bottom of his waistcoat. Fixed Marc with his icy gaze.

"If the cap fits . . ." was all he said.

"Didn't this Miss Emry *die* in the carriage accident with James Knight?"

"So we have all been told. But though there is a grave for James, I have been unable to locate a similar grave for Miss Emry. Tell me why that is, Vader?"

Uhmm, because Arthur neglected to make a fake one for her too?

"You have poor eyesight?" Marc shrugged. "I mean, you do have trouble seeing you are a smart ars—"

"Or the lady is not as dead as some would have us believe." Linwood cut him off. "I do not suffer fools. There is obviously more afoot here. The timing of your presence here goes far beyond mere coincidence."

"And yet, on that point, I can assure you, my presence here is entirely happenstance. I am sorry something of importance to you was stolen. If I hear or see anything that seems related, I will *consider* telling you."

Linwood narrowed his eyes. And then he pocketed the button and straightened his coat sleeves. Never once taking his eyes off of Marc's.

"I will be watching you, Vader. Do not consider this conversation finished."

Chapter 14

Kit quietly tightened the harness on Arthur's gig, squinting in the dim light.

Sunrise had yet to arrive, but nighttime had begun to recede, leaving the sky more gray than inky-black.

After overhearing the tense conversation between Marc and Linwood, Kit realized her blasted brother truly was in over his head. A sickening knot in her stomach twisted and coiled, tightening her breathing.

Gah! Daniel was *such* an idiot. How was she ever going to straighten all this out? She just prayed it wasn't too late to prevent far reaching consequences . . .

She had lain awake for most of the night, her brain cranking on the problem. Kit didn't know what she would do, but she was done with doing *nothing*.

And then sometime before dawn, she had hit upon a course of action. She actually *did* have a faint idea as to where Daniel may be. The more she thought about it, the more likely it all seemed.

It was *her* turn to be an idiot. How could she not have thought of this before now?

Which is how she found herself in the barn quietly hitching a horse to the gig.

You should not be doing this. You will be caught, Virtuous Angel chided. *And then Arthur will have you jailed for horse theft, too.*

Stop being defeatist. We aren't stealing the horse and gig. Just borrowing it for a short while, Wicked Angel replied.

"Going somewhere, Miss Ashton?"

Kit jumped as Marc's voice sounded loudly in her ear, though he hardly spoke above a whisper.

Drat!

She whirled around to see him outlined in the barely-there light, dressed in a long caped great coat, boots and a beaver top hat, tapping gloves against his leg. He cocked a confident eyebrow and stuffed the gloves into a pocket. Challenging her to explain what she was doing.

Though *that* should be fairly obvious.

With a grunt, Kit turned her back on him and tightened the strap she was working on. Driving the gig so much in recent weeks had made her quite adept at the entire process.

But the buckle stuck and she struggled to pull it taut. Suddenly, a warm hand covered hers.

"Here. Allow me," Marc said softly into her ear, arms around her. Shoulders broad and just begging to be confided in. As if she could.

He tugged on the strap and easily finished buckling it.

Stupid man with his even stupider big muscles.

When finished, he turned to regard her with a slow shake of his head.

"Let me help, Kit." His whispered words carried in the faint light. "I want to find Daniel, too. Do you even know where you're going?"

Kit stilled. Debating.

The tension in Marc's body clearly communicated his frustration.

"Please, trust me, Kit. Let me help. I know you are capable and have been through so much—"

That was an understatement.

"—but running off as a woman alone . . . It's just not a wise idea."

He did have a valid point there but . . . Kit bit her lip.

"And running off with a man alone *is* a good idea?" she countered, cocking her head toward him.

"I promise to behave myself." Marc crossed his heart.

Kit snorted softly. "You're missing the point. If it's known I have run off with you, which it will be when we both disappear—"

"You're leaving. By yourself. How is that any better?" He *would* point that out. "Your reputation is at risk the second you ride out of here in that gig, with or without me. At least with me at your side, you will be safe from things worse than a ruined reputation."

I cannot believe you are even debating this. I mean, we could be traveling with him. All those muscles up close to you in the gig . . . Wicked Angel sighed dreamily.

Pardon me? Virtuous Angel chimed in. *You do have a reputation to consider. If you run off with him, you may not be able to return to Haldon Manor—*

Yes, but if we find Daniel, then we can go home and leave all this behind us, Wicked Angel countered. *Any reputation you happen to acquire here won't follow you home. Nothing will ever connect you between here and there. And he is right. You do need protection.*

Kit sighed. The world out there was not a kind place to women. Having Marc along would solve so many problems.

"Besides, I have this." Marc patted a pocket in his coat which jingled comfortingly. Money. "Arthur has extended me some, shall we say . . . credit."

Her shoulder's sagged. She really did need his help. And the money would be useful.

As long as Daniel doesn't steal that too, Virtuous Angel grumbled.

Noting her indecision, Marc stepped close. So close that the smell of leather and wood smoke and *him* surrounded her. He raised a hand and cupped her cheek. His warm palm burned against her cold skin.

"Please, Kit. I won't betray you. I may be a scoundrel, but in this, you can trust me. I will do everything I can to keep both you and Daniel safe."

Kit closed her eyes to force back the tears which pricked. Almost unconsciously, she leaned into his hand, wanting somehow to scoop his strength into her.

Why did he have to be such a *good* man? And why did she feel like she was stringing him along?

Uh, because you are . . . Virtuous Angel muttered.

Marc thought he knew her. And to a certain degree, he did. He knew the person she was inside.

But he didn't understand the enormous gulf that separated them. And she was in no position to enlighten him.

"It's all right to be my friend, Kit." His voice so close. His thumb stroked her cheek, causing an ache to swell in her chest.

Unbidden with eyes still closed, she turned her face into his hand, almost unconsciously planting a kiss into his palm. His skin firm and warm under her lips.

Marc inhaled sharply—a shocked hiss between his teeth.

His other hand snaked around her waist and he tugged her to him, wrapped her against his body, moving his hand from her cheek to cup the back of her neck.

Dawn filtered weakly into the barn. Kit fluttered her eyes open to see him staring at her, dark and intense. His eyes flitted down to her mouth. She knew she should pull back. Kissing him would only make everything so much harder.

But . . .

What would it be like to kiss him? A man of action who was possibly a spy?

A memory to top all others, really, when she thought about it. Something to take with her. A small souvenir from this odd-interlude.

And so instead of pulling back, she leaned in.

It was all the encouragement he needed.

His lips brushed hers. Feather light, gentle. Testing.

She relaxed her mouth, deliberately making her lips pillowy plush.

He probably assumed she had little experience with kissing. That her life had always been as simple and placid as it currently seemed.

Both Virtuous and Wicked Angel giggled at *that* thought.

Marc clearly sensed this. He kissed her again. This time more emphatically. More determined. Gathering her even closer. Turning Kit's brain to mush.

He kissed like he did everything else, with wild abandon, all in. Like jumping onto the back of a galloping horse, no hesitation.

With a soft sigh, Kit wrapped her arms around his head, returning as good as he gave.

Drat! The man *would* be an excellent kisser. He had definitely acquired experience with all his worldwide ramblings.

How could *this* man, of all men, feel so right? How could being in his arms feel like home?

Kit's knees nearly buckled from it.

The horse nickered loudly, startling them apart. Reminding them where they were. Who they were.

Marc's face likely looked as surprised as hers. He was certainly breathing just as hard.

"Well . . ." His voice hoarse, cracking. Cleared his throat. Tried again. "That was certainly . . . illustrative."

He looked dazed, befuddled. Rattled.

She had *rattled* him.

She smiled, slow and mysterious. A bewitched kind of smile.

Before this moment, she would have considered him unrattle-able. An impenetrable Fortress of Meringue. But somehow, she had carved through his walls.

The thought shot through her with a jolt. Burning and exultant.

She *mattered* to him.

And right on its heels, another pounding blow.

He can *never* be yours.

The sinking pit in her stomach opened wide.

He saw the change in her eyes. Nodded his recognition.

"In another time . . . another place . . ." she started, her voice trailing off.

He sighed. Placed his hands on his hips. Regarded her with those cat-green eyes, vivid against his tan skin. Dark hair mussed from her fingers. His gaze tender and kind. Focused.

Lethally beautiful, on every level.

"I know." Regret laced his words.

Part of her howled in protest. How could he agree so readily? How could he not fight for her? For them?

Not that fighting would do any good. Who was she fooling?

But still. She was greedy enough to want his effort.

He took a deep breath, as if gathering himself back together. Tucking away whatever raw thing that kiss had jarred loose.

He stepped around her and took hold of the harness, intent on leading the horse from the barn.

Kit placed a hand on his arm, stopping him.

"It's not your job to save me," she said as he turned to her.

"I know," he repeated.

"I am not a damsel-in-distress."

"Thank goodness. Because I would be a poor excuse for a knight-in-shining-armor. It's not really my forte." His voice wry.

Ah yes. Meringue Man was back.

He turned away and continued leading the horse out of the barn. Dawn had strengthened, lighting the eastern horizon with a faint bluish pink glow.

"Linwood is going to have an apoplexy when he realizes we have left." Kit skipped to catch up with him, falling into step at his side.

"We can always hope. I kind of like the thought of him frothing at the mouth, spluttering in anger—"

"That's not what I meant and you know it. Linwood will consider it confirmation of your guilt." Kit had to point out the obvious.

He just continued to lead the gig. Silence.

"I'm saying you don't need to come with me."

He shrugged. "Probably not. But I don't mind holding your parasol while you fight whatever battle you need."

He stopped and then winked, holding out a hand to assist her into the gig.

"I don't own a parasol." Kit ignored his hand.

"Pity. I was so looking forward to holding it."

With a disgusted shake of her head, Kit took his hand and hopped into the gig, sliding across the narrow seat so Marc could join her, gathering the reins into her hands.

"Are you ever serious?" she asked as he sat down next to her.

"Not if I can help it."

"What am I going to do with you?"

Marc chuckled, low and delighted. "Are you asking for suggestions? Because I am *happy* to offer ideas—"

Kit shoved his shoulder.

"And yes, I am always this utterly shameless." He wiggled his eyebrows suggestively.

"Impossible man." She clucked the horse to walk on.

She was sure Marc suspected Daniel of spying for the French. Everyone did.

And yet, Marc was still here. Helping to locate her brother. Not one word of recrimination. Bless him.

"Do we know what Daniel took?" she asked after a moment.

"No idea. Something which might help the French, apparently. Do you know where you are going?"

"Generally. I don't know why I didn't think to look there before."

A pause.

"And this place would be . . ." Marc lingered, encouragingly.

"Home. I think it quite possible Daniel has gone home."

Chapter 15

Marc snoozed as Kit drove. Well, he pretended to snooze.

Despite several hours of driving, he was finding it hard to relax. Kit sat close, the seat of the gig barely holding two people. He took shameless advantage of it, allowing his knee to rest against hers whenever possible.

He was only a man, after all.

The day had dawned bright and clear, a rarity in early spring. As the sun climbed, they stopped to raise the hood of the gig to provide some shade. Though the sun felt wonderfully warm, neither of them wanted a sunburn. A woolen lap blanket provided extra warmth.

All of which would have ensured Marc drifted off to sleep. But his mind kept churning.

He *should* have been worrying over the trouble leaving with Kit certainly caused. How upset Arthur was going to be. How running off would look to Linwood.

But his brain kept wandering back to the barn and their kiss.

What had he been thinking?

That kiss had utterly rattled him. He was man enough to admit it. Holding her, feeling her lips against his. The staggering *rightness* of it.

Brought to his knees by a nineteenth century lady of mysterious origin.

Go figure.

What was he going to do? They barely knew each other really.

Well, that wasn't entirely true. He had seen flashes of her soul . . . the shy vulnerability she hid behind a wall of confidence. The quickness of her mind, her spunk and courage, not to mention her devotion to family.

That frightening sense of *rightness*—that word again—whenever they were together.

But given everything, he knew dwelling on her was just a masochistic exercise in self-torture. Why, then, had he spent the last several hours agonizing over it?

The gig hit a larger rut, jostling Marc into Kit. He gave up pretending to sleep.

"You want me to drive for a while?" he asked.

So far he had been content to have Kit handle the reins, as she had more experience with it than him and seemed to enjoy it. But he had watched her and the basics of steering the horse weren't too challenging. Unless it was being shot at, their horse was predictably docile.

Kit shrugged and handed him the reins. She had been remarkably quiet all morning. Lost in thought like himself.

"So where are we going exactly?" he asked, holding the reins loosely in one hand.

"Home. Or, at least, a place I have . . . lived."

Ah. What a tantalizing bit of information. Marc rolled his wrist. *Go on.*

"There really isn't much else to say. It's as good a place as any to look for Daniel."

"Does your family still live there?"

A long pause.

"Not . . . exactly." She offered no other explanation.

Assuming Daniel was a spy for the French, how did she plan on returning home with her brother, no one the wiser? And how were they going to visit a home that was not really Kit's home?

Marc swallowed his frustration. A few answers but more questions.

And thinking of questions . . . What about them? What impediment did she see to their being together? For all she knew, he was a baron, possessed of a title and probably some property. Perhaps even considerable wealth.

Not that he was, of course, but she didn't know that.

She seemed to like him. So what was holding her back? Was her family too aristocratic? Not aristocratic enough? Was she engaged to someone else?

That last thought shocked, leaving him with a sinking pit in his stomach. There were just too many legitimate possibilities.

Kit let out a resigned breath.

"I know you don't want to, but we should probably talk about this." She gestured between them.

Marc considered pretending to misunderstand her meaning, but as he had *literally* just been thinking the same thing . . .

"Agreed," he said.

She nodded. "I know why I can't be with you, but I am curious as to your reasons."

Huh. Throwing his own thoughts back at him. He remained silent, unsure what to say.

"It's . . . complicated," was what he finally settled on. "You?"

She gave a soft laugh and then fixed him with a saucy lift of her eyebrows. "It's complicated."

Marc supposed he deserved that. At least she was open to sharing *something*.

But he wanted to know so much more.

No, that wasn't quite right.

With staggering clarity, he realized he ached to know *everything* about her.

Had she slept with a stuffed bunny until she was eight-years-old? What was her favorite childhood pet? The name of the first boy who had dared kiss her soft lips? Did she laugh or cry when reading overly emotional novels?

The depth of his want terrified him. He longed to drag her into his soul and never, ever let her go.

They drove on for a few minutes, Marc absorbing the unexpected emotions hammering through him.

Birds chirped through the trees, loud and excited for spring to come. The fields spread in every direction, green grass pushing through the debris of winter.

Should he tell her the truth?

It was the first time he had seriously considered it. Up until now, it had felt impossible for her to understand. He had no proof of his twenty-first century origins. No cell phone or other bit of technology. It would just be his word.

Though after the events of the previous night, it seemed Kit had a right to know. Before he had merely surmised Daniel was the man who had attacked him in Duir Cottage.

But seeing the same button in Linwood's hand had taken away any doubt. Daniel was either the blackmailer or in league with them. All of which meant Daniel—somehow, someway—knew about the portal and had, at the very least, visited 2014.

The thoughts wouldn't stop running around his head. Daniel had known ties to some kind of French spy network, stealing something critical from Linwood . . .

Europe was at a crossroads, Napoleon on the run. But what if something happened to disrupt that balance? Would the portal allow someone through who would change the course of history? What would it mean for Britain—and the history of the world in general—if Napoleon won this war?

It was almost too terrifying to contemplate.

"Let's make a deal," Marc said. "You tell me your secrets. All of them. And I will tell you mine."

Kit stared impassively out at the countryside. Contemplating.

And then she sighed. "I just . . . can't, Marc. I am so sorry. But it's just too much to explain . . ."

He felt her rejection like a sharp blow to the head. Why would she deny him? He had offered to tell her *everything*. What kind of life before coming to Haldon Manor warranted this level of secrecy?

And then something twisted in his gut.

What if she knew about the portal too? What if *that* was the secret she was protecting? What if she were in on the blackmail?

The thought chilled his blood.

He suddenly could see it all too clearly. Kit worming her way into the household at Haldon Manor, sneaking messages to her brother. Blackmailing the Knights for money, plotting who knows what.

Kit was capable of it. It was all those traits he loved best about her: confidence, internal strength, intelligence, resourcefulness.

Marc swallowed.

Wow.

The whole situation had suddenly delved into a murky place.

But even as he thought it, he rejected the idea. Yes, she had the personality to do all those things. But it wouldn't be in her character to blackmail for personal gain. No, Kit would only do it for some greater good. But what noble cause was she focused on?

Marc let out a long stream of air. Straightened his shoulders. He needed to know everything about Kit and Daniel. Now.

"Kit, enough. I need to know what's going on. I know you are a good person. Again, please trust me. I am on your side."

She shook her head. "I can't, Marc. As I said, it's difficult—"

"You've never struck me as the type who shies away from difficulty. Or perhaps it's my intelligence you question?"

She turned in her seat and fixed him with such a . . . look. And then turned back to face the road, crossing her arms.

"You just need to leave it alone."

Uh . . . *no.* He wasn't going to leave it alone. She had been the one to bring it up, and there was no way she was backing out because the conversation had veered off track. He was going to bait and badger her until she gave him answers.

The whole history of the next two hundred years might be riding on it. Not to mention his own future.

"So you just see me as a pretty face to kiss, but not someone you would trust with the basic facts of your life?"

She sighed. A weary, resigned sound. "Please don't be ugly."

"Or do you find my rank and position in society aren't up to your standards?"

"Just stop this. I can't tell you—"

"Why? How can the truth be any worse?"

"Let it go, Marc."

"I can't. I need to know."

"You want my secrets? Why don't you start by telling me one of yours?"

"Fine. Ask away."

She blinked, obviously surprised he would acquiesce.

"Your sister," she said without hesitation. "What is the precise nature of the spying activities you do with her?"

Ah, that was an easy one.

"We're not spies."

She regarded him for a moment, eyes narrowed. "Why do I not believe you?"

Marc shrugged. "It's the truth. I am decidedly not a spy. My darling sister invented that entire story for Linwood's benefit."

"Really?" Her head went back. A smile tugged at her lips, warring with her stern expression. "She sounds as bad as you."

"Definitely. Which is why I have kept my connection with Emme secret. It's a huge misunderstanding which Linwood has blown out of proportion and no amount of telling him otherwise has changed his belief. I admit it's been fun to play red cape to his bull because—let's face it—I'm immature like that. But there is absolutely no truth to his claims."

Kit pursed her lips.

"Now it's my turn," Marc continued before she could ask any follow-up questions. "Where were you before coming to Haldon Manor? What is your family background?"

She paused. "Fine. I will tell you what I can." She took in a slow breath. "My father was Lord Whitmoor, which title Daniel inherited when my father passed away last year. My mother left when I was about nine-years-old. I took care of my father and Daniel after that point. I am as much a mother to Daniel as a sister.

"Of course, Daniel being Daniel, is up to no good and refuses to return home. But without him, I have no home to return to. There are no other male heirs beyond Daniel. So if he is declared dead, the title and property revert to the crown. I will be left without a roof over my head. Not to mention losing the last person in my family."

A long breath hissed from Marc.

Kit continued. "The house and property are only a secondary concern, I suppose. I need my brother, Marc. Without him, I have no one."

What about me? The thought whispered treacherously through Marc's mind. *You would still have me.*

But he knew that wasn't what she meant. And she wouldn't have him. Not here.

So did she know about the portal and blackmail?

Marc's heart hammered in his chest. What should he do?

It was on the tip of his tongue to tell her. But . . .

Should he?

"Your turn again," Kit said. "Where were you exactly before coming here? What is *your* family background?"

She threw the question back at him, her tone nearly taunting.

Was this the moment? Would he actually tell her?

He formed the words in his head. *Well, Kit, I was actually a martial arts actor working in 2014. Yes, I know, 2014 is two hundred years from now, which explains a lot of my current problem . . .*

He chuckled, a mirthless little sound. "Are you sure you want to know?"

"I just want the truth, Marc."

He snorted. "You can't handle the truth."

Quoting from *A Few Good Men* never hurt.

Now it was Kit's turn to snort, shaking her head. "Please, just stop. You mock my pain."

Marc smiled. If she thought unwittingly quoting *The Princess Bride* in return would help this situation, she was sorely mistaken.

"Life is pain, my lady. Anyone who says differently is selling something."

He couldn't resist, heaven help him. He stared intently at the road ahead of him, guiding the horse, debating what to say next. Should he tell her about the portal?

And then he realized Kit was staring at him with stunned eyes.

Extremely wide, wide, wide, I'm-trying-not-to-freak-out eyes.

"As you wish," she whispered.

Marc would forever remember the sizzling shock of that moment. The jolt that pulsed his spine. The startled ringing in his ears.

What?!

What had she just said?!

Impossible!

It was utterly impossible.

But, when he thought about it, it suddenly seemed very, very possible indeed.

He stared at her, his eyes surely as wide as hers.

"Life is like a box of chocolates . . ." He swallowed, his throat tight.

Sheer surprise reverting him to his American accent.

". . . you never know what you're gonna get." Kit finished, a shaking hand flying to cover her mouth. Tears filled her enormous brown eyes.

"No," she whispered, shaking her head. "No way."

Marc shook his head too. Blinked. Looked ahead at the road, trying to process what had just happened.

And then turned back to Kit, who was still gaping at him.

"Inconceivable." A small wondrous smile touched her lips.

Marc matched her look, a slap-silly grin sliding across his face.

He felt . . . punch-drunk. Staggered by an unexpected blow to the head.

But . . . how?!

Though, really, he should actually *voice* that question.

"How?!"

Kit shook her head, her face still stunned.

"Daniel," she said, her voice breaking. "It was all Daniel."

"But . . . but how could you not know? About me, I mean?" His native accent still on full display.

"Wait! You're American?"

"Yeah, baby. You better believe it."

Kit laughed. "That was ridiculous."

Marc winked. "Red, white and blue—through and through."

"Are you done?"

"Maybe." And then another thought struck him. "I took *Lord Vader* as my alias. Lord Vader! How could that not have, at least, made you curious?!"

"I was already living with a Jed I. Knight!" Kit gestured wildly. "I just assumed the universe had a super sick sense of humor." And then she paused, eyes stricken. "Wait, Jedediah isn't from—"

"Uh, no." Marc shuddered. "Wow! That's a ghastly thought."

"But surely someone else—"

"Arthur knows."

"Okay." Kit absorbed that for a moment. "And Arthur is genuinely from this era?"

"Yes."

She thought more, a frown creasing her forehead.

"I can barely process this."

"That makes two of us." Marc shook his head.

"Why are you—" she said.

"So, how—" he said, at the same time. Their voices tangling with each other.

Kit laughed, that rich laugh of hers.

Marc stared at her, his heart thumping wildly.

She was still the same Kit: tall, saucy, clever, funny.

But now, he could clearly see the modern woman in her. In her confidence, her assured sense of self.

"So, what year were you born?"

She swallowed. "I was born in 1984 in Gloucester. And you?"

"Denver in 1982."

"Denver? I've never been to Denver. I'm more of a coastal American visitor: New York, Miami, San Francisco."

"Well, I suppose I should fess up. I'm not entirely American. My dad is British, and I lived with my ridiculously proper British grandmother most summers growing up. She insisted on elocution lessons as well. Couldn't stand my broad, drawling accent."

They stared again, Marc's eyes wide with wonder. Two hundred years worth of barriers crumbling before him.

What had seemed *impossible* just minutes before was now suddenly very possible—

He wasn't sure if he were massively relieved or incredibly terrified.

Probably a little of both.

Kit tucked her hand through his arm and scooted close to his side, delightfully possessive.

"I've always wanted an American boyfriend." She slid him a flirty look.

It was Marc's turn to chuckle.

"Hey you," he said.

"Hey." She nudged his shoulder.

His eyes flitted down to her mouth.

So *that* was why she was such a good kisser.

And then, for the second time in as many weeks, a shot rang out, the bullet zinging over the head of their horse.

Startling the poor thing into a panicked run.

Chapter 16

"What the—?!"

The sudden bolt of the horse tore the reins from Marc's hands. He grabbed for them, catching the leathers just in time.

Marc pulled backward, trying to calm the runaway horse without much luck. Poor thing. It lead a simple humdrum life, never looking for excitement . . . only to be shot at twice in just as many weeks. The road ran straight for a while, thank goodness, so Marc wasn't too concerned. But the gig jolted alarmingly down the rutted road.

At his side, Kit clutched the carriage frame as they bounced along.

Abruptly, the loud jingle of horse tack announced they weren't alone.

"Take the reins." Marc shoved the leather straps into Kit's hands. She hesitated for a fraction of a second and then, with a determined lift of her chin, took the reins.

That was his spunky girl.

Carefully, Marc poked his head around the side of the gig hood. A larger carriage with the top down pulled by a pair of matched bays thundered behind them. The carriage was full of three . . . no, *four* burley men, some brandishing rifles.

Linwood rode beside the carriage on a sleek, black horse. A pistol in his hand.

Of course. So predictable, it was nearly comical. What had Daniel taken that had the viscount in such a snit?

"It's Linwood," Marc said turning back to Kit. "He's got a carriage full of thugs. Some with guns."

Kit swore, causing Marc to laugh.

"This is hardly a laughing matter." She gritted her teeth, allowing the horse its head.

"True. But hearing a polite nineteenth century lady swear like a sailor just sorta made my day."

Kit rolled her eyes without taking them off the road ahead. "Are you always so dorky?"

"Naturally. It's part of my never-ending charm."

Moving the reins to one hand, Kit dug into her cloak and pulled out a small, silver tube. "I have a rape alarm." She dropped it in his hand. "It's really loud."

Marc blinked at her. And then laughed. Not politely.

"I'll keep that in mind . . . Linwood is known for improper propositions."

"Really? Do tell—"

"Stand!" Linwood shouted.

Kit swiveled to look behind.

"Eyes on the road." Marc tugged her cloak.

"You know I hate backseat drivers, right?" Kit said as she turned back around.

"Don't care."

Kit nodded toward her left side. "I also have a taser in my cloak pocket."

"Anything else?"

"Nope."

"A taser? You know, a handgun would be much more useful in this situation."

Kit tilted her head, giving him a deadpan look, and then moved her eyes back to the road. "Gah. You are *such* an American. Handguns are illegal in modern Britain. Even *you* should know that."

Marc dug through her cloak, finding the pocket, and pulled out a large taser, hefting its weight in his hand.

"Great. Now what?" Marc asked. "I can't very well taser the carriage horses. Animals and people would end up dead."

Kit blinked, her mouth moving, perplexed. "That is true."

"Halt, Lord Vader!" Linwood's voice rang over the sounds of the carriages' jostling.

Even over the clang of the carriage wheels, Marc heard Kit giggle. "He called you Lord Vader."

Marc grinned. Man, and he thought he liked nineteenth century Kit . . .

"You have the wrong people, Linwood," Marc yelled back, tucking the useless taser into the waistband of his pants.

Linwood responded by firing another shot.

Which naturally frightened their horse again. Kit kept a firm hand on the reins, but the poor animal whinnied and continued to run.

Angrily, Marc shouted, "Stop spooking my horse!"

The carriage gained on them. But the road was too narrow for it to draw alongside their own gig. And Linwood didn't shoot again.

Thank goodness.

Their horse still ran, but Kit seemed to have him back under control.

Which was fortunate, as the road curved to the left. Kit feathered the galloping horse around the turn.

"Nice driving."

"Thank you."

Marc glanced behind them.

"Linwood made the turn, though their carriage skid a bit."

"Drat them."

"Drat? No more expansive use of the English language?"

"I decided to spare your tender ears." She handed him the reins. "Here, my arms are getting tired."

Marc took the reins with an unsure look. "You do realize I'm not a pro at gig driving, right?"

Kit shrugged. "That makes two of us."

He tightened his grip on the reins, steadying the horse. "I do believe we are involved in a carriage chase scene."

Kit chuckled. "It's like incredibly cute and horridly dangerous at the same time."

"I feel like there should be some theme music going on."

Kit nodded and then began humming the theme song from *Mission: Impossible.*

Still humming, she poked her head around the side, looking behind them.

"They're gaining on us." She turned back.

"Of course they are. They have *two* horses pulling their carriage."

"Yes, but those horses are pulling four people instead of two, so it should be more even. Laws of physics and all."

"Wait, are you a scientist?"

He could practically feel her eye roll. "Hardly. Just common sense."

"Well, our horse is tiring." Marc gestured to the horse, straining in his braces.

Kit glanced behind them.

"Linwood's gaining," she reported. "We can't outrun him. No matter how cute this entire scenario or how much theme music I sing."

Kit shifted her skirts, looking at the floor of the gig. Marc raised a questioning eyebrow at her.

"Just looking for something to throw," she explained. "Too bad we didn't steal a wagon full of rotten vegetables."

Marc snorted. "You've watched too many 1960s Disney movies."

"*Herbie Rides Again* was a staple of my childhood, I will have you know. Daniel loved that movie—"

"Daniel! Ugh. That's right. Your brother is blackmailing me!"

"What?"

"Your brother. Blackmailing me."

Even with the carriage jostling them, Kit looked stunned.

"Daniel is? Are you sure?"

"Absolutely"

"Why?"

"Give up, Vader!" Linwood's voice howled.

Marc tightened his grip on the reins, ignoring Linwood. "It's all about the portal."

"What?" Kit stared at him.

"The blackmailing."

"Oh. The time portal? What is up with—DUCK!" Kit screamed, pointing ahead of them.

Sure enough. There were ducks.

Hundreds of them, swarming across the road, wings flapping, quacking loudly. A handful of men stood to the side of the roadway, herding the ducks across with long sticks.

Marc hauled on the reins, slowing the horse somewhat, but he still plowed into the birds who scattered out of the way, hissing at him.

"Careful, Marc! I think you hit one." Kit craned around the side of the carriage, trying to assess the damage. "Poor little thing. But . . . wait . . . it's okay. He's up and shaking it off."

Marc had his hands full weaving through the quacking animals crossing the road.

The birds all had black feet, which seemed odd until he realized the animals' feet had actually been dipped in tar.

The horse slowed even more, threading its way through the birds.

"Why are their feet all tarred?" Marc jerked a chin toward the animals.

"A latent sense of fashion awareness?"

"I'll buy that."

"Or it could just be the easiest way to shoe a duck."

"That makes more sense. How's Linwood faring?" Marc asked.

"Eh. I think the ducks are taking their anger out on his carriage. They're trying to climb inside and the thugs keep shoving them out. But Linwood is pushing his horse through more successfully."

She turned back around. "So wait. Where were we? My brother is blackmailing you?"

"Yes, indeed he is. You didn't know?"

"Good grief! Of course not, Marc. What kind of a person do you think I am?"

"Well, I thought you were a nineteenth century lady up until about ten minutes ago, but I was apparently waaaaay off base there, so—"

"Don't be lame. What is Daniel doing?"

"He's threatening to tell the world about the time portal unless we pay up."

"We?"

"Me and James."

"James?"

"James Knight . . . Arthur's older brother."

"Right." Kit blinked and cocked her head. "So correct me if I am wrong, but is this the same James Knight who was killed in a carriage accident with your sister, Emme, and then buried in the parish church-yard? That James Knight?"

"The very same. Though reports of their demise *might* have been somewhat exaggerated."

Kit rolled her hand. *Pray continue.*

Marc edged around the last of the ducks and clucked the horse back into a trot.

"James and Emme are very much alive, married and living in Duir Cottage, among other places, in the twenty-first century."

"Really? That is truly fascinating. I want *that* whole story, but for now . . . Daniel has been threatening them?"

"No, just me, actually. Which makes no sense at all—"

Kit screamed, causing Marc to pull up on the reins, which was just as well. It saved their horse from plowing into Linwood, who had maneuvered his horse around the gig and now stood broad-ways, blocking the road.

The gig rolled to a stop, Marc panting.

Linwood leveled a pistol at Marc's head.

"I do not want to shoot you, Lord Vader, but I will if you give me no other option."

Kit choked and then made a loud asthmatic breathing sound. It was a remarkably accurate Darth Vader impression.

Both Marc and Linwood turned to stare at her.

Kit stifled a giggle and then waved her hand at them.

"Sorry, sorry. Just been wanting to do that for quite a while now."

Marc shook his head. "Are you trying to get me shot?"

Linwood's carriage pulled alongside, the four burley men piling out onto the road. Now that Marc got a better look at them, he realized Linwood had brought a selection of his largest footmen and grooms. Though armed, they didn't look to be well-trained fighters.

Linwood dismounted, gesturing for Marc and Kit to do the same. As Marc helped Kit down from the gig, he surreptitiously slid the taser into her hand.

"That's not going to be much protection against five armed men," she muttered.

"No. But I figure if you take down Linwood, I can probably take out the other four."

She raised very skeptical eyebrows. "Don't get cocky, kid."

Marc grinned and then kissed her hand. "Keep the quotes coming—"

"Enough," Linwood's haughty voice cut in. "This is hardly a morning social call."

Marc half-rolled his eyes at Kit and turned to Linwood.

The viscount stood in the middle of the road, pistol held at his waist, still aimed at Marc. Linwood looked nearly rumpled with his windblown hair and greatcoat askew. Somewhere he had lost his hat.

That said, his cravat remained immaculately tied, and his boots shone with a mirror-like brilliance. What would it take to truly dishevel Linwood?

The four henchmen angled themselves around Linwood. Two had rifles at the ready.

Marc spread his hands in a placating gesture, drawing back into his British accent. "We are unarmed and bear you no ill will."

The servants shifted restlessly, glancing at one another, unsure.

Linwood grunted. "Indeed."

The viscount raised a cool eyebrow, every taut line of his body indicating his unbelief. The quacking ducks sounded in the distance. A breeze tugged at Marc's overcoat, swirling it around his ankles.

Marc calculated his odds. If he took three steps to the left, the four servants would rush him. But he would be between them and their own carriage horses, so they would be loath to fire their weapons. And if they knew him to be weaponless, their guard would be down, having no idea what awaited them.

It was a good plan. Now, he just had to prepare himself.

"Allow me to prove it," Marc said.

With deliberate motions, he slid his arms out of his greatcoat, tossing it back onto the seat of the gig. Ostensibly to show that he was indeed unarmed.

But mostly to free his body. There was no way he could fight wearing that long, bulky thing.

Just to be sure, he pulled off his wool tailcoat too, leaving him just in a waistcoat and shirtsleeves.

One of the footman breathed a sigh of relief to see no sign of a weapon on Marc's person.

Clearly, none of them had any idea what was about to happen.

"Linwood, Miss Ashton and I are trying to help, believe it or not." Marc loosened his cravat as if he were nervous.

"Of course," Linwood drawled, voice oozing sarcasm. "Which is why you stole a gig—"

"We did not steal it," Kit cut in. "It has just been borrowed."

Linwood stared at her for a moment, clearly appalled that she dared speak.

"It's true. The gig is Arthur's and—"

"Enough. You left under a cloud of silence and stealth only hours after the theft at Kinningsley. Given your past history, Vader, how can your actions not be construed as suspicious?"

"My past history? Linwood, you truly know nothing about my past history—"

"Bah! Give up this charade, Vader. We both know that isn't your name. I should like to know the exact nature of your relationship with Princess Pepsi of Toyota Camry."

Kit choked and then erupted into gales of laughter at Marc's side.

"I fail to see the humor in this situation, Miss Ashton." Linwood turned his icy eyes on Kit.

"Oh. My. Word," she gasped, clutching Marc's arm. "You didn't tell me . . . that is so funny."

"It wasn't me—"

Linwood turned his attention back to Marc. "So Miss Ashton is involved with your scheme as well. Is she an agent for Princess Pepsi?"

Kit laughed even harder, resting her head against Marc's shoulder, slapping his back with her hand.

Marc allowed himself a grin. Kit had a decidedly infectious laugh.

However, judging by how still Linwood went, he found their mirth decidedly *un*-amusing.

"I fear you are quite addled in the head, Miss Ashton. Without any further proof and given your recent actions, I must suspect you both of being in league with French counter-agents. Though if you could tell me the precise nature of your interactions with his Grace, Calvin Klein, the Duke of Kleenex—"

"Ohohohoh. Make. Him. Stop." Kit gasped, tears streaming down her cheeks. She shook Marc's arm. "You seriously had nothing to do with this?"

"No. It was all Emme."

"I love your sister so much!"

"I know. I don't know if I want to strangle or kiss her right now."

Linwood's head reared back at that admission. Marc didn't see the point in hiding his identity anymore. Linwood already suspected the worst.

"Hah! I knew Miss Emry was your sister!" Linwood bristled. "Now was she truly a spy acting on behalf of Princess Pepsi—"

"Give it up, Linwood. There is no Princess Pepsi or Duke Calvin Klein. I have never been involved in espionage work of any sort. Emme fabricated the entire story."

Linwood narrowed his eyes. "A convenient excuse. Then who, pray tell, is behind the recent activity in this area?"

"I don't know."

"Ah, of course not. And who robbed my estate last evening?"

"I am not sure."

"You should become a better liar. That button meant something to you."

Marc sighed. "Fine. I think I know who the button belongs to. Miss Ashton and I are trying to catch up with the person to confirm this. And then, if possible, recover what was stolen—"

"Again, I do not believe you. If this were indeed the case, why not come to me immediately with the truth?"

"Uh, well . . . because I was afraid you would round up a group of thugs and go after the criminal all harebrained-like." Marc gestured to the men surrounding Linwood.

Linwood's eyes narrowed at the insult.

Silence stretched.

Kit was wiping her eyes on Marc's shirtsleeves, controlling her laughter. Though she still shook her head every other second or so.

Linwood regarded them for a moment, unmoving.

"I find this entire scene tedious." Linwood's grip on his pistol remained unwavering. "You will tell me where you were going and whom you seek. As this involves me and my property, I will take the search from here."

Kit stiffened at Marc's side. They both had the same thought.

Linwood wouldn't hesitate to shoot Daniel, if needs be. He couldn't be allowed to chase after Kit's brother.

"*What* was stolen, Linwood?" Marc asked.

"I fail to see how any part of this affair pertains to you. Why do you care, Lord Vader? Though we both know that isn't your real name. Is it. . . Mr. Wilde?"

Kit gasped. Loudly.

"Wait. Your name is Marc *Wilde*?" She clutched Marc's wrist.

Marc bowed. "At your service, ma'am."

Linwood gestured with his pistol. "You have not even had the common decency to share your actual name with the lady. For shame."

But Kit ignored Linwood's taunts. Her brown eyes going incredibly wide again.

Marc saw the exact moment when she recognized him. When he forever became that-guy-from-*Croc-nami* in her head.

"No!" she whispered, her hand flying again to her mouth.

Marc barely managed not to groan in frustration. That *stupid* viral post—

"Oh no. Nonononono." Kit looked away and clutched her stomach, placing her hand over her face.

The strength of her negative reaction stung. So he had made a few lame movies. So what? That wasn't the sum total of his existence.

"Ouch. C'mon, Kit. It's not that bad."

Kit just shook her head, turning back to stare at him with horrified eyes.

"I am heartily sick of this," Linwood said. "As touching as I find this baffling scene to be, I must ask you to politely submit to being bound and to go with two of my grooms to Kinningsley where you will await my return."

Kit jerked her head back to Linwood, standing in the road with his men.

She shook her head and then laughed. Mirthless.

"Wow. You are a fool, Lord Linwood. Marc Wilde will destroy you."

"You forget your station, Miss Ashton—"

But Linwood never finished his sentence. Marc had heard enough.

Marc launched himself at the nearest groom who never saw the roundhouse kick to the head coming. The man dropped like a stone.

Kit's appalled response to his career smarted.

Who did she think she was? A judge and jury?

Wait. Why be content with just thinking that?

"How dare you judge me, Kit! Just because you don't fancy my chosen profession—"

As the first groom fell, Marc kicked the rifle out of his hand.

"Me?!" she squeaked, moving behind him, keeping Marc between herself and Linwood. "No, that's not it at all, Marc—"

Spinning the gun around, Marc clubbed another footman with it, knocking the man to the ground.

"Right. That's why you doubled over in horror—"

Despite a few unfortunate movie choices, he was a respected athlete and actor with a long resume—

"You misunderstood." Kit gasped behind him.

The two remaining thugs rushed him. Marc shoved the rifle into Kit's hands. And then he delivered a sharp punch to the jaw of the man to the right, sending him sprawling, while simultaneously kicking the man on the left in the groin, followed by a twirling flying kick to the head with his other foot.

Collapsing him.

Marc whirled on Linwood as the viscount raised his pistol to Marc's head, finally having a clear shot.

Linwood's eyes were wide, wide, wide. He had obviously never seen hand-to-hand combat quite like this.

"Who the bloody hell are you?" Linwood hissed through clenched teeth. Despite being completely rattled, the pistol held steady in his hand.

Marc swallowed. A bullet through the head was really not in his plans. Though, honestly, it could hardly make the situation much worse.

Why had Kit been so upset about realizing he was Marc Wilde?

He could feel her behind him still.

"As the lady said, I am Marc Wilde. Nothing more. I am not a spy. You have the wrong man."

"Why do I doubt you?"

"Because, as I've repeatedly said, you're an ass."

"How dare you—"

And then Linwood glanced at Kit with a sharp intake of breath.

Out of the corner of his eye, Marc saw Kit level the rifle at Linwood.

That was his spunky girl.

At least she still felt loyal enough to help defend him.

"I would carefully consider your choices, Linwood." Her voice unnervingly calm. "You have one bullet in that pistol. You can kill me or Marc, but you can't kill us *both* before one of us does you in."

Linwood darted a glance between them.

"Drop the pistol, Linwood. I have no weapons other than my hands. What kind of coward shoots an unarmed man? Or a woman for that matter? Face me like a man." Marc laced the words with disdain. All of his anger coalesced on the viscount. "Give me the pleasure of pummeling you senseless. It's the least you can do after the way you treated my sister."

"Your sister was hardly here under auspicious circumstances—"

Marc gave a bark of laughter. "What kind of creepy cad propositions a respectable gentlewoman?

Linwood at least had the decency to flinch. As if Marc had flicked scalding water on him.

Marc spread his arms wide, indicating the moaning men on the ground.

"Your actions are hardly those of the gentleman you pretend to be." Marc ticked off Linwood's offenses on his fingers. "You make *in*decent proposals to decent women. You threaten unarmed, innocent gentlemen at gunpoint. You are arrogant and condescending to all those around you. Now drop your weapon and fight me man-to-man with only your body as a weapon. Show me you have even one ounce of courage and honor left—"

"How dare you insult my honor!"

"I dare insult it because I don't think you have any, despite all your preening and posturing."

That finally did the trick.

With an oath, Linwood handed his pistol to one of the grooms who had groggily managed to sit up.

Man, nineteenth century guys were so predictable. Hint that they might be dishonorable and *booyah*. You had yourself a fight.

Marc allowed himself a nasty grin.

This was going to be so fun.

With precise movements, Linwood stripped off his billowing greatcoat and tailcoat. The viscount loosened his cravat while turning to Marc, his face resigned yet determined.

Against his will, Marc had to admit a twinge of admiration for a man who would enter into a fight knowing he was going to be severely beaten.

It *almost* made him feel bad.

Kit cleared her throat behind him, still holding the rifle at the ready. Marc glanced at her. She obviously had a softer heart than him.

"You're going to beat Linwood senseless. Maybe you should have a handicap?"

"Excuse me, Miss Ashton?" Linwood intoned, jumping into the conversation as he meticulously rolled up his sleeves. "I do not understand your meaning."

She gestured toward Marc with her chin. "Marc should limit some of his moves, like no roundhouse kicks to the head or something. Just to make things more fair."

Marc sighed. It was a sensible suggestion and would perhaps level the playing field. Though it would take *so* much of the fun out of the upcoming bout . . .

"Fair, Miss Ashton?" Linwood arched an arrogant eyebrow. "I do not expect *fairness*. I expect an honorable fight. *If* Mr. Wilde is capable of such a thing."

Marc snorted. "Define *honorable*."

"Striking only and avoiding, shall I say, sensitive areas." Linwood stretched his shoulders. "No holding or grappling. No touching an opponent if they are on the ground."

"Sounds easy enough."

"Then we are agreed."

With a nod, both men squared off.

Linwood was several inches taller than Marc giving him a farther reach, though that hardly compensated for Marc's superior muscle mass and years of training and practice.

Marc raised his fists into a typical muay thai stance, as it seemed a good place to start. Linwood matched his position competently. So the man wasn't entirely unaware of how to box, at least. Gentleman Jackson's Boxing Salon, anyone?

They danced around each other for a moment, each looking for an opening. Linwood shot a punch at Marc who ducked and took instant advantage of the opening to deliver a punishing kick to Linwood's side.

Linwood grunted and danced back, fists still at the ready. Waiting for Marc to make the next move.

Marc darted in, blocked a blow from Linwood with his forearm, kneed him in the stomach, knocking the wind out of him, and then whirled and jumped, delivering a powerful kick to Linwood's jaw.

The viscount staggered backward. But didn't collapse.

Spitting blood out of his mouth, Linwood straightened and came again for Marc.

Marc felt a grudging amount of respect for the man. He wasn't a wuss.

They feinted and punched for a moment or two, Marc blocking Linwood's blows with his fists and forearms. Linwood landed a lucky blow to Marc's shoulder, causing Marc to wince.

But Linwood had reached too far with the punch, leaving him open. Marc moved in for the knockout, kicking Linwood in the solar plexus and then delivering a sharp right hook to Linwood's head.

With a moan, Linwood collapsed, landing on his hands and knees on the ground.

Staring at the dazed viscount, Marc was suddenly tired.

Why was he here fighting this jerk?

As Linwood gasped for air, Marc turned to see Kit beside the gig, rifle in one hand and taser in the other.

She stood like an avenging angel, ready to do battle. Hair loosened from its pins and tumbling down her back, cloak twisted, but eyes bright and fierce.

In other words, utterly magnificent.

So many unanswered questions.

He just wanted to find Daniel, get back to the portal, take all three of them home. Put this entire incident behind him.

The grooms and footmen had roused themselves, eyes darting between Marc and their fallen master. Each of them watching Marc with a healthy amount of respect.

"Good fight, men." Marc nodded at them.

Kneeling beside Linwood, Marc dug into his pocket for a handkerchief and handed it to him. Linwood took it and began to wipe the blood from his face.

"I don't think you are a truly evil human being, Linwood. But you need to let go of your precious pride for just two minutes and realize you do not understand everything that is going on here. There is a lot more at stake than merely something stolen from Kinningsley which the French might or might not find useful. For once, trust someone else. Trust that others are intelligent too and can solve problems. We have your interests and the interests of Great Britain at heart. Miss Ashton and I are leaving. We will return to Haldon Manor when we have something to report."

Not caring to hear Linwood's reply, Marc stood and walked over to the gig and Kit. He shrugged back into his tailcoat as she stared at him.

"You were incredible out there." She handed him his caped great-coat. Hesitantly. As if she, too, were afraid he would bite.

He drew on the long greatcoat, unsure of how to respond.

He handed her into the gig and then climbed up himself, taking the reins, clucking the horse into a walk. He skirted around Linwood, who had staggered to his feet with the help of a footman, and continued down the road.

Kit sat silently at his side, leaving Marc to mull his next move.

So she was from the future. That was great.

But why had she reacted like that when she realized who he was?

He was an actor. So what?

Kit sat nearly motionless beside him, chewing on her cheek.

As soon as the gig rounded a corner, leaving Linwood out of sight, she pulled on his arm.

"Stop for just a moment, Marc. I need to say something."

Obligingly, Marc pulled on the reins, turning his attention to her.

Kit placed a hand over his and then raised her enormous brown eyes.

"Let me just set one thing straight, Marc Wilde. You misunderstood back there. You are incredible. And this is precisely how I feel about you."

Without giving Marc a chance to catch his breath, Kit grabbed hold of his coat, pulled him to her and kissed him.

An extremely thorough, hot sort of kiss.

The kind of kiss that melted a man's bones and scattered every other thought from his brain.

A very twenty-first century kiss.

Not one to hold back, Marc gathered her close and pressed a hand between her shoulder blades, clasping her to his chest. Losing himself in the soft give of her lips.

With a sorrowful gasp, Kit pushed away shaking her head.

"I don't have an issue with who you are. But I'm afraid *you* might have an issue with *me*. That was why I reacted the way I did."

Marc frowned. "Why would I have an issue with you?"

She took a deep breath and then covered her face with her hands.

"Ugh! Why is this so hard?" She lifted her head. "Remember that I told you as soon as I could. That I abhor secrets, and I didn't want to keep this one from you. Even though it would have been so easy."

"Is your name not Kit Ashton?"

"My name *is* Kit Ashton, but that's not how you know me." She took a deep breath, eyes pleading for understanding. "I usually go by the moniker La Pochette."

Chapter 17

Kit watched all the blood drain from Marc's face.

He blinked, looked at the road. Went to cluck the horse back into a walk. Stopped. Turned back to her. Shook his head. Took up the reins again, this time clicking the horse into action.

Basically, he obviously had no idea what to do or think.

Kit sat silently, letting him sort through it.

Marc Wilde! She had been laughing and kissing and generally falling *hard* for Marc Wilde.

What were the chances? She had been so relieved to realize they could actually have a life together. That maybe their obstacles weren't as huge as she thought . . .

And then this.

No wonder he had looked familiar. Without those awful blond dreadlocks and completely out of context, she hadn't recognized him. But now, it seemed so painfully obvious.

And that article she had written . . . *yikes*. She cringed just thinking about it.

It had been such good fun at the time. But at the moment . . . face-to-face with him . . . maybe not so much.

After driving in silence for a minute or two, Marc cleared his throat.

"So . . . let me get this straight. You, Kit Ashton, are in actuality, La Pochette? The website owner, editor and snarky voice behind FauxPause?"

"Yes."

"And you, personally, wrote that scathing article about *Croc-nami* and, more specifically, me?"

Kit winced at the cool tone of his voice. But she squared her shoulders and nodded.

"Yes."

A lengthy pause.

"And . . . you don't wish to add anything else?"

Her shoulders sagged. "What do you want me to say?"

"A defense of your actions? An apology, perhaps?"

"I *am* genuinely sorry. Sorry that a decent person like yourself got caught in the middle of everything. But, in reality, I was just doing my job, Marc—"

"You *own* the company, Kit. It's not like someone was going to fire you—"

"True. But it's the brand we've built."

"Mocking others' hard work?"

She flinched. "I deserved that."

"Yes, you did."

He drove in silence, eyes on the road. His expression shuttered and withdrawn.

All vestiges of happy-go-lucky Marc gone. Not even a spot of meringue in sight.

So she had broken through his defenses. That was good, right? But now he had completely shut her out. Rightfully so.

A farmer guided two cows along the road, using a switch to direct them. Marc carefully steered the gig around the animals, face impassive.

An ache twinged in Kit's chest, spreading through her heart . . . a heavy, burning sensation. Her breathing sped up, and she chewed on her bottom lip to stop its trembling.

She *never* cried. She could just imagine it. La Pochette *crying* over Marc Wilde.

It was almost too funny.

Except it *so* wasn't.

You are such an idiot, Virtuous Angel murmured.

Agreed, Wicked Angel chimed in. *You didn't have to tell him. He would have found out eventually regardless.*

That's not what I meant. We don't lie, remember? Virtuous Angel said.

Blah, blah. Who cares? Wicked Angel snorted. *We could have been snogging that gorgeous hunk of manliness for much longer if you two would just shut it—*

"Enough," Kit whispered, sniffling quietly. "I made the right decision. It's better to be honest."

"What did you say?" Marc asked.

"Nothing." Kit pulled her cloak tighter around her.

"Talking to yourself?"

She shrugged, blinking back her tears.

Marc continued, "Is that guilt talking? Or did you decide to carry on a conversation with the voices in your head?"

That was uncomfortably close to the truth. And, fortunately, instantly shut down her waterworks.

"Look, Marc. All barriers are gone. I kept my mouth shut about my past . . . well, for obvious reasons. But I am an open book now. So yes, for your information, I actually *was* carrying on a conversation with the voices in my head."

He swiveled his head to stare at her. Raised a questioning eyebrow.

"Why does that not surprise me?" His voice ironically dark.

Kit swallowed and stared into the leafless, winter trees which lined the road.

Why hold anything back at this point?

"For as long as I can remember, I have broken inner thoughts into Virtuous Angel and Wicked Angel—"

"You're serious, aren't you? You actually do hear voices?"

"Well, it's not like I'm schizophrenic or anything. I think I just sub-consciously divide thoughts into good, bad and neutral. So when it came time to start writing the 'Review of the Preview' column for Faux-Pause, it was simple to have it be a conversation between my ego, id and superego—"

"Do you ever *think* about the people you diss on? How your words affect their careers?" Marc shook his head and then turned toward her.

Kit paused, taking in a deep breath. *Did* she think about them?

Probably not as much as you should, Virtuous Angel pointed out.

"No man—or woman in this case—is an island." Marc gestured. "Everything you do . . . it's like making waves in an ocean. You may not mean to swamp someone else's boat, but it doesn't excuse your respon-sibility either. "

He paused, but he wasn't done. "It's easy to stand ringside and heckle those of us who show up day after day, slogging through our work and dreams. But at least have the courage to hop in the ring yourself from time to time. Own your actions."

Kit bit back a hefty sigh. "First of all, I *do* try to own my actions. Second, I would hop in the ring with you, but I understand it's croco-dile-infested so—"

Marc gave a sharp bark of laughter. Not the amused kind.

"Wow. You are sooooo not in a place to go throwing jokes like that around," he said.

"Too soon, huh?"

"Way too soon."

"Good to know." Kit straightened her cloak. "This is not funny yet."

"Nope."

"Will you ever find it funny?"

Marc fixed her with a long look, eyes disbelieving. Every line of his body communicating outrage and indignation.

Not humorous. Duly noted.

"I don't know. Why don't you tell me?" He shook his head, probably in disgust. "What *is* funny about this?"

It was a rhetorical question. Kit knew better than to answer it.

They crossed a small stone bridge to see a town a short distance ahead. The white-washed wattle and daub walls gleamed between dark cross timbers.

"Look, I know I'm a B-list actor—or D-list wannabe, as you so unkindly branded me—"

Kit flinched again. "Marc, I *am* really sorry—"

He held up a staying hand. "I have a plan for my life. Or, rather, *had* a plan before your little stunt. Millions of people the world over will only ever know me as 'that *Croc-nami* guy.' Who knows where my career will go after this? Do you even care?"

"Marc, of course, I care. You are so much more than just 'that *Croc-nami* guy'—"

"I mean, you can't write some insanely viral post and expect everything to be butterflies and roses for the target of your vitriol—"

"Whoa, wait. What? The post went viral?" Kit's eyes widened, his words sinking in.

"When I left, it had more hits than anything else you had ever written . . . and that's saying quite a bit."

"Wow, really?! I had no idea. That's amazing." And then she saw his eyes nearly bugging out of his head and realized he might not see the situation in *quite* the same way. "I mean, that's . . . not good . . . maybe. Don't they say all publicity is good publicity?"

He shook his head, ignoring her question. "How could you *not* know the post went viral?"

"Uh . . . well, I have been here for a while now. Six weeks-ish and counting. I left a backlog of articles for my assistants to post."

He frowned. "How is that possible? I've been here for only two weeks. When I stopped your horse, I had just arrived. How can you have been here for six weeks?"

Kit sighed. "It's such a long story—"

And then her stomach growled. Long and loud.

The village had drawn closer, and Kit realized she knew this place. Knew this village. It had altered quite a bit over the intervening two hundred years, but some landmarks remained the same.

Like the Golden Rose Inn.

"Look, Marc. We've been traveling all day, and there probably won't be any food where we're going. I'm hungry and I'm sure you are too. Let's stop, grab some lunch and I will tell you everything."

Marc nodded tightly. Kit placed a hand on his arm, drawing his attention.

"And, for the record, I want to know everything about you too."

His arm was steel under her hand, but his expression did soften slightly, giving Kit hope that they could work through this.

Marc guided them into town. Kit smiled at the farmers and laborers they passed. Marc tipped his hat.

The Golden Rose Inn had changed somewhat. In 2014, only the front main building remained, sitting flush with the busy road which cut through town.

In 1814, it was set back from the street a pace and encompassed a two-story galleried yard and stable to the right. That said, the actual building looked nearly the same with its white-washed walls and exposed dark cross-beam timbers. A wooden sign swung from chains over the front door, yellow wild roses painted on it.

An ostler ran out to take charge of their horse and carriage. Marc tossed the reins to the man and then turned to help Kit down, frowning.

"Do you have any idea how this works?" he asked, gesturing toward the inn with his chin. "I haven't a clue."

Kit's mind blanked as she took Marc's hand and stepped down. That was a very good question.

"I . . . don't know. I think you give a coin to the ostler there." Kit subtly leaned her head, indicating the man holding the horse's head, waiting expectantly. "Though if we hit a snag, I will just pretend to faint and that should smooth things over."

Some of the tension eased from Marc's face. A smile tugged at his lips. "See, I had this idea that you were from the nineteenth century and so had experience navigating situations like this."

"There you were so wrong, Lord Vader."

Marc offered her his arm, which Kit greedily took. Lightness settled into her chest. If he was finding humor in the situation, perhaps he could forgive her and move on.

For her part, there was no way she was giving up on him.

In the end, ordering lunch was surprisingly simple.

Kit watched as Marc, in his stuffiest British accent, hailed the innkeeper and introduced them as Lord and Lady Vader. He then, quite pompously, requested a private dining room and hearty luncheon. It was an impressive performance.

"I learned all that from *Pride and Prejudice*. Emme always makes me watch it with her," he whispered to Kit as the innkeeper led them into a dark-paneled parlor with a fire burning cheerfully in the hearth. Light streamed through the mullioned windows, rendering the room quaint and cozy.

Kit took off her cloak and warmed her hands by the fire as a maid delivered platters of food. Most of which Kit recognized: a meat pie, steamed cabbage, mutton stew, fluffy scones and some slices of pound cake.

Once the door closed behind the maid, Kit chuckled. "Lady Vader?"

Marc nodded his head. "Why not? It seemed more believable than saying you were my sister." He doffed his hat, setting it on an empty chair, and then pulled off his gloves. "Even I know claiming you as anything other than my wife or sister would be a complete *faux pas*—"

He stopped, tension suddenly entering the room.

FauxPause. It hung between them.

"Right." Kit smoothed her skirt. "Again, I am truly sorry, Marc. Sincerely. I am committed to doing whatever I can to make this right."

He regarded her with hooded eyes, slapping his gloves against his thigh. She watched emotions flicker across his face: hurt, frustration . . . maybe even a smidge of betrayal.

"Your review stung, Kit. It really did." He rubbed his chest with his free hand, as if massaging some tightness away. Gloves still snapped against his leg. "But who knows? Publicity never hurts and maybe some good will come of it—"

"Exactly! That's what I think too. And, I *do* sincerely apologize. Do you feel it possible, given time, you could forgive me?"

He stared at her, face impassive. After a moment, he shrugged, tossing the gloves on top of his hat.

"I don't know," he said, sliding off his greatcoat. "I suppose it depends on how good your make-up kiss is."

Her entire body sagged at his admission.

"Amazing. I promise it will be amazing." She smiled, letting her relief shine.

He matched her smile, though it didn't quite touch his eyes. "It will have to be."

He studied her for another moment, face unreadable. And then nodded.

Time. He just needed a little time to process it all. Heaven knew, she did.

Marc took a seat at the table and started dishing food for himself, gesturing for Kit to do the same.

She sat and placed a scone on her plate. And then stopped, as another thought occurred, causing her to give a long chuckle.

"What?" asked Marc, looking at her over the meat pie. Eyebrows inquisitive.

"I was just imagining the scene if we had met at a posh party in modern London." Kit reached for a jar of what appeared to be gooseberry jam. "One of those Perez Hilton types would have made sure we were introduced as La Pochette and the 'Crocinator.' I would have made some pithy comment about your missing dreadlocks—"

Marc snorted softly. "And then I would have said something oh-so-dry about people hearing multiple voices in their heads. All in a dignified manner, of course."

"Of course," Kit agreed, smile flitting. "But we would have simply confirmed all our prejudices about each other and never looked beyond that. It's such an interesting twist of Fate for us to be here together. That we had to travel two hundred years into the past and be stripped to our barest selves—"

"Allowing us to see the person behind each of our twenty-first century public personas," Marc finished for her.

"Exactly." Kit nodded.

"Emme has a best friend, Jasmine. She's part mystic, part psychic. Personally, I think she needs to lay off the incense." Marc set down his fork, studying Kit. "Anyway, Jasmine believes the universe will find a way for people who truly belong together to meet. Even across time and space."

Something flared in Kit's chest at his words. Hot and bright.

"What a beautiful way of expressing it." Kit smiled softly, dishing some cabbage onto her plate.

Her breathing eased. He seemed more relaxed . . . his anger would pass. It had to. She refused to consider any other option.

Marc broke open a scone and reached for the gooseberry jam. "So I know some about La Pochette. But I want to know more about the real Kit," he said.

She let out a long breath of air. "Let me start at the beginning. You already know part of the story anyway. My father was the seventh Lord Whitmoor, a title awarded by the crown in the 1820's, if I remember right. My parents married, had me and Daniel, and then my mother ran off with her best friend's husband and never looked back. She died about ten years ago in Thailand."

Marc lifted his eyes, questioning.

"Drug overdose." Kit said the words tonelessly. As if those two simple words could encompass the pain of burying a mother she had never known. Of being raised motherless. Of being the one child on the playground who had only a vague understanding of what the word 'mother' even meant.

Something of her pain must have flickered across her face.

"My father left," Marc said softly, not taking his eyes off of her. "When I was about eight. Emme and I woke up one morning and he was gone."

"I'm sorry."

"Me too."

Marc paused. And then shifted his shoulders, as if moving something weighty.

He continued. "There was so much rage in me over it. So many years before I even understood what the rage meant. Martial arts literally saved my life. It gave me an outlet."

Kit nodded. "Writing and humor were like that for me."

"Jokes made it palatable, at least to other people."

"Exactly. If I could be the funniest, most likable kid in school, then maybe the other kids would forget about my motherlessness."

"Kids don't forget," Marc said, shaking his head as he piled another slice of meat pie onto his plate. "Us or them."

That was truth.

Laughing at yourself and others before they could laugh at you.

The natural reaction to not being wanted by the one person who had mattered most.

"What happened to your father?" Kit slid the question in casually. She intended to stay inside the non-meringue zone as long as possible.

"Died when I was a teenager. Car accident. My British grandma took it hard, obviously. I think she held onto Emme and me even more after that."

"Your mom?"

"She took it all in stride. Looking back, I don't know how she held us all together. She worked as a flight attendant. Still does, actually. You would like her. She's a hilarious, spunky lady."

"I'd like to meet her."

Their eyes met and held.

That sense of familiarity still hung between them. It was more than just recognizing someone from a movie preview. Or sharing a few jokes with each other. Kit saw that clearly now.

It was realizing you had found your tribe. A person who sees the same reality as yourself.

She and Marc were two sides of the same coin. Achingly similar.

Housed in the same soul.

The knowledge caused a pang to rise in her chest, something tight lodging in her throat.

She looked away before she did something stupid. Like cry. Or kiss him senseless.

Or both.

Kit shifted in her chair. "How did you end up here?"

She meant in the nineteenth century. Though, really, it was a better question for her.

Marc grimaced and told her about James and Emme, Georgiana and Sebastian, Duir Cottage, the portal, the blackmail note and arriving to find the trunk and nineteenth century clothes. The short fight with Daniel.

"Daniel . . . can be such a trial." Kit shook her head. "He's a good person, Marc. You have to believe that. He wouldn't deliberately harm you. But you said all this happened about two weeks ago?"

Marc nodded, taking another bite of meat pie.

"I knew nothing about the portal." Kit swallowed. "How does it work?"

"Who knows really." But in between bites of bread, Marc told her all he knew about the portal, its fickle nature, the ties that can bind people across centuries.

"So if we were allowed through the portal because it was the best way for us to meet, what about Daniel? Why was he sent through the portal with you?" Kit asked.

Marc sighed. "I honestly don't know. He and I were grappling, so maybe he was just collateral damage. In the wrong place at the wrong time. Though it was obvious he had been planning to go through the portal—"

"Only Daniel would get caught up in a mess like this." Kit shook her head. "My brother has always been restless. He's a wanderer, just like our mother. He dabbled in drugs as a teenager but, fortunately, never got addicted to anything. I think he was afraid to end up like our mum. But he can't just *be*. His mind never seems to stop. He is brilliant at mechanical things and is the type of person who can pull apart a toaster or grandfather clock and reassemble it, better than new. But ask him to spend an hour in an engineering class and he blows up. He refuses to even look at a computer. I don't know that he has ever even read FauxPause. I don't think he even knows how to turn a computer on—"

"What? How is that even possible in this day and age? Well, not *this* day and age—" Marc rolled his hand, nodding his head. "—our day and age. You know what I mean."

"I'm with you. I can't understand it either. My brother and I are so much alike and yet so opposite somehow. It's like Daniel got the worst attributes of both our parents. He just bounces from one thing to the next, constantly one step ahead or even behind the law. He's smitten with serious wanderlust and often will disappear for a day or two without telling anyone. It's so frustrating, particularly his ridiculous aversion to post-1950s technology. He never carries a cell phone, so tracking him down is nearly impossible . . .

"Anyway, about two months ago, I found some notes of his with the words 'Duir Cottage,' the address and a note listing different articles of clothing and money. It was all stacked under an old bottle of chloroform our father had collected at some point. Obviously super suspicious. Probably related to the blackmail, but I didn't know that. Daniel got super cagey when I asked him about it and refused to talk to me. I thought maybe he was back to his drug habits or something. Then, to make matters worse, he vanished. Just didn't come home. After nearly a week, I was panicked, desperate to find him, thinking he was in something deep this time. So I went to Duir Cottage, just to see what kind of a place it was, maybe talk to the people who lived there. The house was charming and looked entirely harmless—"

"Which it is."

Kit acknowledged this with a nod. "Yes, well, I guessed as much. Anyway, this is the part that is less-than-flattering, but I, uh, tried the doors and found the back door ajar—"

"What?! How did that happen?" Marc's eyebrows raised in alarm. "Perhaps the caretaker left it open by accident—"

"That could be. There were some cleaning supplies in a bucket by the door." She noted Marc's wide eyes. "But, I know, I know. I shouldn't have gone in regardless. I guess I was just trying to find anything that would help me find Daniel and understand what he was up to. I just want my brother to be safe, you know."

"Are you insane? Anyone could have been in the house. You could have been hurt."

Kit rolled her eyes at him. "Exactly! Which is why I brought a taser and my rape alarm—"

"Kit, Kit, Kit," Marc muttered, lowering his head into his hands, pressing his fingers against his temples.

She ignored it. "I snooped around the house, finding nothing—taking nothing too, I have to add—and then stumbled down to the cellar, thinking that the drugs or whatever might be down there. So the rest should be fairly obvious. I went through the portal and didn't remotely understand what had happened at first. The house just changed, and I wandered outside completely disoriented."

She paused and stared at her plate, shredding a scone with her fingers. Then continued. "It was . . . awful. I was seriously freaked out, on the verge of having a full-blown panic attack. I was walking up the road toward Marfield when a nice old lady stopped me. She introduced herself as Auntie Gray—"

"Ah, Auntie Gray. Emme thinks that woman is part witch."

"I would believe it. Anyway, she took me home with her, found me some clothing. Over the next couple days, she acclimated me to this century, showed me the ropes, how to behave. She didn't indicate that she knew anything about the portal or where I was truly from, but I wonder if she doesn't know more than she lets on."

"Yes, I believe she knows a lot about the portal. I wonder why she didn't say anything?"

Kit shrugged. "I should have been more direct with my questions, I suppose. She actually left on the mailcoach about five days after I arrived—something about going to Sussex for the birth of a new grandchild. I would have gone back to her with more questions had she been around.

"Before Auntie Gray left, she introduced me to the vicar who then arranged for the position with Lady Ruby. The only thing that kept me going was thinking Daniel was here too. That I needed to track him down and then find a way to return to our own century. I didn't know, at the time, that Daniel wasn't here yet. He had gone off in 2014 and then came home for a week or two before coming here—"

"And he didn't wonder where *you* had gone?"

Kit shrugged. "Daniel doesn't really think about things like that. He just assumed I was on a business trip. Anyway, once I had my position at Haldon Manor, I snooped around in Arthur's study, hoping to find something that would link Daniel to the cottage or Haldon Manor. Or, at least, information about the portal and how it worked, but I couldn't find anything. And that's where you came in."

They ate in silence for a few moments.

"So . . . your father was an honest-to-goodness lord. What's *that* like growing up?" Marc took a bite of meat pie.

"Not so different, except you hang out with other kids whose parents are lords. Most of them were uppity and arrogant. I think that's where my initial idea for FauxPause came from. I was so tired of being looked down on and wanted to have a voice of my own. I mean, sure my dad was a lord, but the family estates had been given to the National Trust years ago and we were never wealthy. Dad was a history professor at the university in Hereford.

"Don't get me wrong. We were obviously not poor, but we never had the money other peers had. Dad didn't seem to care. He just wanted to spend time in his study, researching the history of the family and area. Daniel and I were left to fend for ourselves most of the time. Which is how I became more mother than sister to Daniel. I fixed dinner, did laundry, cleaned house . . . all of that."

Marc gave a mock-gasp of surprise. "What? No servants?"

"Uh, no." Kit laughed. "*That* ship sailed a good generation or two before my lifetime."

"So, if your father has passed on, Daniel is Lord Whitmoor now? Isn't that how it works?"

"Well, yes and no. Daniel *should* be Lord Whitmoor, but the title hasn't been vested in him yet as Daniel has been reluctant to accept it. And there are no other male heirs, so if Daniel leaves or declines the title, then everything reverts to the Crown. It's all been this ugly mess. The barony was created through a writ of summons, not patent, so Daniel feels like we have options but—"

Kit caught Marc's eyes glazing. She waved her hand. "I'll spare you the details. Basically, when my great-grandfather gave Whitmoor to the National Trust, he negotiated that future heirs could live in the family wing but if Daniel doesn't return and everything reverts back, then—"

"Wait. Whitmoor? You lost me."

"Whitmoor House. The family estate. If Daniel doesn't return and take up the hereditary title, then the family stake in the house automatically reverts to the National Trust. I not only lose my brother, but the house that has been in our family for nearly two hundred years. The house where I live. Which, incidentally, is where we are headed. I think Daniel would go to Whitmoor. The house isn't in the family yet, but I figured it was as good a place as any to start looking for my brother."

"Is it far? Whitmoor House?"

"No. It's not far at all. Just up the road."

Chapter 18

They reached Whitmoor House just as the sun was setting. Kit knew the estate lay only a couple miles outside of town, but even so, it had been shockingly easy to find. So many of the landmarks hadn't changed through the years. The moss-covered stone fence lining the road. The ruined watchtower on top of a nearby hill where she and Daniel had played as children, its windows already empty and sightless.

Kit's heart gave a painful lurch as the impossibly familiar ramparts came into view. The house had its origins in the Middle Ages, but had been added to over the years, lending it a bit of a hodge-podge look. A medieval keep stood in its center, flanked by two Tudor halls which branched into Jacobean wings, the entire whole outlined against the darkening sky.

"So . . . who lives here right now? How do you propose we work this?" Marc gestured toward the large house as they drove up the drive.

"As far as I remember, no one lives in the house during this era. My father was somewhat fanatical about the history of the family. The house stood empty for many years before my ancestor, the first baron, purchased it for a song. So we should be alright visiting it for a night."

"More breaking and entering? Are you sure your brother is the only member of your family with criminal tendencies?"

Kit nudged him playfully with her shoulder.

Marc guided the gig around the house to the stables. There were no signs of habitation, though the stables were clean enough. They even found some serviceable hay for the horse.

Their horse tucked in for the night, Kit led the way back to the house, skirting the main entrance and heading toward a recessed area next to the central tower. A small door with age-darkened wood emerged from the gloom. If she were lucky, the small servant's door would be as it had always been. It certainly looked the same.

Marc raised his eyebrows questioningly, but Kit reached her hand between the door and cool stone wall, finding the groove carved into the limestone. A chain nestled inside which lifted the locking crossbar. Pulling on the chain, Kit pushed the door open.

Go figure. It worked just the same. She and Daniel had been fascinated by that door as children. Such a clever way to provide entrance without needing a key.

She turned back to Marc with a smile, beckoning him to follow her inside.

"Allow me to welcome you to what will become Whitmoor House."

Confidently, she led Marc up a few narrow stone stairs and through another door into the large central medieval hall. She could see the faint outlines of banners hanging from the walls and the enormous ancient fireplace gaping before them. Furniture dotted the room, lumpy shapes covered in heavy cloth.

Kit tugged off her bonnet and gloves, placing them on what seemed to be a table. She felt several strands of hair pop free of their pins. She probably looked ghastly, but the gloom hid that, right? Marc dropped hat and gloves onto the table, too.

"I don't suppose you have a flashlight or some matches?" Marc asked, his voice echoing quietly. "Or maybe you know how to light a candle in 1814?"

Drat. That was a problem.

Kit rotated, studying the large hall. The general layout of the house hadn't changed much, but it was going to be a long night without any light whatsoever.

Suddenly, a noise came from the left of the keep, coming from the portion of the house that would belong to her family in the twenty-first century. Something that sounded a lot like a chair scraping across wood.

Kit jumped and grabbed Marc's arm.

"I thought you said this place was empty," he hissed in her ear. "That no one lived here."

"It *should* be." Kit took a couple tentative steps toward the family wing.

"Kit . . ." Marc said warningly behind her. "It could be anyone up there. Robbers, thieves, French spies—"

"Or it could be Daniel—"

"Aren't they the same thing?"

"Be nice."

But Kit kept going. Through the west drawing room, up the stone stairs she knew so well.

A strong suspicion lodged in her thumping heart.

Marc followed her, his quiet strength lending her courage. Or maybe it was just his huge muscles. She couldn't be sure.

She rounded the corner and saw a light flickering from one of the bedrooms.

The bedroom that had been (wait—would be?) her father's.

She crept down the hallway and cautiously peered around the door. A lean figure bent over a desk in a pool of candlelight.

Just as she had thought. It could only be one person, in the end. Daniel.

And now they had found him, she would finally get some answers, and they could all go home.

Together.

Marc watched a glorious smile illuminate Kit's face. The kind of unfettered, joyous look that knocked all thought out of a man's head.

Not that it was aimed at him.

Kit pushed the door open further, spilling faint candlelight into the hall.

"Daniel," she cried, launching herself into the room.

Marc entered on her heels just in time to see a tallish, dark-haired man stand up from a desk in front of a boarded up window and catch Kit in his arms, giving her a tight hug. Knocking free more of her hair from its pins.

He was younger than Marc had expected, probably only in his early twenties, six or seven years younger than Kit.

"Kit! What on earth!" Daniel pulled his sister back, looking her up and down. "Why are you here? I told you I would come back for you."

And then Daniel lifted his head, seeing Marc for the first time.

Marc had never seen someone's jaw literally drop, but there was no other way to describe what happened.

"You!" Daniel pointed a finger at Marc and then immediately shoved Kit behind him, as if to protect her, obviously recognizing Marc from their scuffle in Duir Cottage.

Did he consider Marc some kind of threat?

The bloody nerve.

"Do you know who this man is, Kit?" Daniel held Kit back with his arm, but she pushed it out of the way and moved to the front of her brother, placing herself between him and Marc.

"Marc Wilde." She gestured toward him. "My brother, Daniel Ashton."

Daniel's eyes were still wide.

"Daniel." Marc inclined his head. "So glad to finally catch up with you. Kit has told me quite a bit about you."

Marc walked farther into the room. Even in the dim light of a single candelabra, he could see the layer of dust which settled over everything. A large bed with floor to ceiling hangings dominated the right of the room. A dark fireplace yawned open on the other wall, flanked by two chairs. The desk that had occupied Daniel sat in between, the candelabra resting atop it. The flickering light cast ghostly shadows onto the wood-paneled walls.

Marc pulled his coat tighter and strode to one of the chairs in front of the fireplace. He wanted some explanations, and he intended to listen to them in comfort. He disregarded the small puff of dust as he sat down.

"I suppose a fire is out of the question?" Marc gestured toward the empty grate.

Daniel blinked and then shook his head. "I wouldn't chance it. Who knows if the chimney will draw correctly. Besides, the smoke would be a clear beacon of our presence here."

Marc nodded and then leaned back, crossing a booted foot over his knee. "So, Daniel. It seems that I owe my presence here to you. Would you care to offer an explanation?"

Daniel stiffened and regarded Marc with cautious eyes.

He said nothing.

"Allow me to rephrase that question, Mr. Ashton. In the last two weeks, I have been drugged and dragged through a time portal, befriended your sister, protected her person, been shot at, fought a viscount, been mistaken as a spy and rode all day in a decidedly uncomfortable gig, all while using a pretentious accent and wearing these ridiculous clothes. Not to mention forgoing modern plumbing and ESPN. All because *you*"—here Marc lingered on the word— "decided to blackmail me and broke into Duir Cottage. So based on this, the least you could do is provide some small justification for your actions."

Daniel's shoulders slumped, and he sank down in the chair opposite Marc, resting his forearms on his knees, causing another billow of dust.

Predictably, Kit and Marc sneezed. Kit swung the desk chair around and positioned it next to Daniel, taking her brother's hand in hers, pulling it off his knee. Long tendrils of hair escaped to frame her face. What would the mass look like down? Marc shook the thought clear. *So* not the time to be dwelling on things like that.

Daniel looked down at Kit's hand and then sat back, keeping her hand in his.

"Just tell us what happened, Daniel." Her voice gentle and soothing. The kind of voice which invited confidences.

Or caused younger brothers to bristle at being told what to do.

Daniel shifted, uncertain as to how he felt about it. Then he sighed, lifting his eyes to Marc. "For the record, I never meant for you to come through with me. I just . . . didn't think."

"Why don't you start at the beginning," Marc said.

"The story is actually quite simple. After our dad died last year, I found myself sorting through all his old papers. I came across a history written by a man named Garvis, who had been a servant to another man he referred to simply as W. At one point—I think it was in the late 1820s, about fifteen years from now—this W was severely injured and became delirious with fever. Garvis recorded W's ramblings which included mention of a portal in the cellar of a place called Duir Cottage."

A chill shot down Marc's spine. So someone else *did* know. Or had known. But who? And how?

"As you can imagine, I was incredibly intrigued by the account. Garvis mentioned things that only someone from our century would know. References to antibiotics and vaccines. It seemed like this W really was from the future or had at least spent time there. I have always loved history, so if there actually was a portal through time, I wanted to try it for myself."

"But why send a blackmail letter? Were you that desperate for money? And why me?"

"Garvis recorded that this W claimed to go by the name Marcus Wilde on occasion."

The tingle along Marc's spine grew, spreading along his arms and legs, constricting his breathing.

No! Impossible! He refused to spend the rest of his life here.

Something of his panic must have shown on his face.

Daniel shifted in his chair, as if he hated being the bearer of bad news. "The past . . . this era . . . it isn't too bad of a place, really."

Marc and Kit stared at him, causing Daniel to squirm a bit more. "I'm just saying I kinda like it. It's a little bit awesome to be a gentleman. To live in a time when people care more about honor and a code of conduct than the latest gadget and what's playing on the telly."

"Well, I have no intention of staying, regardless of the stories this Garvis wrote." Not going to happen. Nope. Never. Marc tapped a hand against the arm of his chair. "So, why the blackmail?"

"Oh, yes. That. Well . . . it actually wasn't blackmail. Not really."

Marc cocked his head at Daniel. "Seriously? Because it felt a lot like blackmail. The whole threatening letter, pay-up-or-else thing—"

"True. I did send the letter, but I never intended to follow through with any real blackmail. I just wanted to see if the portal actually existed before breaking into your house—"

Marc let out a sharp crack of laughter. "You realize your sister had no such scruples—"

"You broke into the house too?" Daniel turned scandalized eyes to Kit. "Kit! Everyone expects me to do such things. But you . . . we count on you to maintain the respectability of the family—"

Kit gave her brother a withering look, the same expression Marc had seen countless times on his own sister's face. He chuckled.

Daniel grinned a maddening-little-brother grin and continued. "Anyway, the roses were a sort of test."

"Roses?" Kit looked between the two of them, the swift motion threatening to dislodge more of her hair.

"Yes. Daniel insisted I place thirteen yellow roses in the front window of Duir Cottage to prove I had received his blackmail letter."

"Exactly! It was the perfect set-up." Daniel looked quite proud of himself. "If there was no portal, you would have completely ignored my letter. But if you placed roses in the window, then I knew that you had something to hide."

"Stupid, sinister roses. Yellow roses represent treachery and death in a lot of cultures—"

"Oh. I thought they symbolized friendship." Daniel adjusted his legs. He really did seem to struggle to sit still. "I wanted to reassure you I meant no harm. Anyway, once I saw the roses, I knew there must be a portal. I mean, I had hoped it existed, so I had been preparing to go to the past. Reading up on this time period. Language, social customs, ways to earn my living. I outfitted a trunk with items I would want and had a costume expert make me some period clothing. I even found some vintage doctor's supplies in things Dad had, including old-school chloroform—"

"Honestly, Daniel, I can't believe you wanted to be a time-travel tourist." Kit shook her head.

"And so you broke into Duir Cottage, determined to go through the portal when I surprised you." Marc's head reared back, a hiss of understanding escaping. "You never intended to influence the Napoleonic Wars or change history. You were just wanting to have a lark."

Daniel at least had the decency to flush and look embarrassed. "History has always been my passion. And yeah, I am really sorry. I didn't mean to hurt you or drag you through the portal with me. I guess I just panicked when I saw you drive up and dumped some chloroform onto my handkerchief just in case. We sort of fell together and ended up going through. The portal wouldn't let me back to get my things, so I was left with just the clothes I was wearing."

"Oh, Daniel." Kit shook her head, setting more curls free. "How I wish I had known. I was already here. I bet the portal is just waiting for me to find you, so we can return together."

Daniel shifted again. Was this his normal restlessness or was he hiding something from his sister? "Honestly, Kit, I didn't know you were here. How could I have known? It wasn't until I saw you in town— and then followed you to the church graveyard—that I realized you had come back too. But once I knew you were here and having to serve Lady Ruby . . . well, I wanted to save you from that."

"You are such a sweet brother, sometimes." Kit patted his hand. "Terribly misguided, mind you, but still sweet."

Daniel continued, "I asked around town after talking to you by the church and . . . wow. There's a Jed. I. Knight *and* a Lord Vader at Haldon Manor? What are the chances?"

Marc allowed himself a grim chuckle. "Well, the Lord Vader was all me—"

"Wait. That's you?" Daniel pointed at him.

Marc nodded. "But Jedediah is his own man."

"Go figure," Daniel smiled. "After leaving Kit that day, I asked around for work and was directed to a tavern in a nearby town. I met some cove who wanted a job done, no questions asked. He was dressed in a dark hat and cloak and had a kerchief across his face. He promised me a significant sum of money if I stole some papers from Lord Linwood at Kinningsley."

Kit sighed. "So of course you took him up on the offer."

Daniel spread his hands in front of his sister. "What else was I to do? I needed money, Kit. I did it for us."

Hands shaking, Kit threaded her fingers into her hair and held tight to her head. Pulling more tendrils of hair free. How much more hair could escape before it all tumbled down?

"You realize those papers are probably going straight into the hands of French spies."

Daniel nodded. "Yes. I sorta figured *that* out once I realized what I had stolen. For the record, I am to turn over the papers to this agent the day after tomorrow—"

"You have them here?"

"Yes." Daniel rose and went to the desk with Marc and Kit following closely behind. "Here they are."

He spread what looked to be schematics for some sort of canon across the desktop.

"This is what Linwood was so determined to hide?" Marc frowned and picked up a page, studying it more closely in the candlelight. The detailed drawing resembled a Gatling gun with multiple barrels. "Aren't repeating rifles and canons a little after this time period?" Marc turned a questioning look to Daniel.

Daniel nodded. "It would seem Linwood is hiding a secret talent for mechanical engineering. These drawings are excellent and, if placed into the right hands, could enable the French to create weaponry decades ahead of its time."

"Which could influence the outcome of the Napoleonic Wars. Oh Daniel, how could you?" Kit whispered.

"How was I to know what I was stealing and why?"

Kit rolled her eyes. "Do you seriously want me to answer that?"

"The man I was dealing with made it very clear that I was not to ask any questions. I just figured they were documents related to a local land dispute or a bill in the House of Lords . . . basically, none of my business."

Marc shuffled through a few more pages. There were seven in total. But there were other pages on the desk, papers Daniel had obviously been working on when they interrupted him.

"So what is this then?" Marc gestured toward the papers Daniel had been writing.

"Well, as Kit just pointed out, I cannot in good conscience turn something over to the French that could change the course of history. So I decided to copy Linwood's drawings but change them enough so the schematics will be essentially useless. That way I can still turn something over to this agent tomorrow and get my money. But not betray my country."

Kit moaned and covered her face with her hands again, rocking back and forth. "There are so many, many ways that plan can go awry, Daniel. Please let me talk you out of it."

Daniel grimaced. "Look, Kit, I know you think this isn't one of my brightest ideas—"

"Bad idea, Daniel. This is a bad idea. A *horrid* plan."

"But Kit, I *have* to meet this man tomorrow. He has people and I need to turn these papers over to him. Otherwise, I become a hunted man. Besides, I really need that money—"

"Why? Why do you need money? Who cares if you become a hunted man? *We*" —Kit waved her hand back and forth to indicate the space between them— "are going home. These spies won't follow us to the twenty-first century. Marc has enough money to see us back to Haldon Manor. I fail to see how any of this is even an issue."

Marc locked eyes with Daniel as Kit spoke, seeing the truth in her brother's gaze. The simple fact that Kit had been missing throughout the entire conversation.

Daniel had no intention of returning home. Ever.

He wasn't a time-traveling tourist. He was trying to build a life for himself in 1814, and these stolen papers were his golden ticket. However misguided and harebrained the idea, Marc had to give him credit for sheer bravado.

Kit, however, would be devastated. She would *never* give up trying to get her brother back. Marc knew her well enough to clearly see that basic fact.

Daniel's eyes communicated his awareness of all of this to Marc, pleading for understanding, asking Marc to help Kit understand.

Firmly trapping Marc in between them.

Marc wanted to punch something. Hard.

Instead, he gave a small shake of his head.

No.

He would not get in the middle of this. It was not his battle to fight. Daniel and Kit's relationship was their own to sort through.

With a narrowing of his eyes, Daniel turned back to the papers. A determined clench to his jaw.

Marc tugged on Kit's sleeve, eyes still on her brother. "C'mon, Kit. Let's leave Daniel to work. You can show me around the castle . . . ehrrr . . . your house."

"But what about Daniel? The papers?" She gestured toward her brother. "None of it matters. We should just head back toward the portal and home."

Daniel stubbornly turned his back on them, sitting back down.

"Come, Kit. It's too late to journey back tonight." Marc reached out and snagged one of the burning candles from the candelabra.

Daniel barely flicked a glance in their direction, intently focused on the papers before him. Not saying a word.

The coward.

Marc threaded his fingers through Kit's and, without waiting for her to argue, pulled her from the room. Allowing Daniel to complete his counterfeit drawings. Not forcing Kit to confront the reality of her brother's choices.

It just figured.

He was caught in the middle of their relationship, whether he liked it or not.

Coward, he thought again. But, this time, the only coward in sight was himself.

Chapter 19

Kit allowed herself to be lead from the room, watching numbly as Marc found another candelabra and carefully lit it. He lifted it up, illuminating the hallway. Furniture and wall hangings loomed at the edges of the light. The flickering candles cast the house into long, leaping shadows.

Whitmoor before the Whitmoors.

She should have been over-the-moon about exploring the house.

She wasn't.

An icy chill had settled through her. Freezing her thoughts. Unconsciously, she took Marc's hand and wandered down the stairs and into the room that would become her father's study. She had always checked on him in here, his head bent over some book or another.

Marc raised the candelabra, chasing some of the shadows of the room away. Details emerged from the dim light. Dark paneling and bookcases along the opposite wall. A large fireplace and a bank of tall windows.

Huh. Who would have guessed? It looked eerily unchanged. Even that same lynx painting stood over the fireplace, its golden eyes tracking her in the low candlelight. She could practically smell her father's cologne lingering in the air.

"This was my father's study." Kit's voice echoed in the quiet.

Marc set the candelabra on the enormous desk in the middle of the room. Even the desk was the same.

"Do you have happy memories of this room?" he asked. Softly, carefully. As if he hesitated to shake her memories loose.

She ran her fingers along the top of the desk, walking around it. How many times had she done just this? Stepping over her father's books in the process.

She swallowed back a tight lump in her throat.

"He wasn't always so distant . . . my father." She nodded her head toward Marc. "Before my mother left, he laughed. I remember bringing my books in here and sitting there" —she pointed to the chair at the left of the fireplace— "reading with him. Talking. Answering his questions."

"I wish I could have met him."

Silence hung.

She turned away from Marc, pulling her cloak tighter around her as she wandered over to study the painting above the fireplace. The lynx stared out at her. Watcher of all her secrets.

A breeze from the chimney stirred her dress and swirled through her hair. More of it had come free from its pins, of course. She could feel tendrils rippling against her throat. The house was as cold and drafty as ever too, it seemed.

Everything felt frozen in time. Breathless. Waiting.

Marc shuffled his feet behind her. The desk shifted as he partially sat on it.

"After my mum left, my dad just sort of . . . drifted away too." She turned back to Marc. The candles flickered on the desk, dancing golden light across his face. "It was like all the light went out of him. I mean, he was there and kept a roof over our heads. But I'm not sure how much he cared—"

"Oh, Kit. Of course he cared."

She took a deep breath. "Maybe. I don't know. He felt distant and . . . apathetic. All the warmth of the man from my childhood just evaporated. *Poof.* Gone. Daniel was all I had left."

"It's why you hold on to him."

"Yes. As much as I can. Though Daniel is slippery at the best of times." She massaged the back of her neck with one hand, trying to relieve the aching tension coiling around her head.

Darkness settled in the room like a weight. Heavy. Lulling.

"It's why I collect friends," Kit said, hesitantly, still rubbing her neck. It was a truth about herself she had never really admitted to anyone else. "When the people who should love you the most—mother, father, brother—just don't, that's what you do. You prove that you *are* lovable by gathering as many non-family people as you can. And then when you have collected an absurd number of real life friends, you move online, create a funny persona and start collecting even more. I know, I know" —she waved her free hand dismissively— "so much has been said about online communities being no substitute for real ones. That they're fantasy, blah, blah. But I've been involved in them for so long now . . . I just can't see it that way. When my dad died last year, there was such an outpouring of love. So many emails and posted condolences . . . it meant a lot to me. It felt like caring and support and . . . community."

Marc didn't reply. Simply watched her. Eyes quiet with understanding.

Kit continued, "Maybe I'm deluding myself. Who knows? Perhaps my family life broke something irreparable inside." She started pacing, one hand still on her neck. Each step slowly dredging up deeper . . . more intimate thoughts. Things she rarely admitted, even to herself. "But . . . being so visible online . . . it changes you. I don't think I really anticipated that. The online stuff can be super ugly. Haters *are* gonna hate—"

"Gotta shake it off." Marc gave her a small smile.

Kit laughed. Startled. She paused, mid-step. "You know, it's a good thing your dorkiness is sort of endearing." She resumed her pacing. "With the online stuff, you have to develop a thick skin, or you'll end up rocking in a corner popping Xanax like candy. But all the negativity has a silver-lining. It forces you to look deep within yourself and examine who *you* are and what *you* want. To find that solid center of *self* that nothing else can touch—"

"So that's where it comes from then."

Kit stopped walking and cocked her head, not sure she understood.

"Your confidence." Marc waved a hand toward her. "I've been wondering what created it. A person doesn't become as self-assured as you are without some opposition. Something burnished and buffed you. Polished you gleaming bright."

Her breath caught.

What an incredibly . . . *lovely* thing to say.

"Thank you." Her voice barely above a whisper.

He shifted back on the desk, as if he had said too much. She studied him in his coat and cravat. More rumpled after his fights earlier in the day, but somehow more appealing. Hair carelessly mussed, stubble darkening his jaw. The man who never took himself or life too seriously. A complete rogue. A completely *lovable* rogue.

And, yet . . . a kind, good man too. Loyal and fair. Those broad shoulders which had supported so much over the years, caring for his mother and sister, moving past the pain of abandonment. A gentleman underneath the wit and banter.

So now what are you going to do? Virtuous Angel murmured.

Wicked Angel offered up a veritable banquet of images as suggestions. Most of which involved kissing and other stuff.

Shoving both thoughts aside, Kit crossed the room, leaning back into the desk next to him. Still trying to massage some of the stiffness out of her neck.

"Here," he said. "Allow me."

Without waiting for her reply, he reached out a hand and pulled a hairpin from her head, casually setting it on the desk behind them.

"Your hair. It doesn't like being caged." He emphasized this point by removing the remaining five pins, sending her long hair tumbling across her shoulders and down her back. "And I think all that happened today is threatening to give you a headache."

Marc threaded his fingers into her hair, clasping her head. Gently massaging her scalp, sending a zing down her spine. Instantly releasing tension.

Kit sighed and relaxed her head into his hands. Eyes fluttering closed.

Heavens but that felt good. *That* was what she needed. She resisted the urge to purr.

After several minutes of muscle-melting massage, Marc pulled his fingers through her hair, watching it cascade.

"So beautiful," he murmured. "Like molten honey."

Kit gave him a smug, all-too-knowing smile.

If nothing else, she *did* have nice hair. Thick and wavy. Her single vanity. More than one boyfriend had fallen in love with her based on hair alone.

"What about you?" She couldn't resist asking. "What has honed you?"

He jerked his eyes to her face, dropping his hands, obviously startled by the question.

"Besides sarcastic online reviews?" he countered, locking eyes with her. Lifted his eyebrows.

Kit nudged him in the shoulder. "I thought you were going to forgive me."

He shrugged. "Well, I plan on it. But I believe I was promised an amazing make-up kiss."

He stood, angling his head toward her. Flicked a look at her mouth. "Though so far, my evening has been decidedly kiss-less, so . . ."

He left the words hanging in the room and strolled to the fireplace, studying the lynx painting with hands clasped behind his back. All nonchalant-like.

Ah.

So *that's* how he intended to play.

"Well, practically *begging* for a kiss certainly takes all the fun out of it," she said.

He stilled and then so very, very slowly turned back to her. Raised a decidedly cocky brow.

"Surely not *all* the fun." His voice held a taunting edge.

Surprised, Kit felt heat wash her face.

You are not going to let that slide, are you? Wicked Angel asked.

Not a chance.

Matching his challenging raised eyebrow with one of her own, Kit leisurely crossed the few steps to the fireplace, holding his gaze the entire time. Noting with satisfaction the slight flare of his eyes.

She stopped in front of him with a saucy toss of her head. Grasped a fistful of his waistcoat with one hand. Pulled him toward her, intent on teaching him a lesson.

She caught a flash of his smile before his mouth captured hers.

Hot and searing. Needing.

She gave as good as he did. He had been promised an amazing make-up kiss after all.

Locked in his embrace, time froze. Everything narrowed down to just *them*. To just this moment.

The taste of his mouth, the feel of his hands winding into her hair, the rapid pulse of his heart under her hands.

"Kit," he murmured her name between kisses.

He was electric. Magnetic.

She had thought to school him, but he turned the tables on her.

Twining her deeper and deeper under his spell. Rapidly losing the ability to even think of a life without him.

But on the heels of that thought came a reminder.

You don't have to live a life without him. You are creatures of the same world.

The thought flitted through her mind with such force that Kit gasped, pulling abruptly away.

Eyes wide and chest heaving, she lifted a hand to touch his cheek.

Gently. Reverently. As if he were a treasured gift.

Marc's expression surely mirrored her own.

Still breathing heavily, he swiped his thumb along her kiss-stung bottom lip, shaking his head. Almost in disbelief.

"How can kissing you get *better* each time?" he asked, voice laced with wonder.

Kit swallowed. And then managed a tentative smile. "Am I forgiven?"

Marc grinned, sweet and sultry. "I suppose. Though I might need just a *little* more encouragement to soothe my ravaged pride."

He chuckled and bent his head, claiming another languid kiss.

After a moment, Kit breathed in contentment and pulled back, nuzzling her nose into his throat, twining her fingers into his soft, curly hair.

Did she want to say anything about pursuing a relationship?

Should she say anything?

Okay, so she knew the answer to *that*. She probably shouldn't. Men could be so easily weirded out.

But . . . she wanted to know where they stood. And Marc was so much more than just a guy she was kissing.

He was a friend. A kindred spirit. And if she couldn't confide in him . . .

"Uhm, so about all that 'this could never happen' stuff . . ." she said, pulling back to look him in the eye.

"What about it?" He kissed the tip of her nose.

"Well . . . all my reasons became non-issues about the time we started swapping *Princess Bride* quotes."

"Mmmmm . . ." He moved to nuzzle her cheek.

"So from my perspective, this uh . . . could actually happen."

Marc didn't say anything for a few moments, content to just softly kiss her cheek and then her forehead.

Dragging out the moment.

"You're not saying anything." Kit's heart pounded.

How was he feeling? What would he say?

"Marc?"

Silence and then, "Just making you squirm."

He chuckled, pulling back.

"Impossible man." She batted his shoulder.

He laughed harder. "Well, if you find you need some make-up kisses, just let me know. I would be more than happy to—"

"Marc—" Her voice warning.

"Yes?"

"Please be serious."

Still smiling, he shrugged. "Fine. I agree. My reasons evaporated too. So maybe this—" Here he planted a soft, lingering kiss on her mouth. "— could actually happen. I say we sort through our current mess and then see where *this*—" *Kiss.* "—leads."

He tugged her all the way into him. Snugging her almost possessively against his body.

Kit reveled in being held by him. All her senses slowed, focusing on the steady thrum of his heartbeat, the press of his cheek against hers. The sway of his chest, almost as if he were rocking her. He shifted, capturing her right hand with his left.

"Dance with me." His words a whorl of air around her ear.

He began to softly sing 'Unchained Melody' by the Righteous Brothers, slow dancing her around the room, her hand tucked up against his chest. Voice low and rumbly in her ear and not too terribly out-of-tune.

She could feel the rhythmic thump, thump of his heart as they moved in lazy circles. Their breathing syncing until Kit wasn't sure where she ended and he began.

It took several minutes for Kit to realize he moved like someone who actually knew a thing or two about ballroom dancing. Surprised, she pulled back with a quizzical look.

"Don't think you've discovered all my secrets, Miss Ashton." He emphasized the statement with a quick foxtrot spin and signature slow-burn smile.

"I should hope not, Mr. Wilde."

"My sister." He finally answered her unspoken question. "I buried myself in martial arts, while Emme focused on ballroom dance. She needed a partner more than once. You?"

Kit shrugged. "Some. I went through a ballroom phase when I was sixteen."

"Excellent."

Instantly, he switched to singing a fast-version of 'The Way You Make Me Feel,' by Michael Jackson, twirling Kit out and around in several minutes of rock-step, triple-step swing dancing.

He was fast on his feet making his singing breathless, but his hands were quick and sure, guiding her through the moves and around the desk and chairs in the room. Her long skirts and cloak made the steps more difficult, tangling her legs.

Kit stumbled once. And then twice. The third time, Marc caught her before she could hit the floor, wrapping both arms around her, dragging her with him into the chair to the left of the fireplace. Holding her tight on his lap.

Out of breath and laughing, they clung to each other. Marc shifted back in the chair, arms locked tight around her waist.

"We need to practice your swinging more," he gasped into her ear.

"It's the long skirt, I swear." Kit chuckled and wound her arms around his neck. A rumbling laugh vibrating in his chest. His strong arms around her.

No one could ever be better than this, Virtuous Angel noted. *No one.*

Wicked Angel just sighed.

Kit cuddled into him. "This is so perfect, Marc. Tomorrow we'll wake up, load Daniel into the gig with us and head back to Haldon Manor. With Daniel, the portal should let us return. We can put all of this behind us."

Kit saw it all so clearly in her mind's eye. She and Marc seated in this very study in 2014, laughing together. Daniel popping his head in to say he was headed out for work. Kit blowing him a kiss and promising to leave some dinner out for him. Turning back to Marc, smiling wickedly at her . . . and then, truth be told, her imagination ran a little wild . . . or *Wilde*, as the case may be.

Both her shoulder angels groaned at the bad pun.

She was so busy picturing their perfect future life together, she nearly missed Marc's stiffening in her arms.

"What will you do if Daniel refuses to return home?" Marc's voice broke through. He sat back, looking her in the eye.

Reality crashed around her with an intensity that was momentarily suffocating.

"He has to come home with me. There is *no* other option." Kit instantly tensed and started to push out of his lap.

Marc tightened his arms around her, holding her firm. "Have you considered what Daniel wants?"

Kit snorted. "Daniel has never *known* what he wants. He just wanders from thing to thing—"

"But what if this *is* his thing. What if this is the life destined for him?"

The fear Kit had been tamping down all evening reared its head.

Noooo, all of her howled.

All the heat in the room suddenly evaporated, leaving Kit cold and almost shaking. She wrapped her elbows around herself. Marc rubbed his hands along her arms, warming her.

"He is my *brother*, Marc."

"I understand that, Kit." Marc's eyes were warm. Gentle. As if he were trying not to break her heart, but fearing he probably would.

"I will not just *let* Daniel go." She pushed away and scrambled out of his lap. Glaring down at him.

"But he is entitled to live the life he chooses—"

"I can't abandon him, Marc. It's not who I am." She turned away and practically stomped over to the desk "I don't give up on those I love."

A pause.

"I am not suggesting you give up on him, Kit. I am merely pointing out that Daniel's vision of his future may not coincide with your own."

She whirled on Marc, still sitting in the chair, legs extended, arms crossed. The candles dancing shadows across his face.

"He is the *only* family I have left, Marc. The. Only. Family." She punctuated each word with a jab of her finger. "Do you give up on your family? Would you stop fighting for your sister?"

He stared at her for a moment and then looked away. Shrugged.

"If it was what Emme deeply wanted, then yes," he said into the shadows, shoulders shifting. "I would have the courage to set her free."

Silence hung in the room. Tense and laden.

Kit clamped her jaw. Tight. "Well . . . then. That's where you and I are different. I won't give up. Daniel is all I have."

Chapter 20

THE GREAT MEDIEVAL HALL
WHITMOOR HOUSE
MARCH 2, 1814

D awn filtered through the shuttered windows in tight beams, turning the great hall into striped bands of floating dust.

Marc sat calmly in a chair facing the small staircase which led to the servant's door.

After their tense conversation the night before, he and Kit had opted to sleep in the large medieval hall for the night. With the exception of the bedroom Daniel occupied, all the other bedrooms were in a sorry state. And though the old keep was drafty, it had several large settees draped in heavy holland covers which provided enough warmth. Allowing Marc to be close to Kit but still separate. She didn't seem in the mood to cuddle.

Kit had gone to talk with Daniel before going to sleep. Their angry voices rang down the stone staircase, forcing Marc to overhear their conversation whether he wanted to or not.

"Just stop all this nonsense. You have to come home." That was Kit. Impassioned. Upset.

"Kit, I know you want me to, but I have things I need to finish here. There is a war on—"

"This isn't *our* war! We both already know how this war ends, and I have every expectation it will end the same whether you're here or not. Probably more likely to end the same if you leave now, quite frankly—"

"You're not listening to me. You *never* listen to me. Just for once, Kit, please trust me."

"Daniel, I do trust you—"

"No, you don't! You're basically standing here, telling me I should abandon everything and go back. Telling me I don't know what I want—"

"What could possibly hold you here? Why do you want to stay here, Daniel?"

"It's hard to explain, Kit. You know I've never felt like I fit in—"

"And you think you will fit in *here*?!"

"Like I said, I left you a letter—"

"A letter?! I never got your letter. I was gone, remember? Get with reality, Daniel. This isn't our world!"

"If you would just try to understand—"

"Understand?! You simply need to drop all these stupid ideas—"

"My dreams and hopes are not stupid, Kit!" Daniel was shouting now too.

"Well, if they stop you from coming home and behaving like a *grownup*, then I suppose they are stupid—"

"I've had enough of this conversation. You can leave now. We'll never see eye-to-eye on this!"

"Fine! Be like that!"

A door slammed, echoing throughout the house.

Kit said nothing about the conversation when she returned to the hall. Though the tense line of her mouth expressed it clearly.

Marc ached for her. He understood all too well why she was fighting to keep Daniel in her life. But he also clearly saw the futility of it.

Daniel was his own man.

He glanced over at her, asleep on a settee. Facing toward him, hands tucked under her cheek as a pillow, the holland cloth pulled over her for more warmth.

She looked adorable. Relaxed. Soft snores escaping.

For his part, Marc had tried to sleep. But it wouldn't come. His mind was on overload. Flooded with images and thoughts and . . . feelings.

He had been pushing back his emotions for Kit for so long, convinced nothing could ever happen.

And now . . .

Now he faced the reality that something could, and quite frankly *was*, happening. They could be together in 2014. Her laughter and spunk and spirit—the sheer vivacity of her soul—could have a more permanent place in his life. He meant what he said about wanting to pursue a relationship with her once they returned to the twenty-first century.

He had expected to feel somewhat panicked at the thought. But instead, he felt only relief. Wave after wave of it. A deep sense of peace.

It felt almost too big to even define, to put into words.

Kit belonged with him. Beside him.

Together, they would work through this whole Daniel mess.

But for now, he waited. Sitting in his chair at the top of the stairs to the servant's entrance. He had a hunch.

Which was confirmed when Daniel crept into the room, crossing toward him. Dressed for travel in a long greatcoat, carrying a rucksack in one hand and the papers stolen from Linwood in the other.

Daniel froze when he saw Marc sitting in the chair and cocked a challenging eyebrow. He strode over and handed Marc the papers stolen from Kinningsley. Marc took the papers and then quietly followed Daniel out the door.

The cold February air froze his breath. Frost crunched under his feet as they walked across the overgrown driveway.

Daniel paused before reaching the lane, turning back to Marc.

"Will you tell her?" Daniel asked without any preamble.

"That you're never returning to 2014?"

"Yes."

"I already have. She doesn't believe me. She thinks she can change your mind."

The lingering memory of Kit and Daniel's tense exchange from the night before rushed through Marc's head.

"She cannot." Daniel snorted softly and then looked longingly up the lane. "I belong here."

Marc nodded, studying the man before him.

It was hard to detect the twenty-first century man in Daniel. He wore his clothes like a second skin, as if he had been born to them. Even his speech fit into nineteenth century patterns most of the time.

Silence stretched between them. A bird *tweet-tweet-tweeted* somewhere in the bare tree branches up the lane.

Daniel kicked gravel with his foot, head down, drawing words out like hesitant treasures.

"It's like . . . my entire life, I've been a misfit. Nothing ever feeling . . . right. I've spent so many years wanting to crawl out of my own skin, feeling like I was broken and wrong. Nothing would ever be whole. And then I come here and . . . *whoosh.*"

Daniel let out a surprised laugh. He lifted his eyes to Marc's, gleaming and bright. The eyes of a man astonished. "I am suddenly . . . *me.* Awakened. I can see myself here. Living, working . . . for the rest of my life. Like everything before was just a bad dream but *this* . . . this is the reality always meant for me." He punctuated his words with an expansive swing of his arms.

Marc swallowed. Daniel's words hit him hard.

Because there they were. The words he had been searching for to describe how he felt about Kit. Expressed to perfection.

I am suddenly . . . awakened. Like everything before was just a dream but this . . . this is the reality always meant for me.

Being with Kit.

Daniel met his eyes, saw the dawning gleam there.

"Do you know what I mean, Marc?" Daniel nearly whispered the words. And then shook his head, looking out over the house and undulating fields with an almost awestruck expression.

Marc nodded. He did indeed.

But if Kit wanted to be part of Daniel's life, she needed to remain in 1814. That was her only option. Stay, abandon her twenty-first century life and retain her brother. Or return to 2014, leaving Daniel in the past.

Where did that leave Marc?

Panic buzzed at the back of his head. Daniel had mentioned this man—Garvis, was it? Who had been (would be?) employed by a man who occasionally went by the name Marc Wilde.

Marc swallowed. His future was, well . . . in the future. He couldn't stay here in 1814. He didn't *want* to stay here—

But a life without Kit . . .

Marc kicked the thoughts away. There would be no happy solution here. Somewhere there would be heartache.

"She won't ever let you go." Marc nodded his head back toward the house. Toward Kit.

"I know."

"She loves you too much."

"She is fierce in her love. She is a good person. A better sister than I ever deserved."

"*That* is truth." Marc paused. And then, taking a deep breath, asked the question he dreaded. "If she decided to stay here with you, would you let her?"

Something flared in Daniel's eyes, as if he found the thought . . . tantalizing.

And then he shook his head. "I would welcome her, but this isn't the life for her. She is too wrapped up in that website of hers and all her friends. She is not an old-fashioned sort of woman. To tie herself here . . . it would chafe, I think. But that is her decision to make. She would always have a place with me, no matter what. I love her, you see. Despite everything, I love her more than anyone."

"Just not more than yourself."

Daniel gave a rueful smile. "*Should* I love her more than myself?"

That was a good question. Should another's opinions and wants override your own?

Marc's silence was his answer.

"Do *you* love her?" Daniel asked.

Marc reared back. Blinked. The question caught him off guard.

He liked Kit. He liked the thought of her. He liked the fit of her in his life, in his thoughts. Oh, who was he kidding, in his arms too.

Kit was just so unlike any other woman he had ever met. So much . . . more.

She made him feel whole, complete. At home. Like every best friend he had ever had wrapped up into one package. Like, without her beside him, life sort of lost its meaning.

Was that real love? True romantic love?

All these emotions were so new to him. It was hard to say.

Daniel stood patiently, an amused look on his face.

"I don't *not* love her," Marc finally said.

Daniel clapped him on the shoulder, wide grin stretching.

"I'll take that. Be kind to her. Be loyal. She needs someone who puts her first."

Marc nodded. And then reached into his pocket and pulled out the two items he had prepared for this moment. He shoved them into Daniel's hands.

"Here. She would want you to at least have these things."

Daniel glanced down at the taser and leather purse filled with coins.

"I cannot take your money—"

"It's not mine. It was a loan, of sorts."

"Well, in that case—" Daniel hefted the purse and then pocketed it.

Marc gestured toward the taser. "You are taking a terrible risk giving those papers to the spy."

Daniel examined the taser. "Probably. But I need seed money if I'm going to make a go of a life here. And all the hard work is already done. Just have to hand over the goods tomorrow night. Thank you for this." He tucked the taser into his coat.

"Would you be willing to do one thing for me?"

"Anything." Daniel nodded, looking Marc intently in the eye.

"Linwood isn't going to let this whole spy thing go until he has someone behind bars . . . or strung up by their neck, which I suppose is the more likely scenario. Would you mind seeing what you can find out for us?"

"You mean, uncover the identity of the spy I've been working with?"

"Exactly."

"It might be dangerous."

"Yes. I expect it will. But it is something that needs to be done. For King and Country . . . for Kit."

A gleam flared in Daniel's eye. And then a wry grin tugged at his lips. "My sister would kill you if she knew you were suggesting I put myself in harm's way."

"Probably."

Daniel chuckled, delighted. "Good thing she can't stop me. I'm on the case. Tell her it was my idea. And, hey, maybe I will come out the hero this time. I'm never the hero. It would be nice for a change."

"Deal."

Marc held out his hand. Daniel shook it with a firm grip.

"I will send you word at Haldon Manor regardless of what happens. Also, I want to let Kit know where I am, if she decides to join me. I am serious about my offer. It would be wonderful to have her here with me."

Marc ignored the sharp pain lanced through his lungs, catching his breath. If Kit stayed . . .

"Perfect." He managed to get out. "We'll wait to hear from you then. Be careful."

"Care for her. Give her my love. And I apologize in advance for the scene you will endure when she wakes and realizes I am gone."

With a soft smile, Marc clapped his shoulder. Daniel returned the gesture, his face alight with hope and promise of his future.

And then, with a jaunty tip of his hat, Daniel strode up the lane into the rising sun.

Marc was sitting in the same chair when Kit woke up, stretching from underneath the holland cover. The sun had risen in earnest, sending beams of winter light into the room. Dust still hung in the air.

Kit saw him and smiled. Marc hated being the one to knock the happiness off her face.

She sat up, looking around. Looking for someone other than him.

A tiny surge of jealousy threaded through him at the thought. At least, he thought it was jealousy. It wasn't an emotion he had felt much in regards to women.

Deep breath. It didn't matter. There were more important things to discuss.

He caught her eye in the filtered light. Held it.

"Good morning, beautiful. Remember that I told you as soon as I could. I abhor secrets just as much as you." He said it lowly, gravely. Letting the sound linger in the room. "Daniel is gone."

As if gravitas alone could stem the imminent explosion.

Kit was on her feet in an instant, darting panicked looks around the large room.

"Daniel," she called. Took a few steps over to the stairs leading into the family wing. "Daniel!"

As if the sheer force of her will could bring her brother back.

Marc stood, setting weary hands on his hips. "He's gone, Kit."

"How do you know?" Kit peered up the staircase without turning around. "Sometimes he just hides and pretends to be gone. There was this one time when—"

"I watched him leave." How that admission cost him.

She whirled, hair flying.

Marc held her gaze. Saw the moment when realization set in. When she understood what he *hadn't* done.

"You let him . . . go?" An entire universe of heartbreak in that sentence. "But . . . but *why?* We just found him. I barely had time to say hello—"

Her voice broke. Her anguish cutting. Sharp. Keen.

She wandered toward him, eyes wide and stunned. Impossibly lovely with her hair sleepy and tumbling down her back. Honey eyes filling with tears she bravely bit back with a trembling lip.

What justification could he offer?

"He's a grown man, Kit." Marc gestured helplessly as she drew near. "He can make his own decisions—"

Probably not his best choice of words. Kit's eyes widened further and then narrowed. Sorrow instantly morphing into anger.

None of which was directed at the man who actually *deserved* her anger. Though Marc was smart enough to keep that thought to himself.

"How dare you?!" She shoved him. Both hands firmly on his chest and pushed. "How dare you just watch him walk away!" *Push.* "How dare you not wake me!" *Push.* "You don't get to make these decisions for me. For Daniel."

Her tears spilled over. Hot. Angry.

She glared at him, chest heaving. She tried to shove him again, but Marc snagged her hands in his. Pulling her up against him.

"What would you have had me do, Kit?" He said it kindly, gently. "Beat him into a bloody pulp so he couldn't leave?"

She pulled on her hands. "If necessary." Said from between clenched teeth.

"You don't mean that." Marc released her. She stumbled back. He spread his hands wide. "Call it honor. I don't beat men for doing what they feel they must."

"Even for me?"

The question hung there.

There was *no* good answer to that.

"Kit, you are not your brother's savior. You can't bend him to your will. Change him. Force him to be that which he is not. All you can do is love and accept him as he is. Set him free to be himself."

She backed away as Marc spoke, shaking her head.

"No," she whispered. "No, it's not a matter of setting him *free*. As I keep saying, it's retaining that one last fragment of my family. That one person who matters more than any other. How could you suggest that I *ever* give up on him?"

"I am not suggesting you give him up, Kit." Marc paused. Scrubbed a hand through his hair. "I am merely pointing out that Daniel has chosen his path."

She jutted out her chin mutinously. Stubbornly.

"Kit, if you want your brother in your life, you might have to reconcile yourself to living permanently in 1814. I can't see a single reason why Daniel would return to 2014. You yourself said he was lost in the twenty-first century. But in this time period, he seems grounded and driven. He likes life here."

Kit deflated. A tear escaped, leaving a ragged trail down her cheek.

"I can't leave him, Marc. I just *can't*."

The anguish in her voice cut him. Slicing deep. Her swimming eyes pleaded for understanding.

Marc reached out, snagging her hand and tugging her to him. Sliding a hand into the silky mass of her hair and bringing her head snug against his cheek. She sagged against him, arms wrapping around his shoulders, sniffling into his neck.

"Hush, beautiful. Hush," he murmured, stroking her back. Soothing. Every slide of his hands communicating his concern. His care.

You are cherished.

You are wanted.

You are needed.

He kissed the side of her head. Tightened his arms around her.

"You can do anything you set your mind to, Kit. If you decide to carve a life for yourself here, you will. It's that simple. You will adapt. It seems you always have."

She threaded her hands into his hair, hugging him in return.

"And Daniel?" she whispered.

"Let's return these schematics to Linwood. Daniel will keep his appointment with the spies and turn over the fakes. He promised he would send word after his encounter, telling you of his location, if you care to join him. In the meantime, you need to decide where you want your own future to be."

Marc swallowed back a lump in his throat as he said those words.

Would *he* give up Emme and James and his mother and his entire life in 2014 to stay here with Kit?

What an unthinkable decision.

He cared for Kit . . . but did he care enough to abandon everything else? That journal Daniel had found about Garvis. Was Marc the one who had leaked the information about the portal? And did that mean he decided to stay in the past after all?

Fate had brought him to this point, but Marc refused to allow his future to be pre-destined. He still had choice. He desperately wanted to be with Kit, but to lose everything else . . .

Would love be enough? Or would he come to regret his decision, resenting her in the process . . .

He swallowed again, mentally shaking his head.

But leaving Kit here with Daniel . . . returning to 2014 alone . . . *that* thought nearly tore him apart.

Both impossible scenarios.

But how could he ask her to do something he himself wasn't willing to do? Namely, leave an important piece of your heart in another time and place.

How could Fate bring them together, only to cruelly separate them again?

Despite a brief reprieve, the impasse between them loomed as large as ever.

Chapter 21

Kit angsted and fumed over her situation all the way back to Haldon Manor.

Angry at Daniel.

Angry at a mother who had left.

Angry at a father who had retreated and ignored her.

Angry at Marc who had let Daniel walk away.

And then angry because Marc had been all understanding and helpful about it.

Which just made her furious at herself.

Because only a truly awful person would be angry with someone for being helpful and kind.

Which pulled her back to being angry with Daniel for making her angry with Marc.

Starting the cycle all over again.

It was a vicious circle.

Daniel just needed to grow up and come home to the life and century into which he had been born.

That was it. Problem solved. End of discussion.

Except, apparently, Daniel wasn't going to do that.

You need to find peace, Virtuous Angel whispered. *This has possessed you for too long.*

Wicked Angel was more obnoxious. She hummed 'Let It Go' from *Frozen* for hours on end.

Neither of which improved Kit's mood.

They arrived back at Haldon Manor well after sunset, cold and battered from the long carriage ride. The house blazoned with light. A welcoming sight. Though really Kit just wanted her bed.

Well, that wasn't true. What she *really* wanted was a long hot shower, followed by some Indian takeaway and time in front of a television with a heated blanket, soft cotton pajamas and two sleeves of double-stuff oreos.

But *that* obviously wasn't going to happen.

And if she decided to stay in the past with Daniel, it would *never* happen. So . . .

As Marc steered the gig around the medieval walled garden and toward the stables, Kit sighed. The thought of getting up the next morning and chasing errands for Lady Ruby made her physically ill.

"Dash it, Marc! Where have you been?" A voice called out from the doorway of the walled garden.

Marc pulled up on the reins as Arthur stepped out of the shadows, walking quickly over to them.

"I heard you pull up the lane and slipped out before anyone else notices your return. Miss Ashton." Arthur coolly inclined his head in her direction. Condemnation evident in every line of his body. "You both owe me a detailed explanation as to why you stole my gig and absconded together. Such behavior hardly reflects well on either of you and is obviously grounds for Miss Ashton's dismissal."

Arthur rested a hand on the gig, glaring up expectantly at them both.

Kit suppressed a weary groan. When faced with serving Lady Ruby or being turned out into the cold night, she would obviously side with having a roof over her head. She doubted Marc or Daniel would let her starve, but the fact that neither man was from this century did limit how much they could help.

Mostly, she was just tired of playing all these nineteenth century societal games.

Marc tensed at her side, clearly having heard her soft sound of distress.

"Good evening to you too, Arthur. We are happy to be returned to your loving care in one piece. Thank you so much for your kind concern in asking after our welfare." Marc's tone was a masterpiece of sarcasm.

Arthur stiffened. "This is no time to be difficult. I have housed and cared for you as if you were my own brother. And this is how you repay me? Have you no thought for propriety?" Arthur stole a look at Kit, obviously trying to scold them without revealing too much. "It's well known you ran off together. Miss Ashton's reputation is in tatters, and I can hardly keep such a woman under my roof—"

"Stop, Arthur," Marc interrupted quietly, frustration evident in his tense voice. "Miss Ashton isn't going anywhere. Turns out, she's from 2014 too. Her brother, Daniel Ashton, is the blackmailer I've been seeking—the one who attacked me in Duir Cottage—

"What?!" Arthur's eyes went wide with shock.

"—Fortunately, Miss Ashton's brother was not actually attempting to blackmail me," Marc finished.

Arthur stared at her in stunned silence for a moment, trying to piece everything together.

"Is *anyone* the person they seem to be?" he finally asked faintly.

Marc chuckled. A grim, dark sound echoing in the night.

"That's a philosophical question for the ages, but not one I care to debate right now. Daniel helped us recover the items stolen from Kinningsley, and we are working to uncover the spy plot."

"Thank heavens! Linwood was terribly upset and rushed off right after it was found you two had left. Of course, Marianne and I and our house guests returned immediately home. I understand Linwood returned to Kinningsley yesterday evening a little worse for wear. I am not sure what transpired, but I know he will be pleased to hear what you have uncovered."

"Yes, I suppose he will. But, for now, we need a way to smooth this all over. Miss Ashton is actually the daughter of Lord Whitmoor in 2014 and is a respected, well-known woman. I refuse to watch someone of her stature reduced to serving Lady Ruby. She needs to be upgraded."

Kit's breath hitched at Marc's unwavering defense of her. He really was just the sweetest—

"Upgraded?" Arthur questioned, clearly unfamiliar with the term.

"Yes. She needs to have a more proper position within your household. Something more like a guest of honor than a servant. I'm sure it's what James would want."

Arthur's eyes narrowed, obviously not liking his older brother being used as a bargaining chip. Marc's bland expression clearly said he would not back down.

Silence hung.

"Arthur, we are tired and have had a long day. We have done much to help you and Linwood—"

"I do not see how it is possible to explain your behavior, Marc." Arthur's shoulders sank, conceding the argument. "It is well-known that you left together. Miss Ashton has no reputation—"

"I say, Arthur, is that you out here in the moonlight?" A voice called across the back terrace. A high-pitched, nasal voice.

All three of them instantly quieted. But it took Jedediah less than a minute to find them.

He strolled through the same door in the garden wall, taking in Kit and Marc still sitting in the gig. A footman followed closely at his heels, moving quickly to hold their horse.

Placing them all in a nice bind.

Biting back a few bitter words, Marc climbed out of the gig, reaching up a hand to assist Kit down. All under the censorious eyes of Arthur and Jedediah. Jedediah, in particular, watched Kit with almost predatory glee.

It was *not* a particularly good moment.

"Well, cousin," Jedediah said, turning to Arthur. "I cannot imagine you would allow people of such deplorable character to remain under your roof. I am sure they can find their way from here." He gestured into the frigid, dark night, his eyes gleaming in delight.

Ugh. He was *such* a jerk.

Arthur stood frozen, obviously torn between propriety and the sense of obligation he felt to both Kit and Marc.

Marc straightened his spine beside her, obviously not willing to go down without a fight.

"I would ask you to speak more carefully around my cousin, Mr. Knight." Marc fixed his gaze on Jedediah. "She has had a long day. While staying at Kinningsley, Miss Ashton and I realized she was the long lost daughter of my mother's sister. Our family has been looking for her for years. I cannot express our great joy in having her brought back to us." He raised Kit's gloved hand in his, bestowing a light kiss on her knuckles. "I must apologize for our abrupt departure from Kinningsley. We had urgent family business to attend to."

Arthur raised his eyebrows, impressed with Marc's story. It *was* almost plausible.

Jedediah, however, looked decidedly skeptical.

"Hogwash, Lord Vader!" Jedediah scoffed. "As if anyone would believe such a Banbury tale. Everyone has seen how you have been panting after Miss Ashton, and now we are to accept that you are *cousins*—"

"Lord Vader! I am so delighted to discover you and Miss Ashton have returned without harm." Marianne rushed past Jedediah, stopping beside Kit to place a concerned hand on her arm.

Was *everyone* outside tonight?

"Did I just overhear Lord Vader saying that you are, in actuality, cousins?" Marianne asked.

"Yes, Mrs. Knight," Kit managed to reply. "It has been a most unexpected pair of days—"

"How marvelous! Why that just explains everything does it not?" Marianne exclaimed, looping her arm through Kit's. "Come inside, all of you. 'Tis far too cold to stand around outside chatting. Let us sit in front of a warm fire, and you can recount your tale."

"But . . ." Jedediah spluttered, "surely the propriety of this situation—"

"Enough, Jedediah." Marianne turned to him, steel in her voice. "Miss Ashton has been a model of virtue and kindness to all of us. I will not stand here and listen to you impugn her reputation. If Lord Vader says she is his cousin, then she is. And as his cousin, there is no dishonor in their traveling together. I will hear no more disagreement on the subject. Is that understood?"

For the first time, Kit clearly saw the resemblance to the viscount in petite Marianne Linwood Knight. Head held high. Eyes snapping. When needed, Marianne could be as haughty and intractable as her brother.

Arthur nodded, an appreciative smile tugging his lips. "Well said, my dear. Now, let us get out of this cold."

He clapped Marc's shoulder and led the way indoors.

And that was that.

HALDON MANOR
MARCH 3 THRU MARCH 9, 1814

Kit welcomed the 'upgrade' from paid companion to honored guest. Even better, the change came with Fanny as her maid, more of Georgiana's altered clothing and hot baths.

Ah. Hot baths. *Such* a luxury.

The next morning, she and Marc returned the papers to Linwood, who through a swollen lip and black eye, grudgingly thanked them for their efforts. Marc promised to let him know if they received any more information from Daniel . . . er . . . their 'source.'

And then, suddenly, there wasn't much else to do. Except wait for word from Daniel.

No more fetching shawls and plating food for Ruby, thank goodness. Though the old lady had *not* been pleased to lose her paid companion. Fortunately, a young woman from Marfield had been found on short notice to help.

Kit's days were her own, so she spent them with Marc. All the while, falling deeper and deeper.

A week passed and still no word from Daniel.

All of her angst morphed into anxiousness. Kit hated just sitting and waiting. She wanted to be out and doing. Searching for Daniel.

His promise to Marc lingered in her head. He was going to send word of his location. She could remain permanently in the nineteenth century with Daniel. All she had to do was join him.

The big question lingered. If Kit decided to stay, would Marc stay with her?

For his part, Marc refused to discuss *that*. Every time she brought it up, he skillfully changed the topic. He obviously didn't want to confront the issue one way or another.

When she finally pressed him, he insisted he was Switzerland. Neutral territory. He wasn't going to make a decision that might sway her one way or another.

His face unreadable. Intractable.

A look she had seen too many times on the faces of men she loved.

Her father whenever she dared speak of her mother. Daniel as she pleaded with him, again, to find a path for himself.

But Daniel has found a path, Virtuous Angel muttered. *You just don't like the path he chose.*

True that, Wicked Angel agreed.

Stupid, dumb shoulder angels. She shrugged them off. Who needed them anyway?

So instead of pressing the issue, she and Marc spent the week discussing their twenty-first century lives.

Her ideas for expanding FauxPause. His plans for future movie projects.

The places they had traveled to, the places they still wanted to go. Common likes (beaches, fast cars and bacon), common dislikes (crowded cities, slow drivers and cilantro) and things they agreed to disagree on (pop versus rap, soccer versus football).

They met early one morning in the walled garden in the clothing they had been wearing when they arrived. Up to this point, Kit had enjoyed the sight of Marc in a full nineteenth century gentleman's getup.

But Marc in designer jeans, tight t-shirt and a leather jacket . . . positively swoon-inducing. It had taken her almost a full minute to start breathing again. Talk about broad shoulders . . .

Granted, he had been equally appreciative of her skinny jeans, green silk shirt, black puffer jacket and knee-high black leather boots. If staring for an awkwardly long time with heated eyes qualified as *appreciative*.

His exact words had been, "Your figure is utterly wasted on those stupid Empire-waist dresses."

And then he had languidly tugged her to him, kissing her long and hard just to emphasize his point.

Each day wedged another chink into her do-not-abandon-Daniel armor.

She felt so utterly trapped between the two men. Waiting for word from her brother. Wondering what Marc planned to do. Trying to decide where she wanted to be. The tension of simple waiting wore on both of them.

So much so, that Kit insisted Marc go hunting with Arthur and Jedediah one afternoon. Giving Kit a break and a chance to spend time with Marianne and tiny Isabel in the drawing room.

Baby Isabel was darling, small and petite with her mother's dark hair. Obviously smitten with her daughter, Marianne loved nothing more than watching others fawn over the baby too. Though barely three months old, Isabel could already hold up her head and reach for Kit's fingers. She smiled and cooed at everyone, eager to talk.

Kit had very little experience with infants, having only held friends' babies a handful of times over the years, but cradling Isabel in her arms caused a curious pang deep in her chest.

Probably just her biological clock ticking—a not-so-subtle reminder she had recently turned thirty.

Though Kit knew it was more than that. She couldn't stop herself from imagining holding a similar baby—a boy possibly—with dark curling hair, green eyes and a mischievous smile. Because why not? It was her fantasy.

The image lanced through her heart. The longing welled painfully, blurring her vision.

She could almost smell that baby. Could feel Marc's arms around her, loving her and their child. She could see them all together, riding in a car, playing at the beach, laughing at a playground. The dream ached.

But . . . in the middle of her daydream, the child shifted, becoming a different little boy. One whose hair wasn't quite as dark, whose eyes were more blue than green.

She saw that same boy sitting in a hallway, watching their mother walk out the door. Never to look back.

That's when the tears actually fell.

She couldn't have a twenty-first century future with Marc without leaving Daniel behind.

And how could she *ever* abandon Daniel the way their mother had?

Swallowing hard, Kit calmly passed Isabel back to Marianne, who quietly handed her a handkerchief in return.

Marianne Knight truly had a kind heart.

Kit expected to remain a "watering pot," as Marianne fondly called her, but Linwood's arrival soon after stemmed that.

His black eye had settled into an eye-catching shade of yellow-green. Watching the stiff viscount tentatively hold his cooing niece as if the baby offended him by being, well . . . a baby, made up for the rest of the day's woes.

It was anyone's guess as to why Linwood visited so often. He probably just wanted to keep a closer eye on Marc. He usually sat silently, casting judgmental looks and stiffly interacting with tiny Isabel. Making everything awkwardly uncomfortable.

Not exactly Kit's idea of a relaxing afternoon.

But until she heard from Daniel, Kit wasn't sure she could relax anyway.

The next day, Kit and Marc were tucked away in the library. Linwood had come to call again, and neither she nor Marc wanted to deal with the viscount. So they were essentially hiding, pretending not to have been notified of his arrival.

The morning light filtered through the paned windows. They were nestled into the window seat, facing each other, her feet drawn under her. Marc's legs stretched out beside her.

"What will you do?" he asked.

She understood what he meant. Was she going to stay with Daniel?

Finally broaching the topic himself, despite being 'neutral territory.'

"I don't know." It was the truthful answer.

He said nothing. Just turned his head and stared out the window. The sun shone weakly through the clouds, dappling light across his face.

"Would you stay?" she asked.

He swallowed and continued staring out the window.

And then finally, after a nearly painful silence, turned back to her.

Eyes sad . . . lost.

"No."

It was little more than a whisper. More the motion of his mouth than any sound.

But she felt it like a hammer to her chest. Hard. Jarring.

She was instantly breathless. Wanting to plead with him. Beg. Find a way.

"Even . . . even with the journal from this Garvis fellow and his association with a man named W? The journal could be a sign you're supposed to stay . . ."

Marc's entire body slumped, sagging beneath the weight of her words. He swallowed. Shook his head.

"Kit . . . the portal let us through . . . Fate brought us together." He fixed her with that same haunted look. "But we both still have free will . . . I care so deeply for you, but . . . though it would be hard, returning to your life in 2014 without your brother would not force you to rebuild everything. But with this—" He gestured toward her, indicating the question she had just asked. "—I would give up not only my family—my sister, my mother, aunts, uncles, cousins, friends—but also my livelihood. My passions, my interests. I would give up my entire world. Start over with nothing."

Something hot and tight lodged in Kit's chest.

"But you would have . . . *me*," she whispered, licking a tear from her lip.

"Oh . . . *Kit*." His eyes met hers, emotions flickering through them.

Pain, sorrow, regret. And then the last one . . . resignation.

She *hated* resignation.

The air between them stretched taut. Marc opened his mouth, intent on continuing the conversation—

Someone cleared their throat. Loudly.

They both swiveled to see a footman standing in the doorway with a silver salver.

"This just arrived for you, Lord Vader." The man extended the tray where a small letter lay folded.

Shooting Kit a quick glance, Marc stood and took the letter from the tray. The footman bowed and exited.

Kit was instantly at his side, hands trembling as Marc opened the note. He tilted the paper, allowing her to read with him:

> *Luke Skywalker belongs to the Dark Side. Padme is a mole for the rebels. Thanks for the taser. It came in handy.*
>
> *Please tell my sister I will await her with 'golden roses' on Tuesday hence, should she wish to join me. I love her so.*
>
>   *DA*

"Jedediah!" Marc shoved the paper into her hands. "And Lady Ruby!"

"Daniel!" Kit sucked in a sharp breath. "The Golden Rose Inn!"

"How kind of your brother to provide me with an excuse to beat Mr. Jed I. Knight senseless." Marc turned toward the door, leaving Kit stunned in the middle of the room.

Daniel's words echoing through her mind: *I love her so.*

He did care! He really did.

Of course Daniel cares, Wicked Angel said.

Hope bloomed in her chest. And he would be at the Golden Rose Inn on Tuesday waiting for her. Did she want to stay—

But all thought fled as a horrifying cry rose from the great hall: "Fire!"

Chapter 22

Intent on tracking down Jedediah, Marc didn't pay attention to the cries at first. But the acrid smell of smoke washed over him just as the repeated shrieks of "Fire. *Fire!* Everyone out!" sank in.

Damn.

He had known this—that a fire destroyed Haldon Manor at some point. But he had never expected to experience it himself.

The smell of smoke filtered through the great hall. No sign of actual fire in the room.

Yet.

It seemed too much of a coincidence to think this wasn't *the* fire. The one which destroyed the old house.

Marc's mind reeled from the revelations of the last five minutes. Jedediah was the spy. Ruby was the missing agent for the Crown.

And if so, what did she know about her son's activities?

Marc dashed across the great hall to see panicked maids grabbing paintings and hangings from the walls, the butler directing them. Marianne ran out the front door, little Isabel in her arms, the baby's nurse at her heels. A glance outside showed Linwood rallying the male servants into a bucket brigade.

The housekeeper hurried toward the entryway, several priceless vases teetering recklessly in her arms. Kit rushed past Marc to help the woman, snatching a falling vase just in time.

"You stay out of trouble," he said, catching her arm.

"You too." She slid her hand into his, giving it a quick squeeze. And then followed the housekeeper out the front door.

Arthur dashed up, eyes wide but otherwise self-composed. Not one for idle panic, Arthur Knight.

"Everyone is accounted for but Lady Ruby and Jedediah," Arthur said. "They are definitely still inside the house."

Of course.

Which reminded him.

Marc grabbed Arthur's arm and leaned in, speaking lowly. "Jedediah is the spy Linwood seeks. He could be dangerous. Ruby is the missing agent for the Crown."

Arthur hissed a breath through his teeth. "I'll look after Miss Ashton," he said jerking a chin toward the door where Kit had just disappeared.

Marc nodded his head. "Thank you. I'll go find Ruby and Jedediah."

"Ruby was in her bedroom, last I heard." Arthur indicated the stairs to the family wing.

Marc nodded again, turning to cross the great hall.

"Oh and Marc," Arthur called after him. "Please be careful."

The smoke was instantly worse as Marc neared the top of the family stairs.

He retreated down to the landing, wrenching off his neckcloth and wetting the fabric in a vase of flowers. Wrapping it around his face, he tentatively took the stone steps again, staying low under the worst of the smoke.

Nearing the top of the stairs, he could hear the fire now. The pop of wood, the rising heat. Smoke poured from the upper hallway to his left.

Out of the smoke, a figure emerged, commando crawling along the floor.

Ruby. Her face bloodied and soot-streaked. Purple muslin mobcap askew and her purple muslin dress torn in places.

And then suddenly, a larger figure loomed from behind her. Crouching. A long sword in his hand.

Jedediah.

Intent only on his fleeing mother, murder glinting in his eyes. The medieval broadsword—most likely borrowed from one of the suits of armor—raised over his head, ready for a killing blow.

"Look out!" Marc yelled, just as Jedediah swung downward toward Ruby's head.

Hearing his warning, Ruby rolled sideways at the last second, the sword embedding itself into the wood floor precisely where her head had been just a moment before.

Jedediah pulled on the stuck blade, unable to free it. And then, instead, grabbed Ruby's ankle before she could get away.

By that point, Marc was on him.

Crawling along the floor, Marc balanced on both hands and swiveled his body, landing a powerful dual kick to Jedediah's chest, sending the smaller man flying backwards into the smoke. Disappearing from view.

Refusing to chase Jedediah into the smoke filled house, Marc backed up and grabbed Ruby's hands, pulling her toward the stairs.

"Jed—" she croaked.

"Leave him," Marc coughed. "He's not worth either of our lives."

The smoke thickened by the moment, stinging Marc's eyes, causing him to hack uncontrollably.

He needed to get both of them out. Now.

Reaching the steps, he took the first three and then turned to slide Ruby onto his back.

But at that exact second, all the hairs on Marc's neck stood on end. Years of training and muscle memory registered the hiss of a sword through the air, aimed at his head.

Marc twisted his neck away just in time to hear the loud zing as the sword glanced off the stone step.

"Jed, no!" Ruby cried, rolling away from her crazed son.

Crouching above Marc, Jedediah ignored his mother and instead swung the sword again, intent on embedding it into Marc's skull.

Go figure. The foppish Jedediah *did* know something about fighting.

With a grunt, Marc stopped Jedediah's arm mid-swing, wrapping his hands around Jedediah's forearm, bending it back at an awkward angle, forcing him to drop the sword down the stairs with a clatter.

"I know you were involved with that other fellow. What did you do with those plans, Vader? The real ones!" Jedediah hissed. "My superiors are not stupid men. It may have taken a few days, but they realized the plans given them were fakes. I need the real ones. I'm a dead man without them!"

Jedediah launched himself forward, fingers intent on Marc's throat.

Marc rolled with Jedediah's hands, using the smaller man's downward momentum to toss Jedediah over his shoulder and down the stairs.

Smoke filled the stairwell, choking, blinding. Coughing, Marc turned again to Ruby, only to feel a sharp pain in his left arm as Jedediah came at him again, bending his wrist back painfully.

"What did you do with the plans?" Jedediah screamed.

Furious and desperate to get Ruby out of the burning house, Marc whirled on Jedediah, kicking him in the stomach with one leg while hooking his knee with the other. The combined moves wrenched Jedediah off-balance, sending him windmilling back. Marc staggered to his feet, finishing off with a glancing right jab to Jedediah's jaw as the man fell.

A loud crash sounded from down the hallway. The house was burning down around them.

From the corner of his eye, Marc saw Jedediah scramble to his feet, dart a glance at the rapidly encroaching fire and run down the stairs.

Leaving his mother to her fate.

Coward.

Coughing from the smoke, Marc crawled back to Ruby and grasped her hands in his, pulling her toward him, ignoring the pain in his wrist, levering Ruby onto his right shoulder.

"Forgive him." She wept into Marc's ear as he staggered down the steps. "Forgive me."

Afterwards, Marc had no distinct memory of how he got out of the burning house. Smoke seared his lungs, blurring his vision. Ruby must have passed out. But somehow, he kept putting one foot in front of the other, staggering across the smoke-filled great hall and through the front door.

Fresh air wrapped around him. He felt hands grabbing him, lifting Ruby away. Cold water splashed his face and soothed his raspy throat as he collapsed on the ground.

Wiping the smoke out of his eyes with his good hand, Marc gulped in air, coughing uncontrollably. Someone placed a cup of much-needed water into his fingers. He lay on the ground, alternating between spasmodic coughing and sipping water.

After a length of time, the coughing subsided somewhat, and he managed to push himself upright.

He was sitting on the lawn, well back from the front of the house. Flames leapt from the upstairs windows, particularly fierce along the right of the house where the family wing had been. Though by now, fire engulfed nearly the entire structure. Smoke rose as one enormous plume into the sky that could probably be seen in Hereford itself.

It was quite the magnificent sight. He almost wished he could take some video of it for James and Emme.

Kit stood with Marianne and the baby across the lawn to his left, well back from the building. Tears streamed down Marianne's face as she clutched tiny Isabel to her chest, unconsciously rocking and soothing the baby. Kit offering comfort.

Kit turned her head, seeing him. Relief washed over her face and she turned away from Marianne, intent on coming to him.

But Marc stayed her with a wave of his hand, coughing again. He was fine. Well, as fine as he could hope to be. And there were others, like Marianne, who could use Kit's help.

Understanding his meaning, she nodded and then, with a wink, blew him a kiss. The darling minx.

His heart swelled, pounding in his chest. Heavens how he adored her.

He blew a kiss right back.

Man, anyone who knew him at *all* would mock him about now. Blowing kisses like some love-sick puppy.

But it wasn't the potential embarrassment that startled him.

It was the fact that he *liked* blowing kisses to Kit. He wanted to blow more kisses to her. He wanted to give her *actual* kisses.

Wow.

He was in so deep.

Part of him was desperate for her to make a decision, so he knew what his future would be. Part of him wanted to remain in this limbo, avoiding the situation all together.

Would she join Daniel at the Golden Rose Inn on Tuesday? Could Marc leave her there with her brother and ride away?

The thought left him breathless, hands shaking.

Which kicked off another painful coughing fit.

After several minutes of uncontrolled hacking, he managed to drink enough water to soothe his throat for a moment. His wrist throbbed from the motion. Marc tested it, pressing gently on the bones. No tenderness, thank goodness, which meant no broken bones.

But when he tried to move it in circles, pain shot up his arm. Definitely sprained. He wouldn't be punching anyone again anytime soon.

His soot-smeared cravat was still damp around his neck. Gingerly untying it, Marc used the long length of cloth to bind his wrist, immobilizing it as best he could.

Aside from singed clothing and smoke-seared lungs, he seemed to be okay.

He lifted his head back to the burning building.

Every able-bodied man—including Arthur and Linwood—stood in lines before the house, passing buckets of water along to toss on the flames.

A decidedly futile effort. Even a host of modern fire engines could do nothing to save the building now.

Arthur seemed to realize this and stepped out of the line, shaking his head in defeat, recognizing that the entire front facade could collapse at any time. He waved everyone back from the engulfed house. Giving up the structure for lost.

Arthur walked to Kit and Marianne, gathering his wife and child in his arms. Marianne instantly sank into her husband's embrace.

Linwood moved toward them and then paused. Arthur, Marianne and little Isabel did make a touching tableau, and Linwood seemed hesitant to interrupt. Instead, he changed direction and, casting a lingering glance at his sister and her husband, the viscount strode across the grass, coming toward Marc himself.

Suddenly, the roof over the great hall collapsed with a gigantic crash, glass shattering. Shrieks of horror spread throughout the gathered crowd. Even Linwood flinched.

So that was that then. The house really was done for.

Marc turned his head to his right, noting that Ruby lay only a few yards away, tended by the housekeeper. Grunting to his feet, he winced his way over to them.

So maybe he needed to add sore muscles to his list of aches.

Collapsing on the ground next to them, Marc hissed when he got a good look at Ruby.

Her face was battered and bruised, one eye nearly swollen shut. With a damp rag, the housekeeper was gently wiping away the blood and soot.

Linwood came up to them with a nod, crouching beside Ruby. Looking between the two men, the housekeeper excused herself, saying she would see if the doctor had arrived yet.

Alone with Linwood, Ruby turned to Marc, fixing him with her one good eye.

"Jed?" she croaked and then coughed, turning involuntarily onto her side.

Linwood patted her back, the viscount somehow looking none-the-worse-for-wear. Hardly a hair was out of place on his head. It was almost uncanny how mayhem never seemed to touch him.

"I don't know where he ended up," Marc coughed, his voice just as gravelly as hers.

Linwood grunted in disapproval. "What happened?"

Ruby waived a hand, as if to dismiss the question as irrelevant, still coughing.

"Please don't bother to dissemble, Lady Ruby," Marc continued. "I know that Jedediah was working as a spy for the French. And that you have long been a secret agent for the British government. In fact, you stopped sending information to your liaison a month or two ago. Every-one has been trying to find you."

Linwood fixed Marc with a decidedly surprised look over Ruby's head. Marc shrugged, like it was all in a day's work.

All the bravado eased from Ruby, her eyes fluttering closed.

"I thought I could stop him," she whispered. "I knew that someone kept betraying us to the French. Someone close to the Home Office, giving them access to our secrets. But it took me a while to understand the covert agent lived under my own roof. I had to come to Marfield, leaving everything and everyone else behind, before I finally realized it had been Jedediah all along."

"Why? Why would he turn spy for the French?"

Ruby lifted a shoulder. "Debts? A chance to prove himself? Who can say. He came upon me earlier as I was writing a letter to a contact in Bath. Confronted me. Beat . . . me. He tried to kill me . . . his own mother . . ." Her voice trailed off in a whisper.

A tear escaped the side of her eye. Marc could only imagine what such an admission cost her strong pride.

"Only the worst of cads would do such a thing," Linwood said, lowly, taut with anger.

Well, what do you know?

He and Linwood had *finally* found a topic on which they could agree.

Ruby nodded and gave a gasp. She fought for control, swallowing back tears.

After a moment, she opened her undamaged eye and fixed it on them. "He started the fire as a way to cover his tracks. He intended to kill me and then make it look like an accident. But the fire spread too fast. I managed to hit him and crawl away. But he caught up with me. If you had not arrived, Lord Vader . . ." Her voice trailed off. She swallowed and then coughed again.

Linwood nodded his head. Decisive. "If he escaped that inferno, I promise he will be apprehended and . . . dealt with. I will personally ensure that no lingering dishonor touches your family over one traitor's decision."

Marc lifted his head and cocked a brow at the viscount. Linwood would be true to his word.

Ruby relaxed, closing her eye again as the housekeeper hurried up to them, the doctor in tow.

Seeing there was nothing more for him to do, Marc wandered toward where Marianne and Arthur stood, watching the burning house. It would likely burn for a while. Arthur still had his arms wrapped around his petite wife and child, stroking Marianne's back soothingly.

It was a touching scene of love and support. Despite tendencies toward self-importance, Arthur Knight was a kind husband and a doting father. The kind of man who matured into a pillar of strength. No matter how hard the going, Marc sensed Arthur and Marianne would walk through it hand-in-hand.

And in that instant, Marc wanted that scene for himself. He wanted to be holding Kit, comforting her, secure in the knowledge that no matter the problem, they would face it together as a team. That her laugh and wit and the sheer delight of her would always be at his side.

He was desperate to see her. To hold her. She had left Marianne to Arthur's care and was now probably helping comfort someone else. Capable. Strong.

He scoured the assembled throng of people, all watching the house burn. Footmen, grooms, gardeners, maids . . . but no Kit.

Perplexed, he threaded his way through the crowd until he spotted Fanny, the only maid he knew by name.

Grabbing hold of her arm, he caught her attention.

"Have you seen Miss Ashton?" His voice still scratchy and rough.

"Miss Ashton? I do believe she was just here." Fanny glanced about with him, trying to see through the crowd. "Well, she *was* just here," Fanny repeated. "Gilbert, have you seen Miss Ashton?"

One of the footman turned his head. "Miss Ashton? I saw her leave with Mr. Jedediah a short while ago. Headed down the lane they were, probably off to arrange more help in Marfield."

Marc had heard the phrase 'my blood runs cold' often enough. But he had never actually experienced it.

The sensation felt rather like . . . one's insides turning to ice.

Go figure.

The panic that washed in *behind* the terror was no better. Tasting of fire and ash.

Kit *had* just been here.

Except, suddenly, she wasn't.

Chapter 23

Marc took off at a run down the lane. His lungs burned in his chest, hurting worse than the most vigorous workout he could ever remember. His wrist throbbed.

But he pushed himself through it. Numb. Terrified.

If something happened to Kit . . .

Nausea crept in at the thought.

After a few minutes of running, Marc had to slow down. His poor overworked lungs couldn't handle any more abuse. His throat on fire. Coughing wracked him.

Coughing which wasn't going to help him sneak up on Jedediah unawares.

Why hadn't he thought to bring some water with him?

Oh, that's right. Because he was stuck in 1814, and water bottles wouldn't be invented for probably a good hundred years. Granted, if he had been thinking, he probably could have found a canteen . . . or, at the very least, a bucket.

After struggling for a few seconds, he managed to quiet his cough, but the sensation tickled almost unbearably at the back of his throat.

Walking as quickly as he could up the lane, Marc scoured the trees and sides of the road for any sign of Jedediah or Kit, fighting to hold his coughing to an occasional quiet burst of air. Spring was just starting to creep into the forest, lending the trees a suggestion of leaves. The lack of foliage made it easier to spot an attacker. But it also made Marc a more visible target.

Nothing.

He carefully peeked around the sharp curve in the lane where he had first met Kit.

Nothing.

He continued on, crossed over the bridge, pausing every twenty feet or so to listen. But he heard only the birds in the bare trees, chirping cheerfully.

Still nothing.

But drawing near the lane which curved off to Duir Cottage, something glinted in the middle of the road. Small and silver. Rushing up to it, Marc picked up Kit's rape alarm.

No!

And then, a faint noise caught his attention.

It wasn't much. Just the sound of scuffling, the muffled cry of a woman.

Kit.

Marc clutched the alarm in his good hand and darted up the lane toward the cottage, staying low, eyes alert and scanning.

He could see nothing out of the ordinary and, each time he stopped, he heard nothing more. The tickle in his throat caught up with him, and he had to pause for a second, leaning against the trunk of a tree, stifling a coughing fit with the sleeve of his coat.

How was he going to save Kit if his coughing trumpeted his arrival?

Firmly swallowing against the itchy sensation in the back of his throat, Marc continued up the road.

After a minute, he came into the clearing where the house stood.

It looked much as it had when he arrived. Shuttered and lifeless. The front door closed. The guards Arthur had set were nowhere in sight. Most likely drawn away to fight the fire.

Crouching, Marc scurried up to the house, keeping his back to the honey-colored stone wall, carefully circling the building. He rounded to the rear and noted the kitchen door was ajar.

Voices drifted out, though he couldn't make out the words. Just the tone.

First Kit's, taunting and fierce.

Jedediah's, loud and sneering.

Creeping forward, Marc peered into the window.

Jedediah stood in the kitchen, his back to the window. Kit was before him on the floor, her hands and feet bound. Soot and dirt on her face.

"Where are the damn plans! I know you and Vader were involved with this. I grow tired of this game!" Jedediah brandished a pistol in one hand. A wicked-looking knife in the other.

"I don't know what you're talking about." Kit lifted her chin bravely. Her eyes flashed with courage, but there was terror there too.

"You lie! The plans were altered. You had to have been involved with the mix up. Both you and Vader—"

"You have the wrong people!"

"I'm going to give you two minutes to change your mind and then I torch this building too. You tied up inside it, of course. A nice little present for Vader to mourn later. Unless you care to start talking . . . "

Kit's eyes widened in fear. But she pressed her lips together. Shook her head. Protecting Marc and her brother.

With a disgusted shake of his head, Jedediah swiveled. Marc ducked down just in time.

Two minutes.

What to do?

He breathed through the panic swamping him, swallowing cough after cough. He couldn't allow Kit to be hurt. What had he been thinking running off without a pistol?

He was tired, sore and had a sprained wrist at best.

Marc examined his options.

Jedediah was legitimately armed and dangerous. Unlike the encounter with Linwood the previous week, Jedediah would show no compunction in killing them both. No matter how he played through different scenarios, one of them could easily be hurt or killed.

There was no time to go back for help.

Kit was in danger now.

What if Jedediah set Duir Cottage on fire? What would fire do to the portal?

Stemming his panic, Marc settled on a single solution. It wasn't the fanciest of plans, but it was the only one his panicked mind could focus on.

Marc ignored the tiny thought which insisted there *were* other plans, but this one got him what he wanted most too.

Creeping back around to the front of the house, Marc examined the rape alarm. It appeared to still have battery power, having not been used. With a deep breath, he switched it on and threw it into the brush beside the front of the house.

The noise was satisfactorily loud, sounding like a hyper car alarm.

Without hesitating, he scurried around to the back of the house, peeking through the window just in time to see Jedediah cautiously head out front to inspect the strange noise.

Marc darted through the partially open kitchen door, meeting Kit's startled gaze. Kit visibly sagged with relief at seeing Marc, tears swimming in her eyes.

Jedediah had disappeared out the front door, but he would find the alarm in less than a minute. It's frantic beeping cut through the calm.

Kit struggled to get free of the ropes that bound her, indicating with a jut of her chin that Marc should help.

They didn't have enough time.

Silently, Marc shook his head and mouthed, "I'm sorry."

Instead of freeing her, he grasped Kit by the waist and pulled her upright. And, then, for the second time in as many hours, he hefted a woman over his shoulder, his wrist throbbing from the effort.

There wasn't time to dash for the trees. Besides, he hadn't the strength.

And that had never been the plan.

The rape alarm still screeched frantically. Jedediah hadn't found it yet. But they only had seconds left.

Without hesitating, Marc made for the closet and cellar door under the stairs. Quickly, he opened the door, set Kit inside. He lifted the large trap door in the floor and then stepped onto the first stair, turning to shut the closet door.

Darkness instantly closed around them in the small space. Their combined breathing loud.

The alarm suddenly stopped.

Not a moment later, he heard Jedediah re-enter the house.

Marc held his breath, as footsteps echoed down the hall outside the cellar door. The footsteps faded into the kitchen.

Only to return as Jedediah dashed out of the kitchen, swearing profusely at Kit's disappearance.

"Vader!" His voice rang through the house. "This can only be your doing. You have to be in the house still. And when I find you, you will both die!"

Marc paused, but only for the barest of moments. Jedediah *would* find them. And who knows what the outcome of that fight would be.

Without hesitating, Marc caught Kit around the knees and carried her into the cellar. The portal loomed ahead, thrumming with life.

Reading his intent, Kit squirmed against his shoulder, butting him with her head. Indicating in every way her sharp disagreement with his decision.

Marc paused.

The door to the cellar rattled.

That was all the motivation he needed to step forward into swooping, falling darkness.

Chapter 24

K it felt the dizzying disorientation of the portal. The sense of falling, falling, falling.

And then suddenly, the world righted itself. Leaving her slung over Marc's shoulder like a sack of potatoes.

Her mind reeled in shock. A figurative version of one of Marc's roundhouse kicks to the head.

Marc had truly done it. He had taken her through the portal.

Leaving Daniel behind.

Without so much as a *by your leave*.

Without. Even. Asking.

But . . . why?!

He was Marc Wilde, for heaven's sake. He could take on one slimy, ridiculous, over-primped—

"Put me down this instant!" She all but shouted the words.

She had long considered his shoulders capable of bearing burdens. And even, quite frankly, of bearing her. But she never dreamed they would carry her away from her brother.

She wriggled emphatically just to underline the point.

Obligingly, Marc set her on the ground with a groan, staggering slightly as he did. His breathing labored, wheezing.

Kit stared down at her tied hands and feet and then, in sheer frustration, tried to free them again. She was starting to lose feeling in her fingers.

"Let me get a knife." Marc choked, stumbling up the wooden stairs, coughing.

Of course. He *would* leave her to stew in the dark cellar.

She was just so . . . so . . . ugh! How could he!

He had no *right* to make this decision for her.

Emotions swamped her.

Loss. Frustration. Anger.

She stood helplessly, tapping her foot as much as possible. Waiting.

When she had gone through the portal last time, she had been too frantic and frightened to really take it all in. Not to mention, the light too dim.

Not this time.

Afternoon sunlight streamed down the steps from the open closet door. Was it really only afternoon still? So much had happened. The fire, Jedediah shoving a pistol into her back and telling her to walk, arriving at Duir Cottage and being tied up.

The light illuminated the cellar with its stone walls and dirt floor. The portal stood a little behind her, its electric pulse thrumming through the ground.

Upstairs, she could hear Marc clattering through a utensil drawer, looking for a knife. And then his footsteps returning to her, backlit as he half fell down the stairs.

Bending down, he quickly sliced through the ropes around her ankles and then moved up to remove the bindings on her wrists.

"Come on." He rasped and nodded his head, retreating back up the stairs. Still coughing.

Kit stood in the darkness, chewing on her cheek. Anger welling up from deep inside.

Though, it was more like fury at this point. Blind, mind-numbing rage.

How dare he!

How dare he make this decision for her. Return her to 2014 without even *asking*.

She glanced back at the portal, half-tempted to walk right back through it.

No.

Before she did that, Mr. I-have-control-issues Wilde could explain himself.

Marc disappeared through the doorway into the hall, coughing loudly, incessantly.

Shaking some feeling back into her hands, she stumbled up after him, nearly tripping on her long skirts. She stopped in the hall, staring at a large antique-looking trunk across from the door to the cellar.

Daniel's trunk.

The stabbing pain of it literally robbed her breath. Sharp and vicious.

She turned and walked into the kitchen, jaw clenched. Noted the greatcoat and beaver hat slung over the dining room chair in front of her.

Daniel's coat and hat.

And then she turned to see Marc. He was at the kitchen sink, guzzling a glass of water.

Drinking water!

He casually dragged her literally two hundred years through time, kicking and (mentally) screaming. And then felt the need to just get a freaking drink?!

That did it. Something snapped.

With two steps, she grabbed the knife Marc had set on the marble island counter. Turning, she flipped open Daniel's trunk in the hallway. If she knew her brother at all . . .

Sure enough, an antique pistol sat gleaming on top of everything else. Guns were generally illegal in modern Britain. Antique ones, however, got a pass.

Snatching up the pistol, she tromped back down the stairs into the cellar.

If Marc wouldn't fight for her brother, *she* would.

"Kit?!" Marc's voice sounded warningly from the kitchen.

Heedless, she strode over to the portal and leaned into the stone.

Nothing happened.

Frowning, she put her back against it and pushed.

Again, nothing.

Turning, she pounded against it with the fist that clutched the knife.

Nothing.

"Kit . . . please." Marc's voice sounded behind her. Soft. Raspy.

"How. Could. You!" She whirled on him, hysteria finally getting the better of her. "How could you drag me through? How could you leave him? Leave me without any choice—"

She turned again, pounding on the portal.

Let me through!! But silently shrieking the words didn't help either.

With a hiccupping sob, she collapsed to the floor, the knife and pistol clattering beside her.

Awful, wracking gasps tore through her. Ugly crying at its worst.

Her brother was *gone*. Lost to her as surely as if he had died—

Wait! He *was* dead. No one lived two hundred years . . .

Which just made her cry harder. And harder and harder.

She would stay here. She wouldn't leave this spot until the portal allowed her to return.

Thoughts of Daniel raced through her mind. Her brother's little hand in hers, teaching him how to look both ways for cars before crossing the street.

Daniel home on school holiday laughing over a prank he pulled on some upperclassmen.

Daniel bent over research with her father, their identical dark heads nearly indistinguishable, voices tangling as they talked.

Daniel's face the day they buried their father, watching the casket being lowered into the family crypt.

Memory after memory washed over her.

How long she lay on the floor, she couldn't later remember. Long enough for her hands to go numb from the cold, for her legs to cramp.

Eventually, she realized only half of her was cold. The other half was tucked up against Marc. At some point, he had sat down beside her on the ground, cradling her against his chest.

Comforting. Understanding.

Well, she didn't *want* that.

She wanted to be angry and hurt. They were much safer emotions.

She pushed away from him, swiping at her tears. Staggered to standing.

"Kit . . ." His voice washed over her, plaintive and quiet. Pleading. He grasped her hand.

She shook it free.

She didn't want pleading. Or pathetic excuses.

She wanted her brother back.

Stumbling up the stairs, tears welling again when she saw the trunk and greatcoat, she walked to the kitchen sink. Turned on the hot water and scrubbed her filthy hands. And then her face too for good measure. Letting her tears mix with the water.

Finally, she gave up and just stood at the sink, tears falling into the running water.

Sobbing and sobbing. As if a lake of tears could return Daniel to her.

"Hey." Marc's hand reached across her, turning off the water.

A linen towel dabbed at her face. Strong hands turned her around. Two fingers lifted her chin.

Still hiccupping, she looked into his green, green, green eyes. Soft and concerned.

Streaked with soot and blood.

That got her attention. She took a step back. His clothing was singed, jacket partially torn, neckcloth missing. Eyes bloodshot.

He looked like she felt.

Gutted. Burned.

"I am *so* sorry, Kit." His voice rasped. Eyes drilled into hers, beseeching. "It seemed like the best solution."

Unable to stand the intensity of his gaze, she glanced down.

And through her swimming vision, noted his wrist. His cravat tied around it.

"You're . . . *hiccup* . . . hurt." She reached for his hand, gently lifting it. He winced.

"I don't think it's broken. Just a bad sprain."

He wiped her wet cheeks again with his free hand.

She snuffled.

"You should . . . *hiccup* . . . ice it."

"Who cares about my damn wrist, Kit?" He grasped her chin again, forcing her back to look at him. "It's not important right now."

"I care," she sniffed. And then jerked her chin out of his hand. "But, then, that's what . . . *hiccup* . . . I do. I *care* about things. About people."

Still angry-sniffling, she stomped over to the fridge, pulled open the lower freezer and dug out a bag of frozen peas.

"At least stop . . . *hiccup* . . . the swelling." She handed him the bag as she walked past. Ignoring his tug on her sleeve.

Grabbing her brother's greatcoat off the chair, she wrapped it around her and stalked over to sit on the overstuffed couch facing the enormous fireplace.

Hiccupping and snuffling.

Burrowing into the scratchy wool coat, breathing in deeply, trying to find some lingering scent of Daniel.

Hoping to hold part of Daniel to her.

Nothing.

The coat smelled like wool and chemicals. New. As if Daniel had never worn it.

Out of the corner of her eye, she glimpsed Marc joining her, the couch dipping under his weight. He held the peas to his injured wrist.

Silence.

Marc broke it first. Voice hoarse.

"Again, it seemed like the best solution, Kit—"

"You said you were Switzerland. More like the former USSR, just taking over everything you see—" She hiccupped again, her voice breaking. "He was one man. One stupid, weak, little man. You're Marc Wilde, for heaven's sake. I watched you take down four armed men in seconds on the road to Whitmoor—"

"Yes, four men who didn't really want to hurt me or you. Four men who were afraid to fire for fear of hitting each other or their horses—"

Kit pulled Daniel's coat tighter around her. Like a cocoon. As if she buried herself far enough into it, she could keep Marc's pleas out.

"Kit, Jedediah tried to kill his own mother—"

"What?" She whirled to face him.

"You were busy with Marianne, so I don't think you got much of the story. I interrupted Jedediah trying to kill Ruby. Daniel must have somehow slipped up and let Jedediah know that you and I were involved in this whole mess. So, he then tried to kill me," —Marc held up his wrist as proof— "screaming the whole time that he needed the *real* plans. I beat him off and managed to rescue Ruby before her son could finish her off."

He paused, shaking his head. And then fixing her with his impossibly green eyes.

"*That* is the man who held you prisoner, Kit. Add in the fact I have an injured wrist, had hefted a woman out of a burning building, inhaled a lifetime of smoke, ran to Duir Cottage once I realized what had happened despite being barely able to breathe . . . Kit, I am so sorry, but Jedediah was armed. And intent on killing us both. I couldn't outrun him—not as I was and having to carry you—and there was a good chance you or I would be injured in a fight. How could I ever risk your life?"

She clenched her jaw, hating that a lot of what he said made sense.

"But you didn't even try. It was like you had made the decision to go through the portal before you even entered the house."

Silence again. Marc looked away. His lack of a response confirming her statement.

"Why? Why take the decision away from me?" she whispered.

He brought his eyes back to hers. "I didn't want—"

"No man is an island." She threw his own words back at him. "Everything you do makes waves in an ocean. You may not mean to swamp someone else's boat, but it doesn't excuse your responsibility—"

"Kit—"

"I want to go back. I want to decide for myself—" Unbidden, her eyes welled up again.

Marc sighed, shifting the peas on his wrist. "I know that. I do—"

"Daniel is *all* I have left. Everyone leaves—"

"I don't. I'm here."

His voice fell between them, the barest breath of sound.

Hoarse and jagged. Yet somehow strong and true.

A jarring punch in her soul.

Stop making sense! She wanted to scream at him. *I just want to be angry right now. Stop with all this . . . reasonableness.*

"I support you and your decisions, Kit." He gazed at her calmly. Sympathy evident in every line of him. "I do. Daniel *wants* to remain in 1814. So if you go back, you should go with a plan to stay there with him. Permanently."

More reasonableness. Stupid man.

"Easy to say with the portal shut and refusing to allow me through."

"Kit, we've been through this. Your brother is forging a life for himself in the past—"

"Yes, you mentioned that. Right after you watched him *walk away!*" Anger surged through Kit again. "You just let him leave—"

"He's a grown man making his own decisions. I respect other's choices—"

"No! Don't you *dare* bring it back to that. You refused to force him to stay."

"As I've said, I wasn't going to beat him up—"

"Right. Or, say, throw him over your shoulder and drag him off—"

"Don't do this, Kit!"

Marc surged to his feet, a frustrated hand in his hair. His uninjured hand. He began pacing in front of the fireplace.

"Just explain to me *why*." She gestured toward him. "Why wasn't I accorded the same respect? Why let my brother go but then turn around and *make* the choice for me?"

"Why? Why?!" Marc stopped. Flung his hand outward.

Fixed her with a look so intense it pinned her to the couch.

Breathless. Unable to move.

"Why, Kit?! Because I don't *love* your brother. When it's someone I *love*, it's a totally different thing."

His words hung between them. Raw. Bleeding.

When it's someone I love . . .

Kit held perfectly still.

"Well," she whispered. Cleared her throat. "I *do* love him. Or I *did*. But I will never get the chance to say that to him, will I? Because that choice was *taken* from me."

And then, suddenly, it seemed there was nothing left to say.

"I'm leaving." She stood, clutching Daniel's coat around her like a talisman.

Marc closed his eyes, shoulders sagging. Deflating in front of her.

"Please don't go."

She shrugged. "We won't ever see eye-to-eye on this issue."

"At least let me give you a lift—"

She shook her head. "No need. I can find my own way."

Sliding her arms into the coat, she moved down the hallway to the front door.

"Kit, please. Try to understand. I couldn't bear the thought of losing you."

She paused. Half-twisted her head toward him.

"I think you just did, Mr. Wilde."

And then slid the bolt on the door, opening it.

Turned back to him, giving him one last, lingering look.

"Later, alligator."

And then she left. The door a satisfying *slam* behind her.

Marc collapsed against the wall in the hallway. Sinking to the floor with his head in his hands.

The door shutting behind Kit mimicked the shattering of his own soul.

He could practically *see* the shards of his heart strewn across the wooden floor.

The one and *only* time he had ever told a woman he loved her.

He groaned, tugging at his hair. Relishing the pain in his sprained wrist.

How could he have made such a *spectacular* mess of this?

Her face when she realized they had come through the portal . . .

Ashen, washed of life. As if her very reason for existing had been snuffed out.

He literally felt physically sick over it.

It hurt.

It hurt that he had hurt her.

It hurt that all her love and affection was not for him.

Which really just made him the worst sort of cad.

He released his head and tipped it back against the wall. Thumping rhythmically. Once. Twice.

He should have tried harder to keep them in the past. He should have shown more respect for her choices.

But for what? To watch her decide to stay in the past without him?

His throat ached from the smoke. At least that's what he told himself.

And his eyes watering . . . that was just smoke too.

Right?

With a groan, he tipped his head into his hands. Gouging his eyeballs with his palms.

Letting the devastation settle through him. The agonizing loss of *her*.

He sat in the hallway until the shadows stretched and the light faded from sunset gold to twilight blue.

He was still sitting there in the near dark when Emme and James walked through the back door, flipping on the lights. Marc blinked into the sudden brightness.

That's right. Just back from their off-the-grid trip to Mongolia. Fantastic. They probably had no idea anything had happened.

James tossed his coat onto the kitchen island and walked around the table. Noting the beaver top hat and trunk in the hall. The open door down to the portal. Raked his gaze up and down Marc in his battered Regency-period clothing.

Raised both his blond eyebrows in surprise.

"You look like hell," he said by way of greeting. "In a nineteenth century sort of way."

Marc managed a gruff laugh. More noise than humor.

"Feel like it too," he croaked, pushing to his feet.

Suddenly, every ache and pain in his body made itself known. His throbbing wrist, his scorched throat, stinging eyes.

Emme brushed past her husband.

"Marc!" She caught him around the waist, hugging him tightly. And then pulled back, surveying his sorry state.

Singed and smoky.

"What happened?" she asked, shaking her dark curly head. "Wait. The portal?"

He nodded.

Emme rolled her hand. *Go on.*

Where to start?

He shook his head wearily. "Let's see. I solved our blackmail case. Interesting twist on that."

"That's a relief," James said, scrubbing a hand through his blond hair.

"Yes. I also beat up Linwood. That felt good."

"Shut it!" Emme pushed his chest. And then gave a gleeful laugh.

"A little bloodthirsty, aren't we, Mrs. Knight?" James gave his wife a teasing wink.

"He so deserved whatever he got!"

Marc managed a faint not-quite grin.

Turns out seeing his sister and brother-in-law so happily in love did *not* improve his mood.

"I also managed to fall in love with La Pochette."

No sense hiding that small bombshell. Emme would ferret it out of him soon enough anyway.

"What?!" Emme took a step back, giving him a comically puzzled look. "As in FauxPause?"

Marc nodded.

"How is that even possible?"

"It is a long story."

Emme sniffed the air. "Wait. Were you in a fire too?"

"Why, yes, thank you for asking. Haldon Manor burned down—"

"Pardon?!" James' eyes went wide.

"No!" Emme exclaimed at the same time.

"It was spectacular. Oh, and you're an uncle, by the way." Marc gestured toward James. "Arthur and Marianne had a darling little girl. Named her Isabel."

James' eyes went even wider.

Emme tucked an arm around Marc, intent on leading him back into the kitchen.

"C'mon, big brother. I want to hear the entire story from the beginning."

Chapter 25

K it woke to drumming rain on her window.

Which was just fine, as it seemed to match her pounding headache.

She wanted to attribute it to time travel jet lag (if such a thing existed), but she knew that was wrong.

It was a love headache.

A headache brought on by too much crying over a man (or brother, rather) who didn't seem to care.

And not enough crying over a man who did.

Marc had told her that he loved her. Well, more or less.

And, yet, she had still *walked out* on him.

Gah! What kind of a person was she? To just walk out on a man like that?

Correction: To walk out on Marc Wilde like that.

She lay in bed, feeling as if a weight the size and breadth of all of Britain had taken up residence on her chest.

The previous night, she had returned home, called her two managing editors and apologized for her absence. Made up a (partially true) story about having to dig Daniel out of one of his scrapes. Smoothed things over.

And then took an absurdly long shower.

The website was doing well, despite her unplanned 'vacation.'

Yes, the *Croc-nami* post had gone mega-viral. Apparently several media outlets had been eager to interview her.

Lovely. So many people wanting to be with her, wanting to have her around.

Everyone but her family. The *only* people who should want to be with her, no matter what.

She staggered out of bed. Pulled a cotton wrap over her tight t-shirt and pajama bottoms. Loosely gathered her hair into a messy bun.

And wandered down the stone stairs of Whitmoor House.

The family wing, of course.

Ironic that. Given she had *none* now.

She was deep into her pity-party. Intent on wallowing there for a good long time. She had already gone through a full package of hobnobs and was deep into a package of shortbread biscuits.

Kit could hear the low rumble of voices coming from the medieval hall. Visitors gaping at the enormous wooden beams and faded banners. The tour guides recounting the history of the building.

How much longer would it be hers? Eventually, Daniel would have to be declared dead. And then, without a living male heir, the entire building would revert to the National Trust.

Gone, gone, gone. All gone.

She wandered into her father's study. His desk stood in the same place in the middle of the room. Heavy, solid. Grounded. Light filtered in, faded and gray, casting the room in blue shadows.

Walking up to the desk, she touched her father's books, his notes. At some point she would need to sort through this room. But she just hadn't been able to face it yet. To box up her father's life. Now to have to box up Daniel's too. . .

It just felt like such a betrayal. A negation of them as people. To what they had meant to her.

She stared out the window for a moment. The rain drip, drip, dripping down the panes. A mimicry of her soul.

She turned away, unable to think about it any more.

But as she did, a flash of white near the fireplace caught her eye.

With a frown, she walked over. There, nestled on the marble mantle, sat a thick envelope. Her name written across the front in sloppy handwriting.

Daniel.

The letter he said he had left for her. How could she have forgotten?

With shaking fingers, she took the envelope down. Walked back to the desk and sat in her father's chair. Opened the envelope and pulled out a stack of old papers.

Wrapped around them was a single sheet of crisp modern stationery. A note. Handwritten, of course, given Daniel's love of a tangible world.

Kit read her brother's sloping hand:

Dearest Kit,

You are probably going to be very, very angry with me when you receive this letter.

But, please, do me the favor of being angry at me, Daniel. Not our circumstances or our parents or, worst of all, yourself. This letter is not about you. It is about me and who I intrinsically am and my decisions. Most importantly, the person I feel I am destined to be.

Let me begin by saying you are the very best of sisters. Because of you, I know I have been thoroughly and unconditionally loved in my life. I know

I have caused you pain and considerable frustration over the years. And for that, I am deeply sorry. You deserved better than my indifference. I wish I had a good excuse for my behavior, but I don't. Not really. But I'll try to explain.

All my life, I have felt like an outcast, a misfit. Like a square peg in a round hole, to use a cliché. This sense of unease within myself has driven nearly all my bad behavior over the years as I've searched for the place where I belong.

After Dad died last year, I think I hit rock bottom. I sat in this room, remembering all the stories about our family. All the history this building had seen. I even pulled out the family journals Dad collected over the years. All the diaries and records our grandparents and great-grandparents and their friends, etc. had written. I think I hoped to find myself through them. And to my surprise, I did.

Literally.

Read through the documents I've enclosed here. Most particularly, the history of a man named Garvis. He tells the story of the first Lord Whitmoor, a wealthy businessman raised to the peerage for aiding the Duke of Wellington in a moment of crisis. This Whitmoor also rambled once in a delirious fever about a time portal. The more I read the account of his history, the more I realized a simple fact:

I am the first Lord Whitmoor. The person Garvis describes is, in fact, myself.

I know you are probably laughing right now and thinking I am insane, but this is a truth I feel profoundly in my soul. This is my destiny, Kit. I do not know my fate from here. Once I realized that the first Baron Whitmoor was, in fact, myself, I stopped reading about his history. I want to live it, not necessarily anticipating more than I already know. But if you are reading this letter, then I am already gone through the portal. To my future in the past.

You have often accused me of not caring about our family, but that is not true. I care more than you can ever know. Most importantly, I care enough (in the nineteenth century) to insist the barony be established through a writ of summons. This means that without a male heir, the barony can continue on through the female line.

To that end, I have sent in documents abdicating my right to the barony (well, in 2014) and insisting that it pass to you, as the only remaining heir. May I be the first to pay my respects to the newly minted Baroness Whitmoor?

Do not mourn me, sister dearest. I am living the life I was born to live, the destiny I am to follow. Know that I am happy and love you with all my heart. Be well. Find the path that makes your heart sing.

Your ever-devoted brother,

W

The letter slipped from her lifeless fingers. Stunned. Kit sat motionless, absorbing the shock of it.

Daniel? Really?

He was just . . . *Daniel*. Always needing her help, always getting into scrapes . . .

But, suddenly, she saw him in an entirely new light. Daniel *was* a horrid misfit in a technological world. He floundered and struggled here in the twenty-first century.

Yet, all the things that were weaknesses in 2014 could be strengths in 1814. His boundless energy, his love of the real and tangible, his charisma and charm.

But how could he *know* that he belonged in the past? It seemed so unlikely. Like another fanciful idea of his.

She set aside Daniel's letter and looked at the other documents enclosed in the envelope.

And there it was.

A history written by a man called Garvis Samuelson. She read his account, of his dedication and service to a man named Daniel Ashton, the first Lord Whitmoor who went by the moniker W.

Garvis stood by his lordship through thick and thin, nursed him when he was fevered and delirious, recording W's ramblings about a portal and odd futurish-sounding things. He even mentioned Marc's name. It was apparently an alias W liked to adopt when he had covert dealings.

And more than once, he referred to his beloved sister, Katharine.

That last bit caused Kit's eyes to mist over.

Oh, Daniel.

She could see her brother so clearly in the record.

As she sat reading, a sense of peace washed over her.

Flooding and cleansing.

She felt almost as if Daniel were there, arms wrapped around her. Assuring her that he was happy.

Be well. Find the path that makes your heart sing.

The words vibrated in her soul.

For the first time in more years than she could remember, she asked a simple question: What did *she* want?

Not, what *should* she do?

Not, what was the *responsible* thing to do? Or who was she responsible *for*?

But just simply, what did she want more than anything else?

The answer hit her immediately. Without a moment's hesitation.

Marc.

She didn't want a life in 1814 with Daniel. She saw with sudden clarity that holding on to Daniel was a selfish desire. A way to prove she was loved.

But you are loved . . .

The thought whispered through her.

Everyone leaves—

I don't. I'm here.

Finally, she allowed the painful happiness of Marc's love to flood her.

A torrent through her heart, washing away all pretense. Cleansing her past.

What did it matter, in the end, if her mother had abandoned? Her father retreated—Daniel left?

Their past choices did not need to limit *her* future happiness.

She could chose to live in the emotional pain of their long ago decisions. Or she could forge a future bright with hope and full of love.

And she did love. She loved her friends, her life, her work . . .

And Marc.

She profoundly, deeply loved him too. Adored his throaty laugh. The way his eyes lit when he teased her.

The way he knew her, accepted her for everything she was, even the ugly bits—especially the ugly bits, actually. That sense of rightness when she was with him.

The feeling of *home.*

So he, perhaps, made a mistake in dragging her through the portal prematurely? So what?

He was human. So was she.

And, in the end, was it actually a mistake? Or more an action directed by Fate?

She needed to talk with Marc. Hold him. Kiss him.

But first, there was one thing she wanted to do—

No, make that two things.

Besides, she was going to be a baroness now, it seemed. And couldn't Lady Whitmoor do whatever she wanted?

She could already hear Marc chuckling at the thought.

Chapter 26

Duir Cottage
Herefordshire
March 12, 2014

The color was gone. All of it.

The world composed almost entirely of shades of black and white and gray.

Marc sat in front of the fireplace in the kitchen of Duir Cottage, trying to convince himself to get up and do . . . something.

But with everything being so bland . . .

Without Kit, he was sleepwalking through each day.

Everything lacked color and flavor and . . . Kit-ness.

And you know who would love the word *Kit-ness* and spend a good ten minutes joking with him about it?

Kit. That's who.

He groaned and leaned his head against the back of the sofa.

He had woken up determined to drive down to Whitmoor House in Gloucestershire and, at least, see her. Let her know he still cared. See if he could do anything for her.

Emme had talked him out of it. Blast her. Something about space and giving it just another day and not seeming desperate.

But seriously, why wait? Would another day make such a huge difference?

And, quite frankly, he *was* desperate. No sense in hiding the fact.

Then, adding insult to injury, Emme and James had taken off, saying they had errands to run and would be back later. Flirting shamelessly with each other as they walked out the door.

Which just made everything hurt that much more.

Kit would *love* Emme and James.

He should drive down to Whitmoor House right *now* and tell her. Who cared what Emme thought?

That settled it then.

He was off the couch and working on stuffing his braced wrist through his jacket sleeve when the front doorbell rang.

What the—?

Drawing the jacket on all the way, he stomped to the front door, determined to send whoever was there away. Probably some lost tourist looking for Haldon Manor.

But when he swung the door open, he blinked.

Surely that couldn't be—?!

A tentative lightness crept in to his chest. Color trickled into his day.

Darth Vader stood on his doorstep.

Literally, some tall guy in a full-on Vader costume, complete with helmet, cape and electronic asthmatic breathing.

"Marc *kaaa* Wilde *kaaa*?" Vader asked.

With a smile that was surely far too wide, Marc nodded.

"This *kaaa* is for you *kaaa*." Vader handed Marc a pillow with the parish church in Marfield embroidered into it. The exact pillow the gift shop at Haldon Manor sold.

Marc raised a questioning eyebrow. Vader shrugged as if to say, *Your guess is as good as mine.*

"I am also *kaaa* supposed to do this *kaaa*." Vader then pushed a button on his chest.

The peppy strains of 'The Way You Make Me Feel' rent the air.

And then Vader danced.

Not *well*. But danced nonetheless. A Michael Jackson routine, circa 1982.

He finished with a flourishing moon-walk.

It was about the awesomest thing Marc had seen in a *very* long while.

Marc clapped appreciatively.

Kit. It had to be Kit.

Only she would arrange something that incredible.

Relief washed through him, breathtaking in its intensity.

And just like that color bounced from the green grass. The sky vibrated a flourishing blue. Birds sang in the trees.

Laughing, he stared at the embroidered pillow, puzzled.

"It's *kaa* a clue." Vader said, gesturing toward the pillow. "Treasure *kaa* hunt."

Ah. That made sense.

Marc slapped the man on the back and tipped him five quid.

And then grabbed his car keys.

James was lounging against a jauntily angled tombstone in the parish churchyard when Marc walked through the gate.

James' own tombstone, to be precise.

Which wasn't nearly as awkward as the large bouquet of yellow roses James held in his hand.

"I'm not sure if you're waiting for a lover or mourning your own death two hundred years too late," Marc said as he walked up.

James shrugged. "It could go either way, really."

James nonchalantly patted his tombstone. It was worn and weathered, the lettering long ago faded. Which explained why none of them had known it was James' until recently.

James straightened and walked over to Marc, handing him the roses.

"Good thing this isn't uncomfortable." Marc took the flowers, a wry grin on his face.

James chuckled. "Kit initially wanted me to dress up as a scarlet partridge for some reason, but I said a firm *no*. Turns out my pride does have limits. Compared to a scarlet partridge costume, just holding yellow roses didn't seem so bad."

"Probably part of her ploy all along."

"She seems like the type who would appreciate the awkward."

Marc laughed at that. And then studied the flowers. What was this clue?

"She said you would know what they meant." James indicated the flowers.

"Yellow roses? Treachery and death?"

"Kit said I was to correct you. These are friendly *golden* roses." James patted them just to emphasize the point. "Not sure how that makes a difference."

As, yes. Well. That did make an enormous difference.

"If your smile were any more punch-drunk happy, I would think your wits addled." James added a deep nineteenth century gravitas to his accent.

"Can't help it. The sun's shining."

"She is an amazing woman. Congratulations. Not that I thought you would ever fall this hard for someone who wasn't worthy of you." James clapped him on the shoulder. "Go find her, my friend."

Though pressed tight against the modern road, the Golden Rose Inn looked remarkably the same, minus the stable yard. A sign with yellow roses still hung over the doorway, though it had been given a bit of a modern touch.

The inside was eerily untouched by time. The man behind the bar directed Marc to the same private parlor along the front of the building with its paned windows and dark paneling. Though the room appeared to be used as an office now.

Emme sat behind the desk, a decidedly amused grin on her face.

Marc nodded at her, his own smile so broad it nearly hurt his cheeks.

Emme took one look at his face and laughed.

Standing, she came and wrapped her arms around him, giving him a tight hug. "I'm so happy for you."

A thought occurred to Marc. "Wait. How did Kit arrange all this?"

"Online social media. I'm not too hard to find."

Marc nodded.

"Did Vader actually dance for you?" Emme asked with a chuckle.

"He did indeed."

"I understand Kit made him do all his dance moves twice for her. Just to make sure."

Marc laughed. "Man, I have missed her so much."

Emme patted his back. "Sit." She turned and gestured toward a leather club chair in the corner.

With a lift of his eyebrow, Marc did. Emme handed him a tablet with a webpage loaded on it.

FauxPause.

"I was told to have you read this."

And so Marc did.

Lessons Learned from Croc-nami

Hello world. Yes, you really did read that title correctly. Croc-nami does indeed have a moment or two of brilliance.

And there's not a drop of sarcasm in that statement.

Usually I would do some oh-so-witty online review involving my id, ego and superego. However, today I have decided to embrace my entire self: the good, the bad and the indifferent. Hence, no split personalities in this post.

So, yes, I actually sat down and watched all of Croc-nami. Not just the two hundred and forty second preview of Marc Wilde's abs (still the best part of the film, but I digress . . .). Croc-nami is no Citizen Kane and will not be bringing home an Oscar. But I do think it is destined to become a cult classic. Which leads me to my next point . . .

There is this part in the movie (right before Mr. Wilde cuts a path through an airport full of crocs with his chainsaw) where he turns to a battered friend and asks: "Why are we killing these crocs for being themselves? They aren't inherently evil. They're just being true to their croc-ish nature."

Which is when I had a personal epiphany. We often metaphorically kill or stifle those we love, trying to force them to make decisions that go against the very nature of who they are. In the words of many a poet and songwriter: If you love someone, set them free.

This has been the painful lesson Croc-nami taught me. Letting go of those I love is hard. But I have to let go in order to have my hands free to embrace my future.

And what a glorious future it is. A chance to be with those who will always be there for me. To create the home I have always craved.

Marc set down the tablet with a deep breath.

"Where is she?" he asked, glancing at his sister.

"Where do you think?"

The answer was obvious. She was home.

"Oh and Marc," Emme said as he turned for the door, "thank you for coming back. I am glad to have you here."

The road to Whitmoor hadn't changed much in the past two hundred years either. The dry stack stone fence stood a little higher and covered in more moss, but Marc recognized the landscape.

A sign at the entrance to the lane told him the house was closed for the day, but a caretaker waved him through when Marc gave his name. Marc pulled down the lane and then parked in the gravel beside the stables.

Walking across the front of the house, he ran a hand along the aged honey stone. Loving the hodge-podge nature of the house. No one was about, but he had a hunch.

Reaching the side of the central, medieval tower, he smiled at the small servant's door. Was even the wood the same? It seemed so ancient.

Sliding a hand between the wall and the door, he found the groove with the chain and pulled. The door swung open.

He walked up the stone stairs and into the great medieval hall. Late afternoon sunlight streamed through the windows, un-shuttered now. Banners hung along the walls and the enormous fireplace still dominated the space. But the room was spotlessly clean and the furniture different. Most of the area was roped off.

No sitting or lying on settees this time around.

But he noted all of this only in passing.

Because there she was.

Kit.

His Kit.

Leaning with her hand against the wall by the first window.

Jaw-droppingly gorgeous in a wine-red satin dress and stilettos.

A retro 1950s dress with a tight waist and subtle crinoline that stopped at her knees, highlighting a fabulous pair of bare legs. Her hair tumbled across her shoulders, shiny and waving into subtle curls.

And make-up. Not heavy, caked on . . . no, that wouldn't be Kit's style. But enough to make her eyes luminously large and her lips even more kissable.

Yet, it was more than that.

With Kit, the external merely manifested the internal. The fierceness of her heart, the quickness of her mind, her spunky outlook on life. The fact that the entire world seemed brighter and more alive because she was in it.

Marc literally forgot to breathe.

Had it really only been two days? It felt like a lifetime.

"Hey." She smiled, clearly not missing the effect she had on him.

Minx.

He matched her smile with a slow, lazy grin of his own.

"Hey you." He walked toward her.

Drinking in every last inch of her saucy Kit-ness.

"Fancy meeting a fine, handsome gentleman like yourself here," she said, heady and breathless.

He gave a look which clearly said he would fancy meeting her anywhere, anytime. He stopped in front of her.

Ever so deliberately, he placed a hand into the wall too, just above her head.

Leisurely perused her from head to toe, lingering on her lips longer than anywhere else. Loving the jump of her pulse in her throat.

Hoping he had made her tingle everywhere his eyes touched.

"Go figure. I walk through the door and find the most beautiful woman in all of Britain. Past *or* present."

Her eyes flared gratifyingly.

He leaned in so close he was sure she could feel the scorching heat of him.

Two could play at this game.

He wasn't a World Champion Flirt for nothing.

"So why aren't we kissing yet?" she asked, biting her bottom lip.

Plump and ever-so-kissable. Teasing. Just to torture him.

Talk about World Championship Flirting.

He reached out and traced his fingertips up her neck, along the silky skin of her jaw. Leaving a trail of goosebumps in his wake.

"Does such desperate begging for a kiss actually work?"

She closed the few inches between them, fisted her hands into his t-shirt, a wicked smile on her face.

"Every. Single. Time," she said.

With a groan, Marc crushed her against him. Lost himself in the lush promise of her lips.

Soft and ever-so-sweet.

Kit ran her hands up his chest, over his shoulders, threading her fingers into his hair. Holding his mouth tight against hers.

It was a *long* while before either of them came up for air.

"Mmmmm." Her breath feather-light against his lips. "I don't know if my hands will ever stop itching to touch these magnificent shoulders of yours." She emphasized her point by wrapping her arms around said shoulders.

Chuckling, Marc gathered her even closer, burrowing his nose into her hair, until his lips were just an inch from her ear.

And then ever so softly whispered, "Itching, eh? That wouldn't happen to be due to a festering rash, would it?"

At *last*. That did it.

Kit threw back her head and laughed. That wicked, delighted, throaty laugh so uniquely hers.

Finally!

Grinning widely, Marc caught her up in his arms. "I won!" he crowed, spinning her around. "You laughed! That means I get one of your secrets."

Kit twined her arms around his neck, hugging him tightly, still giggling in his ear. "You can have all my secrets, Mr. Wilde."

"Like the fact that you actually watched *Croc-nami?*" He set her down, but still kept both arms wrapped firmly around her.

"Exactly! Though that is hardly a secret anymore. I also watched all three *Ninja Pirate* movies, *The Fast and the Spurious, The Docs of Hazard* and even dredged up a copy of *The Codfather.*"

"Wow. I don't even think my own *mother* has watched that one yet. That's an act of true love."

She laughed again and tugged on his jacket collar, pressing her nose into his throat.

"I hoped you would see it that way," she murmured, pulling back slightly.

"I am so sorry. About the portal—"

"Hush. I'm at peace with it." She placed a finger over his lips. "I found the letter Daniel left for me, and it explained everything."

She told him the tale. That Daniel was actually the first Lord Whitmoor—the man who started their family dynasty in the first place.

Marc blinked. Stunned. "So . . . let me get this straight. Daniel is his own great-great-whatever—"

"Seventh," Kit helpfully supplied.

"Right." Marc cocked his head. "Daniel is his own seventh great-grandfather?"

She nodded.

He opened his mouth. Started to speak. Stopped. Shook his head. "That . . . that is unexpected. Isn't this one of those time travel conundrums that should be impossible?"

Kit laughed. "Probably. I'm sure someone somewhere is having a serious conniption fit over it. But it honestly doesn't bother me. It's just one more way in which I'm connected with Daniel. Even though he is gone, I suddenly feel him around me all the time. I mean, he deliberately purchased the house I live in. Established the barony in such a way that I could inherit it. All done with *me* in mind. How could I not feel of his love through acts like that?"

"True. And despite you having different goals for your lives, you still love each other."

"Exactly! And speaking of goals for my life . . ." Kit tugged him closer again, pressing her cheek against his.

Marc breathed in the scent of her hair. Citrus and peppermint. Enfolded her in his arms.

Intent on never letting her go.

"I wish I could promise not to screw up again," he whispered. "But I am sure I will make mistakes—"

"Congratulations on being human. I plan on continuing to make mistakes too. But I promise to never shut you out."

He hugged her to him. Heart too full to respond.

"It's what you do when you love someone," she murmured into his neck.

All the breath whooshed out of Marc at her words.

Pulling back, she captured his head in her hands, holding him tight, pressing her nose into his.

"That's my final secret." Her words a soft puff of air against his lips. Her eyes boring into his. "I love you, Marc Wilde. Heart and soul."

Something stung in the back of Marc's throat. Probably just the lingering effects of smoke inhalation.

Because Marc Wilde didn't cry . . . right?

"Ah, Kit. Darling, wonderful Kit. I love you too, beautiful." He swallowed. Hard. "Am I forgiven then?"

Kit shrugged. "I don't know. How good is your make-up kiss?"

"Uh-mazing." He lowered his mouth to hers.

And made sure the kiss lived up to his promise.

Epilogue

R *eview of the Preview:* Croc-valanche

Ego: *With* Croc-nami *becoming a worldwide sleeper hit, I have been shamelessly awaiting Marc Wilde's return to the big screen in* Croc-valanche. *I have been so excited for this to come out.*

Superego: *Me too! What's not to love? Melting glaciers in the Rockies thaw prehistoric crocodiles trapped in the ice. Who then ravage downtown Seattle only to be stopped by the hunky Marc Wilde in all his abs-solutely stunning glory. It's going to be the must-see movie of the year!*

Ego: *And not just because Mr. Wilde lost those horrid blond dread locks for this sequel—*

Id: *Stop. Just stop. Both of you.* Abs-*solutely? I think a baby panda died just hearing that. Besides, you are only saying all this because La Pochette got engaged to Marc Wilde last week. You are in* love *with this man, making this entire discussion so hopelessly biased—*

Superego: [Long deliriously happy sigh] *I know, right?! It was the most perfect moment of my life. We were on the beach near La Jolla, and Marc went down on one knee and had this incredibly romantic speech about how I was his beating heart—*

Id: *La-la-la-la, I'm not listening to you. Don't want to hear it. It's abs-solutely irrelevant—*

"Mmmmm, I don't think it's *entirely* irrelevant." Marc nuzzled Kit's neck from behind, causing her hands to jump on the keyboard.

She looked up from her laptop and angled her head back, smiling at her darling boyfriend.

No wait. *Fiancé.*

She grandly admired the large diamond ring sparkling on her finger, making sure Marc saw.

With a happy chuckle, Marc walked around the couch and sat down next to her, running a hand into her hair and kissing her cheek. He was in board shorts and flip flops, smelling of sunscreen and fresh air. Showing off those magnificent abs—

"Is it time for Bronco kickoff already?" Kit set her laptop down and cuddled into his chest.

The back half of the beach house where they were staying was all glass, giving a magnificent view of the Pacific Ocean. Waves lapped hypnotically.

"Almost." Marc craned his neck, squinting, trying to see the clock in the kitchen. And then turned to gather her even closer. "I just wanted to sneak back to have a few moments with Lady Whitmoor before everyone else crowded in to watch the game."

Kit laughed softly and relaxed into him. "I don't know if I will ever get used to that, by the way."

"Lady Whitmoor? Or being alone with me?"

"Both."

Marc kissed her head.

"How's Emme feeling?" Kit asked.

"Well enough, I suppose. James is waiting on her hand and foot. She managed to sit on the beach for a bit before waddling—"

"Be nice." Kit smacked his chest.

"I meant *walking* up to the house." Marc gave his best annoying-big-brother laugh.

Kit mock-glared at him.

"What?" Marc asked in response to her look. "She *is* my little sister. If I can't razz her when she's eight months pregnant, when can I?"

"Poor thing. It's only going to get more uncomfortable from here."

"Only thirty-five more days of gut-wrenching heartburn to go."

"I'm sure she appreciated you pointing that out to her."

Marc shrugged and gave a decidedly wicked grin. Kit actually loved the constant good-natured banter between Marc and Emme. They obviously cared deeply for each other.

"Everyone else is finishing the last couple waves and packing up. They should be here any minute."

Kit sighed and just reveled in the beauty of the moment. Of having Marc here with her. Of being surrounded by love and life and, yes, family.

When she had decided to stay in 2014 and allow Daniel to pursue his life in 1814, she had assumed it meant giving up on being with family.

But Marc changed all that.

Why had she never realized how *amazing* it would be to have a sister?

She and Emme had become incredibly fast friends. Forget brothers. A sister was like having a built-in best girlfriend for life.

In fact, Emme's pregnancy had inspired them to collaborate together on a new website, www.KitandKaboodle.com. It was like FauxPause, only geared toward parenting and childhood.

James had also welcomed her with open arms. The elder Knight only vaguely resembled his more serious younger brother. Open and full of life, he made Kit feel accepted just as she was.

And then there was Marc and Emme's mother. Kind and thoughtful, she pulled Kit into the arc of her love. Filling a parent-sized hole in her heart.

Though she still missed her brother and always would, Emme and James and her (almost) mother-in-law and their host of aunts, uncles and cousins made up for a lot. Having lost her family made her appreciate even more how blessed she was.

She and Marc were still cuddling on the couch together when the door opened, letting in Marc's mom, James, Emme and several cousins. Everyone gathered for a family reunion.

Soon the room was full of people, laughing and eating and just enjoying being together. Football played loudly in the background, Marc and James arguing with the referees. Emme resting on the couch, round but radiant, shifting every few minutes, trying to find a more comfortable position.

As the sun set and the game wound down, Marc slipped an arm around her, snugging her against his chest.

"C'mon, let's sneak away. I have been dying to slow dance in the surf with my fiancé. And the moon promises to be glorious tonight."

And indeed it was.

Author's Note

As usual, when writing a story set in the past, I have incorporated select aspects of history and then blatantly made up others.

Some facts that I borrowed from reality and/or history:

The shipwreck in the first chapter truly exists on Fraser Island, off the coast of Queensland, Australia. Called the *Maheno*, the steam ship was grounded there in 1935. It's well worth a visit (and photoshoot) if you're ever in the area.

Gentleman Jackson's Boxing Salon was run by a former boxing champion named John Jackson. Though called a salon or a saloon, it was more of a gym where 'Gentleman' Jackson taught proper fighting and boxing form. During the Regency era, any sporty gentleman of means would take instruction there, learning how to box.

The ducks with their tarred feet were definitely a feature of the era. Livestock was reared in rural areas and then taken by drovers to larger cities for sale and slaughter. Ducks and geese were prized commodities, but their feet weren't suited for traveling over long distance. So they would be dipped in tar, providing the animals with some protection.

Mmmmm, what else? I won't bore you with a lengthy discussion of British laws of primogeniture (succession through firstborn male children), but needless to say, Britain has historically been extremely biased toward male heirs. That said, some baronies and even a duchy or two (the dukedom of Marlboro, for example) are set up in such a way that the female line can inherit should there be no male heirs. There has been strong interest in recent years to include all children in an aristocratic inheritance, male and female (the changes made with the birth of little Prince George a few years ago being just one example).

As usual, I made up a good many things: the town of Marfield and all house names, as well as all websites used/mentioned. For each of my books, I create a Pinterest board of all the visual references I used when writing. So if you would like to see them, don't hesitate to look me up over there. As usual, I'm NicholeVan.

As with all books, this one couldn't have been written without help and support from those around me. I know I am going to leave someone out with all these thanks. So to that person, know that I totally love you and am so deeply grateful for your help!

First of all, thank you to all those who read *Intertwine* and *Divine* and sent me excited emails, asking about the next book in the series. Your encouragement and enthusiasm means more than I can say.

To my beta readers—you know who you are—thank you for your helpful ideas and support. And, again, an extra large thank you to Annette Evans, Kelly Crawford and Norma Melzer for their fantastic copy editing skills and insights.

A huge thank you goes to Lois Brown for her always helpful plot suggestions and insights.

And I cannot even begin to thank my brilliant editor, Erin Rodabough. She has the amazing gift of being able to hone in on problems and provide solutions. Not to mention just being an all-out awesome friend and travel buddy. Thank you so very much.

Thanks, again, to Andrew, Austenne and Kian for your patience and being willing to play Minecraft for hours on end while I wrote.

And finally, no words can express my love and appreciation for Dave. Thanks for always supporting me and listening as I work through problems. Without you, none of this would be possible.

Reading Group Questions

Oh yes, this book has reading group questions.

Why?

Well, the English professor in me couldn't publish this book without making it vaguely educational. And obviously your reading group would show excellent taste by selecting this book—reading groups don't always have to be about the classics and Oprah's Book Club. Sometimes you just need a shameless don't-judge-me read. And any book that has reading group questions has to have redeeming literary qualities, right? So you're totally justified in assigning it.

You're welcome.

1. Throughout the book, Kit is frantic to hold on to her brother. Her relationship with him is more like a mother/caregiver figure than a sister. Do you feel that her attachment to him is understandable? Or should she just have let him go long before she actually does?

2. Unlike the first two books in this series, Marc is a twenty-first century hero. How did that change your reading experience? Did you like seeing a modern man in the past and all the humor it brought? Or did you find it less romantic and engaging?

3. How did you feel about the surprise reveal that happens about 60% of the way into the book? Did you suspect it? Did you feel betrayed by it or did you think it fun? How did it change the way you viewed the action in the book?

4. How concerned should we be over how our actions affect others? How much responsibility do we bear, particularly when those actions are done through our line of work?

5. How do you feel about the conclusion with Daniel? Do you like the explanation of his history or does it trouble you? Why or why not?

6. The next book will feature Linwood as the romantic hero. Do you think it will be possible to redeem him? Is he a truly evil person or just a product of his environment? Why or why not?

7. For me, writing is only fun when I can incorporate a lot of voice, meaning there is attitude and personality in the narration—so you get a sense of Marc and Kit's thoughts throughout the book. Do you find this kind of narration more enjoyable to read or do you prefer the writer's tone to be 'invisible'?

8. When writing historical fiction, you face a conundrum. Do you stay completely true to the language of the period or do you allow it to be more modern (and therefore more accessible to readers)? Some argue that the language of the past would sound colloquial to those of the same time period. For example, a gentleman of 1813 might describe a new carriage as 'bang up to the mark,' whereas my brother would describe his new truck

as a 'sweet ride.' Though the phrasing is different, the words would have the same casual meaning in both eras. Considering this, how should language be used in historical fiction? Should authors use completely modern language, instead of trying to recreate the cadence of older English, in order to more perfectly capture the sentiments expressed?

9. As a writer, I feel the look of words on the page can communicate meaning as well. Therefore, I deliberately used line breaks, non-traditional punctuation, italics and visual cues to help convey tone and cadence. Did you find this helped as a reader, making your reading flow more easily? Why or why not?

10. Alright, let's cast the movie of the book. (Cause hey, we can dream big, right?) Who plays Marc? Kit? Etc. In the movie version, what aspects of the book should be thrown out, condensed or altered? Also, what should the theme love song be?

House of Oak Series

The House of Oak series will eventually feature four books. As of this writing, the books in the series are/will be:

Intertwine (James and Emme)
Divine (Georgiana and Sebastian)
Clandestine (Marc and Kit)
Refine (Linwood and Jasmine)

Turn the page to read the prologue of *Refine*, the fourth book in the House of Oak series.

Refine

HOUSE OF OAK, BOOK 4

PROLOGUE

Timothy Linwood laughed.

Had he known it would be the last time he would laugh, he would have savored the moment more. Reveled in the joy bursting in his chest like so many champagne bubbles.

Instead, he merely cringed when his voice cracked between childish giggle and manly guffaw.

Such was life for a fourteen-year-old.

"Again, again, again!" His four-year-old sister, Marianne, jumped up and down, bouncing her dark curls. Pudgy hands clapping.

Smiling indulgently, Timothy placed the metal boat into a long basin of water set on the stone landing. He twisted the metal flywheel that was the ship's steering wheel, sending the boat churning through the water.

Marianne's high-pitched laughter rang down the curved stairs and across the garden. But, most disconcertingly, through the open french doors at Timothy's back.

"Hush, Marianne. You will wake Mama." He tried for stern, but a wide grin belied his words.

He darted a glance through the doors into the drawing room. Their mother was still asleep on the long chaise, an empty bottle of laudanum resting sideways on the small table beside her. She had already taken two full doses, though it was barely early afternoon.

"Again." Marianne nudged him and then giggled, stifling the sound behind her little hands.

It had all been worth it. The hours constructing the ship, secreting away the materials, working by candlelight, breaking at least twenty-one different rules . . . all to see Marianne's face wreathed in smiles, banishing that pinched, too-old look a child should never wear.

Fortunately, their father wouldn't return from London until next week. And, heaven knew, Mama probably wouldn't be conscious before then. A few more days of precious freedom.

He wound the boat. Marianne laughed, leaning forward with clasped hands, anticipation palpable. He released the mechanism and the toy sprang to life.

Her excited squeals filled the air before she caught herself, covering her mouth again. Timothy lounged back on his heels, smiling broadly. The merriment felt good. Lifting him from the inside out. Hydrogen in his veins, just like those newly-invented hot air balloons he had read about. Quicksilver.

But it was far too short-lived.

"What is this, boy?" A deep voice came from the doorway behind him, the sound skittering down Timothy's spine. The boat gave a final sputter, bobbing to a stop.

Timothy staggered to his feet and whirled around, unconsciously placing a protective hand on Marianne's tiny shoulders. And then looked up, up, up into his father's impassive gaze.

Lean and dark-haired, Charles, Viscount Linwood, still towered over his only son despite the inches Timothy had grown in recent months. Lord Linwood tugged stiffly on his silver-threaded waistcoat, gaze moving side-to-side, taking in the listing boat, Marianne's wide expression, surely cataloging each of the twenty-one broken rules.

Silence.

Charles Linwood locked eyes with him. Timothy had no confusion as to what would happen next.

"Marianne, you will return to the nursery." Words said without taking his gaze from Timothy's face.

Marianne whimpered. Grimly, Timothy unclasped his sister's hands from his leg and gently pushed her toward the door. Her soulful eyes lifted to his, bottom lip trembling.

"All will be well, sister," he said. "Go now."

Without a glance at their father, she ran into the house.

Timothy studied his sire. As usual, his father's face was as expressive as granite. No trace of emotion flickered, anger or otherwise.

A textbook example of Rule #37: *A gentleman is always in control of himself and his situation.*

And its corollaries:

Rule #23: A gentleman suppresses emotion, whether of disappointment, of mortification, of laughter, of anger, etc.

Rule #59: A gentleman never allows his thoughts to be evident upon his visage.

"You will recite rules three hundred and three through three hundred and nine for me." His father clasped his hands behind his back. "Now, boy."

Timothy swallowed, forcing his face into an impassive mask, mimicking his father's expression. Took a deep breath. Recited.

Rule #303: A gentleman does not engage in trade.

Rule #304: Mathematics should remain in a theoretical sphere.

Rule #305: A gentleman does not toil with his hands like a common laborer.

Rule #306: A gentleman does not indulge in the vulgarity of practical mathematics.

Rule #307: A gentleman does not manufacture machines, either with his own hands or with the help of others.

Rule #308: A gentleman does not design or use machines to bring a good to market.

As Timothy recited, Charles Linwood walked to the stone balustrade overlooking the back gardens, rigid back to his son.

"You are my heir." His father did not turn around. Did not raise his voice. "Rule number three: At all times, a gentleman should maintain behavior and a demeanor which honors the illustrious heritage and sacrifices of his ancestors." His father straightened his shoulders. "To engage in trade is a disgrace to the family name. Your actions reflect on us all."

Eyes staring sightlessly ahead, Timothy absorbed each word as a blow. He knew. He *knew* how he should behave. It was spelled out. Literally.

"Why?" His father's words barely a question. "Despite all my endeavors to impress upon you the importance of your duty, why do you persist in this lowering pursuit?"

Timothy swallowed and then locked his spine.

"'Twas for Marianne's sake, sir. I wished to see my sister smile." It was, at least, a partial truth. "Rule number nine."

A gentleman always cares for the needs of his family.

His father turned back to him, mouth tensed, eyes narrowed the smallest bit. An eyebrow rose slowly upward.

For Charles Linwood, it was a catastrophic display of disappointment.

"That is a lie you tell yourself, boy." His voice deathly quiet. Cutting. "You made the toy because you wished to. Your sister was merely an excuse. The rules shall never be placed in contradiction with each other."

That was Rule #301.

"If you truly care for Marianne, you will tame this . . . *proclivity*," Charles Linwood continued. "If you sully the Linwood name with such low habits, you will damage her prospects. Would you allow this silly infatuation to be the cause of her ruin?"

Timothy's heart pounded. Machines were his very breath. Ideas constantly assaulted him, flitting through his brain, restless. Numbers, gears, springs, levers . . .

Even as his father continued to lecture, Timothy noted his father's shadow on the flagstones and, almost unwillingly, mentally triangulated the man's height, the numbers practically visible before his eyes.

"It grieves me greatly to see you thus," Charles was saying. "I will stamp out this stain. I will mold you into a man worthy to bear the title of Lord Linwood. Do you understand?"

Rule #1: A gentleman will ensure that the next generation is raised in a manner worthy of the Linwood name.

There was only one answer to such a question. "Yes, sir."

"Bring that here, boy." His father gestured toward the boat, bobbing on its side in the basin.

Dutifully, Timothy picked up the toy, its metal cold against his skin. It had taken him nearly six months of long nights and cut hands to build. An obsession which had distracted him while he memorized Latin declensions and deciphered Homer in ancient Greek.

Solemnly, he set it into his father's outstretched hand. Charles turned the toy around, studying the curved edges Timothy had carefully formed and filed down. Not a single emotion flickered across the man's impassive face.

Turning, he gestured for Timothy to follow him. With deliberate precision, Charles walked down the curving rear staircase, across the large flagstones, through an arch and onto the back lawn, stopping in front of a small reflecting pond. Once there, his father set the boat adrift in the pool of water. And then with studied casualness, the man pulled a pistol from his frock coat and handed the weapon to Timothy.

"Now, you will dispatch this monstrosity. You will take this action as a metaphor for yourself, blasting away this unworthy part of you." Charles gestured toward the toy.

Timothy swallowed, hard and fast. He would not cry. He never cried. He could do this. It was the barest minimum he had expected if caught.

Images flooded through him. Equations and metal . . . cause and effect . . . even the mechanics of the pistol he now held. As he aimed and then squeezed the trigger, his mind saw the chain of events. The flint descending, scraping along the metal frizzen, creating a spark which landed in the flashpan, igniting the primed gunpowder in a flash of sparks which traveled through the touchhole, lighting the main charge which sent the lead bullet flying from the barrel—

The boat disappeared in a shower of smoke and metal fragments, some sinking into the pond, others landing on the ground around him.

Timothy bit his quivering lip, focusing on the pain, the taste of blood in his mouth.

Rule #23: A gentleman suppresses emotion . . .

A solitary gear—the boat's flywheel—rolled across the ground, coming to a stop against Timothy's boot. He stared as the steering wheel wobbled and toppled over. Which meant he didn't see his father's hand coming.

The blow snapped Timothy's head back, causing him to stagger. He was proud he didn't fall over. Or even flinch, for that matter. And his tears stayed firmly locked away.

Thank the heavens for small miracles.

His sire *had* taught him well.

"That blow is for breaking rule number twenty-nine." *A gentleman will refrain from all displays of levity.* "Remember, this is all for your own good, Timothy. I do not enjoy having to discipline you thus." *Rule #77: A gentleman takes no joy in the righteous administration of just punishment.* "In time, you will thank me for this day, for saving you from this baser part of your nature before it destroys everything you value, including your sister."

Timothy tracked his father's dark head as the man strode back to the house. For nearly the thousandth time, Timothy wondered *why?* Why had God seen fit to give him the gift of mathematics but then doom him to love mechanics as well?

He needed to give it up. For good. Pack it away. He would not risk Marianne. She was the brightest part of his life. With their mother constantly enveloped in an opium haze and their stern father distant and absent, she was all he had. He was all *she* had.

He would see to Marianne's future. Ensure her bright smile remained undimmed.

Timothy looked back down, eyes resting on the solitary gear which had landed near his boot, its spokes perfectly cut and filed. That piece alone had taken nearly two weeks to make.

What did the Bible say? *When I was a child, . . . I thought as a child: but when I became a man, I put away childish things . . .*

Yes.

He would become the man his father wanted.

In a sense, he was no more than that gear, lying on the ground. A cog in the machine of history. A mindless automaton who would preserve the Linwood heritage and honor.

He picked up the gear, slipping it into his coat pocket. This he would keep. A *souvenir*, to use the French word. A remembrance of everything he needed to stamp out of himself.

There was no other way.

Visit www.NicholeVan.com to buy your copy of
Refine today and continue the story.

About the Author

Nichole Van is an artist who feels life is too short to only have one obsession. In former lives, she has been a contemporary dancer, pianist, art historian, choreographer, culinary artist and English professor. Though Nichole still prefers the label 'adaptable' more than 'ADD.'

Most notably, however, Nichole is an acclaimed photographer, winning over thirty international accolades for her work, including Portrait of the Year from WPPI in 2007. (Think Oscars for wedding and portrait photographers.) Her unique photography style has been featured in many magazines, including *Rangefinder* and *Professional Photographer*. She is also the creative mind behind the popular websites Flourish Emporium and {life as art} Workshops, which provide resources for photographers.

All that said, Nichole has always been a writer at heart. With an MA in English, she taught technical writing at Brigham Young University for ten years and has written more technical manuals than she can quickly count. She decided in late 2013 to start writing fiction and has loved exploring a new creative process.

Nichole currently lives in Utah with her husband and three crazy children. Though continuing in her career as a photographer, Nichole is also now writing historical romance on the side. She is known as NicholeVan all over the web: Facebook, Instagram, Pinterest, etc. Visit her author website at www.NicholeVan.com to sign up for her newsletter. You can see her photographic work at http://photography.nicholeV.com and http://www.nicholeV.com

If you enjoyed this book, please leave a short review on Amazon.com. Wonderful reviews are the elixir of life for authors. Even better than dark chocolate.

www.ingramcontent.com/pod-product-compliance
Lightning Source LLC
Chambersburg PA
CBHW020403260626
47156CB00007B/2211